T0115105

MacKenzie
of
Kintail

Jocelyne Forget

Order this book online at www.trafford.com
or email orders@trafford.com

Most Trafford titles are also available at major online book retailers.

This is a work of fiction.
Names, characters and institutions are the product of the author's imagination. All situations
and/or characters are not to be construed as real. Any resemblance to actual events or persons,
living or dead, is entirely fortuitous. In cases where the writer uses actual events, names and details
are changed so the real identity of the subject is not revealed. Furthermore, anachronisms will
be found throughout the book but are voluntary in order for this story to be brought to life.

Nota bene: So that this manuscript shall bear the essence of the medieval era, transcripts are
written in their original languages: Gaelic, French and Latin to be translated in English.

Printed in the United States of America.

ISBN: 978-1-4669-7751-8 (sc)
ISBN: 978-1-4669-7750-1 (e)

Trafford rev. 02/19/2014

 www.trafford.com

North America & international
toll-free: 1 888 232 4444 (USA & Canada)
fax: 812 355 4082

Contents

Introduction

Passion can only be revealed with action, for words are nothing,
unless action is taken.

The author

There are vast periods in life that space and time forgot. Not ignored but unrevealed since no clue can be found for it to be explained. Destiny provides on our path, people and events for us to discover their full range. With diligence and wisdom, they are outspoken by those meant to be their illustrators. Those dark periods are kept by trespassers and might be exploited for selfish, unkind reasons or might be in adversity, the only reason why life itself could be worthy of. There are no coincidences. All that we endure and all those who surround us and learn from, bear a meaning. This is what I believe in and this is the epic that transformed the entire purpose of my own existence.

As I sit in my backyard and watch the sun go down into a diminishing array of nuances while the smoke of my cigar blends in the brisk lower Laurentian air, I cannot recall a single day when "he" wasn't part of my thoughts. Call it adoration, fantasy or fixation, I only know that without him I couldn't have survived my teenage years and thus would not have taken the time to write about this character.

It all began on a late July afternoon when I was about twelve years old. Bored out of my wits, taking a stroll on my bike up and down on Lonergan Street, I unexpectedly heard an odd sound, a lament of some sort. My mother was doing some chores so I did not feel compelled to tell her of my whereabouts, afraid she would ask my help. The sound took me up to the college where my father used to study. Awkwardly, four bagpipers wearing their gears of plaid tartans and sporrans were giving a performance. After a few melodies where I stood amazingly stupefied by the languorous feeling that embodied my soul, I knew Mother would get worried from not seeing me around the house so I raced back wishing that someday, I would hear the rest of the melody in their homeland. From that day on, the complaint of the bagpipe never left me and I started dreaming about a character that grew as I did. He was my soul mate, my twin brother, the one I never had. The one I could talk to when things were at their worse. Gorgeous dark haired and blue eyed, he could face situations that were much too complicated for me to handle. My imaginary friend was there as a silent bystander until one evening in my early thirties, I found a concrete connection that related me to him. There are no coincidences . . .

Chapter First

June 24TH—End of High school—Mont Royal, Montreal, Quebec, Canada.

"Who wants another beer? A promising scientist asks holding a joint in his mouth.

"I do!" Say a few of them listening to the festivities engendered by the Saint-Jean Baptiste celebration as well as their school graduation. He then turns to a friend who's had a little too much of the defended stuff.

"So, what's it gonna be for you Josh?" His answer takes a while to be heard. "I've had enough beer, thanks." He replies turning to the echo of the voice, stoned as one could be, his upper body reeling. He takes the joint from his friend's mouth and inhales a puff. "That's not what I meant . . . are you going to work or will you end up in a Cegep?" Josh turns obviously incapable of focusing on the simple question. "Do I have to give you an answer tonight?" While a few of them laugh at the reply, he moans as he takes a cigarette from the pack squished in his back pocket. "I won't work in a bank that's for sure." The future scientist sheds a flame from his lighter pulling his hand above. Josh tips over a little too low and almost falls down. "I don't think you're in a state to go back home. Do you want to call your mother?" Josh tries to evaluate the question as if it was a mathematical problem but seeing the cell, he picks it up slowly and tries to be as poised as one can be. "Allo m'man, oui tout va bien, je suis encore à Montréal avec des amis . . . non . . . je vais dormir chez Steve . . . (Hi mom, yes everything is fine, I'm still in Montreal with friends . . . no . . . I'm sleeping over at Steve's house)." Josh looks up, approving with his mother's answer. "On se voit demain soir pour le souper . . . moi aussi je t'aime, bonne nuit (We'll see each other tomorrow night for supper . . . I love you too, good night)." Handling the cell in slow motion, an urgent business had to be taken care of; he needed to relieve himself from the ingurgitated alcohol. Adventuring a little further than the first row of trees, he begins his business; avoiding making a mess on his own running shoes. The noise is dimmed by the remote area but the background of music and thousands of people cheering is still present. When he zips his pants back up, an intense sound makes his head tilt. Like a warning, a sort of buzzing plunges all his concentration on getting rid of it. He takes a few more steps deeper in the woods to get out of that ringing tone as if changing place would do something about it. Near the ground a faint light appears a concentration of pale, hazy grey smoke. He looks at it, trying his best to focus and approaches a step forward. The light between the trees is barely making out a silhouette. "Oh Gees!" He tells rushing down. A boy is there, in the last moments of his life, fighting to survive. Blood is over part of his face and traces of fighting are present. Josh bends to hear the heart rate but with all this noise, it is impossible to tell. He rushes the body out from the woods, his own heart pounding like a mad man and brings it gently to the ground. "Steve! Find the police!" He yells pulling out his own jean jacket. At the sight of the endangered youngster, Steve rushes out to seek a man in uniform while Josh does mouth-to-mouth. No pulse is detected and he begins heart resuscitation procedures. The companions from school come close and soon, a group circles around. "Get away! He needs air!" He orders them pounding the boy's heart. Nobody listens and Steve comes back with a policeman. Soon, three more officers arrive establishing a perimeter of security, sending off the too nosy crowd. An ambulance gets called to the nearest road available and two officers clear the rescuer from the body, taking over the heart resuscitation and mouth-to-mouth procedure. Approaching his back against a tree, the teen's legs give in and he heavily falls on the grass. "Where did you find him?" Asks a man dressed in uniform. "In the woods behind me." Replies Josh barely realizing what just happened. "Circle it all around and post two guards until Landers sends a team to investigate. Don't let this one out of your sight. He's the one who found him." He mentions to his partner pointing at Josh. From a distance, the teen looks at all the efforts from the medical personnel to bring the boy back to life but the pale grey light over the boy's face evaporates and a minute later, a pure white light in the shape of a diamond, rises from his sternum over his body and starts flying away. Another man walks out from a pitch black vehicle hooked with a flashing red light. A policeman approaches him pointing to Josh still looking up and far away. The blond man in his late twenties with a scar above his left eyebrow looks at Josh staring at whatever is lifting up from the body and frowns. He then approaches and bends to his height. "Hi, I'm agent Lorne Landers, what's your name?" Josh turns his head, his eyes filled with a smoked gaze, but never answers so the agent invites him to sit in the car. Resuscitation manoeuvres are stopped and the frail body is now being transferred to a stretcher pulled inside the ambulance that just drove in. The white light was already far away in the deep of the night. Far from the crowd and the sound of the ambulance leaving the site, Josh starts vomiting while the policeman opens the back door of the police car for him to sit.

"Unit 1214 responding to emergency call on Mount Royal, this is Landers."

"Yes unit 1214" responds the dispatcher. "Male body of about twelve found by a teen of . . . (He turns to Josh) How old are you? "The teen lifts his head. "Sixteen." He responds weakly.

"Male body of about twelve found by a teen of sixteen in a wood on the northern part of the Mount Royal. The victim is on his way to Sacré-Cœur hospital. It looks like the boy who disappeared two days ago in Hochelaga-Maisonneuve."

A mere silence takes place from the station. "Recorded unit 1214, have a safe evening." Answers the dispatcher before the line cuts.

The agent hangs the microphone, bends his head and raises it right back to look in his mirror. Josh's head is posed against the back seat. His eyes are closed and he is trying his best to calm the pounding within his thorax. All windows are raised instantly and the air conditioning is turned on. Landers turn to the teen "What's your name?" His eyes still closed, he answers. "Jocelyn, but everyone calls me Josh."

"Here's how it is Jocelyn. We're going to need a deposition on the circumstances of your find at the station but you're not eighteen and that causes an issue. Should I call your parents to obtain their consent? I mean . . . you're a little off-set right now." Josh lifts his head from the seat. "I don't have to follow you unless you read me my rights." Landers make a smiling mimic; lifts an eyebrow and turns over furiously. "Listen to me smart ass; I've got a better option. You sit your little touche on the comfy seat while I go and tell your pusher that I'm taking you to the station and you will have a nice evening in our luxury hotel. I'm gonna call your parents and tell them the exact truth, that you found a boy kidnapped two days ago and you and your little brain will make every freaking effort possible to recollect all the details of your find. Maybe a few coffees will help. Then, you will sign the deposition and if we figure that you're not a suspect, I will then drive you home. Is that understood?" Josh turns his face over the window; Steve is there as well as his others friends, waiting. "Is that understood?" The man with no compassion repeats louder. "Yes." He answers realizing that there was no other option. The tall agent gets out from the car but before he shuts it, he tells the one sitting in the back of a last recommendation. "Oh . . . and don't get sick in my car otherwise I'll make you eat it."

Josh gives a glimpse at the man of high stature approaching the group of friends who hid all beer bottles and untouched joints. After a minute chat with his police colleagues, he hops back in the dark car and drives away to the police station. The red light is once more turned on but not the siren. In the back seat, the teen somehow recollects all the intensity of the last hour but like a nightmare, tries to shake it out from his head. His hands are not handcuffed but the grid surrounding the back portion of the car is enough for him to feel recluse and isolated. Landers stops the vehicle in the police station's parking lot and opens the back door. "If you try to escape, I'll shoot both your knees away." He exclaims with no remorse whatsoever.

Josh swallows heavily knowing this was no joke. Like a sheep, he follows the man about twice his size. Arriving at the entrance of the down town Montreal office, the agent takes his magnetised card and slits it in the identification device. Josh follows without a sound but tired from all the booze and cannabis ingurgitated, he feels more and more like throwing up.

The place is condensed, unclean, filled with officers in uniform and he plans to find a waste basket in a rush. "The hospital called." Begins the greeting officer while Landers completes the formulary at the reception desk. "And?" The child was declared DOA (dead on arrival). They are going to call the parents in a few hours. Is that the one who found him?" Josh approaches a small paper basket and starts throwing up. The sound makes the receptionist look but Landers doesn't pay any attention to it. "Yeah . . . where's Taylor?" The officer takes back the formulary. "Gee, let me guess, it's two-thirty in the morning. He might be sleeping." But Landers is in no mood for jokes. "Call him and tell him it's important. We need to talk." Landers brings the teen to a faraway room and closes the door. "Sit." He orders without a smile. Shaking like a leaf, Josh does as he is told on a sturdy seat bolted to the floor. How he wished he had water to rinse his mouth with. Posters on how to obey the law surround dozen of disappeared people. Two desks filled with documents face one another before large and ugly brown filing cabinets. "I need to call your parents. What's your number?" Landers tells approaching a fuming coffee. "Listen . . . please . . . my mother has a heart condition. She thinks I'm over at a friend's house for the night. Couldn't we do that without her knowing about it?" The teen pleads. "I'll talk to my boss about it. Now tell me your full name." The agent inquires bringing over a deposition form. "Jocelyn Laurent Forge." He answers after grimacing to the bitter taste of the beverage. "Fill in the first section and then, write in your own words what happened tonight." The twelve year officer sips his coffee, takes out a prior report from his desk to seek the following procedure, and places it into the upper pack over the right corner of his own desk. After a few minutes, Josh hands the paper over. Lorne looks at it and reads it. He nods in a negative strand and places back the paper over his desk. "You forgot to mention that you were stoned out of your mind, drank beer like a pig and . . ."

"I only had two!" The teen replies with arrogance but the agent replies hastily. "That's a lie! Maybe two beers but how many joints did you have?"

"So! We were celebrating our graduation and I wasn't driving a car. What does this has to do with you? You're not my father!" Lorne's eyes enlarge and he approaches his face to a few centimeters. "Thank God for that. I wouldn't like my son to be a junkie."

"I'm not!! You asked me to come here and sign a freaking deposition so I did. The rest of my life doesn't concern you the least bit!" But the policeman gets more arrogant. "Details are missing on your deposition. Why didn't you write that you saw a light coming out from the boy's body?" Josh's eyes crease under the assumption. "How could you have known?" Landers' objection gets insisting. "You told me." The teen reacts as if thrown into a lion's den. "No, I did not."

"You did without using words. You kept staring above his body. That can only mean one thing." Landers confirms with certitude. Josh shuts his mouth and leans against the back of his seat while the agent pursues the allegation. "The wood was deep dark. The lights were barely entering it. I checked it myself. Was there a light over his body that made you approach him?" Josh stays silent. "Was there?" The policeman insists and still, the teen doesn't answer. At the same moment, a tall white-haired man in his late thirties enters. Unshaved and a misplaced shirt hanging from the side of his pants, he fixes his tie and gives a glimpse to the witness. "There better be a very good reason for me coming to the station at this time agent Landers." He was British, Josh figures after only a few words. The tall man, pale of features, sturdy and unexpressive look gave some hints about his origins. "So?" Taylor says in Lander's direction after reading the deposition. "Ask him a few questions, you'll see." Taken aback, stranded and compelled to a strained environment, Josh uneasily feels the pressure of the interrogatory. "My name is Taylor; I'm the Lieutenant of the missing child division. From the report given here, I see that you have found a child that disappeared two days ago. I would like to know how you found him. Try to recall everything; don't spare any details even if they seem unimportant."

Eyes pivoting from the officer to those of the Lieutenant; Josh's breathing is so deep that the silver cross at his neck rises and falls with every breath. Tears of sweat race down the middle of his back. "We finished our secondary last Friday and this was just an excuse to have another party. Beer makes me sick that's why I only had two and opted for some joints. I called my mother telling her I was to sleep over a friend's house so she wouldn't see me like that."

"What about your father?" Taylor asks. "He died last fall."

"I'm sorry. Please go on." Josh stops a few seconds but clearly wants to get over this. "I . . . I needed to relieve myself so I went to the woods. When I was done, I saw at a certain distance a pale light, greyish, floating above the ground." Still standing beside Taylor, Lorne seems to be more interested in that part of the conversation. "What shape was it?" Taylor asks and Josh opens his hands. "It seemed like a stride of smoke, nothing clear, not even a shape of some sort. I figured that I smoked too much and this was a hallucination but when I approached and touched it, my foot felt something and my hand went from the smoke to the wetness of a cloth. At first, it made me jump but then I realized it was a body. I took it out in my arms and then told my friend Steve to seek a police officer and started doing resuscitation manoeuvres."

"Where did you learn those?" Taylor asks questing for every detail. "One of my sisters is part of an emergency group and she showed me how to do it." Landers cuts in "Why did you do it?" Josh turns over, colours returning to his face. "He was alive at that point." With a creased forehead, Taylor listens while Josh swallows and continues to reveal a little more. "After a while though, I saw a white light, bright like a star hanging over his body. That's when I knew he wasn't with us anymore." Suddenly, Josh turns to the blond officer. "You saw it too; otherwise you wouldn't have brought me here. But you were not stoned, how can that happen?"

Without a reply from Landers, Taylor continues the conversation.

"Let me ask you something Jocelyn, was this the first time you saw a light leave a body?"

"Yes." He answers totally drained.

"In your life, did you ever have other significant findings, things you could not explain, déjà vu experiences? Things you dared not tell anyone else because they were too strange?" Taylor asks more insistently. Josh crosses his hands over, shaking from his legs. "I don't want to answer this." Landers gets more explicit with his questions. "Did you ever dream of someone who's been dead?" Josh looks away and after a pause looks back at the two men. "Three years ago . . . there was this girl who disappeared in Laval. Her face was everywhere, in the news bulletin and posted on retail stores boards all over the area. One evening after doing the groceries, I took one poster home and that night, right after praying, I dreamed of her playing on a wharf with five other kids. My body was above them, they were laughing and the sun was setting. The next morning I called the number appearing at the bottom of the poster and told the police lady that answered, about my dream. She asked me to give my name and telephone number just in case they needed to contact me again. I asked her why and she said that I was the fifth person to call mentioning a river but the first to mention a wharf. She asked a few more details and I told her that the river or rather a canal was long, narrow and right near the wharf, bushes of wild lilies were pushing one against the other. All the kids had bright coloured clothes except for the missing child who was wearing a simple white dress. She looked sad while the others were having fun and then she turned to me and whispered: remember."

Josh pauses once more while Taylor and Landers look at one another. His hands are shaking and, thisty, he takes a sip of the cold coffee. Emotions are too palpable to make him hate the taste or even worry about the headache starting to build up in his cranium. After shutting his eyes for a second, he continues telling his story. "The next day, I happened to watch the news. The police found her body on the river bed close to a wharf. Wild lilies were growing on the berge just like I saw in my dream. So I stopped watching the news for a while. I guess I wasn't ready for that." Taylor draws back his body in the comfort of his chair. "Did you feel you were part of the solution?" The teen turns to Taylor's deep voice without pride.

"I felt that this was certainly the weirdest thing that ever happened to me and wondered why of all people on earth, she chose me to tell the rest of the world where she was exactly. I mean other people saw the river but nobody saw the wharf. Isn't that weird?"

Whenever the Lieutenant talked, the sound of his voice echoed as if it were coming from a mountain. "Who did you pray to? Do you have a guide?" Asks Taylor still questing for comprehension. Josh is listening, but uncertain to clearly get the meaning of the conversation. "What has this got to do with anything? I simply touched the picture and slept. I don't know what a guide is and I didn't pray to anyone in particular."

Taylor sits back, brings his hands together but then, takes the deposition and places it in the basket to be recorded just the way it was written, without all the said details about the vision. "Agent Landers, please bring him home." Shocked, Landers adds a loud "What?" Without reserve. "Just bring him home Landers. End of discussion."

Obviously very annoyed with his superior's opinion, the agent asks the teen to step outside. As soon as the door is shut, Landers explodes.

"Why are you doing this? You know he's got abilitilies. Don't you agree?"

"The kid is under legal age. We need someone older and I have another candidate in mind." Taylor places the report over a dozen others on the corner of his desk.

"You mean that freak that does voodoo stuff? You've got to be joking!" Lorne answers in full mecontentement but Taylor has only one reply: "Don't make me sanction you Landers."

"We're not in U.K. here. We are in Canada where we can speak our mind." Throws Landers pushing his luck but the white-haired British is not the least impressed. "A little respect would not harm very much, would it?" Pivoting his body toward the door, Landers' reply is nothing but polite. "Respect will come when it shall go both ways SIR." The door is then dreadfully shut.

Outside the station, Josh barely lifts his eyes, following the agent who will drive him back home. When they get to the police car, he walks to the far end to the back seat. "Come and sit in the front." Landers offers. "Won't you get into trouble?" As he gets behind the wheel, the agent replies angrily "I don't give a shit tonight." The hangover is coming on strong so Josh lets his body caress the seat and rests his head upon the rigidity of the cheap synthetic fabric. Without further delay, Landers turns the ignition key and takes off to where Josh tells him to. "Why were you so mad?" Josh asks taking breaths of fresh air. "Because that Brit works too much using the protocol; he has no feelings whatsoever and will never use his inner sight." Josh smiles making his juvenile mustache rise. "What's so funny?" Landers ask peeking at his passenger. "We barely met and already you're taking my defense." Still having his jaw contracted Lorne answers with conviction. "Believe me; I can recognize a gifted person when I see one."

The sun is rising into an array of warm colours and even if his head wanted to explode, Josh felt compelled to talk to this stranger met only a few hours ago. It was as if he always knew him. They both start reminiscing about some school flashback making Landers the most profitable student of his time by being thrown out nine times from his French class for courting a girl.

"So what happened?" The teen mocks.

"I married her of course." Landers responds with a happy grin. They both start laughing uncontrollably until Josh asks the inevitable. "You have a gift?"

Lorne continues driving while the sun rays rise up on the Mille-Iles River, making the eyes of the passenger seek a grayish tint that needs sleep. "Can you talk to the dead?" Josh asks with precision. "No. Apart from my numerous functions as an "agent de la paix", I'm a channeler." Intrigued, Josh inquires about the word heard for the first time. "My talent makes me find people like you. Your abilities make your body vibrate and even though I cannot see the aura, I can "feel" that you are special."

"Are there other people like me around?"

"Not as many as I wish there were." After a few more directions, they finally arrive in front of the small bungalow with red bricks. "This is it. Thank you for driving me back." Making the least noise possible, the teen gets out of the police car. Landers on his side, opens his door as well. "If I can make Taylor change his mind, would you like to work with me?"

Surprised, Josh candidly replies. "If you don't shoot me in the knees, I wouldn't mind that."

Landers looks back at the teen smiling before walking very slowly to the quiet house where a lilac is slowly shedding faded flowers.

The following year, a week before Christmas, the weather outside the Montreal office is about to turn to the first snowstorm of the year. Freezing rain is knocking on the windows and the young teen walks in a deserted room, all the way down the corridor and locks the door back. He moves a couple of chairs and silently pushes the table a few feet away. Curtains are drawned to leave the minimum light in. With hastiness, he lies on the floor, head pointing to the north and brings out from his coat, the picture of a disappeared child that he places at his right. Not listening to Taylor who wanted him to learn all the trends before entering the world of astral meditation, the immature adolescent believes to be ready and opens doors to his mind that will forever stay unfastened. He breathes out, each time leaving a longer span between each breath. With certainty about his action, he touches the picture from the tip of his fingers and then completely places the palm down over it. A few minutes later, his eyes start to twitch as if having a dream. The teen's celestial body elevates, leaving the physical one down on the floor, a sensation of lightness makes him able to wander around in the room. He looks at his mortal frame with a sense of wonder but isn't scared. A silver wire is attached from the forehead of the one on the floor to the belly of his "other self" wandering about in the room. He sees the picture beside the body on the floor and feels the urge to look for the disappeared child. Flying high as a kite, a sense of lightness overwhelms him totally. The office is then seen from the top; neither the snow or the cold wind touch him. Somebody knocks on the door and vaguely he hears his name. It's Taylor but now that he's up in the air, travelling so fast, he wants to finish his quest. The knocking repeats itself and Josh concentrates harder not to pay attention to it. The boy of eleven has been missing for four days now and no one saw him after getting bread for his mother at the corner store. No stanger was seen offering him a ride, no missing clothes, discarded item or letter intending an escape were found. Sniffing dogs were at loss with this case and time was running fast against the police squad.

Taylor finally gets the key to the room and is furious to see Josh into that position with the picture of Joey beside him. Closing the door as quietly as possible and moving the curtains a little to bring light into the room, he knows exactly what the teen is doing even though he expressedly warned him to wait a while and acquire more experience. To let him know of his presence, he bends down and touches his left hand.

"Josh, its Taylor. I know you're far but please come back. It's too dangerous, you're not ready yet." Instead of waking, the teen seems to be plunging deeper into his transcendental journey and his lips open a bit. Taylor wants to help him the best he can and decides to bring him back through another method. "Josh, I'm right beside you. What do you see?"

The teenager frowns, his hands becoming freezing cold and words are hard to leave his mouth. "Dust, dust, I don't see anything but I can smell dust and humidity . . . water is dripping." His heart beat begins to escalade and Taylor approaches, enveloping the teen's hand into both of his. "Where is he?"

"He's in a basement or something similar to it."

"Is he alive?"

"Yeah . . . barely."

"Tell me more."

"It's so dark. I can't see anything."

"Are there any windows?"

"No. There's a smell of diesel, it's awful. It's making me dizzy . . . I'm so cold."

Taylor opens all the cabinets to find some cloth to warm him and finally puts his own coat over him. Josh's face becomes paler and he turns his head to the side ready to vomit. Taylor doesn't like it and gets closer to him. "Listen, carefully listen to my voice and come back to it." Josh breathes out, turns his head to both sides and rushes his hands from under the coat and places them in front of him as if walking in the dark.

"There are voices, a banging noise. I can hear a siren. No a horn. It's moving! The place is moving! There's a rumble, the rumble of a motor. His hands and feet are attached with a thick rope. He's bleeding trying to get out of it and he's crying." Josh's head fumbles to the side as he gets in the foetal position. He starts wimping and cries: "Mom, mom, come and get me out of here!"

Scratching his wrists as trying to get rid of a rope, he begins screaming so loud that workers in the corridor begin to wonder what is going on behind the closed door. "Mom, they're leaving! They're taking me away!"

Tears flow from his eyes as he turns his face up and a sudden trembling within all his body makes Taylor realize he has gone too far.

"Jocelyn, hear my voice and my voice only. Leave Joey where he is, come back in your own body. I will help you find the way home. Wherever you are; just concentrate on the wish to come back." Taylor places his hand on the teen's stomach, closes his eyes and tries to make the connection. "Can you feel this? Can you feel the palm of my hand on your body?"

But Josh still shivers and doesn't answer so Taylor reaches for the telephone and dial's Lorne's cell number. "I found him but he won't wake up! Come to the interrogation room at the end of the corridor right this instant please."

The telephone is barely hanged at the other end that the blond agent rushes from his office down to the said room swarming in after pushing his way thru co-workers. The door is left open and a few officers begin to peak in wondering what the commotion is all about. "What happened?" Questions Lorne rushing in the room.

"He decided to find Joey alone. I believe he went too far and plunged into his body."

Lorne shakes his head disapproving. "Josh, this is Lorne." He indicates pressuring his left hand over the third plexus. "Leave whatever you are doing now and come back home." Taylor bites his lips, looking at the scene while Lorne proposes another option. "You want me to slap him in the face?"

"It's way too dangerous." Taylor answers, starting to sweat.

"Jocelyn, you have to come back home, your mother needs you." Desperately says Lorne as a last resort. Still no answer is heard from Josh and his body seems more rigid. His pulse rate begins to drop and his lips are turning blue. Co-workers from the office are pushing themselves at the door to see what is going on. Lorne is becoming more nervous by the second and Taylor cannot imagine such a tragic turn of event for the newest member of his group.

"How about putting his hand in a bucket of water?" Taylor proposes starting to pace back and forth.

"No I got a better idea." Lorne warms his hands together and drops to his knees right beside the teen's shoulder. Everyone stops talking as the intensity of the event rises. Gently pulling up his nape from one hand and placing his right index unto the third eye of the teenager, the agent whispers a few words at Josh's ear that make his entire body fumble loose like a puppet. A minute later, the teen opens his eyes, looks around and starts to scream but Lorne grabs both his arms and then rushes against his body. Taylor sighs and turns his eyes up to thank the Lord.

"It's o.k., you're back." Assures the agent still hanging tight to him.

"Joey is at the old port inside a boat." Josh hushes breathing with difficulty.

"Jocelyn, you're tired."

"No, listen to me! I've seen him. He's at the lowest level of a ship. He's freezing cold. The boat's name is Hillsemere." A policeman at the door walks in. "I'll go and verify if you allow me to Mister Taylor." The white-haired Lieutenant turns to the voice. "Tell the Sergeant to send all available units to the port and block all issues right now. No ships are to leave or come in the harbour until we find the kid and if there's a boat named Hillsemere, tell him to start by that one."

"Yes sir." The policeman answers before rushing away.

Too stressed by the experience, Josh's boby shakes from head to toe and he starts to vomit into the garbage bin. Taylor rubs his back and soon gives him some water to rinse his mouth. "Do you feel better?"

The teen shakes his head positively while Lorne takes off the sweat from his own forehead. His shirt is soaked and the palm of his hands as white as those of a ghost. Lividity is now what can best describe his features, a sense of abandon and emptiness overshadowing the colour of his pupils. "Will it always be like that?" He murmurs to Taylor.

"Well if you would have listened to me, none of this would have happened. With time, you will be able to have control over your emotions. There will be a gap between you and the people you search so you won't be as affected. One last thing, until you can do it on your own; Lorne will be your channeler so you won't get lost and not find your way home anymore."

With half remorse from his action, Josh stands up and lights a cigarette, his hands still shaking.

"I'll be in my office." Throws Lorne walking toward the door.

"Mister Landers?" Shouts Taylor turning about.

"Yes Jacob?" Lorne teases with a tint of humor in his voice.

"What did you secretely tell our young apprentice for him to come back so rapidly?"

"That there were no motorbikes in heaven."

The man with the British accent begins to smile while the teen inhales another time the longing cigarette, wishing it was a joint. A year after being inserted into the department for missing children, Jocelyn Laurent Forge deliberately took the lead into an experiment for finding an eleven year old disappeared in the Montreal region. Nowhere will his name appear in the media until his majority and it was part of the deal. A few cases had been solved in different parts of the world with a similar approach but not on a full time basis for a person under twenty one. He continues to exhales the smoke which he knows he has to quit and places the butt inside an empty soft drink bottle which he knows he also has to give up. He knew the youngster to be there, inside a boat at the harbour. He also knew the boy to have been raped and savagely beaten but he was alive. After four days of trying alone to make a connection, this was the first relevent information to take shape.

While the police are storming the boats at the Montreal harbour, Josh is seated in a city bus bringing him back home, looking out at children playing hockey in the streets of this freezing December day. Playful screams and laughter are heard through the window, their innocence makes him wonder why not all kids are safe from the harm of despotic and deranged adults. He gets off the bus and begins walking home. Since his father died, he uses his own key to get in.

"Allo m'man (Hi mom)."

"Est-ce que tu as faim? (Are you hungry?)"

"Oui, je vais t'aider à préparer le souper (Yes, I'll help you prepare the supper)."

Two hours later, while they finish eating, the phone rings. He runs to it, making his fork fall from the plate of vegetables. "Hello?"

"Josh? It's Taylor. We found him. The boat had already left but we managed with the coast guards to have them stop the motors and make a search. He was in a confined section near the engines. Because he had a tape over his mouth, he couldn't scream."

"That's the reason I got into his body otherwise, no one would have found him. How is he?"

"Shaken and weak but he will survive. He's at the hospital right now."

"Have you contacted the parents?"

"Lorne did. Do you want to talk to him?"

"Please."

Lorne picks up the cell. "Hi."

"Hi . . . I'm really tired Lorne, is that normal?"

"Of course it is. Rest a while; don't worry about it. Jocelyn?"

"Yes?"

"We're very proud of you."

"So am I . . ." When Josh hangs the telephone, his mother turns to him, momentarily leaving the dishes to be set on the counter.

"Tout va bien? (Is everything alright?)"

"Oui, je les ai aidés à trouver un enfant (Yes, I helped them find a kid)." He replies still shocked by the news.

"Tu n'as pas l'air heureux (You don't seem to be happy)."

"Ce n'est pas çà . . . j'aurais simplement aimé que papa soit là (No, that's not it . . . I simply wished dad was here)."

The lady in her late forties turns her head away feeling compelled to finish placing the dirty dishes in the sink. The death of her husband was still too fresh into her mind. Two years had gone by but to Josh, it felt like eternity. Still, no tears would drop on the lady's cheap sweater and her fingers, already wrinkled from working as a seamstress, cling to the dishcloth. He turns away, unable to approve her silent grief and, putting on a heavy coat, exits the back door to sit on the garden wooden table and look at the stars rising above, waiting for a sign from heaven that never comes.

Chapter Second

A man in his late twenties wearing a dark blue and green kilt crosses a faboulous three-arched bridge. The tender heather is glowing with the rays of the sun downing to reach its bed. The hoofs of his horse resound on the rocks sealing the bridge to the pavement of the castle erected long before his days. Soon an archer comes to greet him telling that another master is waiting in the billeterie. Some kind of action has been taken by the Britons in west Lothians and he wishes his advice on the manœuvres. The stairs bringing him to the room seem endless. Again, an injury is preventing him from being in high shape, this time, a slash to his left ankle . . .

Same dream, always the same personage, same castle, the same thirst in his mouth to understand the meaning of it but so many things are higher than this on his priority list. At twenty-five, he wakes thinking that this is an omen of some sort but he has better things to do than trying to associate his *reveries* to any prior events. Job issues brought him all over the planet and this precise castle was never seen so maybe it never did exist but in his dreams. Dawn is now setting in as he finishes his jogging. Its 5:45 on a Saturday and the only appointment he has today is with a very important lady at 9:00 so, for a few hours, he works on files he brought home before he rides his motorbike up to her house. The grey-haired lady is not poor but she was raised with modesty and always feared that she hadn't saved enough after her husband passed away. He kisses her on both cheeks and then pours himself a coffee, adds milk and a dash of honey. She appreciates the fact that he still wore the silver cross bought at Saint Joseph's Oratory so many years ago but makes a comment about the dullness of it. He responds with an elusive reply that it's almost a part of him, never leaving his neck. After he left his parent's house at nineteen, Josh's mother was already a widow and she felt very alone with her two oldest daughters already gone and busy with their own family. He felt compelled to do the more robust chores and visited her as much as he could. It was his way of rendering all the good things she provided him with, like his talent for the arts. A sturdy lady who knew the myseries and happiness of the farm life in the small town of Lacolle close to the United States borders, who used to milk the cows before walking two miles and a half to reach school. Even if she quit right at the end of the seventh grade, she was the most educated in her family and no wonder her three children called her whenever they had difficulty writing something in French. She knew her grammar as well as her knitting. While he moans his mother's lawn, thoughts fill in, swirling crazy in his head. Almost ten years passed since his father died and a little fewer since he started working for Taylor. Karate lessons and painting were not enough to fill his agenda. Travelling about twenty times a year for the job wasn't helping either and now that his latest flame was fighting with him more than making love; it was clear their union was in jeopardy. Constantly implying that he wasn't what she expected of an attentive lover, she would remind him every day that his job was more important than she and hated it to the point that slamming the door was the next best thing to do. So while he was moaning the last stretch of foliage at his mother's, she was bringing her last box of personal belongings to her car and placing her extra key underneath a loose brick beside the entrance door.

Four months later. Vancouver Tribunal, room 105, 11:30 a.m. November 12th.

"Agent Landers, can you please tell us where you were on Wednesday evening, the 3rd of March of this year, around 10:00 p.m?" It was plain to see that the accused lawyer wanted to corner him down with a pre-conceived plot. "In the Montreal office with my boss, Lieutenant Taylor, agent Robert Marchand, detective Morgan from the Vancouver police office and my partner agent Forge." The lawyer approaches the box, looking at his notes "Do you always work this late on Wednesday nights?" Without hesitation, Lorne answers. "After months of investigation, we finally pin pointed the source of the pornographic network so we didn't mind pitching in a few more hours."

"In your testimony, you told us that agent Forge found an irrevocable proof that led you to believe that the instigator was my client. Can you be more precise?" He inquires pretending to read his notes although he knew his response by heart.

"We have been a team for many years and when traditional methods fail, the police send reports to Lieutenant Taylor who then gives us the right to pitch in and find a missing person. In this case, agent Forge came out with links pointing to a Vancouver based group. Before any arrest was made, we had to make sure the leader would be discovered and convicted. Agent Forge found him."

"Can you clearly identify the man you're reffering to?" Without hesitation, Lorne directs his finger toward the accused sitting a few feet away. "The offender is the man sitting there, your client."

"No further question agent Landers." Snaps the lawyer wearing an expensive suit as well as a poker face. The judge tells him to step down; Lorne goes to sit between Taylor and the lawyer representing the Montreal office. "I will now ask to the barr agent Jocelyn Laurent Forge." Josh gets up, very pale but confident that his testimony has to be decisive. The judge turns to him. "Agent Forge, remember that you're still under oath." "I do." He answers seriously then turns facing the audience. The accused lawyer steps in a little closer, making the density and heaviness of the court a little more unbearable. "Agent Forge . . . how would you describe yourself?" Startled with the question the least expected, he tries to be as clear as possible. "I'm dedicated to my work."

"Do you have any family mister Forge, a wife and children of your own?" The man wearing a black toge asks and Josh replies: "Unfortunately, no." The lawyer almost smiles to his response before his following question. "Do you have companions, people you have sex with?"

Taylor's teeth start grinding while Josh frowns. "I don't see where you're getting at." Articulates the witness but his boss does. "Just answer the question mister Forge."

He was there to tell the truth and nothing but. "No, I don't have any sex partner right now." He indicates perplexed.

"So tell me, you're at the prime of having sexual activities and still you are telling us that you are presently living a solitary life. Do you mister Forge have any pleasure in looking at pornographic material?" As puzzled as his face appears, Josh finds words to reply to the despotic opponent.

"My job is to find detracted individuals who are avid of such trash. It is not the other way around. Even before the Internet was applicable, mentally ill people would find ways to savour juvenile fantasies. It is far from being easy to look at children who are serving as sexual slaves to a horde of maniacs who only see it as any other lucrative way to make a living. Too many kids suffer in silence, being abused by strangers or family members and my only wish is to prevent those crimes."

"Agent Landers told us that you and he link to find disappeared children."

"No wait, he does not link." Josh precises. "He makes it possible for me to link."

"How many people would you say you found since you started working for the Montreal police force?" Josh was getting fed up with this moquery and answers with another question. "Dead or alive?" Somehow, the lawyer pauses for a second. "Just answer the question mister Forge." Looking at this man straight in the eyes, the Montreal agent could see the lawyer's aura as green with envy as the next best praying mantis ready to chew out his next victim's head. "One hundred and fifty-two cases were solved by agent Landers and me over the last decade."

A hush comes from the audience. Josh feels like he is the one being judged. He looks out to Taylor whose face is as rigid as can be. After an hour of trying to untangle the web in which Josh got shoved into by explaining his searching methods, the accused lawyer finally ends his questioning with the dreadful "No further questions your Honour." Josh stares into space, totally demolished. "Mister Forge?" Josh hears turning to the Honour presiding. "You may step down." The man sitting higher than anyone else says.

Getting up slowly as if someone hit him with a sledge hammer, he takes a seat beside their lawyer. The next people to stand as witnesses are Robert, a fellow co-worker from the Montreal office, and Detective Morgan from the Vancouver facility. After cross-examining them both for another hour or so, the judge's voice resounds in the court room. "The jury will now deliberate and the court will be adjourned until three o'clock this afternoon."

The hammer is banged once again. The room is no longer quiet and while the accused is discussing with his lawyer, Josh flees from the tribunal to get some air. Out in the Vancouver rain; he lights a cigar, his fourth since he woke. Soon, Taylor, Lorne and Robert stand by his side. His fed-up look is enough to discourage his accolites from mentioning anything about the court appearance. "Let's go for a burger." Lorne suggests but Josh's appetite is bleaked by disgust. "Not for me thanks." Robert walks up to him. "Hey, don't let it get to you like that. This is my fourth court appearance in five years." Josh glances back to the co-worker displaying a revolting scent of two perfumes mixed together with longing to shake his U.K. wits. "This comparution has been going on for ten days now. I'm tired of this nonsense and his lawyer is right. We don't have anything tangible about him really. I just linked into a kid and saw his last moments. That's not concrete stuff. All the videotapes, pictures and USB flash drives were all his accomplices' belongings. None of his fingerprints were found on any of the material." He grimaces his last puff of smoke and throws the cigar tip in the ashtray. From the top of the stairs comes rushing down their lawyer. When he arrives beside them, his face is glowing. "The Vancouver police busted a place last night suspecting a drug sale and guess what they found? Pictures of some of the harassed kids are on the memory card of one of the cameras found."

"So there are more people linked to the network?"

"No, better than that, the teen arrested was not one of the victims or in the racket but just a mere little robber that happened to steel it from the accused's place!"

"Can he testify?"

The lawyer makes a sweet-and-sour grin. "If we drop the drug possession charges, he's willing to testify anything."

Taylor looks at his team and then the Vancouver detective. "That's not right is it?"

Josh walks away and sits underneath the alcove of a bus stop beside a citizen waiting for the next available transport. Strongly pressing his knuckles over the bench, Taylor comes in. "What's your opinion?" When he lifts his face, jaw hardened and his body as stiff as a pole, Taylor's expectation of a rightful answer comes in as quick as a silver bullet hitting a target in a shooting practice. "This guy ruined over children's lives, do you really want me to add more?"

"Drugs also ruin lives and you know that." Josh bangs on the seat and strirs up mad as hell which makes the citizen step out from the comfort of the booth. "There is a balance in this case and it bends so far down to a violated childhood that I wouldn't have any trouble taking whatever proof to send the accused to an exemplary sentence." Josh sustains his stare at Taylor before stretching his neck to reduce the pressure the case is causing. "What a shitty system we've got . . . isn't it too much to ask for deliverance?" After a moment, without adding another word, Taylor walks back to the rest of his team and gives out his decision. Washed and drained, Josh looks out to a lady taking her daughter in the bus. "Watch your step darling." The little dame closes her miniature flower umbrella before entering the public transport and her small teddy falls on the sidewalk. He rises and picks it up to hand it back to her. "Thank you." The mother tells him. How he wanted to tell her to watch her daughter, tell her how to be careful, teach every aspect of protection before something dreadful happened but instead, he keeps his thoughts and only mentions "You're welcome."

He sees the bus drive away; knowing that only a portion of the population would someday live an awful event and his job was to concentrate on those who transgressed that line.

The memory card was new evidence and was brought in as such. Two days later, the Judge looks down at his papers, invites the two lawyers to approach his desk and, when they return to their seat, calls out: "Has the jury reached a verdict?" The first member sitting on the front row raises and reads a paper. "We have your Honour. We find the accused guilty for possession of juvenile pornography and operating a network of juvenile prostitution. We also find him guilty of harassment, bad treatment and domestic violence toward his wife and children." The sentence got quite heavy: fifty-five years behind bars and parol hearing available after forty years. Screams of joy are heard through the room including some of the victim's parents and while the Judge gathers his papers, the Montreal and Vancouver employees congratulate their lawyer as well as each other. Still sitting, Josh turns around and looks at the wife of the accused. Tears are in her eyes and her lips are shaking but even with the sorrow and pain afflicted, he knows it was the right thing to do. While looking at her with apathy, she barely smiles, hiding a deep expression of gratitude and turns her head away. He knew what was going in her mind. She wouldn't be beaten any more but how was she going to survive the shame and financial difficulties that were at her door step? Robert rushes to Josh and with his vivid British accent declares: "Hey Josh, It's done! Let's go out and celebrate!" As the convicted's hands are receiving the deserved handcuffs and is being pushed away, the rest of the audience leaves while talking about the case that will surely appear in the next morning's newspaper.

On the sidewalk facing the stone grey court, the small group gathers for the last time. "So where should we celebrate this event and your up-coming birthday Monsieur Forge?" Their lawyer asks.

"I know a nice bar two streets down." Detective Morgan says condensing his entire file.

"I'll just go to the hotel and rest a bit." Josh replies with all the pressure endured causing a migraine. Taylor turns to his agent and frows. "Are you o.k.?" Unwilling to cast a shadow over the celebration, he simply answers "Just a little tired, that's all."

As the rest of the group walks to the pub, Josh grabs the first cab available. The sentiment of accomplishment was not there and he wonders about the victims' fate, which ones will need medical treatment, psychological support or how many would end their lives. As soon as he walks in his room, he locks the door and opens his shirt, throws away his shoes and socks.

Soon, nausea escalades his throat. His body shakes from head to toe and sweat glides down his spine. To feel better, he takes a shower and drops over the sheets with a bucket right beside. For the next four hours, he sleeps until a knock is heard on the door. Still half sleeping, he puts on his pants. Fumbling over his shoes, he opens the door swearing. Taylor is there with Lorne and Robert who both had a little too much whiskey. "Get ready; we have a plane to catch at midnight." Finally, something he longed to hear. When Josh shuts the door back; he bangs himself against the coffee table and falls down. He gets up grimacing and wonders why his vision is so defective. His right eye only sees a silver screen. No shadow, light or form, just a grayish, morose colour who can't discern any shape or size. He rushes to the bathroom, looks into the mirror to seek any change. Both his eyes are identical in the reflection but something odd is happening, something scarry and uncontrollable.

The following morning, while all in the Montreal office celebrate the group's victory, Josh calls in sick, first time in ten years and takes a taxi to see his ophthalmologist. Nothing abnormal can be seen with the exam so the eye doctor tells his patient that his condition is probably due to stress causing an eye migraine that would soon go away. All he has to do is rest but the specialist insists on considering a full medical exam with his family doctor including a head scan just to be sure. Never has he been sick enough in his life to miss either school or work. He was sportive, had no more interest in drugs or liquor. His only vice was the cigar he occasionally smoked when stressed. As soon as he gets back home, he calls Taylor to tell him the ophtalmologist's opinion who gives him a few days off to rest. By the following Thursday, when he comes in the office to verify some cases, co-workers notice the patch of hair that fell from the left side of his head.

The tests results come back including the scanner report which does not reveal anything abnormal but considering all the physical changes and the blood sample, the doctor's conclusion is depression. With the proper medication and the adequate follow-up, his life would be back to normal in a few weeks. The doctor also insists for him to wear a medical bracelet mentioning his blood type: O negative, and a strong penicillin allergy.

A month later, an hour after getting into bed, a terrible sense of worries about his mother start nesting inside his guts and would not go away. First thing he does is to look at the time. No way was he going to wake her and ask if she was all right but then, a vivid pain in his chess makes him wonder. He picks up his cell and dials his mother's place. The phone rings at least twelve times while he starts pulling up his jeans. No answer. Maybe she was over one of his sister's place. Another strike, this time more severe, draws him right to the ground. He decides to dial 9-1-1.

"Emergency services, how may I help you?"

"Hi, my mother is not answering and I feel that something is really wrong with her. She has a medical condition, is there any way you can get over to her place?"

"Of course, what is her address?"

Another strike makes him cease to breathe. He finally catches his breath with difficulty and gives them the requested address . . . 7a Lonergan Street . . .

When he arrives at her place wearing running shoes, two police cars and an ambulance are disturbing the usual peaceful neighbourhood, with their blue, red and white strobe lights rotating on the houses and reflecting on the snow. The door of her house has been broken down and he rushes in. The paramedics have placed an oxygen mask over his mother's face and are doing rescucitation manoeuvres. He doesn't want to interfere with their work and before long; the lady is placed on a stretcher while they are still pumping back her heart. "Maman, je suis là (Mother, I'm right there)." He assures her right before they place her inside the huge yellow emergency vehicle. In despair, he sees it rushing into the night while neighbours, just like he, feel helpless.

At the hospital, in the waiting room, an urgentologist takes a minute between two cases to keep the son and two daughters abreast of their mother's state. When they found her, her purse was laid beside with the content of the pills dispersed on the floor. This last attack was fulgurent and their mother probably did not suffer before passing away. A vague grab on the shoulder of the eldest daughter seems somehow comforting but shutting like an oyster, Josh holds tight to both his siblings before walking in the room of the deceased. A nurse takes out the electrochoc pads from the bare torso and the respirator from her mouth. The electrocardiogram giving away the last recognition of life sign before a flat line ending the report is teared from the device and slipped into a file at the end of the stretcher. With respect, Josh hides the pale flesh that still has a rose tint. Both his sisters walk in and circle the one who gave them life. "We need a signature for the death report, is there anyone who would like to do it?" Unable to have a single sound cross the barrier of his teeth, Carole the eldest child responds to the request before following the nurse out. Francine stays in the room beside her brother and through her loving nature, finds a peaceful sentence to ease out the sorrow. "Elle est allée rejoindre papa. (She went to join dad.)" Without looking at his sister, he smiles, gives a tender kiss over his mother's forehead and whispers to her ear that he was going to miss her.

Standing in front of his father's monument where the name of his mother also appears without a deceased date, his mind is not there. It seems vacant, full of mist and vapour. Before one hundred elderly people and family members, he looks at his older sister placing dirt over the casket. Francine does the same but unable to obey the tradition, he takes a flower from the commemorative bouquet and gently places it over the dirt. Never would he act exactly like his sisters, and it was not even to defy them. He was different from his siblings, different in so many ways. A single violonist plays her mother's favorite song. Thoughts swirl in his mind, all very happy but his heart is breaking. Reeling in the wind of December, under a crooked oak tree, no tears are rolling down his cheeks but a devastated look fills his gaze. A last prayer is said, a last sign of the cross made.

After the service, the common tradition after a funeral to serve a meal of some sort inviting whoever wants to attend; is held at the reception hall. At the end, when all is left but empty plates and a few celeries, people gather about the three children to offer respect and gratitude.

"Mes sympathies (My condoleances)."

"Merci (Thank you)." He responds bowing to total strangers.

The following lady though, he recognizes from being in his mother's knitting club and her warm words about the deceased make Josh feel like this day was a never ending story. It seemed like more people were at the meal than at the church or was it that he was fed up, wanted to be on his own after this long, long day.

Before entering his own car, Carole gets close to her brother. "You want to stay for supper?" She proposes.

"I'm not really hungry."

"Me neither . . . we'll see."

"Mom, can I go over to Peter's house?" Nicolas, the oldest of her son asks.

"We just buried your grandmother!"

"That's why mom, I have to change my mind from it. C'mon, please mom?"

She sighs. "Come and put other clothes on first."

When they arrive in front of her house, he can almost not recognize it with the new windows, pavement and the huge bushes. In the garage, tricycles have been replaced by cross country bikes. "This place has changed."

"You haven't been here for a while."

"I think last time was Cedrik's birthday back in march."

"Three years ago." she specifies. He turns to her. "That long?"

"I remember . . . . you never forgot to call or send a gift though."

He follows her in. The living room is cosy with a long woolen sofa, a glass table in the middle filled with fashion magazines. "You want a beer?" Her husband asks. "I never drink, he replies. You have mineral water?"

"Sorry I forgot. We have juice."

"Juice will be fine." He looks in the backyard where a play house is perched high in a tree. Some planks are falling and the sign « Private » has now faded. Alan brings close the tall juice glass. "I remember you helping out with it." He indicates also looking at the memento. The tought makes Josh smile. "I had as much fun as they did. Those were the days."

"You can say that again. Now that we've borrowed a second mortgage to pay for their upcoming college, we can only hope that they'll both find good jobs."

"Are they paying back?"

"Are you kidding me?"

During the unusually quiet supper, the dog barks wanting to go out. Carole gets up to take the dishes to the dishwasher and Josh follows, bringing his own plate that he ate with difficulty. A sharp knife falls on the inside of her hand and cuts it open. The wound makes her scream a brief sound and blood jerks out even before the utencil touches the floor. Quickly, Josh grabs her hand, places it under running water and then, compresses it between both the palms of his own hands, making sure his right one touches the wound. Undescribable warmth is felt, making her grimace change from pain to dismay. After a minute, he turns it open, wipes it with a clean cloth. No more blood is shedding and the pain is almost gone. She looks at him in wonder and without any emotions; he leaves his sister, grabs his coat and walks out to the snow filled patio to light a cigar.

Six thousand kilometers away, the scanned page is translated from Gaelic and French to English and the velum relic taken with white gloves is precautiously returned to a vault preventing its deterioration. All alone in the history department, the lady with wooly hair the colour of an autumn sunset, reads the final result to an invisible audience.

It is not so bad to have a gift, only very peculiar.
It appeared that I had many facets to it.
Foresight, prevention, healing, dreamscape, recognition of aura . . .
People would walk miles in the mountains to meet with me.

It was like having something uncomparable to live with,
Something I could use for the benefit of others.
To heal,
To prevent,
To save.
KMK

The lights are shut as she slowly leaves the room and the door is locked. In the hallway, she meets the janitor. "Working late again?"

"I scanned a few pages to work at home during the holidays."

"Won't you party a little during your vacation?"

"When St-Nicholas brings me things to celebrate about, maybe my life will be less boring."

"I'll include you in my prayers asking for a companion."

"Anything but that, my dear."

"Have a good Christmas Miss MacRae."

"You too Mister Johnston, you too."

A week after his mother's body has been put to ground beside her husband, Josh's older sister asks the entire family to come to her house for the distribution of memorabilia. Old black and white pictures are stacked on the table beside silver ware and jewellery. Clothes that could well serve the community are waiting in the closet. "She wanted you to have this; your name is on it." She assures Josh presenting him with a very small blue carboard box. There was no fanciness about it, any ribbon or special card. It was a simple recycled container that fit in the palm of his hand. With immense carefulness, he lifts the top to discover a silver cross filled with marquasite gems. The piece of jewellery was so small that Josh figures it must have been intended for a child's neck. It was a present from his grandfather on his mother's wedding day. "You like it?"

"Well yes, I do but it's so small. Are you sure she wanted me to have it?"

"Oh yes I am. She told me that if you wouldn't take it, then nobody should."

Back at his own place, boots dampered with snow are taken out. He throws his car keys on the entrance buffet, disrobes his shoulders from the heavy police coat and places the tiny box with a few pictures from his childhood on the living room table. Totally drenched from having a day of sorting his late mother's possessions that were not on the will, he sinks in the sofa, joins his hands and places them in front of his mouth. What was her intention? He asks himself. What was the purpose of having a piece of jewellery so small? It wasn't feminine or decorated to the point that a boy could not wear it but still it was odd for him to have been selected to receive such a present. The cross was darkened by time and humidity, so he decides to rub it with soda powder and a tooth brush. Under the lukewarm water, the cross reveals itself to be pure silver and the squared gems are aligned in the four cardinal points. He already had a cross suspended at his neck, one his mother bought him for his fourteenth birthday so the little one had no room to be placed beside this one. Still, he could not discard the memorabilia and felt compelled to leave it at rest before finding the proper utilization.

The Vancouver case made him feel weak; appearing in court and being confronted with a sadist proved to be very demanding. A failed relationship and the loss of his beloved mother only enhanced his fragility. Weeks later, even with the medication taken regularly, his hands still shake, he has trouble concentrating and linking takes much more effort than it used to. So when he comes to work, he avoids the personnel, doesn't have lunch with them and locks the door of his retreat. Mainly working from home, he takes cases one after the other and defines unhabitual working methods by sleeping during the daytime and linking at night. The turbulence of one precise case during his linking becomes a turning point upon his behavior. Holding the disappeared child into his arms while linking, he met what people may call "the beast". The exterior of this grotesque, inhuman creature scared him and whenever it would talk, the savage rumination of an animal could be heard. Right there, still in the deep of his voyage, protectively holding the child, he started reciting the "Hail Mary". The beast's growl becomes stronger, its breath closer and horrific. Strangled by the inhuman claws, the protector doesn't give in, holding the child even closer now reciting the prayer at the top of his lungs. In a last roaring scream the beast disappears, Josh wakes still feeling the grasp of the chocking claws around his neck and makes sure that the silver cross is still the sole item covering his naked body. All he can remember is the shaking of his bed, making him think that an earthquake is taking place and the door of his room slamming so forcefully that the hinges left cracks in the molding. He rushes to his computer to write with precision the setting for the disappeared child and sends it to Taylor. His ears cannot erase the sound of the screaming devil nor the jump he made when the door shut back on itself. From that day on, he decides not to sleep in a bed and to have a brick pushed against his room's open door so it would not shut back. Turtle necks or shirts that would hide his cross would never be worn again and lastly, he decides to wear the small masquasite cross at his left ear to have a better chance at pushing evil spirits as far away as possible from him.

There were two; one magestic, faithful ornament that could be seen
from far and a smaller one to be more apparent.
My left ear would wear it, telling people Mise believed in the
invisible, into His powerful fortitude.
Give me time,
Give me strength.
KMK

The autumn flame haired lady translates the scribbles of the photocopied page into her booklet. She then finishes the last drop of the lukewarm moka coffee before heading out the door and feeding the lambs slowly walking over the dew of the cliffs.

A week later, Josh decides that his mourning is over and he has to come back to reality. Walking in the Montreal head quarters with a huge package, saying hello to all his co-workers, he gets in his office and delicately places his burden against the wall. He gets up on his chair and brings out from his pocket a nail which he drives in the wall with the help of the heavy-duty stapler.

"Josh is back." Shouts a joyous secretary to Taylor. Without wasting a minute, he jumps from his desk to meet with him but unwilling to put too much pressure, he stays in the doorway. When he looks up, Josh is adjusting a magnificent painting on the wall behind his desk. Three archangels are displayed on three different facets, looking the world over for protection. When the young man descends from the chair, Taylor notices the silver cross on his left ear and a t-shirt that is now opened showing the bigger emblem of his faith.

"What do you think?" He inquires to his boss. Lorne arrives short of breath to stand beside Taylor. "It's unbelievable; this must be your best yet." A momentary silence is observed but soon, the three men come together to celebrate the coming back of the long awaited agent.

Head Police Office, Montreal, Quebec, Canada, Early May.

Wearing a three piece suit with a brownish tar colour tie, bounded up to the rim of his neck, Taylor enters the meeting room on the third floor of the investigation complex. He doesn't smile but as always rarely does. Facing a group of the police force, he places a pile of sheets on the table before a white screen. Then, his voluntary chin lifts to meet a group of the police force. "Good morning everyone, we have a report on a white male, about thirthy-two years old, brown hair, brown eyes, no particular distinctions like tatoos or scars, which make handcrafted bombs and places them in school courtyards. We have the testimony of an eight year old that helped Diane make out this sketch. Here is what he looks like."

On the screen behind him, a picture appears. "I want everyone on that specific case before he accomplishes a third felony. Description of his activities has been posted in all the police facilities of the area and . . ." All of a sudden, the orator uses a pitch tone somewhat a little more agressive. "Would someone please wake up agent Forge?" All heads turn to the man whose officer's badge is attached to his belt. Bruised on part of his face, hands and arms, it was clear he was into a fight the night before. "Hey, wow! Look at the cool bike!" A colleague shouts trying to catch his attention. Josh wakes up in a flash, looking around and the group starts laughing. "Jet lags once more mister Forge?" Loudly asks the annoyed presentator. "Guess so Sir . . . I'm sorry." He agrees trying to focus on his boss far away in front of a screen. A paper with the man's profile is circulating around the table while Taylor gives a few more details about the rest of the week's priorities; Josh is not the least interested in taking the portrait.

"That's all for the moment. Good luck everyone. Agent Forge, in my office please." Orders Taylor on a rigid tone. "You're gonna get it this time." A co-worker hushes. "Third time this month." Another adds. The young man slowly stands up and walks away from the meeting room, trying to wave back with his fingers the dark hair that is more than likely misplaced. Obviously, it wasn't going to be a joyful moment with his superior. "Aren't you going to take the picture of the guy we're looking for?" Pleads Diane the artist; pulling up the blinds to let the light come back into the room. Josh turns to the frizzy red-haired lady with the gracile fingers that could draw so well. The early morning sun shines over the city, reflects on the skyscrapers and makes the Saint-Lawrence river shimmer with silver highlights. Taking a couple of seconds to answer back a weak "no", he begins walking away. "Won't anyone tell me why I work so hard for imbeciles?" She whispers. "I heard that." He reproaches on a singing note.

"You could at least fake a little interest!" She blames on a tone he heard a couple of times some while ago. He stops, comes back and sits on the window ledge. "And why would I presume being interested Diane? You know me, I don't lie. I must have fourteen inches of files on my desk. If I start spending time for this bomber; I won't have time for my own cases." He looked ravishingly untamable with his day old beard and the unique colour of his eyes that still made her shiver. "So why were you at this meeting?" His biceps contract, leaving no doubt in her mind that he has started his karate sessions again. "I wasn't, they are repairing the office next to mine and the hammering is driving me nuts. I sort of have a pretty hectic schedule this week with the travelling and my belt exam." He looks at her hands sorting this week's program and the picture of the offender. How he missed them rubbing his back. "Were you not in the States two days ago?" She supposes. Coming down from his cloud, he answers still looking down but then raises his head to look outside. "No, that was last week. I was in Paris two days ago."

How bizarre for her to be interested in his welfare when last time they were this close, she slapped him in the face. He turns his eyes just so she could see the retina being highlighted by the vaporous light above the city's dust. "Our relationship wouldn't have worked and you know it. Robert and I are seeing each other." He heard the rumour through the walls of the office but didn't really want to believe it. Now that she, his beautiful ex-girlfriend proclaimed her non celibacy, he swallows his pride and finds the strength to agree. "Do you still work fifteen hours a day?" She temps trying to ease out their conversation. His answer is now a charming smile surrounded by a dark brown goatee. "You already know the answer to this one."

She laughs while shaking her head. With her hand, she makes the motion of sending him away. "Go on before Taylor takes you to the gallows."

"Brits don't do that, just ask Robert. They just scorch your limbs 'till they rip off." She makes a disgusted face while he raises his eyebrows a couple of times. Walking away to the superior's office, he crosses the long corridor filled with determined officers. Arriving at the demanded office, he hesitates, and then knocks on the door twice before entering. Taylor's office is anything but the one he entered in, ten years ago. It was now all white with black filing cabinets, comfortable chairs and no posters on the walls about missing children but two honorary certificates.

"Close the door and have a seat." The man with the strong accent demands without even lifting his eyes from the papers he's signing. "Apart from falling asleep at another meeting and denting a second police car, what did I do this time?" The man in his late forties closes the file in front of him and plays with his pen before looking up. "What happened to your face? Your opponent was twice your size yesterday or what?" He supposes frowning but the agent doesn't make any comment. "Anyway . . .

a friend of mine called me this morning concerning you or, may I say your abilities and wants to offer you a position in London." By now, Josh had rubbed his arm twice and Taylor knew exactly why his employee filled his agenda to the maximum. "Oh, Ontario isn't so far after all." Josh says taking a more relaxed pose but Taylor adds some precision to the location. "Not London Ontario, London United Kindom."

The lad's head jerks back in disbelielf. Taylor somehow knew the offer would have such a strong effect. "It usually takes a five year residency to obtain a job in this organization but in your case, since it's a transfer, it's different . . . Lorne will be your « assistant » for few months to recruit personnel and then, he will come back here to fulfil his regular occupation. The position is only for you. It could well, if you wish, be permanent." Josh's eyes didn't blink once through the entire announcement. "Robert worked in U.K. in the past, didn't he want the transfer?" He confides inquiring about why he got chosen but Taylor gets quite persistent. "You speak French, English and the sign language; numerous cases were solved when Robert could not handle them and you have uncommon abilities . . . it is clear that you are the one they need."

Making sure that the position of his body was not betraying his state of mind, he leans forward, both hands vaguely open on his thighs and waits for details. With a sceptical stare, Taylor stands up.

"Your salary will be raised by twenty per cent, vast office, bigger than this one actually. You will get a personal secretary, the latest office components, five weeks of vacation and a driver should you need one. Is there anything you want to add or discuss? Any worries?" The agent shrugs his shoulders. "What are the requirements for the job?"

"An elaborated physical is the only thing they are missing. They already have your I.Q. score, that's how they chose you over Robert. So, are you interested?"

Even with the precautions Josh takes, Taylor can still see his employee getting nervous. He swallows painfully, his throat suddenly contracting. "If you feel it's that important then I'm willing to take it."

"Don't do it for me Josh, do it for you. Here, take his card and the contract offer. You may want to take a closer look at it. Oh and Josh . . . I already told him about your depressive state after the Vancouver case so there's no need to worry about that."

Almost jumping from his seat, the agent takes the thick envelope and leaves the scene to go to his own quarters. He places the contract on top of the desk and picks his latest file up. After a second, he pushes the file aside and lets the search engine of his computer do the work. He looks at the name on the card and punches: London Police Force U.K. An entire page appears concerning the institution and all its attributions. He then punches the name shown on the card as the highest authority: Donovan Wilkinson. A few subjects come out so he punches the name again followed by the institution's name. A sole subject emerges and all his attention is derived to the content of the text.

"Strong militant of the police unification's rights, Chief Superintendent Donovan Wilkinson is one of the most respected figures of law enforcement in U.K. After his University studies, he completed his military service and served the country for four years. Climbing his way to the top of the organization, he was recognized to be the most valuable asset in crime reduction and proved to be at the height of his accomplishment to reduce drug and abduction related crimes. At the age of 39, at the height of his career, he lost his son of 19, raped and severely beaten. The perpretretors of the crime were never found and the institutional wizard reclused himself for two months before coming back even more determined to halt this violence and other crime related issues like international terrorism. Behind him are the most select agents . . ."

Josh looks at the screen recognizing his boss at a youger age but even then, John Jacob Taylor already had white hair and as usual, not a hint of smile. In the left corner slightly bigger than the rest stands a picture of Wilkinson. Features of any common British born man, without expression, pale skin, salt and pepper coloured hair, he notices his eyes; deep brown if not black like those of a scavenger. So dark in fact, no light could escape from them.

Four days later later, back in the Montreal office.

The secretary finishes her day and heads to a corner office before leaving for the week-end "Good night Josh." Both feet up on the desk, the young man vaguely answers, still perplexed at the content of the file layed over his thighs.

"Good night Mrs. Thomas". From his right arm, he holds his left shoulder due to another injury in last night's karate class. He lets his grip flick back and forth between the fifth and sixth page of the report, then brings his hands to translate all in the sign language, just so he won't loose the ability to use it. Something seems odd in the description of the facts. The lady pauses a few seconds, staring at the curly haired male sitting underneath his own painting representing the three Archangels, Saint Gabriel, Saint Michaël and Saint Raphaël. Their bodies vaporously suspended in mid-air, the majestic trio is looking down the earthland's surrounding offering their protection. A distant shed of brightness enlightens their features, fluidity of their robes and sublime spreaded wings. The piece is huge, standing over five feet over his head, and four feet wide. The artist made sure that whenever he was to back the two hind legs of his chair to recline; his head would never touch the canvas. With an uncommon dexterity, he painted their angelic faces in different directions, east, west and the last, to dive down over his own shoulders. Every movement, light, shade and colour had been meticulously calculated for this golden composition. A few cardboard boxes are open on the floor with books and desk gadgets. Frames had been taken down, leaving a paler inprint surrounded by dirtier walls.

"Would you like to join me for dinner?" She demands still standing on the edge of the office. "Sorry?" He says lifting his eyes, taking off his glasses and rubbing his eyelids from too much reading. "I was off to a downtown restaurant. Since you are leaving next Monday, I thought we could celebrate." She proposes again to get his attention. "I told Taylor I was to finish this file tonight." He answers turning his head back to the papers again. She starts walking away from the sombre moss green office surmonted with pilled-up documents and open drawers when she hears the sound of boots loudly touching the floor and his calling: "Mrs. Thomas?" The lady in her fifties comes swarming back at the edge of the room. "I changed my mind. I would enjoy your company." Her face lights up in an instant. "Great! Did you come in with your motorcycle?" He starts searching for keys in his pant's pocket. "Not today, rain was in the forecast." Flicking one key after the other to open the desk drawer, they both start putting files away and locking back all the cabinets.

"My car is still at the garage, would you mind giving me a ride? She pleads. Looking around to seek if nothing was forgotten, he grabs his black leather jacket and puts it on. "You were off to a downtown restaurant with no car?"

"Of course, there's a subway station right by. You never take it do you?"

"Too crowded." He reproaches immediately. While she waits at the entrance of his office, he looks around and heads back to a remote shelf to grab a few books and the case he wants to complete. "Who is going to take your files up?" She questions while he places them inside the box. "Some fresh man out from the police academy, Taylor will finish his training." A huge yellow enveloppe is taken and placed above the cardboard box. In it, his copy of the signed contract that ties him with the British office, his benefits and pension plan, liabilities, expectancies. A document of fifty-four pages is inside, including a presentation letter from John Jacob Taylor, Lieutenant of the Montreal Police Office, Quebec, Canada. "Are you leaving anything behind?" The lady asks cutting his thoughts like a razor. He lifts his eyes as he pulls up the heavy box. "I know where you're getting at Mrs. Thomas. I'm sorry, the answer is no." With deepness, she stares at the painting, paying attention to the divine work of art, how it was going to be missed. On his scarce days off, working on it as soon as he would wake, avoiding going out with friends, not answering the telephone, the young artist completed its execution after a full four month period. He purchased the frame and put it on the canvas at his own place. The work was still wet when casted with galvenized finish nails and a six braided metallic wire, levelled at the back. Incomparable pleasure gave birth to the masterpiece with a hint of inspiration from Michelangelo. It was his best yet, everyone told him so. He knew that getting attached to material things was wrong but such intensity was poured into that single representation, that there was no way he could leave it behind. Taking a few steps closer, the secretary smoothly caresses the edge of the frame where he apposed the motto of the security office in Gaelic, the language he wished he knew better: Ri thoir ùmhlachd is sàbhail, "To serve and protect". Mrs Thomas turns back to the artist and he cannot avoid appreciating the gentleness of her gesture. "Let's go." She proposes loudly, now turning to a less emotional individual.

They walk out his ten by ten foot office and stride in front of dozens of pictures behind glass frames, newspaper clippings and articles about missions with outstanding endings. One of the most elaborated memorablia, bigger than the others and mounted up on a sturdy metallic plated frame, shows the entire station staff, all dressed with blue shirts and black pants, gallons and medals pinned up on their hearts and shoulders. On the picture, Josh is seated on the far left, beside Lorne and other colleagues including twelve young, intelligent and beautiful ladies, who all wished the young man would pay a little more attention to them. Hair tailored like the common police crew-cut, he wore his uniform with pride, something he wished his father would have appreciated before going to a better world. "You've been here since six this morning, I've been told. You must be tired. Are you o.k. to drive?" Mrs Thomas asks.

Catching up on the offer, he throws her the car keys. A beeping sound resounds and the doors unlock. The box is placed in the trunk while she turns the key in and a sweet, roaming sound emanates from the engine. "I haven't seen Lorne all day. Where is he?" He snaps placing the file in the glove compartment and locking it. "Taylor asked him to proceed with the Munroe case." He turns to her in a flash. "What about it?" Turning to the main road, she makes sure of not speeding over the limit. "Something came up." He never stops looking at her waiting for the conclusion. "The uncle did it. The one you had doubts on."

Obviously, the news does not make him happy and a faint four letter word evades from the plump lips. "They went to get him this morning with a warrant and then, Lorne was supposed to head home. I waited for his call all afternoon."

He sighs, turns his head to the innumerable lights on Ste-Catherine Street. The sidewalks are filled with people hurrying to their destination. Customers and workers pass by the beggars without digging into their pockets. Mrs Thomas pulls in the parking lot of a cosy French restaurant with trees glowing decorated by miniature white lights. Right underneath the carved wood sign at the entrance, he turns around to lurk at a car that resembles one of his colleague's. Recognizing the wheels deprived of mags, he hurries to open the restaurant's door for the lady. Looking at it once more, he tries to make out the licence plate number from where he stands. "That's Robert's car. Did you invite him also?"

The lady doesn't have time to reply and, as soon as he walks in the lobby, all the staff members from the station loudly shout "Surprise!" Astounded, he jumps at the noise beside Mrs. Thomas who is obviously proud of her acting. Josh's face begins to blush from so much attention. His boss comes forward, grabbing him by the injured shoulder. Grimacing, he starts laughing getting nearer to the group. Other co-workers beer in hand, start teasing. "The Brits are now taking over!"

"Well I've had my taste with Sir Taylor so I guess I can handle a few more."

The group laughs while he gets shaken and hugged by each one of them.

"They've got the nicest bikes." Mentions Robert seated at the far right end, placing high his beer buck. "Yeah, but you can only ride them when it doesn't rain so that leaves you about ten days a year to enjoy them!" Someone else adds.

Josh can't help but smile. Conversations, cheers and vivid laughter start within the group. After a moment, Lorne walks in with spouse and children and again, everybody turns around to start clapping. "So this party was your idea?" Josh asks his partner. "Well of course." Marie, Lorne's young daughter raises her arms so Josh can pick her up. His wife Sylvia gets close, kisses him on both cheeks and hugs the god-father of her daughter.

After everyone has their meal served, Taylor gets up and starts flicking his knife on the side of the wine glass. He then raises it, taking it high. "A toast . . ." Everyone imitates the robust leader with shoulders wide as those of a football player. The man pauses, clears his throat but then adds with assurance:

"We as police officers and peace agents, work hard to protect civilians. Since they have opened this department for missing children more than a decade ago, I'm very proud to say that it has enhanced my personal values, sense of duty and companionship toward other officers who share the same goals." He turns to Josh. "Your contribution has been more than significant and to my own loss, your services are now needed on my motherland." Everyone claps and whistle. Taylor looks at his agent sitting close then, turns his face to look at the other members of the station. "In regards to a teen that grew up to be the gentlemen whom I considered for the last ten years to be a splendidly determined employee and this, with the incomparable help of agent Landers, may the path he will now take, bring other children back home. Cheers!" All raise their glass high in the air and take a sip including Josh with his mineral water and a dash of lemon. Then, all of them put their glasses down to clap hands as Jocelyn slowly walks up to his boss, sturdily embracing him. "We will now present you a short farewell video. Diane, if you may please . . ." Plates and utensils on the table are moved out of the way while Robert and she place the filming device to be projected on the wall. Lights are shut and Marie hops on Josh's lap. Pictures of the old office are the first to appear with Taylor wearing a jacket bearing huge brown squares to the taste of the era. Everyone starts laughing. Lorne is shown in uniform with a wave of blond hair on top of his head that doesn't exist anymore and again, people explode in laughter. The next picture shows a young teen of sixteen at the end of a corridor. Josh is wearing long hair, the hint of a mustache and a pack of cigarettes curled in his t-shirt sleeve. He looks stoned as a rock with both eyes half-way shut and a posture quite decontracted. In the restaurant, no one can resist to smile at the « iced teenager » who had just been hired under special requirements. Josh hides his blushed face behind both hands, laughing as much as his colleagues. A few pictures later, the addition of a fourth floor and personnel, makes them realize how much their group evolved in the last deceny. A few left, two of them died, another few retired. "Remember this one with Robert sitting on Santa's lap?" Soon, another police officer adds his comment:

"How can we forget? He kissed him!" Again, everyone cheers at the memory. When Josh gets to be twenty, a series of rescue pictures come swarming in. Ceasing to smoke cigarettes and dope but opting for an occasional cigar, his body had grown a few inches taller and karate sessions carved it like an athlete's. The following pictures taken two years ago let him appear coming out from a lake, rescuing a four year old. His wet shirt clinging to his torso, jeans full of algaes and mud, his hair dark and trimmed goatee damp and dripping, surround the traits of a man that appear reassuring in front of the crying child. Lorne is behind with other police members, taking care of bringing out the father's body out of the canoe. Fog is emaning from the surface of the lake in this early September dawn. Both men had been called upon that mission in the Toronto Great Lakes area as reinforcements the night before. The result of this recovery leaves a bitter sweet taste about the stunning role they played. Party pictures and baseball gatherings, fund raising events follow before a sombre picture that shows Josh with Lorne and other affiliates, sitting in a room with opened files and lap tops. The men's silhouette barely enlighted by the sorrowing light of a late afternoon last November, can well be remembered with what they called the "Vancouver case".

"Why are you taking pictures, Diane?" Robert asks while the other agents are pointing files, comparing facts and arguing about certain details. "It will be great for our station's album." She hushes. Josh is too concentrated to answer and only lifts his eyes to his ex-girlfriend. "Can you get us a few coffees please?" Lorne asks.

When she comes back with her tray, she places everything in the middle of the table near the laptops and piles of paper work. "See? There he is once more and see this guy in the back? I'm sure I saw him a month before at the camera shop." Affirms the Vancouver detective. Lorne starts distributing the coffees, sees the honey square and places it near Josh's cup. He turns his eyes to the gesture and immediately looks at Diane leaving the room. She remembers, he tells himself silently while he sees her red hair floating away behind the corridor's window. He missed her but then, this case was far too important to let go. Children's lives were at stake and pulling in more than their share into late working hours and court appearances was their glory.

The evening goes on the friendliest tone, Mrs Thomas getting another lift to take her back home. Almost everyone is gone. Taylor is sitting at the deserted table and after thanking one last member of the staff, Josh comes to sit beside his boss.

"If there's anything, anything at all Josh. If you want to come back, I'll understand." The young man wearing a white shirt and a worn out pair of jeans, vaguely nods at the comment while the boss doesn't really know what else to add. He puts on his leather office jacket, avoiding looking at the man who unconsciously saved his life. "Are you o.k. to drive?" The boss asks again. "Yes, of course." He assures showing his empty mineral water bottle. After a pause, Josh looks up to him. "You've been like a second father to me." Bringing to his chest his agent, the white-haired man clings to him tightly. "Get away before I make a fool of myself." Josh pauses a few seconds and from his grey eyes, almost demands pardon. Seing the young man about to leave, Diane quickly gets up and places her hand over on his sleeve. Josh turns around and pauses. "Will I ever see you again?" The lady softly asks.

"I doubt it." He quickly answers. "Then promise me something, don't mind how many hours you spend for work but whatever happens, don't *ever* stop painting." Coming from such a talented artist, the comment is preciously cherished. The young man half-smiles while the lady's eyes turn bright. He kisses both her cheeks, like all French Canadians do, but very, very slowly then, hugs her. The embrace is so warm and sincere that for a second, she stops breathing. Robert understands that the two need a few minutes together. Standing a few feet away, he waits for Josh to let go of his princess but then, the two men approach each other. "Good luck buddy." He smurks punching Josh's shoulder then hugging him. "Watch over her, she'll be a good wife and a perfect mother." Is the reply he gives the man who won her over. Diane tries her best to appear unshaken by the bond while Josh turns his eyes to a white-haired man sitting alone at the end of the table. He bows to him and rapidly heads toward the exit.

It is the first spring night of the year where you can really pull your window down. The brisk air is entering the car. It's eleven o'clock on the radio. At a red light, he reaches for an inside pocket and takes two pills from a container then puts the lid back on. The light turns green but it takes a little while for him to step on the gas. The driver in the back honks and pulls beside. "Hey le twit! T'as pris tes licences dans une boîte de pop-corn? (Hey stupid! Did you get your licence in a pop corn box?)" Turning to the impatient driver, all he says is "Désolé (Sorry)." before stepping on the pedal to speed off in the middle of the night.

Getting off the autoroute at the same exit he's been taking for the last ten years, he drives up to the village center and then turns a few more streets to a remote corner of the city. The fence of the cemetary is of course closed at such a late time and he parks the car in the street facing it. Taking all precautions to make as little sound possible, he doesn't even put the alarm system on just in case a stray cat hops on the hood. Crossing over the pickets is easy but visiting a relative close to midnight may look abnormal. Still, he has to do it, just to try and have some peace of mind. No moon is apparent that night, just a vague brightness coming from the factory lights behind the memorendum of the plane crash victims. The huge cross elevated for the Lonergan priest is the structure he is walking to, then a few paces up; he makes a turn to the left, a dark family stone is there, then the one of his family. The engraving of two birds represents his parents and the liliums, his two sisters and himself. Being the one who drew it, he asked the stone builder to have it engraved. The lady who took the order insisted so much with the approval that he almost decided otherwise. "Once it is engraved, it will last for fifthy years, maybe more. Do you like it? "He wants to reply something like: "No, I don't! I don't want to be the one to draw something for my father's tumb stone but hey! Why should you care for it anyway, you're in there for the money, aren't you?" Instead he replies that he is very happy with the template. In fact, when the final result is shown, it even comes out better than his sketch.

In front of the cold salmon coloured stone he stays up and joins his hands. "Mom, dad, I'm leaving. I won't be coming back to see you for a while. Can you please protect my two sisters? Things are a little hard for Francine these days and Carole, I just think she works too much. So what do you say, can you protect them?" He makes a pause, prays a little more, this time silently. "I love you both and miss you so much." He reveals a little more subtly, kissing the fingers on his right hand and brushing them against the letters forming his parent's names.

Two miles further east, Josh pulls the vehicle inside the garage, the door is slid into place and a light turns on immediately. Taking the envelope in the glove compartment, he then reaches for the cardboard box in the trunk and pulls it out to enter a house where nobody waits for him. The interior has a feeling of loneliness, sadness, desertion. He takes a bottle of mineral water from the refrigerator now almost empty from any food and knocks the door back with his foot. Passing in front of the stereo system, he whispers « music » and a 10 decibel compact starts. Walking down to the basement, he sits at his technical drawing table. With a slow move, he bends his head sideways and with a snap of his fingers, enables the gold lighter that used to belong to his father, to shed a flame on an aromatized cigar. A puff of smoke draws from his mouth when he unintentionally hits the bottle which starts to dance on the inclined table. He rapidly catches it with his left hand before it provokes a splash that could have destroyed what he has been working on for the last few days. Representing someone he never met but in the unsubconscient world, the masculinity of his traits, glorify the avidity of adventure. The angular jaw, the dense eyebrows, the rigidity of the cheek-bones can almost be mistaken for his, but they aren't. The personage's eyes echo the same icy stare the mirror sends him back, evoking the rugged features of a warrior that has seen too much. Far away in his memory, a thought resuscitates.

August is at its peak, summer is a long, unpleasant and lonely season. Twelve years of age, bored out of his wits, he rides the huge bike inherited from his oldest sister. Suddenly, he stops and listens. The wind brings a haunting sound that filters right through him, one he's never experienced before. Without thinking, he follows it more and more avidly. A couple of kilometres down the road, the vision laying before him of four men in kilt, blowing into bags, summound, baffle and hypnotize whatever he ever thought beauty meant.

Captivated by the vision, his breath shortens, his heart skips a beat. With both hands, he disposes of the bike, silently letting it drop on the burned grass in this summer's expiring season. Looking at the bagpipes, it is not sound nor music that comes into his head but angel voices, murmurs from heaven that overwhelm and grasp the young soul. At the end of the rendition, one of the players salutes the child and he returns the politeness bearing a vast smile across his tanned cheeks. While the improvised audience claps and then leaves, he stays there, unwilling to go home because he desires more. No need for him to talk, the musician guessing what the young boy wishes for. The three others companions, putting away their instruments, are not influencing the dark tartan musician. He wets his lips, ravives his shoulders and fills in his lungs. As he orients the long wooden tube near his mouth, he firmly places his fingers on the pipe and squeezes the bag against his ribs. A sultry note comes out, what is later to be compared to the same feeling of a first kiss, honest, deep and true. The boy's knees become weak; he can hardly breathe just as he thinks that he is cuddled by the Eternal. The piper finishes his song and the child realizes that he hasn't told his mother his intention of riding so far. "I have to go mister, thank you. Thank you ever so much." The young voice trembles from excitement. "Would you like to try it?" The musician replies. "I can't. It would be like touching angel wings."

The bag piper stares back and a magnificent smile widens under his oppulent dark mustache. "Come to my country. There are angel wings everywhere." He affirms scorching the « r » in a guttural way. "I'll never forget you." The child lets out. "I know . . ." The huge man replies shaking the child's hair. That same night, Josh dreamed of a warrior with eyes grey like his. It was like some sort of connection, a link to a different era and always did the young boy know that the dream visitor would be a shelter, a refuge to his disturbed childhood where his father drank too much and his mother screamed and cried much more. Comfort always came with the nebulus escape and time let his hero show him a little more every now and then. Eventually other warriors attached themselves to the main character. Soon his wife, a French lady appears. His best friend, hair as dark as a raven and eyes of dyed green, rowed in from the island facing the master's castle. Knights, squires, falconers, masters of the bows, swirled around this man raised with pride and integrity. All those characters had been sketched, drawn and painted over and over again. They were his companions of arm, faithful, the ones he could really talk to without being judged, the ones he could tell everything.

He lifts his hand to un-pin every single etching and carefully places them into a huge portfolio. The phone beside the wide angled table rings as he exhales a puff of cigar. This late, it can only be one person. "Hi Lorne." He answers taking out the shirt from his pants to be more comfortable. "So, are you happy with the transfer?" A last drawing is taken down and he starts to add a little shade under the chin of the subject. "Of course, it's too late to draw back anyway. I'm exhilarated." Lorne knows his buddy, all the intonations of his voice and this one he doesn't like. "Is this another of your ironical moments?" Josh fakes laughter, takes a last puff of smoke before crashing the last ashes into a sand filled canister. "Why don't you come to my place tomorrow night? Sylvia will make a nice supper." A thoughtful intermission sets in so Lorne wants to know the truth. "Are you the one that asked to move?" Josh places the telephone over his thigh and throws his pencil far, screaming through his teeth. He closes his eyes, jerks his head backwards. This is probably the last sentence he wants to hear from his close friend and partner. After calming himself down, he places the telephone back over his ear. "Josh? Are you there?"

"Yeah, I'm sorry. I dropped the phone . . . and no Lorne. Whatever you might think, I did not ask to leave. It's time for me to go on and it's nothing personal. Taylor always thinks ahead and once more, he's right. This is just an opportunity that I have to grab by both fists." Another pencil is taken from a wooden cherry box but now, his right hand shakes so much, that he stops drawing. He lights a second cigar, takes a puff, inhales it and keeps it in a little longer than usual. "So, am I counting you in for supper?" Josh looks at the pair of skis he won't bring and recalls for a second, the last time he was on a slope with his father. "Fine, I'll be there."

Fed up, he puts the drawing away beside other representations of the peculiar character, standing in front of an arched bridge, coming straight out of his imagination.

Completely taking off his shirt, he slowly climbs the steep stairs to the first floor placing the portfolio near large canvases aligned on the wall to be sealed into wooden crates for the trip. Most of them represent distant sceneries, medieval battles, mythological events, ladies waiting at the shore for their men's return from far away quests. His last creation, a magnificent interpretation of Jason charming the dragon, is waiting beside a dozen boxes containing nothing but books.

The water runs an almost silent sound over the well defined body from which a silver cross hangs from the neck. His arms out on the wall in front of him, he lets the warm liquid glide down his spine. Slipping into a comfortable pant pyjama, he walks to his bedroom and opens a singular light sitting on top of his desk. The oppulent bed covered with a dark red throw sliding to the floor is only there to serve the visionary application that it may someday be the nest for some sexual activity like it used to. For now, it only fills the vast, unceremonious room where he sleeps. All the drawers are empty; most of his clothes already donated to charity or packed in a piece of luggage waiting by the door. Right above the sleeping area, a vertical painting in hues of blue represents the dream visitor posing from the back, both arms open, head bent forward. The muscular subject is ducked on his knees. The random of light, shadow and contraction of the back muscles are so realistic that people stare twice, to realize it is a painting and not photography. A strong luminosity glows above the theme, describing the contours of his upper body and base of the nape, slowly shading off to the furthest part of his lower back. What the figure is doing can be interpreted with so many answers and even its own creator doesn't have the exact signification about it, maybe he is praying or so he thinks. By painting it, he figured that the recurrence of the dream would finally cease but instead, it accentuated. There is probably a meaning behind it, the colour, the shape and position of the stranger. Maybe he saw it somewhere. Maybe it was him paying respect to something, bowing in front of someone, maybe . . .

He places the contract over the century old desk, and then opens his laptop. Glasses are pushed against his nose and he enters his pass code to the office link. On the first page, a report from his colleague's intervention over the discovery of a three ton possession of ammonium nitrate is the event of the week. Everyone talked about it but then, he turns to his personal file. Via the link, Taylor sent in three other child missing reports. He decides to look at the one he was working on at the end of his shift, seeking if there is any new development concerning that precise case. With calm, he flips through the pages one after the other. The picture of a thirteen-year-old glares before him, with her name, description and the day of her disappearance. No other details have been added to the computerized file so he prints the picture of the teenager and shuts the computer. He rises from the scuplted chair, takes off his pyjama pants and lies down on the gym mattress set at the foot of the bed. With his right palm, he touches the photograph and breathes in a couple of times, deeply. In front of him, the archway window facing north is barely lit by the whiteness of the street light. His right hand moves up, signing himself by crossing his forehead, his heart and third plexus. Placing both his hands in an open matter on the side of his body, he then exhales every breath of air, seals his inviting lips together and shuts his grey-blue eyes to the surroundings. His right hand slowly lifts to be placed unto his chest, over the Christ's emblem resting on his torso. His head drops to the left (where the past is waiting) and drowsiness takes over. His body tips over to the side and his arm vaporously falls to the floor. The curve of his back leads to the strength of the muscular shoulders, the bicep loses its vigour and the vein appearing in the front of his arms turns to a paler shade of blue. Soon, the tentalising lips open and the breathing changes to a soft harmonious wave, raising his torso up and down in a slow movement.

It doesn't take long before the silver thread appears, inviting him to slide away to another dimension. No wind, no sound, no bright lights. Darkness and tiny starlit galaxies lead the way to the celestial voyage. After a swirl of shades, trees appear, dim sunrays, a passage split in the woods. Five tall birch trees dance into the wind with barely a few leaves on. Something is there, on the ground, on the left side of the path. A white shirt lifted over the head, uncovers a young girl's body. One of her shoes is missing; a damaged bicycle is hidden in a near bush. He concentrates a little more, tries to look around while his feet never the touch the grass. A brownish mass erects in the distance. It looks like a shopping center, huge red and white letters form the mall's name. The vision disappears as fast as it came, the silver thread ruffles back and like a whirlpool, the soul is drawn back into the sleeping body, lying on the floor.

Five hours later, rolling over to his side, he gasps as his mouth becomes awfully dry. His hands and upper body are soaking wet. With difficulty he gets up, puts on his glasses and opens the laptop. Opening the e-mail section of the component, he finds the contact name of Taylor, fills in the blank space with his employee number and the numerical digit code of the case. Without emotion, he writes:

"The victim is in the woods, south-west of the shopping center in Rosemere in between the main street and the parking lot. Her body is under bushes near the pathway close to five birch trees; her white sweater has been lifted to hide her face. The rip of a paper bag is stuck somewhere near. She was probably carrying something. Investigation required for this object. Her bike is about ten feet east from her. The victim has a broken left heel and she was raped then strangled with a belt. Forge, signing off."

He shuts the computer down, takes off his glasses and walks to the kitchen to take a long, tall glass of orange juice. Spilling the liquid beside the container, he swears and touches the rim to finally pour it at the right place. His right eye is playing tricks on him again. The juice is swallowed and with deception, the mess taken care of. The day is about to start. Before long, the young man slips into his jogging gears and starts running on the side of the railroad. Right under the third bridge, about four miles away, the thought of the child seen in the vision comes back, heavier, deeper. He can see what happened in all its atrocity, how she tried to get away but the rapist was too fast, too big, a friend of her mother's. She was selling dope for her, a crack addict. Somehow, this client wanted to get more than what her paperbag contained. Josh starts running faster hoping to chase the images away but, they just don't and with recurrence haunt him until he stops running and shrugs his body down to scream his madness within both hands covering his mouth.

Chapter Third

In front of a brick bungalow of West Island, the door bell rings. "Honey can you get the door please?" When Lorne opens the door, Josh appears wearing a suede coat, dark pants and immaculate white shirt. Of course, there is no tie around his neck. "Glad you could make it."

"Well it is going to be awhile before I get treated with Sylvia's meal." Josh claims giving his pal a savouring Cabernet Sauvignon. A nice fragrance of red roses and a delicate aroma of simmering dish are filling the house. In the lobby, pictures of the kids are filling the walls and a few dolls are discarted on the living room table. "Oncle Josh! (Uncle Josh!)" Joyfully calls Marie before hopping into his arms. "Bonjour ma belle, tu vas bien? (Hi sweetie, how are you doing?)"

"Oui, est-ce vrai que tu pars pour L'Inglaterre et que tu ne reviendras pas? (Yes, is it true that you are leaving for Lingland and that you will not come back?)"

"Ce n'est pas l'Inglaterre mais l'Angleterre où je m'en vais. (It's not Lingland but England where I'm going). Et je pars parce que d'autres gens ont besoin de moi (And I'm leaving because other people need me)." Lorne comes back in the living room and offers his pal mineral water. The guest sits on the sofa all crooked up. "Relax; I won't give you the third degree like Marie did."

"Thanks." He mocks taking the mineral water the host is presenting him. Lorne sits right in front and leans his body forward. "I'm sorry about our conversation yesterday. I should have never said that." Josh stares back a second, then takes a sip. Almost silently, he pronounces words that he wishes would never be said: "Don't . . . you're right. I'm running away, away from Diane, from my boring neighbourhood, from myself actually . . ."

Lorne frowns very concerned about his partner's welfare. "Are you still losing patches of hair? Josh nods in a negative way and gets closer to Lorne.

"I want to move to U.K. because I believe they've got a bigger budget than this country to invest in the searching department. They have far more cases than we do and I want to stop these children kidnapping rackets before they do more damage." Lorne's face turns pale. "There's one born every freaking five minutes for God's sake!" The partner leans forward. "If we have the right amount of money invested to find other people like you and me and a prevention unit, I believe we can do it."

Lorne's wife appears in the living room; both men are face to face, so close, she obviously interrupts a private conversation.

"Do not talk about job issues in this home gentlemen; especially tonight. Is that clear?" Her slender waist, black hair, dark eyes and vivid French accent capture their attention. "Yes, sorry my Love. J'ai une faim de loup (I'm hungry like a wolf), how about having dinner?" Offers Lorne. "Of course." Replies the weavy haired guest, making fun of the lady's crisp intonation.

Two hours later, the children bored with the extention of the meal, go to their respective rooms and Marie wants to be cuddled by her uncle. When he approaches her bed, Josh takes the polka dot llama stool and brings it at her bedside. "Raconte-moi une histoire Oncle Josh (Tell me a story Uncle Josh)." He looks up, searching for inspiration. "O.k. chérie . . . il était une fois un lapin (O.k. darling . . . Once upon a time, there was a rabbit)."

Josh always uses animals to tell the child a story. Bryan their first born, already seven at the time Josh meets Lorne, plays lots of sports with him but never asks for stories. Marie is the opposite, she draws, has her own fantasy world with fairies and gobblins, dolls, teddy bears but her favorite is animal stories from her Uncle Josh. He never gets fed up with the demand. Inspired by the child's request, the police agent is so descriptive with the imaginary character that often, Marie's eyes grow bigger. But now, after fifteen minutes, efforts are made to keep them open. He ceases the story telling, cherishes the innocence of her face and kisses her forehead. Rising from the stool, he places it under the giraffe legged table and starts walking away. "Je t'aime Oncle Josh (I love you Uncle Josh)." Words . . . honestly told that make his heart shiver. "Je t'aime aussi Marie . . . très fort. Bonne nuit (I love you also Marie . . . a lot. Good night)."

Closing the door of the child's room, he takes a deep breath before joining the couple in the living room. The lights are dimmed, the sofa inviting, the setting almost romantic with flowers everywhere. Sylvia is an expert with them, having her own greenery and owning a flower shop. She has a few employees and after years in the business, the French pitch black-haired, is now making plans to buy a second store. "So young man, are you excited? You will meet a lot of good looking young ladies."

"You know very well that the most beautiful are right here." Sylvia starts blushing and giggles behind a hand well manicured but soon, her laughing mood shifts to sadness. "I will miss you so much." She admits between two sobs. Trying to cope with his emotions, he replies with his ever charming smile. "I'm going to miss you and your food and every time I'll see red roses, I'll think about you." "The sense of smell is the one that is most strongly impregnated into our memory." She points out, crying and laughing at the same time. "C'mon Sylvia, your husband will soon be back and work with Robert." He confirms while placing his left hand on her knee but ignoring his gentleness she doesn't let him off the hook easily. "Might, but he won't be you. And Marie, she asked so many questions this week. She knows something is wrong and she's wondering why people just leave like that with no reasons." Josh retracts his hand, his entire body assessing the shock wave. "But I do have reasons." Sylvia doesn't give one inch of pity. "Well maybe you do but she's eight and you're her godfather. She's afraid she will never see you again; England is another planet for her. Can you understand that?"

Uncomfortable with such a revelation, he certainly does not think that he meant so much to Marie. "I'll write to her, I promise. Thanks for the splendid supper, it was delicious. I still have a few paintings to wrap up. Oh, I almost forgot . . . ," he dips into his inside pocket. ". . . I got free tickets to go to the motorcycle show at the stadium. Can you give them to Bryan? Maybe he could invite a friend."

"I will." She responds knowing that as usual he paid for them. "Good night Sylvia, thanks again. I'll be here tomorrow at two." He mentions to his partner.

"Fine, I'll see you then." Lorne answers. The couple step out in the late of the evening following the guest, Sylvia feeling the cold not of the night but of her sentiments. Josh backs up, raising his hand to the lady who bends her head against her husband's shoulder.

Sunday morning. First week in the month of May, day of departure.

Josh brings from the basement his ever longing painting box and straps around a leather belt so it won't open during the travel. His car has been brought back to the dealer and a board in front of the house, mentions the broker who will take care of selling it. As he sits on the antique chair protected with a plastic cover, he starts to caress his bike helmet with the uncommon design of a sea monster coming out from the waves confronting a muscular hero. He places it on the oak desk and begins to wrap it with a bubble sheet. Tightening it with a cellophane paper, he then places it on top of one of the twelve boxes of books. The Three Archangels painting is inserted inside a wooden panel exactly like the multitude of other creations, all ready for the move. He looks at the time on the kitchen clock left behind and as predicted, the van picking up his stuff to be shipped to the Londonian apartment rented by Taylor, backs up in the entrance. Noon comes and only an apple can feed him. The house is now emptied from the furniture donated to the closest church. By early afternoon, a taxi arrives and Josh hops in with his luggage and they drive off to Lorne's place. The autoroute is anything but busy on this Sunday afternoon; most travellers are heading in the other direction toward the blooming scenery of the Laurentians. He starts checking his to-do list in his head. The car had been sold; the bike, the house being taken care of, paintings and books are already on their way. He called both his sisters and paid a last farewell to his parents. Still, he feels like he's missing something, being emptied from within but no regrets are felt, no sorrows but a drowning beatitude of melancholy coming from something that didn't work out. Diane found a more suitable lover in Robert and that was fine with him but even this assumption is not good enough to make him feel better. He is far from being drenched with a savouring sense of satisfaction, always being hungry for something although he doesn't have the slightest idea of what that could be. She was the one that opened his eyes only after a few dates. She never did move in with him and after only a few rendez-vous, did she feel like she would never be happy with a man like that. Twenty-six and a half he thinks. A quarter of a life gone by without having been satisfied but for a few instants, always thinking about a way to stop the vicious circle of child molestation. When Diane told him that their relationship could not evolve, he did not even cry and clearly understood her point of view. She promised to stay friends with him and no one had to know that they shared the same bed a couple of times. Her kindness was almost like a sad song that made you feel happy by crying over it. Since then, no one cuddled beside him at night. Unvoluntarily, a sadness expression evades from his mouth as the taxi rides over the river that gave birth to the Thousand Islands. A last bridge is crossed before finally cutting him from the first part of his adult life to lead him into the second act.

The taxi leaves him in front of his colleague's house. Marie is already seated in the van beside her favorite doll. Bryan has got his iPod on so loud that the music can be heard through his single ear plug. Sylvia hops in and Josh takes place on the back seat with the kids. The partner comes out in a flash, carrying his suitcase to the trunk of the car. He rushes back inside and comes back with his airplane ticket before buckling himself in the passenger's seat. Sylvia turns around. "Marie, est-ce que tu es attachée?"

"Speak to me in Ingland mommy." The mother looks at her insistingly." Have you got your seat belt on Marie?"

"Yes, I do." Josh turns to her, the side of his lip smiling. With her big brown eyes, she makes a sign for Josh to bend down toward her. "I need to practice if I want to go and see you."

"So should I talk to you in English from now on?"

"Of course and later, you can teach me the sign language."

"O.k." he replies using his hands.

"She's got less of an accent than you dearest." Lorne tells his wife. "Do you want to walk over to the airport?" She cuts short a tad offended. "That was just a joke my love."

"No it wasn't." Bryan says from the furthest seat. "Be quiet young man." His father tells him while checking his passport.

The ride to the airport takes less than twenty minutes and when they park the van, everybody is excited, all except Josh. Travelling more than twenty times a year, the thrill is far gone. After checking themselves in, they have to wait for two hours before boarding, a time where a dozen televisions are all set on the same channel to report the finding of a missing child.

« A young girl of thirteen has been found in the woods near the shopping center in Rosemere yesterday morning, her body . . . »

Josh looks at the television set, both his hands in his pockets; head tilted on the side, a sad expression covers his face. Lorne watches him from far, knowing this was one of his cases. The news report is barely concluded before the partner suddenly leaves the waiting area to go outside. From where he sits, Lorne can see him light up a cigar, something he's rarely done so early in the day.

After an hour and a half, the drenching climax of leaving family behind fills the small group. Lorne grabs Marie in his arms while Bryan moves in closer. Sylvia is making last recommendations, talking from nervousness, asking about details she already knows. Lorne puts Marie back down and voluptually kisses his wife on her red, red lips stopping with this remarkable action, the incessant flow of words. Josh is further away looking at the scene, wishing he also had someone to share the ultimate bond with. "Don't worry, everything will be fine." Is his reply while both his large hands cover her slender hips. The tention of the departure getting heavier, Lorne decides to cut it short. Sylvia walks over her husband's partner. "Sois prudent (Be careful)." She advices close to his ear.

"Quand lui apprendras-tu ta condition? (When will you tell him about your condition?)" Josh questions the unapparent pregnant lady before she closes her eyes and holds him stronger. "S'il-te-plaît, ne lui dis pas sinon il ne voudra pas partir (Please don't tell him. He won't leave if he knows)." As they detach their bodies from one another, her pleading stare can only be understood. "If you say so, then I'm willing to observe silence." Approving, she walks back near Bryan and Marie comes close.

"Jocelyn, I have something for you." Out from her back pack, she takes out a neatly folded paper. He opens it and a drawing of him appears surrounded with dozen of children. "What's this honey?"

"That's all the children you saved. That's your family."

Tenderness is all over her face, a simple paper drawn by a child with honesty and belief is worth more than anything in the world at the moment. A lump prevents him from speaking for a second so holding the paper with one hand he bends down, opens his arms wide where the little girl pours herself into. Softly, he caresses her pale brown hair while she wraps her arms around his neck. A sharp musical note is heard with the recommendation for passengers leaving for Heathrow airport to proceed to the designated gate.

"Josh, we have to go." Lorne indicates coming close. A last hug, this one somehow stronger ties them together but then, she's the one who lets go. A last hurried kiss from Lorne to his wife is the last thing done before both agents wave goodbye from faraway.

The seats in the business section are very comfortable. Both are accommodated beside one another and after buckling himself, Lorne takes out his laptop to verify the incoming messages. All of a sudden, air becomes rarefied for Josh, sweat drops roll down his forehead and his throat seems to compress together. Lorne lifts his eyes, only to see his co-worker having a panic attack. He rises from his seat, takes off his partner's coat in a rush. "Can I have a glass of water please?" He asks the flight attendant. Josh is having trouble breathing, his hands and knees are shaking, eyelids are slowly refracting to the light. The blond agent looks through his partner's pockets for a bottle of pills. "Not this one." Josh plaintly says. "Where is it?" The partner asks rushing for the find.

"It's in my coat pocket." The flight attendant is back with a glass of water, waiting by his side. "How many do you have to take?" Lorne asks after finding the right container. "Two . . ."

Bringing them close to his mouth, the water is then approached for him to swallow the medication. The lady comes back with a wet towel and places it on his forehead. His shaking hand trying to hold it, Lorne takes over and tilts back his seat. "Will you be fine to fly sir?" Josh looks up to the beautiful lady and nods affirmatively. "Do you need anything else?" She then asks Lorne. "No . . . thank you, not for the moment." Touching Josh's arm, she wants to be reassuring. "I'll come and check on you once in a while." His heart pounds too hard, he feels like throwing up but after only a couple of minutes, the pills start their effect and slowly, he begins to feel relieved. Lorne shuts his laptop and examines his partner. "We can postpone the flight if you want to." Josh withdraws his head, taking the towel away. "I'll be fine." The seatbelt sign lights up and he reaches for the security device. Because his hands are weak, it takes him two tries before he manages to clasp it in. "What would happen if nobody was there to give you your pills?" Josh takes another sip of water and without looking back at him, answers. "I'd just faint."

"So it did happen to you before, didn't it? This is madness for you to take on another job." Josh stays silent while Lorne insists. "In fact I think it's . . ."

"Shut up will you? Just be quiet. I want to get away, leave everything behind and start anew. Just respect my decision, please." He now feels drowsy while the plane leaves the ground and tilts to the east. His head touches the seat and for an obvious reason, feels heavy.

Lorne gives a last stare at his partner, stubborn like a mule and takes off the glass of water from his hands before he falls into a forced sleep.

He wakes up a little before the arrival at Heathrow airport the next morning, a few minutes before seven. Lorne is besides reading the headlines of the newspaper and turns over "Hi sleeping beauty." Josh rubs his eyes. "Did I sleep all the way in?"

"Looks like it. You must be hungry. We'll land in about an hour. Can you manage?"

"Yes, no problem." After unbuckling his seatbelt, he goes to the bathroom. Washing his hands, he looks at the reflection in the mirror. The dull pigmentation of his cheeks, the paleness of his eyes and the creases surrounding them, make him look anything but joyful to be set on a new adventure. How he hates to play games, planning an escape or simply defying the truth. This face isn't his. The long fingers touch the lukewarm water, approaching his features. Sweat slides down his colar while he looks at the reflection in the mirror. Am I worthy of this new position? He thinks eyes filled with sadness. "Are you o.k.?" He hears from the other side of the door accompanied with a knock. "One moment please." Hurrying to wipe down the droplets still hanging from his cheeks before opening the door, he gives passage to the next would-be occupant and excuses him for the time taken.

The plane is rapidly taking a drop of altitude when the pilot speaks in the microphone. Planned as scheduled, they land at 08:10, local time. The weather is a pleasant fifteen degrees celsius, six degrees higher than the place they left. Passengers gather their personal effects and everyone seems eager to get out. The lady seated on the other side of the alley makes eye contact. He stops, inviting her to go before him. "Thank you, it's very kind of you." She replies. Again, Josh nods, too shy to place a single word.

The Londonian airport is much busier than the Montreal one. The ceiling is high, the light coming through it, is dimmed by the cloudy skies. Still feeling a bit drowsy, he walks over to the luggage circle ramp and bends to place his hand bag on the floor when someone bumps into him. "I'm so sorry." He claims with a strong accent. The man with light red hair looks anything but what he said. "No, it's my fault. I shouldn't have bent in the middle of the place like this."

"So you're fine?" The traveler asks the new arrivant. "I'm perfectly sure, thank you for asking." The man wearing a casual tan coloured jacket puts two fingers up to his head. Josh gives little attention to what seems to be a tatoo on the inside of his wrist and quickly, the man walks away. For a second, Josh is desoriented, the first of his many jet-lag effects. He sees his luggage coming and stretches out his hand for the reach but the motion is useless and soon, the luggage circles out. "I'll get it." Lorne proposes already in possession of his own.

When their last suitcase is retrieved, they both walk down the inevitable corridor for a last search of terrorism devices. Walking then to the last section of the airport before walking out of it, a man wearing a dark rain coat approaches them.

"Mister Landers and mister Forge?" Both turn about. "Welcome to London, sirs. Mister Wilkinson asked me to drive you both to the London Police Headquarters." He offers showing Josh and Lorne's picture with the written demand. As soon as their feet set in on the pavement, a limousine's door open and their luggage is placed in the trunk. A few minutes later, it stops in front of a grey twenty-storey building. The entrance is a thick bullet proof fort where two security guards stand vigil and a receptionist greets the incoming visitors. Josh cannot avoid feeling a shiver from the coldness of the place. Everything is set in tempered glass or icy steel, no plants, paintings or left over pens to trouble the desolation of the decorum, making him feel unwelcomed. Without a doubt, he can percieve the emanations of waves coming from different technical devices. "Mister Wilkinson is out at the moment. Would you like to leave your personal belongings while you meet with his affiliate, Sergeant Hockart?"

"Certainly, here they are." Lorne says taking the lead, giving away his luggage and Josh's. "This way gentlemen." The guard let them pass through a magnetized and infra red security archway before following the corridor to the elevator. There is almost no difference between the flooring and the wall panels. Everything is as sobre as a moon crater and problably colder. In less than fifteen seconds, the elevator drags them to an office on the tenth floor. The guard knocks to the side of the door and a bald man, tall as a wall with no proeminent belly, lifts his head. "Sergeant Hockart, agents Landers and Forge have arrived."

"How are you doing mister Forge?" He lets out presenting his hand.

"I'm very well Sergeant." He answers only tilting his head downward. Hockart retrieves back his welcoming fingers and turns to Lorne who on the contrary is more than happy to grab the welcoming greeting. "It's nice to meet you Sergeant."

"Likewise Mr. Landers, so how is Jacob?" Hockart asks as he encourages them to sit. Lorne handles the whole conversation. "Just swell. He's giving training in Toronto this week."

"He really got accustomed to your weather, didn't he?"

"He even tried skating a few years ago and now practices the sport every winter."

"I'll be damned . . ." Hockart says sitting on the edge of his desk.

"He really made his place with us. Everyone likes his little accent."

"What accent?" For a minute, the newcomer thinks he insulted the British. "What I meant is . . ."

"That's quite alright; we think the same about visitors." Hockart replies giving him a friendly tap on the shoulder. Both start laughing while Josh seems unaware of the conversation engaged. His ears are buzzing like crazy and his face is white as a ghost. Being a very expressive man, Lorne continues his boss' description. "Taylor is very strict, never laughs, and barely takes holidays. Can't get any better I guess." Hockart invites both to follow him. "Fine person that Taylor. Too bad he enjoys your country so much."

"I think it's mainly the job he does that makes him stay there, certainly not the weather." Hockart agrees with a smile and then invites them to the cafeteria. "Come with me; let's grab a bite to eat."

An hour later, the trio is almost done with their lunch. The buzzing in his ears is now gone and Josh looks around, still unsure about the new environment.

"You don't speak a lot agent Forge." Reproaches Hockart. "Don't mind him, he's a little shy." Lorne reassures. Josh never liked his buddy to be so specific or overprotective upon his person but he was right. He gets up to get an apple so Hockart takes advantage of the situation to speak to Lorne in confidence.

"I received your IQ scores a while ago and even though you both scored above average, you are aware that these kinds of tests don't proove anything in an emergency situation."

"What are you getting at?"

"Mister Forge seems to be a very qualified worker but unstable. No, the word I'm looking for is not unstable but he seems to be too sensitive toward specific issues, especially with weapons. In this institution, if you let your emotions take the better hold, you're bound to put yourself in a precarious position." The Sergeant had been there and most probably talked from past experiences but Lorne would have done anything for his partner to be sitting in his new office knowing how much it meant to him. "He won't be on the street so he doesn't need a gun anymore. His job is mainly office work so where is the problem?"

"We simply have to be the best, that's all. And just like any governmental institution, the entire world is looking at us." Lorne makes a pause, thinking how he would speak his mind about the issue. "With all due respect, if Josh wouldn't be so sensitive, he certainly would not be able to make so many connections. That's what makes him special. When he walks into a room, he never leaves anyone indifferent; he's got this charisma that you have to be born with. His integrity is quite unbelievable and I've never met anyone like him before, he really has a gift. Just . . . just let him show you how he works . . . once. I'm sure you will be convinced." Josh is back at the table looking at both men, knowing he interrupted their conversation. "You want me to get another apple?"

They walk up to the following level, barely exchanging words before getting to a vast and plentiful office. The room is set in a corner of the building, on the northern side of the eleventh floor. "This will be the place where you will work for the next few years

mister Forge. Your every wish will be granted considering your
fidelity years and the ostensible loyalty you have proven in the last
years at the Montreal office. And, as choreographed by Lieutenant
Taylor, mister Landers will be joining you for two months to find
qualified personnel to work for you." The young agent walks
around the office, looking at the window facing north just like he
asked. He then takes a few steps in the vast office freshly painted.
The furniture, three desks, chairs and filing cabinets, simple but
sturdy, feel cold. No paintings or fixtures adorn the walls. He
approaches the corner windows which offer a view on St-James
Park. "How long have you been working for Wilkinson?" Josh
asks to the Sergeant behind him. "Eighteen years."

"And what do you think of him?" He demands without facing
the man of authority. "I'm sorry?" Hockart retorts surprised.
Josh turns, thinking that maybe he didn't hear the question.
"What do *you* think of him?" The Sergeant looks startled, having
never been asked this question before. "I guess the word that
would best describe my feelings toward my superior would
be respect." The Sergeant answers while scratching the tip of
his nose. Josh nods, understands that the British trend of being
immensely discrete wears many robes. "Would you like to meet
your secretary? Hockart asks changing the subject. "Yes, yes he
would!" Lorne replies immediately, hoping that the lady will be
as gorgeous as the flight attendant.

"I'll be right back." The bald man gets out of the room,
leaving the door open. Josh standing in front of the window;
looks again out to the distant park. Lorne gets closer thinking
that his partner had second thoughts about the job. "Why did
you ask what he thought of Wilkinson?"

"Provocation; I wanted to see if his aura would change and it
did. He also rubbed his nose."

"And, what do you make of it?"

"That only means one thing. He's lying . . ." On the street
down below, a scuffle between teens soon attracts a few Bobbies
coming from different directions. The teens are soon escorted to
an incoming police car. "Good day." Surprised, Josh and Lorne
turn to meet an employee. "Hel, hello sir, my my name is Wilfrid.
I work in the the office next to yours."

"Nice to meet you Wilfrid, please come in." Josh answers.

"I I I hear you're Canadian and you speak many languages."

"I have that facility." Admits Josh.

"I always wa wa wanted to learn French."

"It's . . . different."

"Women love it though." Assures Lorne with a wink. "I I I don't have a wife. I'm sort of . . . attached to my job." Wilfrid's stutter makes him shy but he seems honest and Josh likes that quality. He smiles back to him and before long, Hockart walks back in with a plump lady in her late forties with the hint of pilosity under her nose. "I'm m m on my way." Ends Wilfrid leaving space for the new secretary.

"Good bye, I'll see you soon." Josh exclaims to his office neighbour.

"Good day mister Forge, mister Landers. My name is Mrs Long, Brenda Long."

"It's nice to meet you." He replies declining the handshake he was being offered. She rapidly withdraws her fingers but Lorne is as welcoming as can be.

After spending a couple of minutes explaining the way he preferred the filing system done, Josh lets Lorne get on with other details and walks away. The skin over his face is still pale, his eyes cannot focus on the park trees and his hands are shaking so much that he presses them one against the other. Lorne is at the other end of the room watching from the corner of his eye, his co-worker's well known travelling effects. Once again, he takes the lead. "If you don't mind, I think we will leave it at this for the day. We both need to rest a bit and I prefer we'd be at our best in front of Mr. Wilkinson."

"I understand and will advise him of your decision. You will need my presence to leave the premises though." Claims Hockart.

"Jocelyn, I'm exhausted, let's go to the apartment and sleep for a few hours."

Taken out from his state of semi-consciousness, he nods, pays his respect to Mrs Long and both follow Hockart out of the office.

The elevator doors close and descend the eleven floors to arrive to the lobby where the Sergeant asks the receptionist to call a limousine. "A cab will be just fine." The young agent replies unaccustomed to such a special treatment. The receptionist makes the call and turns to continue working on something else. Eyes slowly falling and starting to feel nauseous, he takes off his identification badge and leaves it on the counter beside Lorne's. Looking around, he can see in the entrance many cameras, four of them pointing to the reception desk. Their luggage and laptops are soon brought back by one of the security guards. "So we will see you in the morning gentlemen." Confirms Hockart. "Good day Sergeant." They both reply before grabbing their possessions. "Good day sirs." Both walk to the door where they have to wait for a signal to let another security guard open the door. Luggage in one hand, carry-on on the shoulder and laptop on the other side, Josh breathes out, finally enjoying fresh air even if a frail spring mist is drapping everything.

As soon as they get in the black vehicle and reveal their destination, the cab driver replies that road repairs are underway a little further east and they will have to make a detour. "Fine, just go ahead." Lorne instructs while Josh feels drowsy and opens his window.

The city resembles Montreal; chaotic, noisy and crowded. But soon, an immense library announcing a book fare attracts his attention. His head turns to it, trying to catch the address but the black cab makes a right turn leaving him without the information. "What was that street we were just on?"

"Rochester Row sir; would you like to stop?" He questions decreasing the speed. "No, no. I just want the street name for now." A few minutes later, near the Victoria underground station, the car driver stops his vehicle and pulls out the luggage right up to the entrance. Lorne pays for the fare, giving a little extra while Josh catches his stuff. The place is made of chiseled stones, a bay window gives in to the street, and dead flowers from the prior blooming season are in pots escalading the set of steps. He takes out from an envelope one of two keys and turns it in the lock, giving the other one to his partner. Inside to their left, is a simple and basic living room furbished with only a three seat sofa, an armchair and a table. Twelve boxes of books and as many paintings trapped in plastic bubble wrapping, are waiting in the hallway. A bedroom is next to it, filled with a double size bed, followed by a bathroom. A small kitchen is the last room giving in a courtyard that needs weeding. "There's kind of a wee small problem here." Reproaches Lorne. "I saw the bedroom too; don't even think of me sleeping beside you." Josh walks back to the corridor where there's a staircase. Step after step, hopes are high to find a second bedroom but when he pushes the panel in, he only finds an attic filled with dust and forgotten cartons. A small window where light doesn't dare come in is forced open. Lorne soon follows and deception can also be read on his face. "I'll go find a hotel." Exclaims Lorne dusting off the window ledge. "No, don't. You'll keep the downstairs room and I'll fix this place up."

"Are you certain?"

"Of course but first, let me take a nap." Josh says coming down the stairs. "Sure." Lorne takes his luggage to his room. "What would you like for supper? You want to go out?" The young agent's coat takes a flight to the sofa and he discloses the too tight cuffs of the beige cotton shirt. "I don't know . . . maybe later." When Lorne pops in the living room again, the dark haired newcomer is fast asleep on the floor. He looks at him and smiles before taking care of placing his clothes away.

The following morning, a taxi brings the two agents back to the grey, twenty stories building. Hockart has been in for a few hours now. It only takes a phone call to his quarters to come and greed them at the reception. "Good day mister Forge, mister Landers. We have a busy schedule ahead. First, let's meet Chief Superintendent Wilkinson." The doors open to a long marble alley with armed guards. Cameras are all around; metallic receptive panels surround the entire corridor. Both men are searched in two different ways; going through a magnetized probe and a manual check. "You're clean." Admits the armed guard. Josh stares back at him for being a tad too manipulative to his liking. The other security guard talks into his microphone and waits to give his reply. "Sir Wilkinson will now receive you both." The heavy steel door opens to a spacious office with lofty bullet proof windows, overlooking London. When they walk in, the highest figure of security on the land gets up to greet them.

"Here at last! Gentlemen, won't you enter." Wilkinson exclaims. To their surprise, Taylor turns around. "It's a pleasure to meet you sir." Answers Lorne, heavily shaking Wilkinson's grip.

"Good day sir." Responds Josh standing behind with both arms at his back. "Please, take a seat." Invites the leader showing the chairs at Taylor's side.

"Were you not supposed to be in Toronto all week?" Lorne asks. "The meeting was cancelled so I thought I would come and see an old friend." Behind them the doors are quietly shut by the guard, the room becomes noiseless and the ochre wall behind the powerful British figure makes it easy for Josh to visualize the aura of the man with so many responsabilities. Dancing from immense white lines to shadowy red stripes and darker areas, the young man's eyes are examining the fluctuation of the shades. Barely listening to the conversation, Taylor suspects what his protégé is doing. "How long have you been working for your superior mister Landers?" Wilkinson interrogates.

"Twenty-two years." He answers comfortably sinking into the leather seat.

"What about you mister Forge, how long have you been working for John?"

"I'm sorry?" He replies coming out from his bubble. "How long have you been working for Lieutenant Taylor?"

"Ten years, two months and (Josh starts counting in his head) eleven days."

"You will turn twenty-seven on November sixteen." He claims reading a set-aside file. "That's correct."

Wilkinson makes a fast substraction in his head. "So you started working under eighteen? Isn't that against the law for a Provincial institution?"

"I finished High School at sixteen and was available. On their side, they needed someone right away."

"Is this a common business for North Americans to work before they're actually allowed?" Wilkinson asks Taylor but Josh cuts in, not wanting his boss to be jeopardized. "I only received the minimum wage until I got to be eighteen. It was a shared agreement. I figured that the two-year training I received was worth it."

"How many disappearences did you solve in the first year?" Josh turns to Taylor and wonders. "With the help from Lorne and my boss, I found a couple, maybe ten."

"Ten is the correct answer." Taylor precises.

"And in the last ten years, how many cases were solved?"

"Gee, I don't know. One hundred and something I guess. I lost count."

"One hundred and fifty-two cases were solved, to be more precise." Taylor replies.

"It is not a lot when you know that only in Quebec, there are about seven thousand disappearances per year and ten percent of thoses are revealed to be serious and unsolved after a week." Josh adds knowing the statistics. Wilkinson gets up and sits on the edge of his desk. "I've got a responsibility toward this institution as to how the money is spent and your contribution has certainly been one of the most valuable yet but I was wondering if you could concentrate more on living individuals." The man of high rank barely looks at Lorne while he makes a stand-still upon Josh. "Waves between dead and alive people aren't the same. At first, when I started working, I had reluctance going to a certain space but then, I figured that this was the lead to the living people. Most of the time, my link is a picture. As I deepen the structure between my energy and what's left of the person who disappeared, I restructure my impression. Only when I wake do I know if the person is alive or dead, never during the course of the linking. When I work with Lorne, while he's chanelling, he makes me talk so it's totally another way of getting the message. When I work alone, it's quite different."

"Which method is easier?"

"Working with someone is less dangerous. That's the reason our program will include a channeler for each voyant."

"What could happen when working alone?"

"You could easily get lost and stay there."

"Why?"

"The danger lies when it's peaceful. So peaceful in fact that it takes all your strength to come back. It's very awkward to let go of all the pain and trouble of this earth. To wander off into a space where time doesn't exist is very attractive. Well, for me anyway. When I work with Lorne, he makes me get there. I look, search, find and then he brings me back. When I'm alone, I could wander off for hours and still feel the urge to go further. I have to fight against my own will to come back. You have to understand that when you're into that dimension, it's like a drug; it gets you addicted because it's so attractive. Most of the time, you get wrapped by so much love, it's undescribable, almost too pleasing. And on the contrary, when things get ugly and forces want to hold you back, it becomes very hard to come back. It's like an electrical field. You need a strong mind to back off these energies."

"Are you on drugs when you do it?"

"Concentration would be harder and it might even be dangerous to do so. Anyway, my mandate is to look out for people who disappeared and I believe that, whether dead or alive, all individuals are worth looking for."

"I see your point of view about dead people but I see it as a waste of time." The young agent cannot approve with the reply and still feels deeply about the departed ones. "I've heard of your son. Were you not glad to finally put him to ground? Letting him have a decent burial and trying to go on with your own life?" The leader swallows heavily and places his hands on the desk while the newcomer continues, pushing his luck a little too far. "A human being is still one, well after his last breath. That's why we have fond memories of the ones who crossed our path, the reason why we transmit souvenirs and teachings. Death as common people know or hear about is merely another dimension, but far from the end of life as we perceive it. From what I have encountered up to now, it is my belief that everything is connected." Josh makes a small pause and then continues. "I believe that an investment in such a department might bring you parted opinions and even you may doubt it. You don't even have to tell me of your own life's presumptions or hell and heaven's visionary interpretations because I can see and feel the distance that you want to keep with people who think like I do . . . I am an irregularity in the system. God gave me a gift and I haven't got the slightest intention of forcing you into changing your beliefs because you're the kind of person who won't ever have faith in what you cannot see and I can accept that. I've been judged all my life, mainly by my own family so your opinion doesn't really matter, only the results and believe me, you'll see them." The young Canadian grayish-blue eyes are confronting Wilkinson's until the leader retracts himself to his chair and presses his body back to be soothed by the leather comfort. The reply given in a low tone is deep and unagressive.

Used to the young lad's stubbornness and particular beliefs, Taylor warned the high rank commander prior to this meeting. Over the decade he had been working with him, the British born Montreal Lieutenant knew the youngster to be different from all other people he'd ever met before, cherishing his individuality and unability to act hypocritically. The lad was authentic, knew what he wanted and what he was capable of. Extrapoling his abilities, he felt as if the Lord granted him with an uncommon blessing and was surely not going to let anyone misjudge him or think less of him because of it.

Whipped by the strong utterance, Wilkinson takes a moment before giving his last answer. "People on the fourth floor are waiting for you to complete both your identifications. Mister Forge, mister Landers, welcome to the London Police Force." Taylor discretely lifts his lips in contentement while Josh raises his chin with pride. "Thank you sir." He concludes before leaving the cold office.

Being transferred to a far away room, the newcomers are asked to undress completely and wear a smock that attaches in the back. To Josh, another recommendation is asked. "The cross also." Snaps the employee in charge of the examination. "I never take it off."

"Take off the cross please." The employee insists. Leaving it into a white plastic container, Josh is then brought to the next chamber. A sample of blood is taken, heart rate, weight, height. A physical endurance test is carried out followed by another heart rate report. A fourth employee comes close with a camera and an extended photo session takes place. Every birthmark is photographed. Size, colour and location are recorded. "What's this?" The London employee asks about a long strike covering the left side of his rib's cage. "I was born with it." Josh answers without looking at it. "Looks like a sharp knife cut. You think it was the doctor's?"

"I only know that my mother suffered for many hours to have me."

"Did she have a caesarian? The scalpel could have slipped."

"No, it was natural child birth. That I'm certain of, because she told me she was in so much pain that she wouldn't see me for the next three days." The employee brings his eyebrows together, takes a picture of the slain and makes sure that it is added in his file, right after the fingers and retina imprints. "I usually wear my hair shorter but I lost part of it a few months back on the left side and tried to hide it."

"That detail is already mentioned in your file. We were advised about everything there is to know about you even before you set foot in this edifice. My job is simply to record today's picture and tests."

"So you guys make other identity cards each time there is a physical change?"

"A picture is taken everytime a wrinkle appears, sir."

"Oh . . ." Josh's eyes pivot toward another security guard standing as rigid as a pole. There is no way to tell if this is a joke or not. Another doctor, an ophthalmologist, comes in to finish the physical and complete the questionnaire. "You have been under medication for the last six months. How do you feel now?"

"I started to cut back on them."

"How is your eyesight?" He questions testing his pupil with a miniature flash light.

"Better."

"Do you feel any trembling with your hands?"

"From time to time but mainly when I'm tired."

"Let's check your sight." The doctor makes him stand in front of the panel where letters are printed from large to small. "Left eye please and cover your right."

« E,Y,H,U,G,K,O,M,N,Z,A. »

"Excellent. Now do the same thing with your right eye."

« E,Y,H,U,G,K,O,M,N,Z,A. »

"Perfect. Now please stand up and close your eyes. I want you to touch the tip of your nose with one hand, then the other." As told, Josh does the exercise but a mere hesitation comes from the right movement. The doctor notices it and writes it down. "Follow my finger and tell me when you cannot see it anymore." The doctor pulls it far and with his left eye, his side vision stops at eighty-five degrees but on the right side, a mere seventy degrees is accomplished. Concern can be read all over his face. "Please sit." The doctor suggests and doubtful, the newcomer does as he is told. After writing a few more notes which seem like an eternity, the doctor finally says a few words. "Your right eye is still a bit defective. Your sight from this eye is blocked by something. I will have to investigate. We will have the results only in two days and considering today's physical, you are accepted but will have to get another shooting exam to obtain a revolver permit on this continent." For an instant, Josh cannot believe how much this simple sentence could transform his life. "Can I still drive a motor bike?"

"You will have to be doubly careful by turning your head at intersections. Let me just insist on the fact that if any changes occur, you feel pain in the back of your head or start shaking uncontrollably, you really have to consult again and I insist on it. In the mean time, I will make the papers for you to have a brain scan."

"I already had one last December in my home country."

"Yes, we know but it might have been done too early to discover anything and then, maybe not. I only want to make sure that nothing is nesting. It may take a month for you to have one because of the waiting list but still, I really feel you should have it."

"I understand."

"Your medical report will be sent to Hockart. You can now go to your office and settle in. If something comes up with the results, you will be the second person to know about it." Half-dressed, pulling up his shirt sleeve, he thanks the doctor with a huge smile and a sincere thank you. By the window, he can see his partner in a smock answering inevitable questions before he can also be accepted by the agency, even on a temporary basis.

The following day is a quiet one. Both their passes are handed out, each limiting them to certain floors. Just like any of the other 215 employees, they will be taken every morning and given back every night but their identification papers are to be worn at all times. By noon, they had been introduced to most of the personnel in charge and were sitting at the cafetaria with their treys full. As always, Josh chooses a place near a window. "How did you sleep last night?" Lorne questions.

"Why don't you ask me why your snoring sounds like an on-coming train?" Josh digs into his salad after adding pepper and dressing. "You want me to move out?"

"No, that would be ridiculous. I'll soundproof the place with a panel and then put a gym mattress over. That ought to do. Did you call your wife?"

"Yes, I did this morning. Marie didn't want to go to school."

"What happened?"

"She complained about being feverish when her temperature was very normal."

"She probably misses you and wants to stay home with her mother."

"That's what Sylvia figured. So anyway, I said I was to log on to the house every day before going to bed. That way, it will be four o'clock their time. She will see her daddy and it won't seem so bad."

"Good idea." Josh rubs his right eye and cannot focus right.

"Is it bothering you again?" Lorne asks sinking his fork in a slice of bacon.

"Yeah . . . it also did while I was having my examination yesterday."

"So what happened when they asked you to name the letters off the panel? Don't tell me you failed the test?"

"I didn't but the side vision on my right eye is lower than my left and I will have another shooting exam."

"I have to take it as well because I'm old, don't worry about it." Josh smiles while Hockart is coming toward them at a fast pace so both suddenly change the conversation. "Gentlemen, sorry for interrupting your lunch but a few colleagues would like to know more about your methods. Would it be possible for you do do a linking this afternoon?" Lorne looks at his partner, and then turns back to Hockart. "My partner didn't sleep very much last night. I think it may cause a problem. Josh, what do you think?"

"We'll have to try it out." His sentence is barely over that Hockart claps his hands together. "Good! What do you need?" Josh finishes his mineral water and answers: "A quiet and dark room where I can lay on a gym mattress and some water for when I wake."

"Do you need candles or special music?" The Sergeant inquires.

"No, none of that nonsense is necessary."

"Fine, I think I have the right place for you. Be at the lobby in thirty minutes and wait for me."

"We'll be there."

The same afternoon, Josh and Lorne are brought to a room where lights are dimmed, no outside noise to be heard. The youngest is lying on a gymnastic mat, Lorne standing by his side. "What do you see Josh?"

"I can see . . . I can see your huuuuugggggge nose . . ." Josh opens his eyes and sits, manifestly disappointed. "See, I knew you were too tired." Repeats Lorne.

"I'm sorry. I just can't do it today, maybe tomorrow." He articulates getting up and putting his shirt back on. Hockart's expression becomes heavier and he gets close to both of them. "You're just going to quit like this?"

"I'm sorry. I'm simply not up to it today. There could be a dozen of reasons why but I just won't appeal to any of them." Right there, under an opened mouth police Sergeant, the young man leaves the picture of a disappeared child on the table and walks out of the edifice.

In a café close to the office, the young man sits at a table near a window, overlooking the street. Putting his hand on a famous newspaper, he rapidly seeks the big articles and bored, flips the paper back on the table. There is nothing for him to do but clear his head to be in shape for the next morning. A few pounds are left on the table near the bill. Foggy weather is making him miss the Quebec spring, full of melting snow and bright, sunny days. Surely, there will not be any sugar shack party in the area, for there was not one single maple tree in sight. A lot is there to admire on the busy street but mainly what attracts him most, is the architectural design, vast memorials of war heroes and highest representation beyond the Prime Minister, their dearest Queen. Her name or association, is seen everywhere on the streets, the façade of restaurants, stamps and money. Her symbolistic attribution is the pride of the British people. Even if seventy percent of inhabitants proclaim her majesty and court too expensive to afford, her dignity and devotion translate in admiration. Turning to his right, the London Tower appears in the distance. How can he be in this town without visiting it so he buys a disposable camera at a convenience store and heads for the tourist attraction. Dozens of visitors are just like him, getting up to the last level. A little blond girl wearing a pied-de-poule weaved coat with a black velvet colar is staring at him. Certainly trying to guess what country the visitor is from, she is grimacing. Everyone gets out of the elevator and arrives at the top of the iconic legacy where black crows are standing vigil, looked after by the deep red clothed Beefeaters. The view could have been fantastic if it hadn't been for the lingering fog. Unlike the guards with their tall plushy hats, Josh knew these guards could talk to visitors.

"How long have you been working here sir?" Josh questions walking away from the tourists' crowd, rubbing the volatile's sombre chest resting on a brass pole near the guard's shoulder.

"Over twenty years sir."

"I'm not a local. This is my first time in London, I'm Canadian."

"So I've noticed."

"It's my accent isn't it?"

"You seem to be a foreigner mainly because of your features, sir. Rarely do we see dark haired people with light-coloured eyes. I have been to your country a few years back. It's lovely and people are very friendly."

"Well, thank you."

High above them, a fastened door locked by double hinges intrigues the visitor.

"What is behind this?"

The man in his sixties looks back at Josh with a solemn stare.

"This is the tower where prisoners were taken before being judged. History almost took its toll here."

Josh stops rattling the bird's chest and flips his eyes back to the guard. There was something in the way he chose to tell the words, a deep, deep sorrow, palpable with each syllable.

"Are you talking about common prisoners?"

"I'm talking about Scottish invadors scanding their depreciation for monarchy."

"When people starve to death, it's really hard to convince them that a crown bears the weight of equity but . . . who are we to judge what happened hundreds of years ago?"

The Beefeater could not and would not argue with the visitor.

"Have a nice day sir. Enjoy your visit on the British Isle." He adds politely ending their dialogue.

"Thank you sir, have a nice day too." Josh bows and so does the guard, getting back to position himself near the ledge. The crowd is only a few paces ahead and with a few steps, the visitor walks toward it. He turns back; to take a picture of the guard but no one is there any more, neither the man wearing the deep red coat nor the bird with the black plumage. Turning his head to each side of the tower, no one can be seen in the mist. Perplexed and almost with regret, he hastens his steps to join the rest of the group.

There was a vast cloud over the sea, Éire was far behind. The small boat was sliding over to Caledonia. The wind was absent and anyone who knows the water manners could predict that it would have mounted twice by the following sunset. Father has taken this obsolete sea way to meet monks on the green island and then bring Mise to an isolated land, saying it was for my own good. All I could foretell was that Father left me to be on Iona to learn, grow up and eventually become a man. Companions like Gaël and Lochland, future masters of Mull and Skye, were there to help. The three of us fought together so many times that wooden fence pickets were missing from the lamb barriers and made farmers angry at our borrowing. It is Ney my fault should I presume that we cannot aquaint real metal ones, must I say. But they would not believe that it was all to be better and stronger so that we may, one day brave the Norse warriors away on their villain ships. Dia (God) help me through this period of my life since I shall be on the Sacred Island for the next eleven years or so. Mise, with hope, will survive this long hardship of salvation. Gracing Lochland for his teaching of the words, I here stand sheded in by a single candle to relate my myseries, my outcast while Father wars against the red uniforms by the side of MacRae the elder. I only recall from my brothers vague memories and from Mother, the fragrance of magnolia into her hair. Who is there amongst us who shall say that my recluse would be worth something, or even more, anything at all. I now here stand, a young fragile human close to puberty, who shivers in the dark while Father gathers the twelve apostles and their Leader dispersed on the continent. It will take moons to reconcile of their magnificence, he said. It will take seasons before they become into his hands the pleasure to bring them out to their rightful owner again . . .
                                    KMK

Inside a flat in downtown London, the red-haired lady places her note pad, French, English and Gaelic dictionaries on the side and rubs her tired eyes. Dispersed on the table, are pictures of the rooms in a Highland castle, mostly what was affixed to the rock walls. She's on her way to the book fair where her last book is being presented. Tired, she lets loose her pencil down and pulls her body backwards. Her friend, the owner of the flat, walks into the kitchen grabbing the french exercise book and randomly opens a page.

«Par . . . fois je vais à la ci . . . . té—té? What the . . . . it's in French . . . you're still wasting time on this?" Annoyed, the historian grabs all the papers and dictionaries into a pile. "It's far from being a waste of time and I do it mainly because it's part of my re-insertion into the single life of doing what I want to do, when I want to."

"What about checking out firm butted rich lads out in bars? Wouldn't that be a way to let the hour glass drip to a better use?" Charlene raises her eyes and then drops them back before grabbing everything and placing it in a leather sack.

"None for me thanks. No need for a punching card anymore."

"I swear Charlene; they're not all ignorants you know. I met a fantastic guy last week."

"Oh yes? And where is he today?"

"He . . . had to go back and meet his wife about the divorce papers." The red-haired gives her friend a fed-up stare that needs anything but precision.

"Thanks for letting me sleep here yesterday; I'll see you later at the fair." She hopes before closing the door.

With a bunch of documents in her sack and a box filled with her latest book, the red-haired takes the city bus toward the library where she is presenting her new novel. "What is in the box dearest?" An old lady sitting beside her asks after the ride as begun.

"A book I wrote. I'm presenting it this week-end. This is my second one."

"So you're a successful writer?"

"Not yet but I intend to be."

"Oh, you will alright. I can see it your eyes." With a shattered walk, the old lady gets up and leaves. How ironic was it that a total stanger had more faith in her then her divorced husband. The wealthy insurance consultant who never gave room for her to emancipate, was finally out of her life. At thirty-two, it was time for her to be happy. When she enters the library, gliding under the banner welcoming people to the event, a breath of fresh air fills her lungs. Writers from different countries are all over, tables filled with books are evenly placed to greet future buyers and literacy icons. After a few hellos, she places herself at the kiosk corresponding to her contract, at the far end of the alley with a smile on her face. Happiness is in this room, transmitted by the writers, editors and publishers who all pitched in to give their best, presenting something worthy to be delivered. For two weeks, they will meet nothing but happy people who cherish books as the ultimate companion of self-indulgence.

The next day, the two newcomers head to Hockart's office, the youngest wearing old jeans and a t-shirt. The British officer is surprised at the common outfit in the prestigious organization. Nevertheless, he welcomes him like a guest of honour. "So mister Forge, how do you feel today?"

"Much better, I've had a few hours of sleep. Sorry about my clothing. I didn't have time to buy another suit and the one I have, is too wrinkled to wear."

"Don't worry about it. Here are both your cellulars. Laptops and business cards will be available shortly. Now do you think that we can proceed where we left off yesterday?"

"No problem Sergeant."

Back in the quiet room, lights are once again dimmed. Josh lifts his shirt out wearing only an undershirt; does some relaxing stretches and lies on the mattress.

"Why is he taking his shirt off?" Hockart says to Lorne, hushing.

"Connecting takes a lot of energy. At the end of the session, it will be as if he ran for miles."

"Oh . . . I'm sorry. I was not aware."

Lorne brings close the picture of the eight year old again. Josh makes the sign of the cross over his forehead, his torso and lastly, his third plexus. With a synchronised tendrum, he exhales many times deeper and deeper. With his right hand, he touches the picture that Lorne is holding, and then quietly places his hand back on the one resting over his chest. Eyelids are shut. A few minutes of silence are observed before Josh violently gets up and starts looking for an exit, creeping and circling around the room. Hockart jerks at the gesture but Lorne tells the Sergeant to keep quiet by putting an index over his lips. Josh starts crying and fumbles down in a corner of the room, scratching the bottom of the wall.

"Got to get out, I've got to get out." He yells between tears.

Lorne walks a bit closer. "Josh?" The young man turns, afraid and hides his head under his arms.

"Don't hurt me!"

The blond agent immediately figures that this is not his colleague he's talking to, but the missing child. "I won't hurt you Michaël. Can you tell me where you are?"

"I'm stuck in a hold by the bay."

"What bay?"

"Where the ships are, I wanted to play sailor. The floor fell under me and I'm stuck with rats! There's no way for me to climb up again." Josh starts crying again, his face petrified by fear.

"Listen to me Michaël. Just tell me what boat you're in and we'll be right there."

"Most of the paint is off. It used to be white with a blue line. I heard my mom earlier on the dock, I screamed back but she didn't hear me." Josh is still acting very nervously, clinging to the wall that he's trying to escalade and then pushes it with his shoulder until it hurts. Lorne gets closer and slowly touches his friend's forearm. "Everything will be fine Michaël. Just relax, sit down."

"The rats will eat me!" Josh shouts pushing invisible rodents with his feet. Unable to calm him with simple words, Lorne holds his partner tighter, locking his shivering arms with his own body. "Shutttt . . . Get down, close your eyes. I'm right here. I'm right beside you."

Hockart is looking at the scene, unvolontarily creasing his eyebrows, bringing his hand toward his mouth. Josh turns about, frantically looking around. His respiration is fast and tears unvolontarily spread over his cheeks while sounds of fear break the silence. Lorne immediately places his right hand over Josh's eyes while the other protects the back of his head.

At first, « Michaël » opposes himself by grabbing the savior's forearm but the older agent resists being tossed away. To his ear, he whispers a few words and Josh immediately fumbles to the floor, his neck drawn backwards. Hockart has the most troubled look in front of the scene.

"Have you got enough information to get the child?" Lorne asks while gently placing his colleague in a more comfortable position.

"Yes we do. I'll send someone over there right now." In a rush, the Sergeant leaves to send policemen over the area described.

Half an hour later, Josh has his neck up, head rested against the wall. The upper part of his body is glowing with sweat. "There you go." Concludes Lorne giving his buddy a bottle of water. "Are you o.k.?"

The man resting avidly gulps down and nods. "Did I talk enough?"

"Yes, don't worry; officers from his hometown have been called."

"They better do it fast, he has a fever."

"Why?"

"The rats bit him."

Two hours after the demonstration, the finding of the eight year old is confirmed and word spreads out fast that the two newcomers solved the case. Shocked and amazed by the procedure, Hockart walks back to meet the two agents visiting another department. "I don't know how to express my gratitude, this is simply unbelievable. Wilkinson will be overwhelmed with this report. Taylor was right, you two are amazing."

Josh bends his head, clearly shy about such a demonstration of happiness.

"Thank you Sergeant." Agrees Lorne. "I think we'll just head back to Josh's office for the rest of the day. We have many other files to look at."

"Yes of course, I understand."

Hockart watches the two men leave, the youngest one in a slow and shattered walk, completely drained and supported by his faithful companion.

Later that same day, a tranquil supper in a restaurant gives the two men the opportunity to discuss their working day. Looking at the menu, Lorne first speaks out.

"C'mon, say it . . ."

"I hate it when you do that, you're worse than my mother."

"Hate what?"

"Know that I've got something to say."

"Well it's not very hard. When you only have pitty talk for more than an hour, I know that the little mouse circus inside your head is frantically swirling."

The waiter comes by. "Have you decided gentlemen?"

"For an entrée, I will take the chef's salad and then, I will have the trout with baked potato." Josh answers giving him his order.

"And you sir?"

"Your sirloin steak with shrimps looks very tantalizing. With it, I will take a side order of mashed potatoes with lots of butter and half a decanter of your best home red wine."

The waiter turns to Josh. "Any wine for you sir?"

"Water will be fine, thank you."

The waiter nods, takes both menus and goes to the kitchen to place their order.

"So where were we . . . oh yes, I was merely suggesting that as a partner of yours, I may have the right to know what's on your mind."

Josh takes a sip, lifting his eyes in a bothered matter. "I don't think we'll make it."

"Make what?"

"Find the right people to do what we intend doing in such a short period of time." Josh stays quiet, forcing his jaw, looking deeper.

"Oh no!" Replies Lorne. "I'm not staying longer than two months! I've got a wife and kids and if I'm not back by mid July, divorce papers will surely be heading my way."

"Well then, we have a problem. If Hockart wants us to solve so many cases, we'll have less time to find the right people to work with me when you'll be gone. Have you seen how many Mrs Long has prepaired for us?"

"You're forgetting the other boxes laid by the wall."

"I thought that was her stuff."

"Unfortunately while you were recuperating on the sofa, I happened to check them out. Some of them are as old as you and I."

"Gees . . . ."

"And that's not it, Hockart has got . . ."

"O.k., I get it."

Josh's salad is brought over. A basket of bread and churned butter is placed in the middle of the table.

"Thank you."

"You're welcome sir."

As soon as the waiter is far from hearing distance, Lorne smiles and cannot wait to tease his buddy. "You hate it don't you."

"Being called sir? Of course I hate it."

"Better get used to it, you're in London lad."

Josh takes another bite and somehow, for no reason at all, his head turns to the entrance on his left. Waiting to be directed, a tall, red-haired lady in her early thirties is there. Wearing comfortable shoes and a modest raincoat, she has in her hands a leather brief-case filled to the edge. Josh follows her with his eyes until she sits. As soon as their eyes meet, a feeling of déjà vu overwhelms him but afraid to appear rude, he slowly brings his eyes back to his meal. Lorne fakes to drop his napkin to the floor to see who he was looking at. When he rises, the inevitable comment comes out from his mouth.

"Nice . . ."

"No, that's not it. I know her."

"This is your first time in London. How can you say that?"

He raises his shoulder. "I'm not sure but I know that this is not the first time we see each other."

At the end of the supper, Josh rises. From the corner of her eye, the lady attempts a look. "What are you waiting for?" Lorne asks.

"No . . . this is not the place."

"Oh, so now you're being romantic?"

"I just mean this is not the place where I should meet her."

Looking astonishingly perturbed, Lorne opens his mouth. "I give up. It's too much of a hassle to find you a mate." After finishing his supper, Josh leaves his buddy so he can call his wife and kids. "I think I'll go out a bit."

"You? Going out? I don't believe it. Be my guest."

When most people found comfort in being entertained, Josh only wished to bring in more work home but the Sergeant thought that this week's sessions were quite enough. After all, the meaning "getting out" was probably too fat a word. He only planned to walk a mile or two before going to sleep and like every evening after supper, he lights his favorite cigar. Being the last of his cancer sticks, he enjoys it more than all the previous ones. A convenience store stands a few steps ahead and nonchalant, he walks in. The place has a million things to sell, candies, tourist maps and Queen's keepsakes. Music plays in the distance, something a little eccentric, coming from behind the wall.

"Do you sell this brand?" He demands to the employee showing the empty cigar box.

"I'm afraid not sir but would you care for something similar?"

"It's either that or I quit smoking."

The salesman brings it up the counter and proposes two brands, right after checking the tar percentage. Josh then places a few nutritive bars on the counter beside it. After paying, he starts walking away but then comes back to the counter.

"Where does this music come from?"

"From the upstairs floor, it's a coffee-bar kind of place with drinks, a short menu and musicians. It's called Ladder's refuge. It can only be reached from the other side of the street so you have to make a u-turn. The sound can tell you how much the place is soundproof." The salesman throws laughing.

"Well, at least you can have a free hearing of it."

"Tonight it's worth it but last week was the pits."

Josh smiles and thanks him before leaving, this time for good. Back on the street, the mist starts to fall again its humidity down on everything. Stray cats are avoiding getting wet by walking under the low roofings and all the people he encounters, are walking shedded under umbrellas of all kinds. Soon he reaches the opposite side of the street and arrives in front of the said place with orange and violet neons trembling in the rain. In the stairs covered by red rigid semi circular roofing, a couple is close together, sharing a cigarette with a pint of dark ale at their feet. The place looks cosy, dark like a jazz club with a persistent tobacco aroma and a tint of canabis. Reaching the higher level, he stops at the entrance, unknowing if he has to wait or just walk to the first available table. A young lady waitress, barely twenty, comes up to him with a tray under her arm.

"How many will you be?"

"I'm alone." He answers in a flash.

"Come this way." She answers with her beveled black hair almost sweeping off his chin. Her short skirt, or rather the hankerchief that served as one, was probably red but in the dimmed light, it was hard to tell even the fabric in which it was made.

"What will it be?"

"I'll have anything non-alcoholic."

"You're driving aren't you?"

". . . yeah." He agrees avoiding getting into details.

A band of four musicians is playing under a blue light, the latest of their repertoire, something a little jazzy, a little funk. Resting his shoulders against the wall, Josh sees a few listeners staring back. The place is probably frequented by the same crowd over and over and any newcomer stuck out like a sore thumb. The waitress comes back with a juice mixed with sizzling water and a dash of lemon.

"That will be five pounds."

Josh takes out ten and after getting his change back, gives three as a tip. The young woman in the tight skirt bends and in a languorous voice approaches his face, almost to kiss him.

"If you need another drink or anything else, just lift your little finger, I'll be right up . . . or down." Her eyes are brown, deep as a cavern that could engulf you. Her inviting shiny lips and firm breasts are quite appealing. For a few seconds, he only stares at her, surprised by the proposition. "I'll remember that." He replies his eyes wide open. Sweat almost appears on his forehead. It has been awhile since he got such an offer from a total stranger. His sexual thirst had to be filled as the one from his mouth but inadvertently, it could not be this way. Not with someone he met five minutes ago, not in such a place and certainly not in the backstage of a cosy bar on top of a greasy counter. He places the tall glass back on the table, throws in the slice of lemon to impregnate the juice with its bitter taste. The band finishes their song and under a few clappings, the singer addresses the dispersed audience.

"We will now take a short break and be back in twenty minutes."

Feeling like a dog in a bowling alley, he tries his best to fill in the gap in which it was best to be sitting alone in a bar. Another waitress is circling around him like a vulture, bending to other customers like a sensual viper in a very suggestive way. She then secretely handles them small packets of white powder. A sexual desire unvontarily rises in him and as expected, his waitress comes back. She places her thighs right against the edge of the round table, offering her intimacy. He asks her to approach and with a winning smile she bends down.

"Don't waste you're time." He coldly tells her.

"Are you guay?"

"Not in this life."

"So what brings a solitary man to this joint then?"

"I'm new in town. I need to find out where teens hang out."

Un-hiding a laugh she approaches bends down and picks up an empty cigarette pack lying over the next empty table. "So you enjoy teens more than adults?" God, did it really sound like that? He asks himself.

"Do you have a light?" He asks opening his coat to grab his cigar box. Discretely, he shows her his agent identification paper.

The expression on her face radically changes. After hesitating, she brings out a lighter and he bends a cigar to it.

"You're on duty?" She proposes.

"I'm always on duty." He exhales twice but before she leaves, he calls her. "What's your name?"

"Everybody calls me Shadow." She simply answers. He reaches into his pocket and finds a card from his old office and scribbles his cell number. She places herself in between him and the other customers.

"Don't do that. You're the one that's wasting time." She whispers avoiding co-workers to hear.

"Don't you want to make it easier for other kids who may be in trouble? Didn't you have it rough?"

"That's none of your business."

"I'm afraid it is. Well maybe not for you but for the hundreds who get into trouble each year."

She stares back while he finishes his drink, gets up and leaves a fifty pound note under his card. With the same un-hurried pace, he leaves the bar. Shadow looks at the money and quickly grabs at the same time, the business card with the police emblem before anyone else sees it.

The frail tempering of the rain makes the street-lamp shimmer on the sidewalk. Police sirens are screaming near by, the noise of cars speeding in the night, the sound of two men fighting, one of them obviously drunk, swearing like a madman. Nothing was new, nothing had changed from his hometown, and the pain of loneliness was still there, hanging in the back of his mind. He shuts his eyes for a second, thinking that maybe it was a stupid idea to leave everything behind, believing that a new town would change his future. It was now close to midnight and the traffic was urgently passing in the city. London is a place where it rains two thirds of the year and the month of May was no exception to that rule. Trees are scarsely divided by sidewalks; people are rigid in their manners, even in their walk. Solemnity is everywhere. Food has barely any sugar if not for the crème brûlée and sadly, he looks at the iron fences wondering if they are as lonely as he is. When he arrives in front of his apartment, his cellular phone rings. Looking at the number, he frowns and answers immediately.

"Forge." He replies.

"Good evening sir, my name is Lucy. I work at the police headquarters with Sergeant Hockart. He asked me to contact you."

"Is there a problem?"

"Mister Landers is already at the office. There is an emergency."

"What is it?"

"Details can only be given in private, sir."

"Can I at least talk to Lorne?"

"I'm afraid he's not available. Mr. Landers is already with the Sergeant at the moment sir."

"Tell them I'm coming."

Half an hour later, he is back in the entrance of the sombre building where two agents bring him to a counter and give him a special permission pass. This late in the night, none of the regular passes would work.

"Sergeant Hockart instructed me to issue a pass that will now give you access to the building at all times. Just enter a seven to ten digital code right after the insertion of your card. And please, make sure it has nothing to do with your telephone number or birth date, sir."

"Can you do me a favour?"

"Of course, sir."

"Can you stop calling me sir?"

"We cannot favour any familiarities in the institution."

"If you call me Josh, Jocelyn, or Forge it's going to be just fine, believe me."

"I will try s . . . agent Forge."

This place was as rigid as the Russian parliament, maybe even more. Or, was it that his hometown office was rigourous only when needed? Even in Ottawa, did he feel less strangled by the system, less shocked by the pressure of the royal scepter on his neck.

"I got my code."

"Insert your pass in the slit, let it out and press the keys for the code you have chosen."

"Now what?"

"The system will ask you to do it again for confirmation. Don't write that code anywhere, just remember it. Only you and our security system will know it."

Josh presses the eight numbers again. A green light appears and the two inches thick bulletproof glass doors open. The two agents follow, inserting their card as well. A long corridor leads them to elevator doors where again, the pass has to be inserted. Josh is standing near the side panel very decontracted while the two other men stand as straight as l'Arc de Triomphe in Paris. They're going down and when the doors open, Josh is amazed to see all the commotion around. There are at least thirthy people affaired in front of computers, looking at maps. Lorne is right there in front of a table with two opened files.

"Good evening Josh." He greets his buddy.

"Hi, what's up?"

Hockart lifts his head. "Two girls disappeared; they went off to school yesterday and never came back. One is thirteen and the other fourteen."

"Why did you wait so long?"

"Because of their age; we have to wait twenty-four hours before initiating a search."

"What's that got to do with anything?"

"They are considered young adults and in our country, there is a certain protocole regarding the age of the disappeared."

"I don't believe this."

"Anyway, we wouldn't have called you so late if one of the mothers was not deaf. Her husband does speak the language but we wanted to reassure her with somebody from the police department who can communicate with her. You are the only available agent that can speak the sign language."

Josh's patience is lowered to a minimum. "You know what? I really hate your stupid waiting law."

"We do not tolerate any assumption over our system in here mister Forge." retracts Hockart.

"O.k. let me rephrase that. The fact that a disappearance is not reported in a shorter period; makes mister Lander's and my own job a lot more complicated than it should. You always tell parents of teens that they have to wait an entire *freaking* day before any procedure can be deployed?"

"We do it all the time, every child that is more than twelve is . . ."

"Your system has got to be changed." Josh says with both his hands firmly pressed against the table. Hockart is forcing his mouth, pushing his fists against the wood slab as a gestural refusal of any comprehension.

"Mister Forge, come in my office right now."

"No I won't! I want to meet the child's parents first. I want to see what Lorne and I can do with this case then, you can stuff me shit all you want."

A pin dropping could have been heard. The silence in the room is intolerable, someone has to break it. Hockart turns his gaze to the far end of the room where lights are dimmed. A nod from the head comes from a man sitting at the far end. Right after, Hockart picks up a near by telephone.

"Miss Thorn, are the kids parents still in room B-12? . . . Fine, I will be there in a minute. Come with me." He then demands Josh and Lorne after hanging up.

The tone used like redemption, sounded like a fed up and extinguished one. Walking to the end of a concrete tunnel and rising to the second floor, Hockart leads the duo to a far away complex, opposite the main entrance.

"I don't like your attitude mister Forge, you are not here to tell us do's and dont's." Retorts Hockart without turning his head.

"I'm sorry it's a package deal. I only hoped that Taylor had told you so."

"Oh he did alright but unfortunately, he also said that the two of you were the best recovery agents he ever saw in his entire life." He concludes opening another steel door.

Hockart was tall, huge with a grip that could surely sent anyone to the ground in a jiff. He had been to war, seen things that no man can erase from his mind and come back from it with no decoration but a patriotic sense of duty. Working in this London police office was the next best move to have a quiet life and raise a family, or so he thought. He enters his pass into the verification slit again and then presses his digital code.

Guided by the Sergeant, they rapidly walk to a further room where the parents of the disappeared teens are waiting. The room is a square dark place where a table filled with papers takes most of the attention. Recent pictures of the two young ladies have been brought. Coffee, bottled water, tissue boxes are there in between descriptions and pictures, strengthening the parents' anguish over their missing kids. Notes have been taken about their last whereabouts, last clothing description. Parents have been told to bring in recently worn shirts to be sniffed by tracking dogs. One of the mothers is using the sign language, translated by her husband. Before sitting, Sergant Hockart presents Lorne and Josh to the parents and inside officers. Staying far from the group, Josh takes an overall look above their heads and he soon realizes that one of them is clearly more powerful than the others. He lets his hand discretely spread across both pictures, gazing at what emanates from it.

"Agent Forge, I'll let you introduce yourself to the deaf mother." Invites Hockart.

Josh walks over and sits in front of the lady whose eyes are red, her hands squeezing a t-shirt damp from holding it too long. Even if the colours are dark and gruesome at the moment, he can see the potential of her aura's receptivity.

"Hi, my name is Josh, I'm an agent working with Sergeant Hockart." He confirms in the sign language as well as out loud.

A sound, sort of a suffocated scream comes out from the lady's mouth. Rapidly, she says her name, Janet Simms, explaining that her daughter Mandy and her best friend are both missing. She starts making signs so rapidly that he has to gesture out to calm herself down.

"I'm here to help you. Whatever is written down; I would like you to tell me again, in your own words. When was the last time you saw your daughter?"

"Yesterday morning, just before leaving for school." She gesticulates.

"Does she take the bus?"

"No. The school is only half a mile away."

"What about the other girl?"

"She came to get my daughter. They both left together."

"Do they always do that, leave for school together?"

"Yes."

"Were your daughter's grades bad recently?"

"Mandy had difficulties in some of her courses but we've had help from a tutor. Everything was getting better until last week."

"What happened last week?"

"We had a fight."

"What was the fight about?"

"We quarreled about her coming home too late after supper."

"Ask her if the girls were seeing any boys." Lorne lets out.

Josh makes the appropriate sign and the mother replies with vagueness.

"Is your daughter on drugs Janet?" Lorne precises and Josh translates.

The lady keeps silent. Lorne comes closer.

"Ask her again." Lorne insists.

"Janet, I know this is hard but we can't avoid it. Is your daughter taking any drugs?

"I don't know." She replies almost losing control of herself.

"If she is on something or you feel that she is, we have to know and you don't have to be ashamed about it. Do you understand Janet?"

It was as easy for Josh to converse in this language as French, his mother tongue or English, the language used back in school. Everything he learned language wise was because of his father, the one person he wanted to communicate so much with. Reticence is felt from Janet but then, Josh makes another sign: "Please, tell me more."

"My husband has been complaining about beer and liquor disappearing from the cabinet and I could have sworn I bought capplets of aspirin and other medications last week . . . money has also been missing from my purse. We had a big fight about that too."

The young agent makes the sign Thanks then rises and walks away with Lorne and Hockart.

"What do you think of hypnosis?" Josh proposes to Lorne.

"Won't work, she's deaf; there's no way I can reach to her brain. Did you feel anything with the pictures?"

"I didn't feel anything."

"What does it mean: that you didn't feel anything?" Hockart inquires.

"That they are more than likely still alive or not in an immediate danger." Lorne says turning to him.

"Well, that's good." He answers sighing. Getting back to the table, the Sergeant takes the lead into telling the parents what the procedure will now be.

"After consulting with these two gentlemen, we now feel that the girls are still unharmed. Their picture has already been sent to every police station in U.K. and all the patrol cars will receive it as well. We will deploy all efforts to find them. Now, please go home and try to rest. We will call you as soon as something comes up." They all stand up; the husband of the deaf lady cannot avoid asking what is on his mind. "Will you call us if you find their bodies?"

Standing away from the Sergeant, at the other end of the table, comes out a voice, deep, strangled by fatigue.

"They're not dead if that's what you mean." Josh replies out of nowhere.

The father strangely looks at him without a smile, a tear dropping to the side of his face while he translates to his wife. "Are you sure?" The other mother articulates.

"Have faith, they're just . . . out there somewhere." He concludes from his profound voice, looking back at the shredded stare, translating it into the sign language. The father nods, half-believing the power of the words.

"Go home; we will call you if something comes up." Repeats Hockart.

Both fathers share a grasp and thank the group for their time. A sustaining look bridges between Josh and Mandy's mother, one of hope. The door then shuts behind them. Smiling pictures of both teenagers are left on the table. He raises his eyes from them and looks at Hockart.

"I believe you have something to tell me Sergeant?"

"Not tonight. I'm too tired to start an argument."

"You're about to faint." Says Lorne to his companion. "C'mon, let's go back home." Hockart waits for both, leading them out the headquarters to a black bumpy taxi that will drive them back to the apartment.

The following day, every possible action is put in place on the U.K. ground to find the two teens. With Lorne's help, Josh deepens his thoughts and tries to find them. All he can see is big weels and signs. A lot of noise is tumbling through his ears but nothing valuable is perceived so the traditional method is used. News comes in a little after 22:30 from an undercover female police officer. The two girls have been seen at a bus station in Yorkshire and a discussion at the nearest police station was established with the parents. "Well done." Hockart shouts to the officer on the telephone. Everyone is tired and while file papers are being piled to be brought back to their office, the Sergeant cannot avoid commenting the two newcomers. "That was an easy one. I wish they were all like that." He comments with a smile. "And I wish it wouldn't happen at all . . ." The young agent replies.

Josh gets up, takes his coat and leaves the room without paying any regards.

Chapter Fourth

Like an endless sorrow, the rain is once more battling against the window. The curtains he forgot to draw before falling over the gym mattress are flying in the air. His shirt is open, something he has no recollection of doing, like not hangning his police jacket that is spread on the attic's floor. The keys in his jeans pocket are pointing on his hip muscle, more than likely, the reason for his waking. His boots are still on, compressing the swollen feet. Without hesitation, he takes them off, pulls out the socks almost ripping the seams of the soles. How he hated getting up like this, exhausted and still dressed. He looks at his watch attached at the belt loop. It's a little after one thirty. Afternoon already, getting close to two o'clock, he thinks. What day was this? It was probably Sunday. Yes, more than likely, it was Sunday. Turning to his side, he gets up from bed, streches out his back, carefully avoiding hitting his forehead on the angled roof. Feeling like a baseball bat striked him on the back; he goes to take a shower, bringing fresh clothes. Showered and freshly shaved, leaving a clean-cut goatee, he enters the kitchen, pours himself a strong coffee. The pot is halfway empty. Lorne certainly had his two cups already. He walks to the living room, leaning against the entrance post.

"Did you sleep well?" The older agent asks without turning his head, still punching keys on his laptop.

"I sort of didn't have time to get into my birthday suit. I was so tired; I didn't even remove my boots."

"That's the way I found you when I got in. You argued not to touch them, answers Lorne looking at notes then turning to his computer. Maybe it won't be like that every week-end."

"I don't really mind, there's not much else to do." Josh replies taking a sip of coffee as he looks out the window.

"Are you kidding me? This is the place for museums, theatres, libraries, cafés, C'mon you jerk. Just get out and enjoy yourself for a while."

"I checked out a bar Friday evening. I thought it could be a teenage hideaway."

"Anything interesting happened?"

"I left my card to one of the waitresses. Anyway, do you want to go out this afternoon?"

"I don't know yet. Let me call home first. Marie still doesn't feel well."

After checking the time, Lorne dials the long distance call.

"Let me talk to her." Proposes the man who just woke up. The co-worker hands the phone right away. "Bonjour Sylvia c'est Josh, tout va bien? Non rien n'est arrivé à ton mari, je voulais simplement parler à Marie un instant (Hi Sylvia, it's Josh, is everything alright? No, nothing happened to your husband, I only wanted to speak to Marie for a second). Est-ce qu'elle est là? (Is she there?). She's coming; he tells Lorne . . . Is this Marie? (He takes a funny voice), this is mister Rabbit. I've heard you're sick?" On the other end, Marie is laughing.

"Uncle Josh, how do you like Inglign?"

"It's England sweetie and without you, it's the most boring thing around."

"Isn't there (cough) anything good to see like paintings?"

"Might, I haven't seen anything yet because I've been working with your dad all week."

"Its Sunday here, isn't it Sunday there too?"

"Yes sweetie, it is but we're already in the afternoon."

"Aren't the painting or book houses open on Sundays? You like books don't you?"

"Of course I do."

"I'll go on the Internet and find you a book store."

"While you're searching, can daddy talk to your mom?"

"Yes Uncle Josh." Josh hands the receptor back to his co-worker and immediately, Lorne starts talking in French but with the most repressible English accent. Josh finishes his coffee with a glare in his eye, looking out the damp window. How he wished he had a wife to call, children to talk to and care about.

"Josh, Marie wants to talk to you again." After a vivid laughter, Josh hangs the telephone after getting the « ins » on what to do in the glorious city. He walks to his room, gets his jacket and puts it on before checking the content of his wallet. "Did you ever think about the fact that your police coat might scare off ladies?" Josh turns his head. "What are you talking about?"

"Don't take it bad but when you're off duty, you should really take your job out of your system, wear something else . . . Act a little lighter. I could go with you and choose some other clothing if you want to."

"No way, I don't like your odd sense of fashion."

"For God's sake Josh, it wouldn't be bad if you inserted yourself a little more into the British society."

"I am, I'm taking your daughter's advice and going to a library."

The streets are wet from the morning shower and a smell of gas coming from all those vehicles in the suburban area, float in the air. Gentlemen wearing round hats and umbrellas pass by. Ladies with pale features and classical wearings, accompany them. Same as in Montreal, there are too many people, not enough trees. The only real difference with this country is when people noticed that you were a visitor; they were infinitively gracious by greeting you with a smile or by telling you "good day". His feet stop in front of the library where the fair is on. The boldy lettered banner hangning over the classical building's entrance invites people of all ages. The stairs leading to it are like a stairway to knowledge; discussions amongst the visitors are varied. He stops just short of the doorway. "Come in, don't be afraid." He hears in the back of his mind. Just like when he was a teen feeling lonely, a voice is heard, a comforting, and pleasing, deep one. Dad, is that you? He replies without using words. No answer is revealed. The grown man knew it wasn't his father's voice but everytime, he would ask . . . just to make sure.

Tons of kiosks filled with books appear. Readers from all ages approach the litterature freaks, men and women from all over the world who all had versatile interests but one, the quest for knowledge. In his mind, a thought flirts its way in. If he had to make a choice between reading and painting, it wouldn't be an easy one. His mother was the one who first taught him to paint but it was his father whom he saw read everyday that introduced him to be so respectful toward books.

"Good afternoon, I'm the organizer of the book fair. Who do I have the pleasure to meet?" Josh turns in a flash unknowing the middle-aged with thick glasses was addressing him. "Forge."

"And where do you come from mister Forge?"

"North America."

"Let me guess, Canada."

"Exactly."

"Quebec region?"

"Undeniably yes."

"Are you a writer?"

"No, I'm only a mere servant of the words."

"I hope you will enjoy yourself. Nice meeting you sir."

"Thank you." Josh says really impressed. The organizer turns to the next incoming visitor.

"Good day, who do I have the pleasure to meet?"

The place is immense and with all the respect for book publishing, no foods or drinks are allowed inside the building. He looks around feeling a connection, a shared interest with fellow readers, listening to volubile orators' bringing their audience to ravishment by talking about the content of their latest novel or recent edition. Works about Michelangelo and Da Vinci are under his left arm as he hands in a couple of pounds. After a few stops over to inquire about recent works, his eye catches a glimpse of whiteness above somebody's head. Intrigued, he approaches to the furthest wall of the room, where a lady is explaining the content of her studies to a visitor. Her hair is long, and the red blazing colour dances with blond highlights. Her clothes, very modest surrounded by a shawl with a drawing of Celtic knots, enhances her pale traits. Dropping on her chest, a fine necklace is laid. Recognizing the lady he saw at the restaurant, his arms hold the books already bought and he approaches the counter to fake a vague interest in her work. "How do you do sir?"

"I'm fine, thank you." He replies continuing to read the back cover of her novel.

"Are you familiar at all with the Book of Kells?"

"I'm afraid not."

"It's the Celtic Bible written by Saint Colum Cille and his twelve followers on Iona, a Scottish isle in the north. My book relates how it was written, the reasons for it but mainly all the epic that surrounds it. I tell how lucky we are that it is now protected in the Trinity College in Dublin."

"So you're Irish?" He suggests lifting his head.

Completely breathtaken by the lividity of his eyes surrounded by deep dark eyebrows, she hesitates before speaking out. ". . . Scottish" She finally exhales.

For an instant, a frail moment in time, he feels completely numb and unmistakably captivated by the essence that emanates from her. He couldn't stay like this, in total admiration and has to find a way to get a hold of himself.

"Why?" He clearly asks.

"Pardon me?"

"Why . . . why did you write your book? I mean, it's a very long process. What are you trying to obtain by it?"

"Well, it's not my first and even tough the gain of the Bible is beyond comparison, the quest in this volume is oriented to the casket that protected it."

"Let me guess. Was it filled with precious stones?" He then concludes completely surprised by the fact that he wasn't shy with her.

"It wasn't filled with them but was encrusted with them. You must have known about it to make such a comment." She replies with a sweet singing voice.

"Simple deduction, when people are interested in something, there's usually one reason for it and more than likely, it implies profits."

The lady's brown eyes suddenly burst out in flames as soon as he evokes the lucrative aspect attached to the casket. She didn't like being judged, especially by someone she'd only known for two minutes. "And you *sire*, are probably a policeman working from his office or is totally judgemental for inticing such a rapid conclusion. Looking at the way you dress, wearing black to go unnoticed and displaying clean fingernails, I would definitively go for the first option. And, your accent tells me you're more French than anything else so of course, your ancestors' legacy left you with a short temper." He looks at her, squinting his eyes but she raises an eyebrow which makes him smile. "Clever deduction Mrs?"

"Charlene MacRae and its Miss." She answers offering her hand out.

"Sorry, I don't shake hands."

"So you're germaphobe on top of that?"

"Let's just say, I don't shake hands."

"Soon, I will have a third book out this one taken from the memoirs found in the castle near my mother's place."

"When will it be out?"

"It will be commercialized as soon as I finish translating it."

"Translated from Gaelic?"

"Most of it is in Gaelic but a few sentences are in French."

"French memoirs found in a Scottish castle? Very odd isn't it?" He comments while pulling out his wallet to pay for her book.

"That's what I'm desperately trying to elucidate." She approves.

"Well, if you've got your hands on something you can't understand, maybe I can help?"

"I don't think so. I like challenges. Now, how should I dedicate this mister the policeman?"

"Just write the first thing that comes to your mind."

Somehow, right this instant, all the noises around her seem to disappear. He can almost hear his own heart beat faster, heavier than ever before. She stares back and for a moment, loses the ability to write. "Would it be too rude to ask where you come from?"

"From a country that has four seasons, Canada."

"Will you be here for long?" She articulates eyes lowered on the blank sheet to write.

"I'm afraid so. I have applied to a job a few streets away from here."

"You're under contract at the Police Headquarters?"

"Correct."

After a second, her hand becomes agile and the pen flows over the first sheet of the thick work. Finally, she hands the book out with a glow out of this world. "Well if ever you miss your country and would settle for two seasons, you can come and see me in the Highlands. Here is the editor's address who can easily reach me." With precaution not to be touched with his right hand, he takes the business card presented, looks at it making out the words Kyle of LochAlsh and places it in his wallet. "What are those two seasons?" He inquires.

"Wet and damp." The red-haired lassie (young girl) replies with a hint of humor. He can't help but crack a sudden smile.

"Now that you know where I work, maybe you'll grant me the honour of your company once more. Merci Miss MacRae, it's been a pleasure." He ends tilting his head with respect.

"Wait! I don't even know your name."

"Just ask for the French guy with a short temper, everyone will know who that is." He mocks with an authentic smile. The book is cherishly placed up with the other ones against him and slowly, he walks away. She looks at him disappear within the crowd toward other booths, stretching her neck up until an old man comes to her counter and asks about the content of her novel.

For the next week, both agents concentrate on recruiting personnel for the future department. After getting their approval from Wilkinson, methods to find such defined candidates were as varied as sending faxes to other offices or posting a notification on the web. The following day, twenty people replied and by the fifth, just over fifty-five.

"When and where will we meet them?" Josh asks putting down the advertisement.

"The meeting will be next Wednesday morning in the room where we met the two missing girls' parents."

"About that case, whatever happened to them after they were brought to the police station?"

"Their parents went to get them."

"Where were they?"

"Both were hiding at a friend's house. When they got intercepted at the bus station they were on their way to leave to another town. Mister Sims called back Hockart and told him that things were evolving at a slow but peaceful pace."

Josh shakes his head approving. "Listen, I need some air. I'm going out for a walk."

"But we have a ton of work to do!"

"I'll do it when I come back."

Before another comment is added, Lorne closes back his mouth and returns to contacting the candidates.

Once at the foot of the stairs, he takes a cigar and lights it. It wasn't his brand and surely the taste was miles away from it still, his bad habit could not be tamed. No rain is falling on the sleeves of his coat but an invading mist, torturing you to the bones. He exhales before taking long strides toward the main road and crosses at the lights. People are rare on the streets on this Sunday evening. A few blocks later, he arrives in front of the library where he engaged a conversation with a gorgeous red-haired. He walks up the stairs only to see a man sweeping his broom inside so he knocks on the clear door.

"It's closed."

"I know." He shouts at the janitor through the glass. "Is the book fair still on tomorrow?"

"No, it's been on for two weeks and ended today at six."

Deception is making his face sore and he suddenly feels like he missed something very important. "Thanks." He murmurs to the janitor obviously deceived.

"Don't mention it." The man wearing grey pants and a similar coloured shirt with the name Bill sewed on, replies.

As if somebody just cut the air permitting him to breathe, Josh sits on the cement stairs of the library. He wanted to see her one last time, how he desired to listen to her projects, maybe take her to a restaurant, maybe tell her he had a busy week and it was nice to see her again.

"She must have been beautiful." He hears coming from behind. Josh turns in a flash intrigued. A man is sitting, his back leaning against the wall with a bag by his side, probably hiding a bottle of some sort. Pivoting his body back in its original position, he hisses hating all drunks on the face of the earth. "Don't hide yourself behind your feelings, it's only natural. You know where she lives, she gave you her card. Go and see her, she's waiting for you."

That was it! Who was he to tell him what to do? Josh turns in a flash but only to see that no one is there. His mind was playing tricks on him and it sure wasn't a joint that did it this time. He rises, places both hands in his pockets and strolls on the streets until loneliness makes him light another cigar. When he turns his head, a sign on the other side of the street catches his attention. Motorbikes, old and new flash out in the dark of the night. Black, grey, red, gorgeous English made bikes with all the clothes and garnments can be seen through the window protected with rigid metal bars. An idea germinates in his mind and half-an-hour later; he enters the apartment rushing to his upstairs room, leaving only the wind at his back for Lorne to feel.

The first thing he does is check how much money is in his bank account; plenty is there. Second, where the heck did she say her editor lived? Kyle or Loch something, so obviously he figures that she must have lived close to his place. He knew that loch meant lake but for Kyle, he had no idea. He takes his wallet, opens it to find her business card but its not there. Somehow, it must have slipped taking out a bill. He rushes to his desk, picks her book up and flips it to the back. Hair flowing in the wind, she had gorgeous features and eyes of a fairy. He shakes his head, brings his glasses up to his nose and starts reading. Charlene MacRae, majoring in ancient studies, she had a couple of books to her account. Teacher at the Edinburgh University . . . no, her address is not mentioned. How could he be so stupid? He takes his laptop and types in the search engine the name Macrae. About two thousand names come up and he then realizes that the name could also be spelled MacRae. He looks at the book once again and decides to try the Editing House. It is now midnight, a time so unfortunate to receive a phonecall but he figures he could leave a message. "You have reached the Blackburn-Thornhill

House of Editing. Due to renovations, we are presently closed and will re-open our doors on Monday the 21ˢᵗ of June. Until then, you can leave us a message after the tone." A loud beeping is heard but taken by surprise; Josh doesn't speak a word and hangs up. The date mentioned is still weeks away and he figures that there must be some other way to reach her. He punches MacRae for name and Kyle for the city. Twelve names come up while hers is still not there. He eliminates all the male names, now only five names come up living at Kyle of LochAlsh but he figures that reaching her had to wait until the morning. Fully awake and much too excited to wander off to dreamland, he gets down to the living room where it is pitch-dark. Lorne's laptop is now closed and all the papers are placed aside in a pile. He goes to the kitchen, takes the biggest bottle of water, catches the stack of papers and runs back upstairs. Sitting at his antique desk, he pushes his glasses up against his nose and enters his eight digit code to gain access at the police headquarters and start to work. First, he enters all the names that responded to the offer of « Working under a controlled environment to provide assistance toward a security department centralized in the heart of London ». This approach was so vague and obsolete that he wonders how people even dared to respond. The candidates varied from seventeen to fifty-two years old. All living in the U.K. for more than five years and having no criminal records, two very important criterias. He recalls how intimidated he was to meet Taylor the first time around and wanted another approach. Developing a plan for it was probably the best issue yet so he had to make it good, proper, concise. He grabs his cigar box, lights one and starts punching the keys like a mad man.

At seven in the morning, Lorne is looking for his papers and walks up to his partner's room. The laptop is now closed. The vial of water is empty and three cigars buts fill the ashtray. Josh is laid on his back with no shirt, jeans un-buckled at the waist and keys far away on his desk beside his driver's licence. As he walks by his side, Lorne sees that this time, no socks or boots are on. The sun rays, pale and shallow are percolating through the open window. Rarely did he ever see his partner's body rise under such a sweet pulsation. His face, even bearded, looked like a child's and he knew that under those dark and lush eyelashes were eyes tinted with a greyish-blue palette. The lips a tad open; let the young man breathe a soft breeze. His right hand turned to the skies, showing the evidence that he was blessed with a special gift, a six-legged star right above his head line. A sudden urge to let him sleep comes to mind but priorities make him decide otherwise. "Jocelyn, wake up." First, an eyelid opens but then falls back.

"Jocelyn, it's seven, wake up." The young man flips to his side and exhales keeping his eyes closed. "What time did you go to sleep?" Lorne reproaches.

"No idea, four maybe."

"Are you o.k. to go to work?"

"Sure." He replies but stays on the bed.

"Coffee is ready."

"I'm coming."

At nine o'clock, Josh and Lorne scurry into the grey building saying good morning to everyone they meet. The security code is entered and the elevator takes them to the new office.

"Good day Mrs Long. Is Sergeant Hockart in?"

"I presume so, let me check." As she takes the telephone, Hockart steps in the freshly painted office. "Mister Forge, I wanted to have a talk with you."

"So did I." He assures while plugging his laptop. "Lorne, Mrs Long, if you'll excuse us for a few minutes."

Lorne looks at poor Brenda. "Let's go for a coffee." He proposes closing the door behind them.

"You want to go first Sergeant?" The young man asks finishing placing his papers and offering a seat. Clearly staking that no one was to tell him what to do, the Sergeant takes a controlling position by opening his legs, anchoring them to the ground and unvoluntarily clenching his fists.

"You and mister Landers solved four cases last week but there are about one hundred and twenty-five more."

"I know. That's why Lorne and I prepaired a plan last night and . . ."

"You prepaired a plan?"

"Well, let's call it a concept. You guys have been doing it all wrong and because you have much more to investigate on your territory, we need to work in a different way. After discussing it with mister Landers, we both have come to the conclusion that this is the best way to work in your country." He expresses showing Hockart a report containing a dozen pages.

Skeptical, the Sergeant takes the essay and starts reading a couple of pages. He gets to one paragraph and shakes his head.

"Wilkinson will never agree to this."

"We'll meet with candidates on Wednesday morning and I would like him to assist."

"Do you have any idea who you are talking about?"

"Of course I do, the Chief Superintendent of the London Police Force."

Hockart shuts up, breathing hard, shaking his head. "I've never met anyone who confronted Mister Wilkinson before this day."

"Aren't you happy about it?" Josh replies with a stupid mimik. "Your own copy is already in your e-mails." He concludes. The Sergeant takes the pile of paper and places it back on the desk before walking out. Being an artist by nature, Josh always doubted himself but never let anyone see it. His convictions surpassed all given efforts and he believed or at least hoped that a certain number of people would stand behind him.

At the end of the day, looking at his opened laptop, the blue setting that appears before linking to anything, stares back. Hands joined in front of his mouth, he closes his eyes, praying. He punches in the file where five names MacRae appear before a telephone number. First, he calls the University.

"Would it be possible to speak to Miss MacRae, she's a history teacher at your faculty."

After the receptionist takes time to consult her list, her answer is that this teacher will not be back for another week due to exam periods. He politely asks for her address but already knew the answer that it was confidential information. Josh shuts his cell, looks at the list appearing on his laptop and begins calling the most probable individuals.

"Hello, I would like to speak to Charlene."

"You have a wrong number."

Second name in line has the same answer. The third number is dialed but the address gives out the city of Dornie.

"Who?"

"Charlene MacRae." He repeats.

"There's no Charles here young man. Do you want to talk to my daughter Irma?" Asks a partially deaf lady. "No, thank you very much." He answers quite loudly before the telephone is helplessly hung up. Fourth number in line, Josh perseveres despite of all these obstacles.

"Hi, I would like to speak to Charlene MacRae."

"No one by that name lives here. Good bye."

"Wait! Don't you know her? She's a writer, she's got red hair down to the middle of her back, brown eyes, she . . ."

"Listen mister, this is not a mating agency." The click resounds and stunned, Josh decides to dial the last number. "Hello?" A sweet voice answers.

"Hi, I'm looking for a lady by the name of Charlene MacRae. Is she there?"

"I'm afraid you have the wrong number."

"Isn't there a way to . . ."

The telephone once again is hung up. Staring out in deep space, he pulls on his mustache. Lorne comes in with Brenda giggling at the agent's last joke. With a sigh, he closes his cell, knowing that personal matters could not be mingled in with work.

"May we?"

"Yes, come in. I added some notes to your questionnaire so maybe you could take a look at them before you meet the candidates."

The partner brings the sheets over to his desk and for a moment, studies the content. Brenda is affaired into her working space, setting up files and checking incoming e-mails. "Transcendental is spelled with two e's and two a's mister Forge." Insists Lorne rapidly discovering the mispelling. "Just correct it please; you know my force is not with the English

language." Lorne looks down at the paper again and jumps."
You want twenty candidates? Why twenty?"

Without looking up, Josh answers: "Because it's a nice
number". Shrugging his shoulders, the co-worker is far from
agreeing to the number of people involved.

"Wilkinson will never agree, look at the salary involved."

"Never mind that, just concentrate on the questions we will
ask." While he pays little attention to the incessant comments of
his partner still arguing, Josh has a new case he has to elucidate.
The name of the disappeared is Tommy Sacks, seventeen years of
age, elite student of a London private school, and oldest son of a
wealthy family. Printing the photograph and the details about the
disappearence of the teen, he rises to get the copy. "Brenda, can
you tell me what happens to the files after we are done with it?"

"You mean when the matter is concluded?"

"Yes."

"A police report is going to be associated with the file and
whatever the outcome of the investigation is; all cases will be
kept in chronological order in the same drawer and will have
their own reference number as they are created, that way the
files are easily retraceable."

"What happens if I have almost no details about the
disappeared? For example, what if I don't know the date he
went missing, his age or his real name."

Approaching until he reaches the secretary's desk, he then
stays poised by her side.

"Do you at least know the sex?" She inquires still looking at
her screen.

"Let's say it's a boy."

She points to a part of her screen on the left side. "The next
icon is used as a filter and can select whatever detail can be used
to retrace the subject. Let's say it's a boy so, just press on the
gender selection which will offer you three possibilities, male,
female or unknown. If you have a vague idea about his age, you
can select one of theses choices: Under 12, between 12 and 21,
over 21 or all ages. Press filter and you will have a restrained
variety of subjects that will help you clarify your next option like
hair or eye colour and so on."

By that time, Lorne has come closer to the secretary's desk and Josh is actually squatted by her side, arms crossed in total admiration at the device. "What about if the person we are looking for has got a scar or a disability, have you got an icon for that?"

"If you want to add a specification which doesn't exist, you just have to begin the search engine and press this button to have a new selection but, whatever has been recorded prior to that option, will not appear because it hasn't been selected when we first entered it."

"And who does that?"

"Sergeant Hockart's secretary, Lucy. She does it for each of the employees that work here." A long silence settles in, one where Lorne just knew what his partner was getting at. "Would you like me to ask her in?" Brenda proposes.

"The protocol of this place will certainly require that I talk to Hockart first."

By the afternoon, both agents are seated in Sergeant Hockart's office. Their idea to add a few more icons in the searching device has been approved and Lucy steps in after she has been asked to meet the newcomers. Extra hours were to be scheduled for her and Brenda to store in data in the new icons. Old cases were digged out and remastered with adequate details, duplicate files were finally amalgamed and a final transition permitted to clear out the settled documents. By ten o'clock, working all alone in his office, Josh rubs his face and stretches out. As he is about to close his laptop, his next door neighbour Wilfrid happens to walk in the corridor and stops in front of his office. "You you work late also?"

"I want to have our department organized before we meet the applicants. You have been invited haven't you?"

"I did but but I fear that peo people will laugh at me so so I will not talk, o.k.?"

"Did you have that problem when you were a child?"

"Yes." He answers while Josh offers him a seat and somehow wants to know more about his office neighbour. "Were you scared of your father?"

Wilfrid becomes evasive about the subject by telling that his father was strict but fair, that all the punishments he endured were all to make him a better man. His wording is as nebulous as a cloud but his body reveals a lot more. Without wanting to play psychoanalyst, it was evident to Josh that the co-worker suffered from an abusive parent. "How would you like to express yourself better?" The young man asks avoiding using the word stutter. Wilfrid nods his head ironically smiling at the proposition. "I, I've been to so many spe specialized people, Sergeant Hock Hockart sent me to trauma doctors after the incident and and nothing can be done . . . I'm afraid."

"What incident?"

"Nev-nevermind, please I don't want to to talk about it."

Josh's body jerks forward, trying his best to enter the man's carapace. "Let's make it clear Wilfrid. On Wednesday morning when Lorne and I will meet the other candidates, you will not benefit from any favouritism because of your unabilty to speak your mind freely. Chief Superintendent Wilkinson and Lieutenant Taylor will be on the other side of the window checking our every gesture, our single syllables and every intonation. If there is any doubt in their minds that the concept of having a specialized department for lost kids becomes too difficult to be brought to life, they will simply cross it out from their budget and save thousand of pounds. If on the other hand, we show them how much we care about this project, that we're willing to sacrifice self-pity and raise our goals to finding more missing people than they ever expected, then I think that you and I are speaking the same language." Staring back, Wilfrid stays poised but Josh's shoulders lower and hands open, he almost begs the man whose inferiority façade needed to be destroyed. "Why did you apply for that job anyway Wilfrid?"

"My my father beat me until blood wet through my my shirt and . . . (he creases his eyebrows) my mo mother was so afraid of him . . . I escaped and she, she died shortly after that. I know it was my my fault but . . . I, I wan wanted to survive. Now it's my turn to to help o others."

Unable to stay of ice, Josh immediately gets close to him. "It's going to be all right and when you'll be ready, Lorne may have the solution to help you."

Unable to speak, Wilfrid swiftly chooses to escape the scene while Josh is shattered. Tired and hungry, he decides that this day has been long enough to walk back home and get a well deserved sleep.

Two days later, very early in the morning, Lorne holds a first meeting for the new department, where eight candidates out of twenty-five sign a confidentiality agreement which stipulates that all they will see meet and do inside the institution will be kept secret. After they are brought in quarters bared from anything but a long table and chairs, Josh stands outside the room facing the two-way mirror. During three hours, the applicants are questioned about their abilities and ease to travel in deep space. The meeting ends and Jocelyn heads back to his office without being seen and waits for his partner, questioning himself if the advertisement was set up the right way. "So, what are your impressions?" Josh asks looking out the window. Lorne scratches the back of his neck before sitting down. "A few of them are suitable for the business while a few others need guidance but . . . my main concern is your behavior. I don't think you'll have the patience to teach them anything." Josh turns around to face him and throws. "I'm no teacher, you know that and that's the reason why I need a good channeler. Isn't there anyone in this group who could do it?" With a poised attitude, Lorne raises an eyebrow. "Let me place another ad and by next week, we may have other candidates you'll be more apt to work with. "Cool, I guess I'll see you back on Monday then."

"Where are you off to?"

"I need a couple of days to clear my mind, that's all."

A few streets east from the office, febrile he walks in the motorcycle store. An hour later, wearing leather chaps over his jeans and a matching coat, he is off on the road with his favorite helmet. An extra headgear is attached at the end of the seat. The 1800 cc black apparatus is incredibly sturdy yet manoeuvrable and the provisory licence to ride it is arranged by the store. After filling the gas tank to the rim, he takes the highway leading to the Highlands, some ten hours of driving away from London. All he prays for is that rain does not stop his plans.

Bikes have no secrets for him but driving on the side opposite to what he is accustomed to, is an epic in itself. After a few minutes though, learning the trend becomes easy even for the turnpikes exits. By early afternoon, he reaches Carlisle getting off the M6 highway and on to the A74 road. At four, he stops at Stirling where William Wallace made history. A huge tower is erected in his honour and looking at it from the pic-nic area with a chicken sandwich in hand, he promises to come back and escalade each of its stairs to the top. The A82 brings different landscape where black-faced sheep and Heilan Coos, long red-haired cows, wander quietly grazing on the green pasture. The wind is nothing but a caress on his face. The sun, playing hides and seeks between the cumulus clouds, make the ride enjoyable but fatigue starts to envelop him. He estimated that his arrival time at Kyle of LochAlsh would be around twelve counting all the stops he made either to eat or check the map. Right before eight, he enters the legendary valley of Glencoe where a massacre took place between two clans. The road is above moors filled with bushes coming over the swampy, unsteady grid of rocks. The colours escalading on each side are filled with mauve heather and only a few houses still rise from the deserted agglomeration. Beauty with a tint of sadness surrounds him and while he sees from the corner of his eye two hinds running away on his right, he thinks how fragile and engaging living here must be for them. Then, from out of nowhere something is obstructing the path. To avoid hitting the mass without leaving the road, first he decelerates and then is forced to clench on the brakes to their limit. The machine dances before ejecting him on the pavement where he rolls a few times. The stag responsible for the sudden stop, a huge male beast of about five hundred kilos looks at the man layed on his back. Josh tries to rise but the pain is awful. His left leg hurts so much that he feels it is broken and the glove of his left hand ripped from the abrasive of the asphalt. He takes off what's left of the gloves, protection glasses and helmet, pushing them away. The sound of the hoofs are coming toward him and fearing he will get stomped on, Josh looks up frightened. The beast begins panting over his coat. Strangely, it doesn't seem to be wild.

"You scared the hell out of me." He throws getting on his knees.

But the stag shows no sign of leaving the road and stays close. Josh finally rises up, breathing hard and grimacing, opens his coat and touches his rib cage then his leg. Surprisingly, nothing is broken on his body but when he turns to the bike . . . bad news. Swearing until his mouth is dry; he turns off the engine and brings it back up so the carburator doesn't drown. With a kick of his boot, he places the foot rest and verifies the front wheel. Much of the impact was absorbed by the crash bars and what may have been a serious accident, revealed to be a tremendous result of sheer luck. In his back pocket, he searches for his cell but finds it a few feet away on the road split in two. In his coat pocket, his reading glasses protected by a rigid casing, are also broken on the side and one lens is cracked in half. He lifts his face to the *cervus elaphus* nonchalantly looking back.

"The bike is brand new, what were you thinking?"

The stag moves his head surmounted by wide antlers one of which is missing a couple of spikes. It then approaches his muzzle to the human. Now half-mad, Josh presents his open hand. The rough and wet tongue licks his palm taking all the salt it can. Josh's fingers precausiously move forward. Intimidated, the beast backs off a step. "I won't hurt you, you know that."

Thinking that it might be hungry for something else than twigs and shrubs, Josh takes a grain bar from the side luggage and opens it. As soon as the treat is offered, the animal comes forward and engulfs it. Unable to resist the charm of the occasion, he starts petting it on the forehead, a little paler than his bright red-brown fur shedding last pieces of a winter coat. Right after his last bite, the majestic creature turns away to join his two hinds. There, stranded in a place he doesn't know, in a valley where any sound echoes until it loses voice, he stands, looking at the sun slowly dropping to reach the horizon. His left leg is hurting like crazy. No smell of leaking gas is present but still, he takes no chance and sits further away. The sky turning to a deep shade of cerulean blue gives life to bright white stars deepening the Milky Way. Mist starts rolling down the edge of the cliffs to embrace the moors and sounds of uhulating owls' echoe in the distance, warning mice of their approach. Nowhere else on earth has ever made him feel so small and without the interruption of this incident, he would have run through the valley without seeing its beauty. He raises his neck to the vastness of the open drapes of the night.

"I wish you would see that mom." He prays out loud but thinking it over, she may well have contemplated the scenery long before him. He sighs, concentrating his energy on walking back to the bike but his leg starts swelling and his ankle can barely breathe through the rim of the boot. He knows that if he detaches it, he won't be able to put it back on. A fox or something about the same size runs in front of him on the road. He wonders why no cars come in either direction so, for a second time; he makes a halt to look at his map with his lighter. The next town is Ballachulish, quite a few kilometers away and he fears that the bike may need servicing.

"Doesn't anyone come this way at night?" He screams into the valley.

The echoe replies the word night a couple of times before fading with the droplets of water on the carpet of the moors. With hesitation, he turns on the key and surprisly, the motor starts roaming. A feeling of satisfaction reassures him. He hurries to place the map back into the side luggage and mounts the motorcycle hastening.

Scatterred lights from the village can be seen after an iron bridge. It is now ten on a Wednesday night in the last week of May. A time where school is not finished and workers are probably heading for bed. It seemed so bizarre for a traveller to come so late at night in this little town. After taking what seems to be the main road, he reaches a convenience store offering gas and talks to the employee through an opening in the glass.

"Hi. Do you know where I can find a place to eat?"

"At this time?"

"Yes, I crashed my bike a few miles away in the valley and . . ."

"You were in Glencoe at night? Are you mad?" His accent is the most adorable thing he ever heard with rolling « r's » and singing fluctuations.

"Well it wasn't what I planned to do really." Replies Josh joking about it.

"Are you hurt?" The employee asks.

"My leg is bruised. No big deal."

"Wait, I'm coming." He shouts taking his coat.

"No, no, you don't have to do that. Just tell me where I can sleep for the night."

The employee shuts all the lights, turns over the sign to CLOSED and locks the door behind him. "All the hotels and restaurants are not open because it's not high season yet. My boss won't be mad at me for closing two minutes earlier and helping out a lad. I'll take you to my place."

"That's way too nice. I cannot accept."

"Nonsense, my name is Ian." He offers opening the door of his truck, an old greenish vehicle with an open trunk.

"And I'm Jocelyn but everybody calls me Josh."

"Is the bike damaged?"

"Nothing serious but I'll have to take a good look at it."

"Follow me then."

Ian's truck stops in a gravel parking lot. A modest cottage stands by the edge of Loch Linnhe where only a few bushes enhance the rigidity of the stones. Josh takes his stuff and slowly follows him to the basement. The place is simple, a table and two chairs fill up most of the space in the kitchen. Two single windows and a backdoor disturb the singularity of the space. A bathroom with no bath and a bedroom is all that extend from the place where he stands.

"You're clearly mad to cross Glencoe after night fall."

"It wasn't dark when I got into it. And what's the big deal about it anyway?"

"There are spirits and you don't want to wake them."

"Of course . . ."

"You don't come from here, do you?"

"I'm from Canada and I've just been muted to work in London."

"And what brings you over to Scotland?"

"A writer, you know anyone by the name of Charlene MacRae?

"It doesn't ring a bell."

"Her editor lives in Kyle of LochAlsh and I was on my way over there to see if somebody knew her."

"What did she write about?"

"Her last novel is about the Book of Kells."

"I see . . ." The garagist says almost laughing.

"What's so funny?"

"Everybody's got a different idea about the book. Some say Colum Cille was a savior, others an opportunist, that the Bible should not be in Dublin, bla, bla, bla."

"And what's your own opinion?"

"That there are far too many religions in this world and that it doesn't put bread on the table. You want a pint?" Offers Ian extending his hand into the refrigerator.

"No thanks, I never drink."

"You must be hungry. I'll make you some soup."

"I don't want to impose."

"It's no bother at all and it's nice to have some company. Just make yourself at home."

Josh puts his belongings in a corner of the room, and then sits at the kitchen table stretching his left leg. Looking around, a picture of a bagpiper with his costume stands right beside a calendar where the week starts with Mondays.

"Who's that?"

"My old man, he works as a road builder but whenever the occasion presents itself, he's a piper." For an instant, Josh recollects the image of the four musicians he met in his hometown some fifteen years ago at the foot of the college in Ste-Thérèse.

"Is he part of a group?"

"He's in the village band and whenever they are selected, they go to Edinburgh to get a shot at the Tattoo contest."

"And what's that?"

"Gee, you really don't know anything about this country, do you?"

"I'm afraid not."

"The contest is held to determine the best bagpipe players over the world."

"That must be something."

"It is one of the highest honours around here. Here's your lentil soup."

"Thanks." Fuming in a bowl of modest porcelain is a thick liquid, brownish green with lumps. On his left, crakers are placed with butter and a glass of water. The soup looks disgustingly awful but the smell is simply telling him to dig in. Blowing on the filled utensil, his shaking hand slowly brings it to his dry mouth. To his greatest surprise, the repulsive colour has nothing to do with the smell and reveals itself to be smooth, caressing and dearly filling. This lentil potage is the most extraordinary pea soup he ever tasted.

"You like it?" Ian asks as he opens a bottle of dark ale.

"It's the best one I ever had."

"My 'ma made it. She always makes me a batch depending on what's available. Her best is at the end of summer where she crops everything in her garden."

"That must be a treat." Approves Josh taking a cracker and spreading butter on it.

He looks at his knuckles scraped and blood dropping. Quickly, he knots over a paper napkin while Ian sits in front of his guest. The Scotsman takes another long draught before digging in the cupboard. "Now here's the real treat, they're called scones." Right by the tea pot, the canister opens on tenderly placed flat cookies decorated with fork holes. The soup is finished and the empty bowl taken away by the host. The visitor takes one cookie and clearly appreciates the desert so rarely taken.

"Please tell your mother that they're delicious." He replies after chewing his bite.

Pouring tea into a cup unmatching the saucer, the man with disproportioned legs brings it close.

"Take time to enjoy your tea, I'll prepare your bed. The shower is right there if you need to use it and tomorrow, after breakfast, we'll take a look at your bike."

"You're very kind Ian."

"Don't mention it."

The table is pushed in a corner of the kitchen. The tall Scott takes one of the two mattresses of his own bed to make Josh's improvised sleeping area. A few blankets are then added to cut short on the humidity. After a warm shower, sleep almost comes easy for him if not for the dwelling pain in his leg.

The next day at dawn after breakfast, both men take a look at the motorcycle and Ian brings a tool box just in case.

"How did you do that?" The mechanic asks looking at the partially broken windshield, torn brake handle and dented gas tank.

"I avoided a stag."

The man wearing his mechanic's clothes looks at Josh and starts giggling.

"Hey! That's not funny. I didn't want to hurt the beast." Josh replies offended.

"I'm sorry", Ian chuckles. "It's only because Harry caused three accidents in the last two months and since we are the nearest garage, people come to see us first."

"Harry . . . you have names for all your stags?"

"We are that caring only to the ones who give us business."

The event was almost too weird to be true. The bike was damaged, his leg was bruised and this incident could have been far worse.

After checking the whole wiring system and fixing minor repairs, Josh wants to pay his host but Ian clearly refuses the money and tells the visitor that hospitality is a common trend of the Highland people. So after he thanks him again, Josh brings his things, ties it to the bike and takes the next road that brings him deeper in the northern part of the U.K. As the road takes him closer to Fort William and deeper in the Highlands, the scenery drastically changes. There he meets a shepherd near his retirement age. Missing a few teeth and his breath smelling of whisky and lagger, he continuously talks and in ten minutes, Josh knows his entire life story. The coat he wears is made of sturdy weaved wool covered with a safety fluorescent jacket. Nevertheless, the man is an icon in itself, unreservedly telling Josh about the history of the region and a few of its inhabitants. "If you continue north instead of going west, you'll arrive at Loch Ness. All visitors go there."

"Thanks, I'll remember that."

Journeying across Scotland is mainly sharing a meal with the locals, admiring the nature's blend, sipping on a warm tea but time prevents him from straying from the plans he made. At every corner, black faced sheep, Highland shaggy cattle known as Heilan Coos, farmers with border coalies greet him, welcoming him to their country. He waves back to total strangers, hears the laughter of children whose heads are mainly covered with variations of red or brown hair. The vegetation is scarse, mainly composed of vegetables seen in his home country but as the weather changes and the clouds embrace the top of the cliffs, he realizes the need for heavy clothing and why the inhabitant's complexion are anything but tanned. When the rain sets in mid-afternoon, he enters a pub at Ault-a-Chruinn, a small town at the foot of the Five Sisters of Kintail Mountains. He shakes his wet hair and rubs his boots against the tightly weaved hay carpet at the entrance. The place is filled with the aroma of pipe tobacco and the essential lagger drenched from a pump on the dark coated oak bar. So that people would not trip over his swage, he takes the furtest seat in the house. Right away, a lady comes forward.

"Greetings, what will you have?"

"Do you have a menu?"

"Just look over there on the board."

"Sorry, I can't read that far."

"Today we have lentil soup, haggis, trout, salmon and kippers."

"I'll take the salmon with vegetables if you have some."

"Will you have whole wheat or white bread?"

"Whole wheat, please."

"What will you drink, lagger or beer?"

"Do you have mineral water?"

"Of course, will that be all?"

"Maybe I'll have some tea afterwards."

"Tha." For some reason, he knew that *tha* meant yes and his choice for a meal was only attributed to the fact that he had no idea what haggis or kippers were. People in the pub are not that different from the one in the bars of Montreal. Some are noisy, others quiet but there is a feeling of antiquity floating in the air, either coming from their conversation or their clothing. The banners of different clans posted all around, give a sense of belonging. Taking his map out and placing it on the table, he calculates how much distance is left for him to get to the Kyle. The waitress brings the loaf of bread with churned butter and the mineral water. A loud argument erupts between two locals sitting a few feet from him. Words spoken in English are often circled by those of another language but somehow, Josh has no problem figuring out that the two men with auras red as roosters are old friends having one too many laggers. "I'll fight you for it!"

"Oh yeah?"

"Aye!" A fierce banging from the broad hands shakes their table and everything on it. Clients start cheering at the engagement and soon both men take their coats off. Josh lifts his eyes above his broken glasses, everyone but the two fighters and him bang their glasses on the table tops in harmony while the two men aggressively walk up to the bar. "Give me mine Peter."

"Mine first!" Josh lifts up his neck to see what kind of weapons they will use and prepares to duck before a shot is heard. Their back so wide and their arms the size of trunks, hide whatever they are offered by the bartender. "Here, get it over with." He simply exclaims putting something over the bar. When they turn around with darts in their hands, Josh is relieved while the clients align themselves behind the two opponents. The waitress comes back with the meal. Taking the map away from the table, he greets her with a smile. The broiled salmon is covered with small potatoes, herbs and lemon slices. Beside the fish lay a few turnips and marinated baby carrots from a season past. "Buidheachas (Thanks)." He answers without thinking. "Fàiltich! (Welcome!)" She replies surprised.

Somehow, he knew what to say but had no idea how it came into his mind. It simply was. Figuring that he must have read or heard it somewhere, he pays no further attention to it and sinks his fork in. The succulent meal is completed by a fuming tea and when the waitress comes over to bring it, it's accompanied by a small plate which he did not order.

"Compliments of the chef." Drops of toffees and a piece of short bread are appetizingly displayed over a paper doily. Usually, Josh never had desert, a simple habit taken from childhood when he got sick from too many candies at Halloween but now, it was hard to refuse. "What's the reason?"

"For speaking Gaelic, where did you learn?" ". . . Books I guess."

"I hope you will have a good stay." She wishes placing the bill on the table.

He nods and takes out his wallet. Leaving a tip, he places the desert in a folded napkin and goes to pay at the bar before crossing the doorway.

The town is like a set back in time, grey stones piling up on the sides of the pavement, vividly coloured flowers hanging from the windows with lichen climing up to the tiled roof tops. Children don't have motorized bikes but the simple and vintage ones with tall handles and slim tires. Ladies wear hats embellished with feathers and half-length coats to hide their sturdy calves. Only a few teens are different and evoke a new wave by listening to their i-Pods, their conversation probably turning around the latest songs, which is going out with whom in the class and their plans for an eventual summer break. Whatever took him to such a distance into this far away land had something to do with the fact that he wanted to do some soul searching, get away from the turmoil of the city and finally take a really relaxing vacation. A tought about his mother infiltrates his mind. She would have liked to see the black-faced sheep; it would have reminded her of her childhood farm. With his right hand, he clenches to the silver cross at his neck and tighten his jaw. Now she was gone, leaving the best part of her behind. She had taught him almost everything he knew, how to be fair, how to be grateful to others and to have confidence while angels are surrounding him. He never asked her but she probably had a six-legged star in the palm of her right hand too. She was so receptive to whatever pulled him in to serving the police corps for the search of children, that it couldn't be any other way. He starts reminising about all the good memories he had because of this wonderful person. He misses her . . .

Chapter Fifth

In all her incommensurable wisdom, Mother Nature makes the rain stop and a bright sun comes out from behind the clouds. The road follows Loch Duich and entering Dornie, the biker stops for a small break. Taking the last draught of his bottled water, he perks an ear. A sole bagpiper is playing a melody and the sound echoes throughout the mountains. The melody comes afar, yet curiosity makes him follow it. Riding slowly, he arrives at a last curve almost touching the grass of the cliff and amazed; parks in the gravel and turns the engine off. Right before his eyes, the bagpiper is playing in front of a castle. "His" castle, the one he has been drawing for years.

Sandwich in one hand, chewing rapidly and gulping down a soft drink, Charlene finishes translating another passage from French.

Won't you be there anymore? The voice asks.
I will always, I reply.
Let there be messengers to foretell you that your quest is not in vain.
Mountains await you, trails of dusk and liatrids will pass before your eyes until you see it.
When you will, your heart will break and tears will come because for so long you will have missed it and the rush of seing it once again will rejoyce you more than any mortal will ever do.
KMK

Taking a moment to admire the flow of the words, she then places a bookmark over a scanned sheet of paper and inserts it into her sack. She looks at the time, shakes her head and hops into her car to reach her mother's house.

In the heart of the Highlands, he gets off the bike. Key in hand he weakly crosses the road and stops to stare at the fortress. Like the apparition of a long lost love, tears come rushing down his eyes. All those years of waiting to see if his imagination wasn't responsible for the recurrent dream, burning questions now enter his head as to how that bastion is now on the path he followed. The bagpiper standing near the moor finishes his song and starts placing his instrument back into the casket. "Excuse me sir, what is the name of this place?"

"This is the irresistible Eilean Donan castle."

"Can we visit it?" He questions walking closer. "The season doesn't open for two more weeks. I'm prepairing myself for it." The piper rises back to face the visitor filled with deception. "Oh . . . I will have left by that time. It's getting late and I should be on my way. You know a place where I could have a bite?"

"Irma may accommodate you. She has a Bed & Breakfast at the end of this road." Unhurried, he starts to walk back to the motorcycle but then turns around. "Thanks and by the way, your music is lovely, it fills the empty spaces."

"Thank you lad, may the wind always be at your back."

Josh cherishes the comment, puts his helmet and ignition on and at the end of the dusty road, stops the bike once more. The wooden house is painted with a dark blue coat and windows have a trimmed yellow border line. Three stairs lead to a rudimentary porch where a hay carpet with the word "Fàiltich" (Welcome) is embossed. Shyly, he knocks on the door and waits. Nobody answers so he knocks again a little louder. A lady in her early fifties comes to answer; she has a dishcloth in her hands and seems to be busy with chores. "Yes?"

"Hello, I was wondering if I could have a bite and a room before continuing my way to Kyle of LochAlsh." The lady looks at the tall young man leaning on his right leg. She then takes a glimpse at his scraped knuckles and the deep scratch over his left sleeve. "What happened to you?" She inquires pointing out to his hands.

"I had a little accident with my bike." For an instant, her silence makes him think that he should leave but surprisingly, she opens the door and welcomes him in.

"I'm not really prepaired for visitors. Usually, we only get them when school finishes and that won't be for another two weeks but if you're not fussy, I may have something for you."

"You think it would be possible for me to take a shower and sleep a little before supper?"

"Yes of course, I'll just go and get some fresh sheets to make the bed. Just make yourself at home in the living room. Don't mind my mother, she's a little deaf."

He goes to get his pack-sack on the bike and comes back in to walk in the living room where an elderly lady watches television. At first, she doesn't pay attention but suddenly, she turns to him. "Did you repair that damn faucet?"

"I'm sorry?"

"The faucet young man, did you repair it?"

"I'm a traveler madam. I'm seeking a room for few hours and a meal."

"Oh . . . well in that case, you can call me Amanda. Can you bring me the bottle in the cabinet and the glass beside it?" He bends to the furniture in the corner of the room and leaves both by her side. The lady's plump fingers take the liquor; she fills the chiseled glass to the rim and swallows the first half in a single gulp. "You want some?" She articulates. "No thank you very much." The owner of the B & B comes back in the room and approaches Josh. "The room whether you take it for the night or a few hours will cost twenty pounds per day and meals are included. Would you like to see it?"

"I'm sure it's fine." He confirms following her to the front room used as an office and grabs his wallet.

"I need identification papers for insurance purposes." As he takes out his driver's licence, she can see his agent's papers and asks for both. "Just sign here after you read the conditions." She insists handing him both both cards back with a key. "Your room is the second door to the left on the second floor. Now if you'll excuse me, I have to prepare supper."

The conditions were very simple: No smoking in the room or house, no damages to the furniture or stealing. Quite simple and quite legitimate, he believes. The stairs to the second floor are hard for him to climb and he cannot wait for a soothing bath.

Dropping his pack-sack on the floor, he immediately fills the tub with hot water. A few minutes later, he sinks in the warm liquid while looking at his thigh. A blueish colour is now covering most of it so he figures that his leg must have hit the handles to get such a result. The scraped knuckles are burning under the soap lather and a sore shoulder makes him waggle his limb to get some kind of comfort. Things could have been tragic and considering his luck, he kisses the silver cross at his neck.

Exhaustion makes him fall flat on the floor and an hour later, he wakes as rejuvenated as if he had an entire night sleep. The aroma filling the kitchen is noticeable all the way to the stairs he is now descending. "Mister Forge, please take a seat."

"It smells wonderful." He exclaims taking the place she proposes. Irma's mother comes to sit on his right and the owner brings over a fuming cauldron to the center of the table. The aroma of roast beef covered by vegetables impregnates the entire room and Irma begins to serve everyone. First, she takes the visitor's plate. "No meat for me please; I'm vegetarian." Irma's shoulders go down. "I'm so sorry. I should have asked." Used to this reaction, Josh puts her at ease. "Vegetables will be just fine."

"Shouldn't Charlotte be here by now?" The grandmother snaps. Irma places a plate filled with vegetables in front of the visitor and makes sure to offer him condiments and freshly baked bread. "She should have been here hours ago."

As Irma finishes her sentence, the sound of a car door shutting is heard and moments later, a lady in her early thirties walks in. Josh is digging in the plate and reaches for a piece of bread. "Hi mom, hi grandma; whose bike is it?" As she sits, Irma answers her daughter's anticipated question. "It's our guest's motorcycle. How was your trip?"

"It was great! I sold all my books and . . ." Josh looks up and almost falls from his chair from seeing the beautiful red-haired he met at the fair. She recognizes him right away but Irma is all intrigued: "Mr Forge, are you alright?"

"Yes, yes, I'm fine." He assures his face all red, composing with the faux-pas. The young woman's mouth hangs open. "Mister the policeman, what a pleasant surprise but what are you doing here?" Putting the knife down and replacing his napkin, he shyly avoids looking into her eyes.

"I was on my way to Kyle of LochAlsh to seek out people who might have known you." She sits and while her mother serves her a plate, her face still shows the shock of seing him in her mother's house. "I don't quite get it. You wanted to see me?" His cheeks now blush to a deeper tint of crimson. Both are facing each other and a smile is shared. "Do you know each other?" The grandmother suggests.

"We met at the book fair a few days ago." Replies Charlene still incredulous of his presence. "Would you like more potatoes mister Forge?" Irma proposes. "Certainly." He answers bringing up his plate.

For a while, he listens to her talking about the exhibition and cannot believe the turn of events. Something strong brought him up here and it was anything but luck. It was a remarkable twist of fate. After supper, the habitual tea is offered and with eyes gazing at the intensity of light emaning from her, he contemplates the lass.

"My husband was an officer during the war." Begins Amanda out of the blue.

"Is that right? Please tell me more." Replies Josh. "He won a few medals and wherever he went, his bagpipe followed him."

"'Ma, mister Forge doesn't want to hear about this." Irma cuts off.

"On the contrary, I would like to learn more about your customs. What's this passion for the bagpipes?" All heads turn to him. "What did he say?" Amanda asks her daughter. "He wants to know why bagpipes are so important to us."

Afraid he may have offended them, he places his fork down to listen. Amanda straightens her curved back; lightning seem to come out of her wrinkled eyes. "The sound that comes from the pipes is warning the opponent that we will never surrender. As long as there is air in them, the warrior will breathe and nothing will ever stop him. Do you believe in the Divine protection young man?"

"I do believe in it."

"Bagpipes are Scottish angels, whenever and wherever you hear them, you know that they are shielding our people."

"I see." Unwanting for her host to get cornered with a thousand questions on his first night, Charlotte cuts the discussion short by taking his finished plate away.

"Would you enjoy a desert mister Forge?"

"None for me thanks."

"What time is it?" Amanda demands. "It's almost eight." Her daughter replies.

She takes her cane and lifts herself up from the sturdy chair. Josh goes beside her.

"Would you like me to help you?" He suggests offering his arm.

"I'm certainly capable to go about in my own house young man!"

Startled, he withdraws his body avoiding getting knocked with her wooden stick. While she goes away to the other room, he begins to clear the table.

"Guests in my house do not do that mister Forge."

"It's no big deal. I don't believe that I deserve all your good favors. I literally imposed myself on you all."

"How about taking our guest to get Wooly in, Charlotte?"

"Sure mom. Grab your coat and bring your tea." She orders dipping her hand in a pot waiting on the pantry. Using the front door, she takes her tightly weaved three quarter length coat, gloves and hat while Josh takes his own motorcycle coat. "Who's Wooly?"

"He's our eldest male sheep. All the others are probably in by now but he's strong headed and won't come in by himself. He's probably wandering in the back fields and we have to bring him in because of the nocturnal beasts like wolves." Using a pathway beside the fence, they climb up the hill. Arriving at the top, they both walk on what looks like ruins of a house and turns around to admire the castle majestically standing before the loch. Sipping on the lukewarm beverage, he cannot believe the spectacle before him. The wind makes his hair swirl about and for the first time, she sees the reflection of the cross earring on his left ear. His eyes are shiny and she wonders if the coldness of the night is responsible for it.

"Didn't you tell me that your name was Charlene?"

"That's my pen name. My real name is Charlotte but I really don't like it."

"So how should I call you?"

"Charlene will be just fine. How come you're not working, are you on holiday?"

"My superior needs some time to study my latest proposal so I decided to take a few days off."

Climbing up one last hill, she sees that he grimaces taking a slower pace. "What's the matter? Are you hurt?"

"I met a very friendly stag." At his answer, she starts laughing.

"It wasn't very funny, believe me. This animal was huge."

"How did you hurt yourself?"

"I put the brakes on too rapidly and flew over the handles. I remember putting my arms above my head but that was merely a reflex. I rolled a couple of times and woke up seconds later looking at the creature."

She laughs even louder. "You preferred to hurt yourself instead of the stag?"

"Well yes. I'm the one invading his territory, ain't I? He could have been the last of his kind and I would have been responsible for his extinction for all I know." She smiles nodding her head, clearly knowing he mocked her. The tinkling of a bell is heard in the distance.

"Wooly, Wooly, come back here this minute!" The sheep continues to eat without paying attention to her call but then she approaches it and feeds it with a piece of brown sugar taken from her coat pocket. "He's got a sweet tooth." She affirms rubbing the back of its neck. The aminal follows her down to the shed where the females and two other males are already gathered in for the night. She gives it a second piece of sugar and locks the door back. The two horses are brought into a much bigger place and while she gives them hay and water, her interest in the newcomer is unveiled by her questions. "How would you like to visit the castle?"

"I've been told it's not open yet."

"You're right. The season has not even started but my mother is the gate keeper and she's got a key." The expression on his face could not hide his feelings and with pleasure, he accepts the unexpected invitation with delight.

The gravel road leading to the arched bridge makes him realize that the width was meant for horses or very narrow carts. "When was it built?"

"Figures show that the first stronghold was erected under the reign of Alexander II between 1214 and 1250. In the early part of the fourteenth century, William Wallace, he's one of out major heroes, took refuge here. The MacRae's were always elite members of its protection but in May of 1719, the English rebelled against whoever was part in the Jacobite rising to gain a pretender to kingdom and thus destroyed the castle using three frigates, the Worcester, the Enterprise and the Flamborough, well at least, that's what the history books tell us." She turns the key to the massive oak door. Entering the hall, she locks behind her. The humidity within the walls can already be perceived, an odour of wetness lingers. She cracks a match and illluminates the surroundings. "There must be one near." She lets out talking to herself.

With his neck up, admiring the banners barely lighted by the pale sundown coming from a window in the next room, his mind is too preoccupied to even ask her what she's looking for. A light, frail but constant, suddenly comes from the oil lantern she just lit. Unlike other castles he visited on past journeys, this one made him feel like he knew every corner of it. She makes him visit the first floor and comments whatever is around in the kitchen area. "Do you mind if we go upstairs?" He snaps.

As they climb the circular staircase, a feeling of compression rushes in. His heart starts racing, breathing becomes difficult and images of a lengthy room ignite in his brain. Sounds of people talking in a different language fill his brain, the smell of scotch can be perceived; the sharp metallic sparks of iron blades left on the sturdy table are seen by the light of a chandelier. Placing his right palm over the stone wall, he stops to catch his breath.

"Here we have . . ." Explains Charlene holding the oil lamp up. "Are you o.k.?" She inquires looking back at him.

"Yeah, sure." He replies trying to recollect his thoughts to the present moment. "This is the Billeting Room, a place where the owner of the castle would often come and sit with his peers. As you can see, the ceiling is vaulted with stones placed horizontally and the window is very far from the table thus making this room a safe place for meetings."

"Isn't there another hall where they would meet, somewhere with a fireplace?" Charlene looks at him wondering how he would know about the other room. "It's not your first time here is it? Or maybe, you saw it in a book?" Strolling further with the lady trailing him, he enters a chamber called the Banqueting Hall, a place with massive walls and a humongous fireplace. The minute he walks in, a feeling of belonging sets him off guard and alerts all his senses with its vitality. Charlene becomes quiet as he tries to conceal his toughts together. Sitting on the window ledge, he presses both hands together. The force that he brings to his palms makes his knuckles turn white and blood starts flowing from the recent injuries. "How could you know about this room if you've never heard about it before?"

Josh remains silent, staring at the floor.

"Have you got a fever?" She murmurs concerned placing her hand over his forehead. He turns to the lady in a flash, breathing out in surprise. "I'm sorry?"

"You look like you're having a fever and your hands, they started bleeding again. Let's go back home." Nodding, he follows her out like a lamb knowing that this first encounter with ghosts of the past was enough for the day.

Magnetically attracted to her, he follows the lady back to the house. The fragrance of her perfume leaves a trace in the wind that he voluntarily inhales. A light resting on a wood table is on in the hallway while Amanda is asleep, sitting in front of the television with an empty shot glass with a hint of brandy. From the kitchen, Irma is setting the table for the next morning.

"Just go to your room and I'll bring the first aid kit." Charlene proposes to the guest.

"What's wrong?" Her mother demands.

"Mister Forge has a fever; it's probably due to his bike crash. I'll take a look at his hands too, they started bleeding again."

Leaving the door of his room open, he takes off his coat and waits, sitting on the bed. When she enters, a box filled with bandages is laid beside him. First, she takes his temperature and while he sits mouth closed on the thermometer, she disinfects his hands. When she gently pulls his right hand up to put the bandage on, he resists and tries to talk by mumbling a mere negative sound.

"Oh, just shush you big baby." To his surprise, she doesn't feel the habitual tingling people experience when touching the inside of his palm. First she takes off the blood with a tissue damped with alcohol and then applies ointment. Rubbing it gently, she then wraps it with a clean bandage. "Here, you look like a boxer ready for his next fight." Taking the thermometer out from his mouth, she reads it underneath the glow of the lamp. "102 . . . that's a nice fever you've got. Would you like to show me your leg?"

"It's only bruised. I checked it earlier. You can call me Jocelyn if you wish."

"Ghyslaine?"

"No, Jocelyn or Josh, whichever you like best."

Giving him two caplets and a glass of water, she touches his cheek with the back of her hand. "If your fever hasn't come down by tomorrow morning, we'll have to go to the hospital." She is sweet, nice and caring. He looks at her in silence while she takes the first aid kit. "Now you should sleep a little and if you don't feel well, my room is right next to yours." How desirable was she with her long and vaporous red hair, circling the pale face enhanced by beautiful chestnut eyes.

"Are you always this considerate with your mother's clients?"

"I'm nice only to the ones who avoid endangered species."

A last look to her sympathetic face will be the true remedy to his fever. Placing a few sheets on the floor, no pillows as usual, he lies down with his head pointing north. For the first time in many weeks, he had the most peaceful night sleep where his dreams are not haunted by work.

In the morning, Josh wakes to see Irma pruning some trees in the back and joins her. "Would you mind if I stayed here a couple of days?"

"Of course not, it's still twenty pounds per day, payable in advance."

"Sure, no problem, here's the money." Handing the requested amount, he can also see from the corner of his eye Charlene coming toward them. "You look better this morning."

"I am."

"I'm on my way to Iona. Would you like to come with me?"

"Is that far?"

"It's five or six hours away. I could show you on a map."

"I have one, wait a minute." Taking it out from the side casing, he places it on the porch. "See, this is where we are and there is Iona, she points out on the unfolded paper. So, how about it? Would you like to join me?"

"I will on one condition, that we take the bike." He insists folding it back.

"Oh no, I'm not mounting that frail carcass of metal and wires with no roof above my head!"

"As you wish."

She stays silent for a minute. "Won't you argue a little?"

"I'm done arguing with a lady."

"So you're coming with me by car?" He looks at the skies, turns to the direction of the isle and faces her again. "Cumulus nimbus never lie, it will not rain for the next ten hours so there's no excuse for not taking the bike." She places her hands on her hips in discontent and breathes out. "I don't have a helmet!" She argues.

"I have an extra one for you. It came with the bike."

"Will you be careful?"

"Very."

"Even if a stag jumps in your face?"

"I promise."

"Well then, let me get my bag."

"The wind will pick up your dress and you may get your leg burned by the pipe so you should wear pants and leather boots." She's about to go inside when he stops her again. "Oh and, you may not like the chilling factor on your hands so if you have leather gloves, which would be best . . ."

"Gees . . . how about if I wore armour with a shield and spike?" Unhappy about taking the motorcycle, she walks in the house still mumbling while Josh cannot hide a winning smile.

After stowing her luggage in one of the side bags, he starts the engine, bends to her height to adjust the helmet over her head, and gives her protection glasses before climbing on. Irma and Amanda watch the lady get in the back of the motorcycle for the first time in her life. "How do you mount this thing?"

"You climb on just like you would on a horse. Put your foot on the pedal like you would in a stirrup, grab my shoulder and then flip your other leg over." Her first attempt is a bit unsteady and without elegance, she finally succeeds. "How do I hang on?"

"You have two choices, the bars behind you or the waist of your driver." She chooses the seat bars at her back. The motor has revolved a few times so he asks: "Ready?"

"Ready!" She admits and before she has time to wave back at her mother and grandmother, Josh has already started to ride out the dirt track to get to the main road out of Dornie.

As promised; Josh carefully drives out to the A87 roadway until they reach Invergarry. The trip takes most the day and it was next to impossible to have a decent conversation with the motor running. Taking a break at lunch time, they have plenty to talk about and Josh discovers that she is six years older than him. Divorced from a wealthy insurance consultant who didn't leave her much but a bitter feeling, she decided to get a master's degree in history and teach at the Edinburgh University. When it was Josh's turn to talk, he never hid the fact that his finding methods were eccentric and got into the way of people's common principles. Choosing his words, he tells her about the power of belief, the electricity within each body and whenever the complexity of the terms stopped her from understanding, he explained it in simpler words. One thing was certain; it was much too early in this relationship to tell her all the fine details of his visions. It would certainly create a shiver down her spine and make her run like hell.

A step back in time, that's what this country was all about. Nowhere on earth, did he ever feel so good, not even in his home town. Missing his mother like crazy, he feels empty and vulnerable but the presence of the lady friend makes the pain more bearable. When they reach Oban by mid-afternoon, they take the ferry to Mull and ride from one tip of the island to the other. Arriving at Fionnphort, a small boat brings them to the sacred island of Iona. The water dancing in the bay is of intense turquoise; used fishing boats are resting upon the shore where the white sand contrasts with the red highland cattle grazing the long verdant grass. Once again, he is delighted at the view before him. The Abbey graciously standing around seventy odd houses is the predominent edifice as well as the main attraction. He follows the lady to her habitual B & B tended by a middle aged couple. As son as you enter, a fireplace takes most of the space in the room except for a wooden counter that serves as the reception desk. "Hello Miss MacRae, how are you doing today?"

"Just fine, thank you." She replies scratching her scalp. "Same room as usual?" the owner suggests.

"For me yes but I was wondering if you had a second room available for a friend who's visiting."

"That's awfully regrettable but maybe you forgot that the convention for priesthood is taking place this week. All the rooms on the island are booked solid."

"Oh shoo . . ." Visibly uneasy, Josh cuts in. "If it would make you more comfortable, I could sleep outside, I don't really mind." Charlene looks at him, almost wanting to slap him on the arm for being so ridiculous. "No, that's fine, we'll take the room. Just bring us a couple more blankets and we'll manage." She grabs the key and walks to the room on the second floor, places her small piece of luggage at the foot of the only double bed. He closes the door behind him, still bothered about the situation. "I could . . ."

"Don't say another word." She interrupts putting her hand up. "You have no idea what sleeping outside means here. It's damp, cold and hungry beasts are wandering around. We're two responsible adults. There should not be any problem for us to sleep in the same room without any big consequence. Should it?"

"I guess not."

"Supper time isn't until two more hours. Would you like to go to the beach for a little walk? My legs feel numb."

"That's the price to pay for a first ride."

On the eastern tip of the island close to Strand of the Seat, while bright orange beak coloured puffins fly about, Charlene playfully takes a few stems of Echinops and weaves them together. "I used to come here with my parents on holidays, that's how we met the owners of where we will sleep tonight. Her husband is a fisherman just like my father used to be so they had plenty to talk about."

"Used to?" He inquires taking a rock and throwing it into the ocean making a few leaps. "Yes, he died a long time ago, I was fourteen. Gusting winds of a hundred miles an hour came out of nowhere while he was at sea. The hail made his boat tip over and only four men survived, one had his two legs amputed and another one drowned. My father's body was the only one that never resurfaced. So after one year, he was considered lost at sea and only then, did my mother receive any kind of compensation; it was pretty hard at his funeral to have an empty casket. She cried for days hanging on to his favorite scarf."

"It must have been hard on you."

"Financially, my mother was broke. That's when she decided to take back her own mother with us and turn the house into a Bed & Breakfast. At twenty-five, I got married, but after five years of constant arguing, I decided that I wasn't meant for him. He blamed me for everything including the fact that I could not get pregnant. Anyway . . . it's all in the past now. I saw him a few months ago with his new wife. He still has no kids but I hear he's very happy."

He could tell by the way she spoke about her last relationship that it still hurt inside but just like him, wanted to erase this period of the past and move on. Her hair floating in the wind makes swirls like the waves ashore. Walking barefoot beside her in the whitish sand with the sun behind makes him realize how attractive the island is.

"After supper when the lights will dim, I'll take you to the Abbey. That's when it's the most beautiful."

"I'm sure it is."

The supper enhanced by a fresh catch is a total immersion into the local way of life where the guest finds himself amused at the endless fisherman's stories. As usual after his last bite, he gets out to smoke a small cigar. Soon, Charlene joins him with a shawl over her shoulders. The sun is setting and one by one the porch lights come on.

"It's colder than yesterday night. Isn't it?" She expresses looking at him without any jacket.

"I'm always warm. I wouldn't really know the difference."

"Would you like to go to the Abbey now?" She hides her hands under the wool and tries to warm herself.

"I would." He squishes his cigar in the sand filled canister set by the flat rock of the entrance and they begin walking up the gravel road toward the edifice made of stones. Quietly, they enter the place. On their right, two dormants sepultures representing the Eighth Duke of Argyll and his wife lay immobile beneath their marble tomb. Walking up to the second row of wooden chairs, Charlene sits inviting Josh to join her in the nave. A few penitents are sitting around, most of them with faces wrinkled by old age and fierce winds. Monks from different ministries silently pray in respect. The high ceiling, finished with thick wooden planks, rises above them barely lit by the dozens of candles burning scarcely around. It is a moment of collectiveness and serenity. Josh quietly breathes in and closes his eyes before joining his hands together. Charlene has another way of being thankful; she peacefully looks at the crucifix set on the priest's offering table. Slowly, images inside Josh's head plunge him into a secondary state. Visions succeed one another, he sees monks screaming and running from the blades of invaders dressed in dark clothes with rims of fur. Their weapons decorated with abominable representations and bold lettering, pursue the terrorized brothers. Heads roll down until the assailants find and walk away with a casket containing a precious book. Ruby red blood flows on the tiles and a silence worse than screams, resound within the walls. Josh's breath shortens and his hands clasp tighter together, a simple involuntary reflex for protection. The attrocity of the scene is beyond words while innocents are murdered by pagans. He wakes in a flash, reassured that this present day doesn't involve barbarians trying to kill him. Still, the surprise of the attack, the corpses spread all around and the fastness at which he got precipitated in, leave him perplex about the event. Slowly, he rises from his chair and walks forward to the altar. He lights two candles, one for his parents and the second for the Abbey's victims. Charlene comes near and lights one of her own. He steps back to admire the chivalry depicted on the walls and engraved on the columns with knights mounting their tamed beasts. The ashened sun is coming through the window on the western side and attracted by something powerful and strong, he turns to Charlene. She stands in the light with her shimmering personality, modest clothes and radiant hair. But it is the aura irradiating from her that attracts him most, an array of intense glittering, emanating from her entire body and not only from her head.

"Good evening sir, welcome to Iona."

A male voice makes him turn around. Facing him, a monk wearing the traditional dark brown robe deprived of any fanciness, joins his hands and bows.

"Likewise." Josh responds in a low voice to keep from disturbing the praying faithful.

"Is this your first time on the island?"

"It is." Charlene comes forward. "Hello Brother Don, how do you do?"

"Miss MacRae, I'm glad to see you again." He confides taking both her hands in his. "I see that you have brought us a companion this time."

"Mister Forge works in London. For a few days, I have the pleasure of taking him around the country and the first place I wanted him to see was of course your sanctuary."

"Your spiritual value will forever be welcome. Are you a fervent adept of the church mister Forge?"

"I believe in God." He precises without going into details. The monk places his hand on Josh's shoulder and immediately feels a tingling. Both stare at each other for half a second and the resident withdraws his hand instinctively, understanding that the visitor is no common lad. "I wish I could stay and have a more elaborate conversation but other obligations are calling. Please excuse me."

"Nice to see you again Brother Don." She concludes. Josh bows his head in respect and soon, the monk leaves them both to enter a cabinet on the right side of the nave. Charlene raises her eyebrows. "That's strange; he usually chats for hours with me."

"About?" Josh inquires. "Everything and nothing really, he's an expert on the history of this place and not only on the transcripts found in books." She precises.

Both are slowly walking back to the door and he opens it, letting Charlene take the first draught of the brisk evening air. "What do you mean?"

"Well there are a few more details than what is written, probably because most people couldn't read in those days. They mainly relied on an orator to tell stories. His great-grand father was one of those who transmitted the words of the Bible to an audience in the village. He collected whatever he could find about the casket, either verbally or drawn and showed it to me. Most of whatever is told is far more interesting than what is put down on paper."

"And what did you learn from his story telling?"

"You have no idea of the constant struggle the guardians of the book had to go through to keep it from invadors."

"If what you are saying is true and jewels decorated the casket, what will you do with your precious find?" He begins lighting another cigar.

"Give it back to the Irish."

"Don't you want to keep it for yourself?"

"Of course not, that wouldn't be right. The Book of Kells is the Celtic equivalent of the Dead Sea scrolls and is already at the Trinity College in Dublin. The casket belongs with it and so do the jewels." One could tell from her body language and expression that she was telling the truth. Getting back to Mrs Pratt's house, he lets her enter first and ascend the stairs. Shutting the door to their room, he evidently feels the discomforting situation. "You mind if I take my shower first?" She suggests.

"Of course not, you have something to read?"

"I've got the notes for my next book. Here, you can even correct my French if you want to."

"How come you have French and Gaelic words in your notes?"

"Why anything but English? Take a guess . . . I believe they had to hide a thing or two from the enemy." She turns around to enter the bathroom with a nightgown under her arm. Placing his stuff beside the couch, he takes off his shirt and goes to get his glasses in the improvised bagage. Because she forgot her hair brush, Charlene comes out of the bathroom and suddenly stops. Revealed by the lamp beside the bed, a game of light and shadow plays on the man's muscular back free of fat. His hair close to the darkness of a black bird, crowns the top of the head that now bends as to ease a tension in his neck. Perfectly still, she takes a minute to admire this disturbing spectacle. Never has she seen such a carved body, not too developed or too frail, just right. He gets up, a pair of broken glasses in his hand and turns to her. "Is there anything I can do?"

"No, I simply forgot my hair brush." She immediately explains getting back in the bathroom with it while he sits at the table, unveiling the content of scanned papers. A lot of work needed to be done but almost half of it was completed. The letters which seemed to hold memoirs were written in the most fluid handwriting while their content was like a repertoire of the everyday life in a castle from a maître-des-lieux's point of view. Many of the passages are already translated by Charlene, bringing to light a life filled with adventure, terror and passion for a country.

I am, so therefore I pray for the welfare
of this campaign that will decide if the partnership with
Lochland from Skye, Gaël and Ciarán from Mull will be what will
prevent us from the assaults of the British. Ethan is a new member to
my troops, a fierce fighter whom I shall
consider a precious ally.

Whatever master MacRae decides for Mise, I shall observe.
Both his sons still being in the entrails of the Tower,
I shall be the one to gain them back from their recluse setting that will
otherwise terminate their lives.
We shall all take a boat tomorrow before dawn with fifteen other
companions to free them and shall I lose Mo life, only with honour
will my blood be left upon the Saxon shores.
KMK

Josh looks at the original hanwriting, masculine yet fluid, executed sometimes in a language he has barely encountered, Gaelic. He only knew that it originated in central Europe in the early Iron Age, and reached the northern part of what is now Scotland by the La Tène period, the later Iron Age. The language's first intention, like all others, was to asset its adepts with the superiority of communicating among themselves without the ability of the opponents to understand. The last sentence is half-written in French. Josh looks at it, repeats it out loud frowning. Charlene comes out of the shower her hair all wrapped up with a towel, and he turns to her.

"English people did not understand Gaelic so why would he bother writing in French?"

"His wife was French, her name was Sarah."

"Who was he, the owner of the castle?"

"No, well, I don't know. That's my main issue. I have looked over and over for his initials in the castle registry and found nothing. KMK doesn't stand for any of the castle masters but a certain Kenneth MacKenzie was living there in the late 1200's and the person I'm looking for died when Eilean Donan was attacked in 1719. All through the book, he writes of his ascension as being the one making decisions, giving orders, etc. So, I really don't know who he is or as a matter of fact if the book is a fraud; I had it evaluated with carbon 14 at the University and they confirmed to me that it was written in the eighteenth century."

He takes off his glasses and she begins brushing her hair placing the wet towel back in the bathroom. "Where did you find the manuscript?"

"The Trust Fund had employees coming in to repair part of a wall that started to crumble on the lower level and they discovered a metal box. They called me right away. Just like the Book of Kells, the writing on sheep skin is the only reason for its survival. If it would have been written on paper, barely anything would have survived three hundred years and this man knew it."

Josh stays silent for a moment. "There are no numbers on the pages. How would you know if you have them all?"

"I'm the one who scanned the copies." She precises. "I've been wondering; do you have Celtic blood?"

"No why?" Her hand slowly rises to his ear lobe and with curiosity; she admires the small metal emblem. "The earring you wear looks like it comes from our country."

"It used to belong to my mother."

"Where did *she* get it?" With a simple twist, he takes it off and presents it to her.

"It was a gift from her father on her wedding day."

"So *he* was Scottish?" She proposes inspecting it.

"No, French. His name was Adrien Dorais."

"The name is quite French, but this is Celtic, I would bet my life on it." She replies handing the jewellery back.

"Believe me; I have no trace of this country in me except the bruise on my thigh." He ironizes walking in the bathroom.

Half an hour later, he comes out with his jeans back on.

"Why have you got your pants on?"

"I usually sleep in the nude." He confirms taking off his belt and placing it over his luggage. "Mrs Pratt prepaired us some herbal tea. You want some?"

"Sure." She already had a first serving of the fuming tea so she bends to serve the visitor. "We've talked a lot about what I do for a living but I would like to know more about you. How come you chose that field?" She demands curling up her feet under her. Unfolding the thickest blanket, he spreads it over the floor and sits on it, laying his back against the couch. "Every time my father got drunk, I ran from the house. I fled a lot and sometimes got myself in sticky situations just like these kids. So

I've been there and things could have gotten far worse. I was lucky."

"You say you've done it a couple of times, what made you go back home?"

He blows on the fuming tea and takes a sip before answering: "Starving."

They both start laughing. He has the most gorgeous smile, she thinks while resting her hand over her cheek. But then, the laughter dies as he places the tea cup away on the night table. "Seriously, I believe that there is a lot to do to prevent kids from running away, being mistreated or kidnapped. I just want to do my share."

"Do you believe that we're on earth to accomplish a specific mission?"

First, he turns his gaze away but when he faces her again, she knows his answer will be very thoughtful.

"My mother would think that but my father would not. Both had faith in God and while my mother hung on when things were tough, my father turned to booze to cope with his miseries. If both had the mission to raise me, they certainly encouraged me to find my own way to prevent other kids from enduring what I had gone through."

For an instant, she looks at the man sharing her room and almost wishes he would kiss her good night. When Josh realizes that the romance could easily begin, he slips down to the ground and grabs another blanket. "Good night Miss MacRae."

"Bonne nuit Monsieur Forge." She concludes before turning off the light beside her.

During the night, he wakes and sits, hearing some kind of noise outside. He buckles his belt, puts on his leather jacket and barefoot, quietly descends the stairs. The fire is almost out with only a few branches fuming. Inaudibly, he closes the door behind himself and looks around to locate where the sound of a metallic banging comes from. The door of the church is open and a light sheds from within. Attached to the tall cross in front of the Abbey, he sees the silhouette of a horse grazing the spring grass. At first, Josh thinks that the stirrups are making the repetitive clatter but he then realizes that the sound really comes from within the church. He leaves the horse after petting it and walks in. In the entrance, the wind sends a sword knocking against the surface of the pillar it is tied to. The fact that the sound echoed all the way to his room makes him perplex. Far from only being a weapon, he admires it like a work of art shimmering under the light of a thousand candles lighted beyond the nave. His fingers touch the blade where the words *Luceo Non Uro* are engraved near the hilt and a leather band is strapped around the handle. The horse and sword belonged to someone near he figures but yet, no one is in sight. Approaching the altar by the center alley, he finally sees a man, back and head bent on the first step. As receiving a blessing, his arms are open on each side and his fingers spread apart. Wearing a kilt in the hues of blue, green and black, the penitent's feet are covered with boots made of reversed skin. The soft yellow light coming from the candles makes his shadow vibrate. Josh is a few feet behind waiting and suddenly, the man joins his hands together, puts them up against his forehead to cross himself. There is no fear to make the newcomer run away but an enormous curiosity, when the warrior turns his head Josh sees a strong ressemblance with his own features. Same jaw, same nose, same dark and wavy hair but longer, beard cut in the same way and the exact replica of his own eyes. "You have travelled a long way. I've been waiting for you."

"Who are you?" Josh pleads. The warrior's lips rise to a candid expression and he begins to walk toward him to stop only inches away. "Don't ever leave your weapons, always wear them." He advices. A piercing light comes from the way he stares and yet, it doesn't scare the visitor. The warrior's voice is more profound than his, ponctuated with a rough accent. "Who are you?" The young man shouts once more.

"Who do you think?" The man's jaw hardens and violently, he clasps his muscular hands together. Josh wakes in a flash, raises his back to sit. Out of breath, his heart beats like a war drum and he looks around. The rain batters against the window and Charlene is sound asleep in the bed beside him. Only one way to find out if this was real, he thinks. He grabs his coat and rushes out. No prints are left from the horse shoes in the grass because of the rain still pouring. He goes straight to the church and tries to open the door but it is locked. He knocks a couple of times; water is dripping over his head making the colour of his hair even darker. It must be five or six in the morning. The sun is up but hiding behind thick clouds that are releasing all their content.

"Yes?" A young monk finally says after opening.

"Can I come in, please?"

"Is there an emergency?"

"Sort of, it will only take a moment."

The monk lets him in and realizes that the caller is barefoot. "You're going to catch a cold." But Josh is not listening and walks straight up the altar under the wary eyes of the monk. "Is there anything I can do for you?" He proposes from the entrance while Josh looks at the floor and table for any traces of the warrior's presence. Nothing can be seen, no mud, no piece of fabric, no wax from the thousand candles. Brother Don arrives and looks at Josh who seems to be searching for something.

"Mister Forge, you are earlier than the rest of the priesthood." With both hands crossed, the priest comes toward the young man whose gaze is still locked unto the floor. "Are you well?" The man of faith asks again so Josh lifts his head, turns his face away and takes off the garment almost ripping his lobe. "I'm sorry. I lost my earring yesterday." He pretends as an excuse. "Ah, here it is!" He says faking to pick it up from the floor and putting it back on but Brother Don looks at him suspiciously.

"God answers our most precious wishes." Admits the innocent monk returning to his chores. Josh discretely keeps looking on the floor for traces of mud or wax. Resigned, he lifts his head before looking like a fool and begins walking toward the door.

"Mister Forge?" The visitor turns around to the Brother, and stops. "Some questions need not to be explained." Deception, dismay and even angriness can be read all over his face with the reply; so he walks closer, almost defying the man of faith. "My life is either black or white, there is no place for a grey zone and everything I don't understand, I need to find an answer for."

"If you possess any kind of faith, because I'm sure you do, just let it be." Brother Don clearly knew something, Josh could feel it. Either that or he was a total idiot. Without paying any form of respect, the traveler walks with a decisive pace to exit through the front door. Rising his face to receive all the tears from the skies, he stays like this for a minute, trying to comprehend the meaning of his last vision, if vision it was.

"Where were you?" Charlene articulates waking up, rubbing her eyes.

"I paid a little visit to the Abbey." He indicates closing back the door.

"You always go out barefoot with no sweater?"

Leaving his coat on the back of a chair to drip off, he takes a t-shirt from his things and puts it on. Apparently, he won't answer her question so she changes the subject. "Are you hungry?" She supposes getting some clothes from her own luggage.

"Yeah . . ."

"Come, Mrs Pratt makes the best pancakes ever."

Chapter Sixth

Her course was the reason for her visit on Iona and it meant taking a few pictures inside the Abbey. While she concentrates on the painted windows and roofing method, he runs over last night's event in his mind and thinks about the sword attached to the column. Rising from his chair close to the nave, he walks back to the entrance and approaches the circular post made of rough cement. Thinking over the way the sword was attached to it, he glides his fingers to feel the support. There are no hooks or nails from the roof that could allow it to have been hung so close by. He takes a candle, ignites it but the light it sheds only reveals a small section at a time. Gently, he strokes the post, searching for any trace left by the weapon when a little lower than expected, a dent is found as if something hit it repeatedly.

"Found anything?"

Interrupted, Josh takes the light away from his discovery. "No, I was looking at the engraving on top of the column."

"They were made in the 1200's when this place was turned into a Benedictine monastery. Well, I'm done with the pictures. We should be on our way if we want to be home for supper." He nods and follows her to get their luggage. After thanking the Pratt's for their hospitality, they both hop back on the bike, cross the seaway to Oban and ride back to the Highlands.

After a few hours sitting on a bike, her legs feel numb again and a small discomfort invades her lower back. Still, she smiles about the adventure. She hesitates and then asks the inevitable. "Why are you like that?"

"Like what?"

"The word psychic comes to mind but I guess you don't like to be tagged with it."

"It's very disturbing isn't it?"

"Well, to tell you the truth, I don't know how to take you."

"What do you mean?"

"Well since you have more perception, maybe you already know what I'm thinking right now."

"It's not because I can see the aura of people that I know exactly what they are thinking. Besides, I need to be receptive and in an appropriate environment. If I'm too tired, it just won't work."

"What about now?"

"You mean, if I see yours?"

"Correct."

He turns his head to her. "Have you ever seen aurora borealis in the sky?"

"I have."

"Right now, it's like one with hues of soft pink and fine lines of purple over a white backround. It comes and goes with each of your heartbeats, like a wave coming and going on the shore."

"Is it nice?"

"It's one of the most beautiful ones I've ever seen. In fact, that's the reason I was drawn to you at the fair."

Visibly troubled by his response, she is about to get inside when, he touches her arm. "Charlene, wait please." She turns around and looks at him holding tight to his helmet as if he needed something to cling on. "I want to thank you."

"Me? Why would you do that?"

"You took my mind off a few things."

She smiles and takes his right hand. "The pleasure was all mine." With that said she whips her hair about and enters the house leaving the door open for him.

"Amanda! Irma! We're back and all in one piece too!"

When he arrives into his room, he takes another look at his laptop and cellular phone. Evidently, nothing had changed from the fact that they were both irrefutably broken so he walks down to the kitchen to find Charlene's mother. Already prepairing supper, she is stuffing poultry with bread crums and spices.

"So how did you enjoy Iona?"

"It was quite amazing. I really liked it. Would you mind if I made a phonecall to my partner in London?"

"Not at all, take all the time you need. I'll just put in on your bill."

First he calls his cellular number but he doesn't want to leave a message to the answering machine. He takes out a card in his wallet and dials the number that appears underneath the logo.

« London Police Headquarters, how may I help you? »

"Hello this is agent Forge. I would like to talk to agent Lorne Landers."

"One moment please."

After a minute, the familiar voice is heard again. "Agent Landers is not available at the moment. Would you like to leave him a message?"

"No . . . yes, tell him that Josh will call him back tonight on his cell."

"I'll do sir."

"Thank you." He hangs up the heavy black receptor back to the wall. The last time he saw a telephone this big was at his grandmother's when he was about eight years old. "Guess I will have to use it back again tonight."

"Don't worry. My daughter has a cell but because of the mountains, the signal often cuts. Just use this telephone again."

"I appreciate it."

Amanda comes in, walking slowly helped with her cane. "Hello young man, are you here for the leaking faucet?"

"Ma, this is mister Forge. He's not the plumber, he's a guest don't you remember?"

"Where is the leaky faucet Mrs MacRae?"

She sighs, visibly embarrassed. "It's in the downstairs bathroom next to her room."

"Do you have any tools? Ratchet and things like that?"

"Jocelyn, you don't have to."

"I'll just take a look at it and if I cannot fix it then you can call a plumber if you want to."

She places the poultry in the warm iron oven and disappears for a minute. Given tools and different sizes of plastic washers, he first shuts the water, pulls the pipes apart from the sink, cleans the old pieces made of sturdy metal and places them over a sheet of newspaper. He then does the same thing with the faucets. Charlene happens to walk by in the corridor. "What are you doing?"

"Making your grandmother happy, I used to watch the plumber fix whatever was leaking at my mother's place so I have a vague idea about what to do." He assures cleaning the pieces.

"I thought that pencil pushers didn't like to get their hands dirty."

Concentrated on the task, he barely looks at her but still gives a reply to her comment. "I never considered myself an office type of guy since I hate being trapped into those concrete boxes." After putting some adhesive tape on the mesh of the pipe, he delicately inserts the washer and fastens one piece into the other. He then turns on the knob for the water to flow again and tries the faucets. Water is no longer leaking. "Here you go; you can tell Amanda that the faucet is fixed."

"Gees, this is so embarrassing."

"This is nothing compared to the hospitality you and your family are giving me."

"Grandma, your faucet is fixed." She says walking away but suddenly realizes that she has to return to the castle and bring back the oil lamps to be filled.

Josh gets down on his knees and grabs the newspaper but a title captures his attention: "London's protection structure soon to be remastered". He dusts off the broken washer and rusts from the text and takes a good look at it. "The press will soon learn about a restructure in the ranks of the popular U.K. organization. Sources tell us that all major funds will be forwarded toward security and . . ." It was a small article, barely noticeable overheaded by Scottish preocupations.

"She's very happy and thanks you." Irma confirms coming back near.

Shocked and upset, Josh grabs the newspaper, tearing away the page of the article. "You look pale, are you alright?"

"Of course, just tell me where I have to put back the tools."

"You've done enough. I'll take care of that." Amanda appears in the corridor. "How much do you charge for the repair young man?" Confused with Josh's presence, Amanda takes out a few pounds from her wallet. "Nothing today madam, it's our good deed day."

"Oh, well in that case how about a glass of whisky?" She replies placing her wallet back into the pocket of her apron. "I'm sorry, I don't drink." He protests while washing his hands.

"Funny, you're the second man to tell me that this week, or was it last week . . ." While the old lady shudderingly strolls to the living room, he walks upstairs to his own retreat, closes the door and the first thing he does is check the date the story was printed on the side of the newspaper; yesterday's date appear. The article is quite clear about the vision of the organization that will no longer tolerate any incident, even the smallest about infiltrations or suspects about terrorism in the country. All other departments will suffer compression or will even be abolished. He puts the paper down and has only one thought: why was he transferred if not to work for the kids? He has to get back to London and the sooner, the better. Taking whatever he brought with him, he puts it back into the packsack and carries it downstairs. Irma is in the kitchen placing clean dishcloths in the drawer and happens to look at Josh. "Are you leaving?"

"I'm afraid so. Something came up. Here's a little bit for the extras."

"That's way too much." She protests looking at the few more pounds.

"No please. Take it. I arrived here quite uninvited and you went out of your way to make me feel welcome. Where is Charlene?"

"She's still at the castle."

"Thank you, thank you very much for your hospitality."

Attaching his luggage on the back of the motorcycle, he takes his leather gloves and places them beside his helmet on the gas tank. Walking on the bridge made of rocks, a race against the clock is cheating him out of quality time. As he reaches the sole tree on the western side of the fortification, he looks around and admires the island of Skye casting its shadow on the Loch. Prey birds are diving down to capture fish bringing them back to their nests. Charlene arrives by his side with a couple of empty oil lamps.

"I have to get back to London right away. I'll give you my cell number. You can call me in a few days when it's going to be repaired."

He scribbles down the digits on a piece of cigar box cardboard and hands it to her. When her head rises, their eyes meet and she can tell how much he would have wanted to stay longer to get to know her better. "If I don't do this, I'll regret it for the rest of my life." Without a second thought he gently cups her face in his hands and sweetly kisses her lips. Any doubts he may have had a second ago about his impulse, all vanish at the contact of her soft mouth. The desire and will, the essence in which they both capture each other's breath reveal their common passion. It was the first step of a new beginning. Distancing one another, he still has his eyes closed to savour the seductive touch. Reluctantly, he heads back to his bike her hand in his and hops on it. Before long, he rolls away while the sun, just above the hills, cast a shadow on the magnificent castle. Walking up to her mother's house, Charlene stays inside looking out the screen window, wondering about the coincidence that put this man from another continent on her path.

Dornie was covered with deep, deep dew. All that echoed around was the high pitch squeal of the capercaillies. The deers stood all around. Only I was odd in the decor, my feet floating toward the dim sun that was forcing itself through the Caledonian fog. Overlooking the peaks, the zephyr was dawdlingly blowing while I would breathe its splendour. Praise the view for it is on this very mountain that I want my eyes to rest on Mo last breath.
KMK

The sound of a motorbike ceases in front of the Londonian flat. It's four in the morning and the door opens to soon be discretely shut. Josh takes off his soaking wet coat, damp boots and helmet to leave them on the carpet of the entrance. The rest of his stuff is brought upstairs in his room. Lorne appears in the doorway of his room. "Hi!" He articulates with sleepy eyes.

"Hi." Josh responds far from using the same cheering tone.

"I had a message that you would call back tonight. I thought you would only be here later."

"So did I but this came up." He throws handing his partner the newspaper clip from his back pocket. Lorne lifts it with precaution because part of it is damp. "Is there anything I should know?" The young man asks while unfastening his leather chaps.

"Where did you take this?"

"I got it in Scotland. I was over there for a few days." He lets out while pulling down his jeans.

"I have no idea what this is . . . what the hell happened?" Lorne shouts looking at the broken laptop, cell and glasses laid over the working desk. "I had a little encounter with a friendly stag."

"How did it happen? You got yourself in an accident? Where's the car?"

"I did not rent a car."

"Don't tell me you got yourself another bike? You know how Taylor and I feel about you riding one!! He happens to look at Josh's bruised thigh. "Good Lord! How did you do that?"

"I hit the handles before flying over them."

"You could have gotten yourself killed."

"I'm not dead." He reasures putting on his jogging pants. "Let's get down to serious business. I want to know if you heard anything about our department getting cutbacks or even be dismantled."

"No I did not. This newspaper clip might be false. C'mon Josh; it's the middle of night. Why don't you get some rest?"

"Can't . . . I got too much on my mind." Lorne looks at his partner and thoughts rise. "Last time I saw you so hyper was when . . . You met someone, didn't you?" Josh keeps silent and avoids his penetrating stare. "Did you?? How is she?" Lorne asks all excited. "Remember that red-haired that was in the restaurant the first week we arrived?" Josh cuts short taking a towel to rub the back of his wet hair.

"What about her?"

"I met her again at a book fair. She gave me her card but I lost it."

"You mean this one?" Lorne takes the business card neatly placed on Josh's desk.

"Where did you find it?"

"In the entrance, anyway, tell me more."

"We talked for a while; she told me that she's a history teacher at the Edinburgh University as well as a writer. Something inside told me to pursue her so as soon as I got out of the office after Wednesday's meeting, I rented a bike and bought a map. I rode on the highway until I arrived in Scotland after taking a few breaks. The scenery in the Highlands is totally unforgettable and right up to the Glencoe Valley, everything was just great. I took my eyes off the road to watch some deers. Next thing I know, this huge beast stands in front of me, blocking the road. It must have weighed a thousand pounds. I tried decompressing to the max before putting on the brakes but it was too close. Avoiding it, I just flew over the handles and landed flat on my back."

"That still doesn't tell me how you met the lady."

"Wait! I'm getting there. In the next town, I got help from a mechanic checking the bike and he only did minor repairs. I got along the road, making a few stops thinking the whole time that I should reach Kyle of LochAlsh to meet with her editor. But when I arrived in Dornie, my leg was hurting way too much and I had to rest. I got attracted to the sound of a bagpiper who was playing in front of a castle who then directed me toward a B & B at the end of the road. That's where she lives but the weirdest part is not the fact that I met her again but the castle standing before her house."

"Were you not impressed to find her there?"

"Our paths were meant to cross but the castle could not come to me. I had to go to it."

"You sound so odd . . . did you smoke some funny weed?" Slightly insulted, Josh walks up to the desk and takes his portfolio. He opens it and takes out a dozen drawings, places them to face Lorne. "This is what was standing in front of me." The partner picks up one of the sheets representing a castle. "Aren't those the drawings that were in your basement?"

"I've been sketching; painting and dreaming this fortress over and over since my teen years and I never thought it actually existed. The bridge, the main edifice and the roof, everything is the same. It just took my breath away."

"What do you make of it?"

"I don't know but it sure is some coincidence."

"There is no such thing as a coincidence in this world." Lorne advises lifting his eyes up. "Anyway, it's the middle of the night and there are still a few hours before I'm off to work to meet with Hockart." He adds yawning.

"Really?"

"He asked me to meet with him at eleven o'clock."

"Wake me up an hour before you leave; I want to go with you and find more about the newspaper article." Josh insists with eyelids still wide open.

The bastion, fortress of my heart, stands at the mouth of the sea. From the roof, the Five Sisters of Kintail can be seen and on a clear day, from the other side, the rest of the world gazing back.
People, forgive me to love this bastion with so much vigour and beyond human limits.
I will fight for it, give all my possessions and abilities for it to stand endlessly where brother Eilean first set foot and decided that this nest would protect the wrapping of the precious.
KMK

Charlene puts the last period on her translation and places the sheet away in her sack. Nothing can make her fall asleep and her thoughts irremediably converge to the man who passionately kissed her at the foot of the fortress. She turns off the table lamp and wraps herself in thick handmade bedspread, eyes as wide open as the moon above the loch.

Hundreds of miles away, Josh lies on the mattress up in the attic, unable to fall asleep, thinking how sweet her lips tasted and the lingering aroma of her perfume still floating around in his memory.

The next morning, last week of May, London Police Headquarters.

Josh is speaking to Taylor on the telephone about the newspaper article.

"If it bothers you so much, I'll ask Wilkinson about it."

"No I will. I was just wondering if you heard anything about compressions. Anyway I'll see you later."

"Sure lad."

He walks back near the window where Lorne, the Sergeant and another employee named Miller are sitting. The cafetaria of the grey edifice overhangs one of the most destructed cities back in World War II.

"Your procedures differ from one case to the other. Can you explain?"

"Linking « through » the missing person makes it faster for me to find her or him even though Lorne doesn't like it."

"And why may I ask?"

"I believe that it's more dangerous." The blond agent immediately replies.

"What makes you think that?"

"I've done it. Your heart rate is faster and the way to get "back home" is less obvious. The further you get away from your physical body, the harder it gets for you to come back."

"Transcendental voyaging is totally new to me. I guess you both are the professionals on the subject and the furthest thing on my mind is to dictate your actions." Hockart's assistant agent Miller is all ears but for some reason, Josh cannot hide a certain apprehension regarding the obsessive manœuvres he repeats over and over again, cleaning his utensils. While the others seem to enjoy talking about job procedures, Miller rearranges his tie about thirty times and cleans his spoon more often than that. He suddenly looks at this watch and rises. "May I leave now Sergeant?"

"Yes of course, I'll see you later."

"Good day mister Forge, mister Landers."

"Good day." Repeats Lorne following with his eyes the deranged man. Josh nods and for some obvious reason, feels sorry for him. Hockart takes his cup signaling to the two agents that their break ended. "Would it be too impolite to ask what happened to him?" Josh hushes.

"No, no, I guess not. Agent Miller was with Wilfrid your office neighbour and another agent named Fraser when they were asked to make an inquiry in a jewellery store about two and a half years ago. We suspected the owner of doing some unclean business. After they got there, an armed robbery took place and both fired back. The robbers replied and got control of the situation and the owner was killed. When the ambulances arrived, Miller was in shock and he now has that feeling that if things are not done in a proper order, something tragic will happen again. So he has been diagnosed with OCD, Obsessive Compulsive Dissorder. Wilfrid had stopped stuttering when he started working in our office but after that incident, he started again."

"What hapened to Fraser?"

"He quit the police force right after and was never heard from again. As for Miller, it's easy to see that he has been traumatized by the event. He's been in consultation ever since and is much better now. At least he doesn't count backward from sixty-five now."

"Why that number?" Lorne throws.

"Because that's the number where one of the robbers started to count down the remaining time they had to execute their felony." Josh creases his eyebrows. "You still have the report of this case?"

"In the archives yes. We even have the video from the surveillance camera."

"I would like to take a peek at it if you don't mind."

"The case was never closed. The stolen jewelleries were never retrieved and probably sold on the black market."

"I'm not interested about that. I'm mainly concerned about Miller's reaction to the event." Lorne looks at his partner, frowning while Josh pays no attention to him. "I will get the report and the video out for you." Hockart lets out as he gets up.

"Thanks." Josh answers before the trio walks up to the elevators, crossing a few of the other agents, all wearing dark suits, white shirts and bound up to the neck stupid strangling ties.

"I've had a request last evening from Mister Wilkinson." Starts the Sergeant. "Would you mind being filmed? I already asked your superior about it and he said that it was up to you." Having never been asked such a question before, Lorne turns to his partner, waiting for his reply. "I don't see any problem with that, do you?" Josh pauses and takes advantage of the moment to ask a question of his own. "Before we do Sergeant, I do have to ask you something and it puts me in a very delicate position."

"Just asks mister Forge. I'll answer to the best of my knowledge." He takes out the newspaper clipping from the inside pocket of his jacket and shows it to him. Hockart takes it, reading silently. "Where did you get that?"

"It was in a Scottish newspaper three days ago." Hockart gives it back without any explanation. "Is it true Sergeant?" The youngest asks waiting for a reply. The man of high rank still doesn't answer and walks into the elevator. Both agents follow him in. As soon as the doors are shut, the man in his fifties turns to them. "Wilkinson will see you this afternoon concerning this."

Josh's shoulders go down. "So it does involve our presence?"

"I'm afraid so."

"Did he at least get the proposal about my program?" Arriving on Josh office's floor, Hockart leaves the door open. "If you want my advice, you better get another offer with half the effectives that you asked for otherwise your project will be cancelled all together."

"What about the kids? What about all the money that was supposed to be injected and the contract I signed?"

"That was before other threats came in last week."

"You mean terrorist?"

"We have received serious threats against Mister Wilkinson. We simply have to divert the effectives for a while. As to how that information came out in the newspaper, I have no idea."

"How long will I have to wait to get what I was supposed to?"

"This afternoon, two o'clock sharp in Wilkinson's office. He will tell you all about it." Hockart announces walking away letting the door close by itself. Josh has his mouth open and suddenly turns to Lorne. "Did you know about this?"

"Of course not but I'm leaving in a few weeks. Does it really concern me anymore?" Josh furiously begins pacing in his office; Lorne is a few steps behind. Mrs Long is pressing on her computer new file names and preparing documents. "Can you excuse us for a moment Mrs Long?"

As soon as the door is shut behind her, Josh explodes. "He has no right!"

"Josh listen, calm down. Wait to see what he has to propose first."

"I'm telling you, I did not come here to be screwed with other functions than finding kids."

"How can you say that? You haven't heard him yet." Josh places his hands on his hips, exhales and bites his lip. He goes to the door and opens it back again.

"Mrs Long, please come in." She sits at her desk and prepares herself to continue was she was working on. "You remember the report I sent you before leaving?"

"You mean the one with your department structure?"

"Exactly, did you plan a budget for that?"

"Roughly but I did not include it with the program before sending it to mister Hockart."

"Can I see it?"

A couple of clicks later, the budget appears on her screen. The figures are astronomical for twenty employees.

"Can you show me the figures if you cut it down to twelve employees?"

"Wait! I'm still not done with pin pointing the ones with faculties." Protests Lorne.

"How many did you get so far?"

"Eight."

"So that leaves room for a few others. Go ahead with two more Brenda."

In his excitement, he calls her by her first name which makes her smile. The frontier is now broken, a gap she thought would always stand as a wall between them. After she made the requested adjustments, she turns the laptop to face him.

"Look at the figures. It's much better."

Looking at the screen, the young agent nods approvingly and satisfaction lights up his face. "O.k. now, I would like you to get the best insurance for everyone: invalidity, pension plan, dental, eyewear, medication and survivor's assets."

"We already have a good insurance plan with the company."

"If so, I want to see it and I want it to be effective the first day they are employed. I want it to be added to their salary and not substracted from it."

"I'll see what I can do."

"What will you do if he still doesn't let you do it?" Inquires Lorne.

"I'll trow myself off a bridge." Josh snaps checking other papers over his desk.

Brenda turns around with her eyes as wide as those of a gold fish's.

"He's joking…" Lorne precises to the poor lady unaccustomed to Josh's dark humor.

Same afternoon, two o'clock sharp.

Both newcommers are sitting in front of the highest representative of the London Police Force. He's looking at his screen, considering Josh's last attempt to finance the inexisting department. "Twelve employees are much less expensive but I'm afraid it just won't be possible in your own division mister Forge."

"*Agent* Forge please." The young man insists getting irritated.

"Agent Forge . . ."

"So why the hell did you make me leave my Montreal office, bring me all the way here, give me an office, a secretary and finally employ Lorne to find participants? Your manners are really obscure mister Wilkinson."

"We received threats last week, serious and verified threats."

"And you never received those before?"

"Of course we did."

"So why take these new ones seriously?"

"They were directed toward the entire institution. Over the last years, it has been more and more difficult to recruit personnel and the only way to do it is to raise their salary. Their training takes months and looking at past figures, only 45 % make it to the end. Your department doesn't exist yet. None of your employees have been hired. It's like killing the unborn in the womb. No damages have been done and we definitely need qualified employees in the security zone. You could train a few of them to find activists, could you not?"

Josh sits on the edge of his seat, pointing his index on the master's desk.

"I've already got about one hundred and fifthy files in my cabinet ready to be looked at and new ones keep adding up every day. I thought they were the real reason for my transfer but I can see you're nothing but a liar and opportunist."

The young Canadian's greyish-blue eyes are confronting Wilkinson's until the leader lowers his head to simulate reading the report lying over his desk. The reply was meant to set the tone of their relationship. Josh could not and would never be tamed. Silently sitting beside his partner, Lorne tilts his head to the side, waiting for Wilkinson's reply. Josh was provocative, honest and sharp-witted too much sometimes but his partner knew that it's the only way his job could be done. Wilkinson recalls Taylor's warning about the young lad's stubbornness and particular beliefs. Over the decade he had been working with him, the British born Lieutenant knew the youngster to be different from all other people he had ever met before, cherishing his individuality and integrity. The lad was authentic, knew what he wanted and what he was capable of. Exploiting his abilities, he felt as if the Lord granted him with an uncommon blessing and was surely not going to let anyone underestimate or think less of him because of that gift. Whipped by the strong utterance, Wilkinson takes a moment to question the young psychic again, trying to corner him once more.

"The security of a nation is at stake. Consider this opportunity agent Forge. Just work in Sergeant Hockart's security department for a while. That's where we really need you."

Josh rises from his chair and starts walking away.

"Agent Forge!" Wilkinson rigidly shouts.

Josh turns to face the leader and speaks words without remorse. "If that was your plan from the beginning, then I'm extremely disappointed. I don't like being lied to and you should feel the same." With assurance, he starts walking away again. Lorne rises from his chair as well and before long, Wilkinson sits alone in his vast and cold office.

Back in the apartment, Lorne serves Josh a plate of pasta while he brings two salads on the table. "And to think he wanted to film us! For what reason? To know how we do it and then gracefully thank us? I can't believe this!" Concludes Josh out loud.

"Calm down, there must be a solution."

The younger one places both his fists together, against his lips as if wanting to suffocate a scream. Lorne looks up to his buddy.

"You're going to explode. Can't you just stop thinking about it for a second?"

"This is all I ever wanted." He pleads grabing his fork attempting to eat without conviction. Lorne risks a stare.

"Can you be a little less precise?"

"All I hoped for was to have an office, have a lot of people working with me and not for me. A secretary who would take care of the paperwork so we could concentrate on the cases."

"By the way, you remember Mandy, the daughter of the deaf mother?"

"What about her?"

"She wanted to thank you personally."

"Tell her to make it fast because I don't think that I'll be in London for much longer."

Lorne keeps quiet and continues to eat, drinking a glass of wine while Josh sips his mineral water. The young man's aura was furiously engaged with his thoughts and soon, unable to eat anymore, he dumps what's left in his plate into the garbage bin. Lorne's shoulders go down. He gets up, takes the bottle of wine from the refrigerator and fills his glass to the rim.

The next morning, the stumping of Lorne in the staircase does not even disturb the deep sleep of the man lying on the floor of the attic. "Josh! Josh! It's Taylor. He's on the phone. Here!"

The man sits up in the London flat; half awake, and beard unshaven scratching his back. "Hello Sir."

"What the heck happened? I called your office and Mrs Long told me that you left yesterday in the middle of the afternoon after you met with Wilkinson."

"Yep, that's what happened."

"Josh . . ."

"I showed him my concept of the structure for the department. I cut back on my own salary to have ten co-workers instead of twenty and he didn't approve so I left."

"Just like that? I don't believe it. You're not telling me everything."

"He said that we would have to abandon the project and my next option was to work for Hockart in the security department."

"He never told me about it. So what are your plans?"

"You know me well Sir. I'm usually more persistent and you know I won't give in but yesterday, it was clear that I had to leave his office before making a big mistake."

"I'll be there the day after tomorrow. Just be patient until I arrive."

"You're coming to London?"

"There's nothing like a Brit to argue with another one."

Josh starts to laugh. "Thanks Sir."

Two days later, 13:00 o'clock sharp.

Taylor, Lorne and Josh are seated in Wilkinson's office where only the grey colour of the clouds is coming trough the windows.

"So, you brought in the cavalry." Reproaches Wilkinson glancing at Josh.

"Sir Taylor proposed the meeting so we could conclude an arrangement. He thought that since you are both born on the same grounds and have been to school together, maybe . . ."

"Jacob, how long has it been since you've been reclused into the Canadian wilderness? Things have changed here and elsewhere in the world. Don't they have television or Internet in Montreal?" Wilkinson interrupts abruptly the agent.

"Oh C'mon Donovan, don't give me that bullshit . . ."

Josh and Lorne cannot believe that their superior is using such a familiar language. ". . . you think that because these guys can find lost children that they are able to find terrorists? Their minds just don't work that way."

Wilkinson stays quiet under the assumption. "You keep telling me they are the best."

"Yes but in their particular field." Starts again Taylor leaving his body toward the leader. "Finding kids has nothing to do with searching for a deranged activist who wants to put bombs everywhere."

"Isn't it?" Wilkinson comfortably sinks his back into the leather chair and crosses his legs.

"No it's not. Children have souls, they are sending in waves for other people to hear. These guys are like receptors catching on stimuli. People with malignant plans are deliberately cutting their waves from the rest of the world and want to be found on their terms. They are diametrical opposites of the victims. We are talking about kids Donovan, lost kids, just like your own son."

The leader's shoulders drop an inch and his jaw suddenly hardens. "Nobody saved him, it was too late."

"So, is this some kind of revenge?" Taylor attempts.

"Of course not, I only think that the menace of terrorist acts is compromising the security of far more people than the safeguard of a few kids."

Josh takes a turn at trying to work some kind of settlement with Wilkinson.

"You are right sir but I was under the impression that I was welcomed into your walls for the same purpose as my previous job. If you had told me that my career would tilt toward Sergeant Hockart's security department, I certainly would have answered negatively."

"I've got a solution." Firmly suggests Lorne speaking for the first time. "Agent Landers?" Now asks Wilkinson interested in hearing a decent proposition.

"Well, none of the eight candidates have been hired yet. How about discerning the ones with specific talents into one group to find kids and the other ones will be working over in the security department? We can find other candidates when the budget will allow it."

"What do you mean by specific talents?" Wilkinson repeats now facing the blond haired agent. "What Lorne means is that for some people like Josh, linking can be as easy as breathing. They can see the aura of people and are adepts of spatial interaction." Replies Taylor. "What about the others?"

"Some people can read minds, walk beside pedestrians and see their illnesses, feel whatever their intentions are. Those candidates might be the ones you're looking for to work in the security section." Taylor speaks clearly and without technical terms so his college buddy can see an opportunity. While both agents impatiently wait for an answer, Wilkinson places his elbows on the armrests and slowly joins his hands by the fingertips. "Fine, I want to meet the eight candidates tomorrow morning at nine o'clock in the investigation room. I'll be behind the glass beside you." He adds pointing at Taylor. "I want to know everything: your methods, who will be in which department and for what reason."

"Fine Donovan, we'll be there. Won't we gentlemen?"

"Of course we'll be there." Confirms Lorne.

"Yes Sir." Replies Josh sitting so rigidly that he feels his neck stiffen. Both employees find it hard to contain their enthusiasm. As for Taylor, used to wearing a poker face, this meeting is no exception.

"You may all be excused." Concludes Wilkinson turning his eyes back on the pile of papers in front of him.

Back in Josh's office, he and Lorne start to contact the candidates once more and when Wilfrid's name comes up, the youngest immediately turns to his colleague. "Wilfrid is afraid to talk in public because of his stuttering. Is there any way you can help him out?" Without any effort, a compationate response is signaled.

"Well, if he asks me, I don't mind. Did you know he was one of the first to apply?" Lorne precises bringing in close a bundle of papers. "He told me. It must mean a lot to him." Taylor looks at the program while Josh takes off his coat. "Whenever we'll be done with contacting the applicants, I'll see him." He adds while Brenda places in a stack, the signed confidentiality contracts of all the people interviewed at the last meeting.

The rest of the afternoon is concentrated on the questions that will be asked for the new interview. Taylor pitches in a few questions recalling the encounter with the young one a decade ago. On the corner of his desk, Josh finds a sealed envelope with a case number. "Mrs Long, you know what this is?"

"Sergeant Hockart's secretary brought it in; she said you asked for it."

The date stamped on it, two years and a few months ago doesn't ring a bell so he looks at the paperwork: Case number 121456-07, Robbery at Carnagy jewellery store, London. He now remembers. It was Miller's robbery case gone wrong. He inserts the surveillance camera film into his laptop and begins watching the unfolding event. A date and a running clock appear at the bottom of the image. Two agents show their badges to the owner. He recognizes Miller and co-worker Wilfrid standing on the left but the other agent's face cannot be seen because of the angle. As mentioned by Hockart, it was probably Fraser. A minute later, three robbers enter the store with cannon chiselled rifles. The three agents turn around and pull out their weapons while the owner gets shot. Two of the gun men aim and order them to drop their guns and lay on the floor, head facing down. The one that killed the owner comes close and ties their hands and feet with plastic straps. The third one jumps over the counter; pushes the victim away from the cash register and starts taking its content. He uses the butt of his rifle to break each of the glass display panels to collect all the jewels and places them in a sport sack. By now Josh figures that the alarm went off and just like his father's robberies, this one takes under two minutes to be executed. While Miller and Wilfrid lay still face down on the floor, their partner turns to his side and watches the robbers leave. Josh stops the film and rewinds it up to that scene, freeze-frames that moment and enlarges it. The film leaves him perplex so he takes the report and begins to read: Agent Ralph Miller and Agent Wilfrid Armstrong both received medical treatment that lasted respectively six and nine months. As for Agent Colin Fraser, he quit the London Police Force two days after and has never been seen since. None of the robbers was arrested and the case was never closed. Josh looks at the screen, intensely staring at Fraser's features and wonders; if this was his first time in London, why did he feel like he knew him.

21:00 same evening, Lion's gate restaurant, near Trafalgar Square.

Taylor rises a glass of Cabernet Sauvignon and brings it to his lips. "So what have you been doing on your time off lad?"

"I've been up in Scotland."

"Really? How was it?"

"He crashed his bike over a stag and broke his laptop before going to see a belle." Lorne volubly recites between two bites. Taylor chokes on his wine at the revelation. "Did anyone ever tell you that your mouth is bigger than your brain?" Josh upbraids his partner. "Well if you would have told the story, it would have taken two hours."

"Is it true?" Taylor turns to the youngest, still amazed.

"Yes."

"All of it?"

"I'm afraid so."

"Tell me how it happened."

"I was on my way to the Highlands and in the Glencoe valley, this huge stag came out of . . ."

"I mean, the lady. Who is she? How did you meet her?"

"The first time our eyes met was in this restaurant. She was sitting a couple of tables away."

"And he didn't want to meet the lady here. He said that it was the wrong place for a decent conversation." Cuts Lorne. Taylor pivots his head from one man to the other wondering and wanting to know more. "Why don't you just shut up and let me tell my own story." Suggests an impatient Josh.

"Because Taylor is only here for a couple of days; he doesn't have time for the details."

Josh raises an eyebrow and slowly turns his head back to face his boss. "Anyway, I didn't feel a restaurant was the appropriate place to introduce myself. A few days later, I went to this book fair and there she was again, selling her own material."

"So she's a writer?"

"And she's also a history teacher at the Edinburgh University."

Taylor takes another sip, savoring the sweet taste of heady liquid and a discrete smile appears at the corner of his mouth. "How long has it been since you've had a lady friend?"

"I don't know . . . a few months."

"If you don't count Diane with whom you had a liaison for about two months last year, you never really had a serious relationship. Maybe the fact that you had to protect your right hand during the act had something to do with it."

"Oh Gees . . . did you really have to mention that?" Josh asks getting a notch above annoyed. "So when shall we meet her?" Taylor pleads.

"It's all quite new and she's working a lot."

"Keep me posted then."

"I will, I promise."

At the end of the meal, the three men stand outside the restaurant.

"Won't you come and stay for the night at the apartment?" Josh suggests to his boss.

"I already rented a room a block away from the department but thank you for the offer. I'll see you both tomorrow morning at the office."

Taylor hops into a cab and disappears within the winding traffic. "You think that Wilkinson would have changed his mind if Taylor hadn't been there?" Lorne mocks getting down the stairs. "No way, he already hates my guts."

"That's because he doesn't know you yet. When he'll know you inside out, then he's really going to despise you with all his might." Josh starts laughing and punches his colleague on the arm.

When he walks into his room, it's almost eleven. He borrows Lorne's cell and dials the telephone number where an eighty year old lady answered *there's no Charles here* a week ago. On the fourth ring, he's on the verge of turning off the cell but then a voice, half woken is on the other end.

"Hello?"

"Charlene? It's Josh. Am I disturbing you?"

"No . . . I just finished my last correction."

"Maybe I should call tomorrow?"

"No! I mean no . . . it's nice to hear your voice."

"Now that I know the way, I could be there in six hours."

"Aren't you working tomorrow?"

"Of course I am but if you want to see me . . ."

She starts laughing and he closes his eyes to the sweet sound. "It has been a long time since I've made a lady laugh."

"And it has been a while for me to do so." For a minute, both stay silent wishing distance could be compressed with a snap of the fingers. "Can I kiss you good night?"

"You may." She smurks placing her sheets away.

"Can I choose where?"

Her lips rise to the offer and a giggle is heard. "Yes." He makes the discrete sound of a kiss with his mouth. "Where did you kiss me?" She whispers enjoying the playful conversation. "I kissed your hands because you have no idea how much I wish they were holding me near right now." Her mouth opens, unable to reply to such a sweet declaration from his heart. He swallows, breathing hard, meaning those words that freed themselves from the barrier of his mouth. Faintly, almost inaudibly, she pronounces her last words. "Good night handsome traveler."

"Good night darling lady." He teases on the same tone. Then, a few seconds later, the telephone on her end is hung. He flips the cell and places it on Lorne's desk before walking up to his lonely room.

That night, the dream he has is as vivid as ever. He sees the castle so far in the Highlands and approaches its front door using the arched bridge. There is no one beside him or standing on the grassy grounds or the edge of the moors. The oak door is pushed to let him enter and as if he always resided there, he knows exactly where his steps will guide him to. First he follows a corridor, then a set of steep, shallow and grey stairs. The air above to the second floor is somewhat less humid and colder. When he walks into the Banqueting Hall, ten men and two women, one of which is his wife, rise and bow down their heads. He replies to the gesture then takes off the sword attached to his leather belt to place it on the back of the only chair that is empty. His hands, rugged and wearing many scars, grab the carved wood as he sits. All imitate the gesture, heads turning to him, his wife on his left side.

"An toirt cho trobhad." The words spoken with a deep voice, his own voice, wake him up. He sits up, troubled by the scene. He searches on the desk and grabs the first available pen or pencil; a drawing pencil. He takes a white sheet from his pad; he rips it out and writes down the four words. The night is still around and he can hear the lament of the soft rain from the open window. Why was he always dreaming about the castle, he asks himself? Now that its occupants are part of his dream, it seems that there is a reason behind all this but, nothing comes to mind and he's more and more puzzled. He rests the paper by the side of his bed and turns on his back to try to continue sleeping.

At 8:45 the next morning, both men wearing dark suits walk back in the institution. Lorne has a matching tie but Josh keeps avoiding the binding around the collar. When they arrive, Taylor stands in the entrance. The doors open to a long marble alley with the usual two armed guards. Cameras are still all around; metallic receptive panels surround the entire corridor. Both men get searched again with two different devices.

"You're clean." Affirms the armed guard with a Welsh accent.

Another policeman speaks into a microphone and waits for a reply.

"Mister Wilkinson will now receive you." The three of them ride the elevator up to the fourtenth floor. The heavy steel doors open to the spacious corner office overlooking the city of London.

"I never imagined myself being in a do-or-die meeting before." Declares Josh before entering. When they walk in, the highest figure of security on the land gets up to greet them once more. "Gentlemen welcome back. The candidates are waiting in one of the interrogating rooms but I wanted to meet you here first. The investigation regarding those people reveals that they have no criminal records and they are as pure as snow. They already signed a confidentiality agreement. So now they are all yours."

"Let's do it." Josh agrees.

The four men get into the elevator while surveillance is all over the edifice. The doors open to a white corridor and Lucy greets them.

"Hello Mrs Thorn." Lets out Wilkinson.

"How do you do sir?"

"I'm doing very well, thank you."

Josh and Lorne smile at her while Taylor simply avoids looking at the young woman in her early thirties. Wilkinson turns to his right with the group and stops before an immense window.

"I will be waiting here and listening to your conversation. Taylor will tell me who will be apt in which department and for which specific reason."

"Fine." Approves Josh letting Lorne enter the room alone. He closes the door behind him, bringing the paperwork.

"Why aren't you going in?" Wilkinson expresses.

"You'll see." He grins taking off his jacket, rolling up his sleeves and loosening the top button of his shirt. While Wilkinson is all surprised to see Josh beside them and not in the room, Taylor never lets his eyes off the group. The microphone is turned on and the three of them begin to listen to the interview.

"My name is agent Lorne Landers and I'm here to meet each and every one of you because you all applied for this job opportunity for a specific position. We'll have a few tests at hand to determine your degree of perception. The first one being that I'll think of a number and you will write down what you think it is. I'll then individually ask your answer."

"Will that be your only criteria?" A man in his forties inquires with precipitation.

"You must be John."

"I am. How did you know?"

"Because you're forty-two."

"We are three candidates in our forties."

"Yes but the two others did not ask any questions and you're the one who has been off work the longest. The two others still work and don't really need that job. Can I continue now?"

"I'm sorry."

"Thank you. So . . . John, what's your answer?"

"Nine."

"Leighton?"

"Can't see a number, I'm sorry."

"Cameron?"

"All I see is four, like four legs."

"Nicole?"

"I see yellow with dots. No numbers for me."

"Samantha?"

"I don't see anything but I can smell blood and dirt. I've got a weird taste in my mouth and I'm thirsty."

"Andrew?"

"The number is twelve."

"Wilfrid?"

"I'm . . . I'm thinking that it might be twelve also."

"Jack? Can you please tell us what number I'm thinking about?"

"You're not thinking about a specific number mister Landers. You're only projecting a vague image of a jaguar eating its prey in the middle of the savannah. The number twelve appears on the bus behind the animal and the number ten is on the licence plate. The colour yellow with polka dots is evidently the animal itself and the number four is the two legs from the feline and two from the prey, sticking out in the air."

Behind the glass, Josh smiles while Taylor and Wilkinson are all ears.

"In which group will he be?" The leader questions.

"The kids' one." Replies Taylor.

"What about the other candidates?"

"Samantha is using her olfactory senses more than anything; she should be in the security group. Am I right Josh?"

"I agree."

"What about the others?" Wilkinson asks trying his best to comprehend the discernation.

"A few more tests will determine their group. Taylor Sir, are you ready?"

"You can go in whenever you want to." The white-haired British answers, holding a list of the candidates on a clip-board where a few notes have been scribbled. Josh turns the doorknob and quietly comes into the room. When some of the guests turn their heads toward Josh, Taylor writes their reaction beside their names. The agent then takes a few steps, grabs a chair and sits beside his partner. "Hello, my name is Jocelyn Forge. I'm also an agent for this institution. It is my job to recruit the best people for two special divisions."

Behind the window, Wilkinson begins talking without turning his head from the glass pannel. "Do you miss it?"

"What?" Taylor questions also looking at the group.

"Do you miss the action, being in the field?"

"Barbara and Nathan's death changed all that."

"Did you make any more transcendental journeys?"

"Just a few when the job demanded it. After meeting Landers, I showed him everything I knew and then I coached Jocelyn but it was almost useless."

"Why? He wouldn't learn well because of his young age?"

"Are you kidding me Donovan? The only thing I had to teach him was to have control over the hastiness in which he plunged himself. There's only one thing about him though."

"What is it?"

"He's a polarized individual, either you like him or you don't, just like he would in return." The two high ranked officers turn back to the agents where the recruiting slowly starts to take shape.

It is now well after working hours and Josh is still up in his office with a single light on. Taylor walks by and sees the glare by the open door. The young man stops rubbing his temples, face down on a load of papers and lifts his head.

"So have you reached an agreement?" Taylor throws coming in.

"We did for a few ones but not all of them."

"How many did you choose?"

"Four."

"Well, that's a good average, isn't it?"

Josh places the front legs of his chair in suspension like he used to do at school when he was bored and gently throws his pen on the desk. "No, that's not good Sir. Lorne is leaving next month."

"I just talked to him. His departure will be postponed for a few more weeks. Wilkinson wants to film you both to learn more about your methods."

"Hockart already asked us. When do they want to do it?"

"Everything is set up for tomorrow morning. That is, if you agree." For an instant, the young man keeps quiet to think it over. "What if the film ends up in hands that don't deserve it?"

"It won't. The codes Lorne uses will only be known through hypnosis. We will only be the three people to know them.

"O.k. then, I agree."

"Why don't you go to sleep?"

"I want to finish this first. What time is it anyway?"

"It's close to ten."

"Ah shit, I promised Charlene I would call her at seven." Taylor smiles at the comment and gets up. "Good night lad." He ends stepping out while Josh takes his repaired cell and starts dialing.

Cloak and dagger, mist and shiver.
Behind the pale sun I wait for you to be near again.
Nothing is missing around, but the most important.
All the fortunes in the world could not compensate.
Do you feel the way I do?
Can you not hear the beating of my inner drum shedding apart
everytime you walk by?
Tell me you do, tell me it's reciprocality.
For the bounding started the moment I saw you.

*Now, the tread is between us, pulling, getting heavier and stretching
to its limits.
Forever you are my home.
KMK*

Charlene is totally caught in the rapture of the moment and languishes at the verve in which this phantom's profoundness is laid on velum to last forever. She sighs when suddenly her thoughts are interrupted by the ring of her mobile.

"Charlene? Yes . . . hi . . . it's Josh."

Chapter Seventh

The following morning, the foursome walks to a vast room in the main building. Although it's airy, there are no windows to capture the glow of the day. Making sure that Taylor's recommendations have all been observed while Lucy is setting up her writing space, water and cans of soft drinks are plentifull, a telephone in case of emergency, towels, a hard gym mattress, a table with files set into a metallic box and a few sturdy chairs are provided. The secretary will take notes, helped by a tape recorder and further down the room, a camera is placed on a tripod to film the session. Lorne and Josh are introduced by Sergeant Hockart to two British agents working on their team while a third one sets the lense so it can capture most of the room.

"You feel up to it?" Lorne asks his colleague placing his jacket on the back of a chair. "Sure." He admits his eyes sweeping the place. Josh removes his shirt, shoes and socks placing everything under the long table. Lorne rolls up his sleeves and loosens his tie also to be comfortable. Wilkinson's eyes revolve as both adults play fight and, accustomed to his men's way of relaxing, Taylor is not even paying attention to them and simply opens the first file. Knowing the eminence of the session, Lucy verifies that her lighted pen works fine and gets ready. After a few karate grasps, Lorne squeezes his co-worker's back muscles while Josh moves his neck from side to side. He then speaks to him in a lowered tone. "Each file will be brought to you, one after the other. We have twenty-five in all but we will stop when I see that you can no longer concentrate."

"Is the number of the case mentionned behind each file?" Josh suggests.

"It's written at the bottom of each picture and inside the first leaflet." The young man turns to face his channeler. "Fine, now can you just ask those guys to take their cells out of here? They're projecting ions." Lorne smiles and goes to meet the rest of the party requesting them to place their cellular telephones somewhere out of the room. Taylor walks toward his agent and speaks out: "Jocelyn, the place is yours, son." Josh nods and the camera is turned on. The young agent raises his neck, heavily exhales a couple of times, shoulders and arms are relaxed by shaking them. He breathes in one last time to put his brain in the right mood, in order to capture outside waves. He then lies flat on his back and crosses his forehead, mouth and heart; a simple ritual to calm himself, should things go wrong. Both his feet are pointing toward the camera. He shakes his left hand and leaves it open palm up, gently raising his right one and places it over his third plexus. Then, he slowly closes his eyes to the present world.

You could have heard a whisper or the flaps of a dragonfly go by.
I shall not be alone while I ask your hand to guide Mise into darkness,
where murmurs turn to turmoil.
Now screams. All that is heard is loud screams, shriekings,
Unbearable sounds into my mind.
The tunnel is long, dark and coldness makes Mise sweat from
scariness.
Crossing the Styx, searching in the above or down-bellow skies, in
between redemption and eternal fires, I shall walk, or should I say,
glide.
But I shall not be alone . . .
KMK

Charlene puts her pen down and somehow keeps thinking about Josh, missing him.

In the confined space, as quietly as possible, Lucy gives a first photograph to Lorne who brings it over to his partner. Placing himself on his right, Lorne bends and barely touches his forearm. Without a word, the youngest opens his glassy eyes, lifts his hand to the picture, presses his palm against it and closes back his heavy eyelids. The forearm unhurriedly falls back down, getting in contact with the cold floor beside the mattress. After giving the picture back to Lucy, the blond man returns to his pal once more, verifying the body's restful state by placing his hand two inches above it, observing his respiration. Everyone waits for someting to happen. After about ten minutes, a shiver makes Josh's body shake, his back arches and both his hands cross above his head for protection. Lorne comes closer.

"Can you hear me Josh?"

"Yes."

"What do you see?"

"Water . . . he drowned. He's been there for days and his enflated body started to decompose."

"Where is the water running to?" Lorne demands in a low tone.

"Close to where he is, there is a red roof and it looks like a farm. A rusted wheel is close. His body is stuck by a farm crank in a ditch. Most of his corpse is covered with mud. He probably tried to swim out of it but sank in."

"Can you rise above and tell me a little more about the setting?" Josh exhales, his fingers compressing tighter on his thorax and his head tilts to the side.

"Chimneys, there are two huge red chimneys, a sign with horses. There is a white fence, a long white fence." Lucy is writting everything down when another agent comes close and writes on her sheet: surrounding area Leeds.

"I have to get out!" Josh screams so Lorne presses the palm of his hand above his to secure him with his presence.

"You're not him; you're only visualizing the scene. Just listen to my voice and come back to it." After a small interlude, the youngest comes out of the state and opens his eyes. "Number two?" He proposes.

"Number two it is." Replies Lorne.

This time, the older agent presents the picture of a little smiling girl of four, with long blond hair and huge brown eyes. How the dark hair officer hated to see kids being brought in situations where they could be harmed. Loving most human beings, he had this wish that all were born equal, born with love, tenderness and raised with good will but the reality of mistreatment for so many, was a toll he could barely endure. Whenever he stumbled across young children who were violated in any way, he felt sad, touched by the ravished innocence. He just had a feeling that this one would be difficult for him to handle. Still, with profoundness, he raises his palm up and presses it against the vinyl photograph. When Josh's eyes close, his hand brushes against Lorne's who captures for a moment the essence of the waves and gets pulled back against his own will. He hushes a curse before getting up again. Fifteen long minutes tick away. Mouth open, body set on the side, Josh seems to be sleeping when all of a sudden, he turns his head, raises his back and sits. Everyone in the room is startled except for Lorne and Taylor. Getting to his knees, he raises himself up. Walking to the northern wall, he starts scratching it with his nails. The camera turns and focuses while Lorne gets close. He realizes that his pal entered the body of the disappeared instead of standing aside. Furious at first, Lorne approaches his pal and addresses himself directly to the child. "Hi, what's your name?"

"Aïsha."

"How old are you Aïsha?" Four fingers are shown. "What are you doing?"

"I'm trying to get out. Mommy is going to be furious at me." Lorne leans over deepening the connection by asking questions. "Why?"

"Because I did not listen to her, she told me not to get into strangers' cars and I did. The man said he had a nice puppy to show me and he would give me candies." Josh's eyes start to water and he begins to cry. "I want my mommy!"

"I'm going to help you out Aïsha. Look around and tell me what you see." Eyes wide open, Josh turns walking in the perimeter of the room Aïsha is stuck in. "There is a bed, a door, my doll, a pot for my pee-pee."

"Are there any windows sweetie?"

"Yes, there is one."

"What do you see outside the window?"

"I can only see the sky."

"If you got on the bed, would you see something else?"

"I think so."

"Go, love." Lorne requests for a chair to a security agent and helps Josh to climb on. Lucy tries to focus on writing the details but just like the rest of the group apart from Taylor and Lorne, is just so intrigued about the happening that she has trouble concentrating. Never in her life has she witnessed someone go into a trance and she just knew that the two Canadians were not faking any of it. Standing on top of the chair while holding his partner's hand, Josh has this infantile stare, stretching up his neck to the imaginary window. "Can you see something other than the sky now?" Lorne precises.

Josh flares back with a mad grin. "I see a car bumper. I want my dolly!"

Lorne's eyes widen, Josh leaves his partner's grip, starts biting his nails and with the other hand, begins clasping at something invisible. Lorne attracts Lucy's attention and points to a towel. She gives it to him and he rolls it in a rush, bringing it over. "There's your doll honey. Now tell me, can you see the licence plate on the car?"

"What is a licence plate?"

"There is a board with different numbers and letters underneath the bumper. It's like the name of the car. Can you see that?"

"Oh yes! I see it."

"Can you read it to me?"

"I don't know how to read. I can draw it though."

"That's great Aïsha." Again Lucy rapidly gets involved and hands out a pencil and a sheet of paper clipped to a board. Lorne helps Josh gets down from the imaginary bed and places the paper in front of him. "Now please draw the numbers and letters honey."

"Can I draw a nice puppy first?"

"Not now love. Please draw the numbers and letters from the licence plate first. Can you do this for me?"

"Fine . . ." Josh hands out the fake doll to his partner. He takes the pencil from his left hand and starts making an M. He gets back on the imaginary bed, lifts his head to the window that doesn't exist, gets back down, and writes another letter then a few numbers. After the seventh marking, Sergeant Hockart silently gets closer, totally amazed. "I'm done!" Josh proudly says sitting up, belly out. "Do I have to draw the bolts?"

"No honey. That's o.k. I only need this, thank you very much. Now you can draw me a puppy." Lorne gently takes the sheet from Josh's hand that still wants to draw and asks for another piece of paper. Lucy comes in closer, hands down a few more, wide eyed, almost afraid to near the man who is acting like a four-year-old. Josh gets close to the floor again, places his feet in an « x » position.

"That's a bird besides my puppy!" He proudly shouts.

Lorne looks at his patner and doesn't like the fact that after twenty minutes, he's still into the child's brain. "Aïsha, it's late. Can you go to sleep?"

"That's all I do except when the man comes to touch me. I don't like it when he touches me . . . he says that he wants to play with me and I'm his toy . . . whenever we play his game, milk comes out of him."

Lorne's heart just makes a swirl hearing the revelation but still, tries to stay poised. "Here love, I will take your drawing, you take back your doll and go to sleep. I'll do my best to bring you back to your mother." Lorne puts the sheet and pen down while Josh squeezes the fake doll close to his stomach and raises his thumb to place it in his mouth, curling up both legs. The older agent touches his pal's hair to soothe him down, letting him fumble to sleep. Lorne frowns, clearly fearing the depth of his colleague's state. He places the tip of his left thumb on Josh's « third eye », the area a little above the center of his eyebrows on his forehead and with the other hand, holds the back of his head. Approaching his lips close to his ear, Lorne whispers a few words and Josh's arms immediately fall lifeless as if pulled by a string. The "doll" rolls away and Taylor approaches his employee to set him in a better position.

"He's going too deep." Declares Taylor.

"I know, I don't like it either." Reveals Lorne. While the young man is on his back resting, Hockart exits the room and imperatively dispatches one unit per case. Lucy is now the only one really watching the young man sleeping. Still mesmerized, she gets up from her chair and walks a little closer.

"Don't touch him!" Lorne warns from where he stands. She abruptly stops, takes the pen and sheet and quietly walks back to the table. So many questions need to be answered but suddenly; all is interrupted by Josh's waking. Turning over slowly, he then gets up in a rush, recalling everything, fastening both his fists, shouting at the raging vision of the litlle girl being so viciously exploited.

"Shut the camera!" Taylor orders.

Everyone is taken by surprise while Josh marches to the furthest end of the room, posing his arms out on the wall, pushing and screaming through his teeth. Wilkinson orders the cameraman to stop filming. Immensely troubled by his reaction, Lucy stares from where she sits eyes wide open. Josh has his head down, turning his back to everyone, raging with madness, fiercely banging his hands flat open on the wall. His back muscles are tense and everyone can see how disturbed he is by what he just experienced. Taylor in his habitual compassion comes right beside him and exchanges a few words while rubbing his back. The young man turns away from the others, circles the floor, looks down, breathes hard, wanting to punch out something, someone, especially the pedophile. Taylor lets the sentiment of rage that overwhelms his man race out and after a soothing grip over his shoulders; Josh comes back to the center of the room, both hands on his hips. "Lagger time . . ." Throws Taylor.

"You want a beer?" Wilkinson corrects looking at Josh. "No sir, I never drink . . . It only means to take a break." Knowing what the term meant, Lorne hands a bottle of water that Josh engulfes in a single gulp. He walks a few steps to sit at the table, near Lucy, his body loosely laid back on the wooden chair, eyes wandering far away. "I'm sorry." Josh says to Lucy very low. "Why are you excusing yourself?"

"Some cases are really hard to take and it makes me too emotional."

"Please, don't apologize. You only want to punch him while I want to kill the bastard. Fortunately you and I both know it's against the law to make vengeance a private business."

Lorne leaves the rest of the group and asks Josh to join him in a corner of the room to have a little discussion using French so the British will not understand.

"Mais bon Dieu, que fais-tu?" (In God's name, what are you doing?) Lorne shouts absolutely furious.

"Quoi?"(What?)

"Tu sais de quoi je parle. Tu vas trop loin. Tu prends la place de la victime au lieu d'observer et çà, c'est loin d'être bon, tu le sais très bien. (You perfectly know what I'm talking about. You're going too deep. You're taking the person's place instead of visualizing from aside. That's not good and you know it)."

Josh jerks his neck backwards, placing one of his arms around his stomach, drinking the cold water with the other.

"Est-ce que tu m'écoutes? (Are you listening to me?)" Lorne imposes with a furious stare.

"Mais oui, je t'écoute (Of course, I'm listening). "

Lorne clenches his teeth together but then, in front of the other agents, catches his buddy's neck with warmth. "I don't like it. Look at the way it's devouring your guts. It will be too demanding to do the next ones if you take this procedure."

"I always connect this way when I'm working from home. It's so much easier and faster. I can find more kids this way, living ones anyway. Isn't that what Wilkinson asked for in the first place?" Lorne gets his hand out and firmly places it on Josh's wrist facing him. "Oh God . . . don't get into this. Don't think of it as a race. I know you want to give your best but everything will catch up to you if you try to speed things up." The younger agent nods, knowing his buddy to be right. "Don't let it overwhelm you. Go with the flow but stand your ground far from the child." He continues. Lorne stares at him with a sharp look. "Have you been getting help?" The young man doesn't answer, discretely biting his lower lip. "Will you answer me? Have you been getting help?" Lorne repeats, insistant and finally Josh answers: "Yes . . ."

"Well then, ask your guide to stand back as well. Ask his support but let there be a distance between you and the one you're looking for because *you're* going downhill and much too fast to my liking. If you don't, I'll have no choice but to cancel further sessions. Understood?" Josh lets air out of his lungs and shakes his head in a « yes » gesture, going back to the hard mattress. He lays again, places his hands in the usual contemplative manner and waits for the next picture.

Three more findings and many hours later, Josh wakes exhausted. The camera is switched off a last time. Reclusing himself far from his acolytes, the linker lowers his head down over his knees. Sweating like crazy, he just feels like a drunk with a hangover. Lucy brings him a cold soft drink and crouch to his height. "Do you need anything else?"

"I'm sorry?" He articulates coming down from a cloud, turning to face her.

"Do you need anything else?"

"No, thanks . . . I'll be fine."

"I'll be right there if you need me." She offers before walking away. He lays his head against the wall, looking at her with eyes halfway closed. "Do you know that you're white?" She turns around. "Well yes, I'm a British, white person."

"No . . . what I mean is that all around your head, you're white. Your aura is practically as pure as snow. There is only one little part over there that is green and yellow." He expresses pointing to the left of her head. She smiles, not clearly understanding what he is talking about, thinking that the man in front of her is not completely back from his parallel world. He slowly blinks and speaks again.

"I've got a friend back in Scotland who's almost as pure as snow . . . just like you. She'll be here soon; I can't wait to see her." Lucy smiles while Josh closes his eyes and starts fumbling down. "I miss her . . . , I wish she was here now." He faintly lets out. She helps him lay his head on a folded towel and takes from his hands the can before it spills all over. Soon after, he is deeply breathing and the caring assistant cannot avoid being touched by the demanding effort the young man pushed himself into. She takes another towel to clean the sweat from his body and covers his shoulders with a blanket. Josh is into his own little world, unaware of his surrounding except for the sound of his own heartbeat which he tries to bring back to a restful pace.

The next day, early in the afternoon at the cafeteria of the police headquarters, a glass of milk in front of him, Josh grabs a paper napkin and asks for a pen. The agent close to him hands it out. Searching for something, he looks around. There is a poster of the United Kingdom on the wall, displaying the merits of the Police Task Force. He walks up to it and stares. Walking in, Lucy gets in line to buy her meal and joins him. "Do you feel better?"

"I'm fine . . . just a little sore between the shoulders."

"What are you looking at?"

"Do you have a map where we can see the metro stations?"

"The what?"

"Metro stations . . . subways."

"You probably mean the underground. I have one in my desk."

"Well, if you don't mind, I would borrow it." Around her is a light, a pure bright, shiny one. The way they look at each other reflects an irremediable bond that has nothing to do with sexual attraction. As Lucy goes to fetch the map, Josh returns to his table where he immediately starts sketching. Hockart, who just walked in, takes a peak over his shoulder. "What are you doing?" He inquires intrigued. "I think that there is a link between some of the cases." He precises to the Sergeant. "In three of them I heard noises. You know the one that is typical to the wind in a tunnel? And this, (he shows the drawing) is the pattern it took."

"What do you make of it?" Taylor wonders getting involved in the conversation.

"Might be an organization or as we've seen before, a pornography network. I'm not certain about this but I think they mainly operate using the underground. Lucy went back to her desk to get the map. Maybe by comparing my drawing with it, we'll end up with something a little more concrete." Hockart turns rapidly to him giving some insight. "If child abduction had happened in the underground, the cameras would have recorded it."

"Everybody knows that, so I think that victims are being spotted taking the underground and then are followed until they reach areas where there are no cameras or witnesses. If we could spot the abducters in the stations, I believe we could be on to something."

"Do you have any idea of how many underground stations there are in the city?" The Sergeant reproaches again. Josh raises an eyebrow, appalled by the reply.

"We will still take that clue into consideration." Wilkinson rapidly concludes. "It was a very interesting session yesterday. When other details about the recovery come in, Hockart will let you know."

Later, that same afternoon in the Sergeant's quarters, the man of high rank stands before a table in front of many agents and the leader of the organization. A police officer swarms in the room and without unrestrained joy exclaims: "Aïsha has been found!" So while everyone is shouting screams of relief, Josh simply joins his hands and bends his head down to thank the Lord above for His grace and mercy.

The following day is the last one of the week, the 1st of June. After watching the video of the last session, analysing it and breaking down the methods to be taught to the future members, the leader looks at his watch and gets up. "Everybody worked really hard this week. You may all leave early." Cutting short their extended shift on a Friday by fifteen minutes and thinking it's a treat, is so Wilkinson, Taylor thinks. No one's arm has to be twisted to scram out of the grey building in different directions, Josh in his own: Heathrow airport. A middle-aged lady is standing behind a booth on the right side of the main entrance door, selling flowers. When Josh turns to her, the ressemblance with his mother strikes him so hard that he stops walking. Approaching the scentful kiosk, he is suddenly appealed by an arrangement of orange lilies, similar to the ones his mother grew around the house. "Good evening. Would you like to buy a bouquet?" The lady proposes holding in front of her the fragrant deployment.

"I'll take these." He points toward the ones that look the freshest.

"What colour of ribbon would you like?" She requests carefully wrapping the prized gift in cellophane paper. "Mauve . . . purple." He translates choosing a far away roll and reaching for his wallet. She lets the ribbon swirl down a meter, cuts it and with agility circles it around the package. With a smile, she presents the flowers to the customer. His mind wanders off to the time when he used to cut all the splendid orange lilies around his mother's house and sold them to neighbours so he could buy her a gift. When he snaps out of the moment, the lady is gently calling out to him. "Here is your change sir."

"Just give it to charity please." He convinces her slightly tilting his head and then enters the modernized and busy airport. Josh's vision is affected by the burst of the glowing neons and the sound in the intercom makes his ears buzz. Walking up to the designated gate, he sits, places his coat and flowers aside and opens his shirt another notch. Before the tinted windows, he takes a glimpse at planes landing and taking off. Nothing here was like the Montreal airport where you could not have that view anymore. The compression sounds of the engines still impress him. How something so heavy could fly, is beyond comprehension. Thanks to precursors like Leonardo, farfetched theories prooved to be true. He would have been proud . . .

Down the corridor, there is a family leaving on holidays, all happy and joyful. A few feet away, a young inconsolable woman is saying goodbye to her boyfriend maybe for a few weeks, maybe forever. The young man is trying his best to cheer her up and through his aura, Josh can see his sincerity. From afar, he looks at their mixture of dim turquoise and yellow lights, bleak as can be. The visitor sitting all alone with flowers beside him, knows exactly why most men do not open up as easily as women . . . he feels the same. Being taught by his father not to cry or show emotions, he resolutely decides to open up to the lady he hopes will always be by his side.

Leaving Edinburgh, Charlene was supposed to have touched the ground half an hour ago. Waiting always makes him worry and dark thoughts invade his mind. With nervousness, he compresses his left fist and takes deep inhalations to calm himself down. Even though it had only been a few days since he last saw her, it felt like months. Just the thought of her makes him feel weak, walk on air, even changes his strict life pattern. When passengers finally start pouring out of the restricted area, he springs on his feet, anticipating. A group of about two hundred people crosses the line, and then without warning, doors flip back to shut tight like glued. Deceived and perplex, he waits in front of them dumbfounded. When he is just about to throw the flowers in the garbage, one of the twin doors opens again letting through a limping red-haired with a broken heel in her left hand, her lips arguing toward the inanimate object. She looks so mad but he cannot help to find the unfortunate event hilarious. Furious, she sits, takes a pair of sneakers out of her suitcase and puts them on. "Bonsoir Charlene (Good evening Charlene)." He greets her, amused. "And to think I paid a fortune for these lousy sandals!"

"You had dinner yet?" He inquires holding a mocking comment at the edge of his tongue. She looks down at herself wearing a skirt and inappropriate footwear.

"I left the University catching the first cab I saw, we got stuck in traffic, the plane left late because the hydraulic something or other wasn't working and now this . . . what was your question?" Before he picks up her luggage, he remembers about the flowers. "That's for you, let's go for a bite."

She momentarily forgets about her fashion misfortune. "They're beautiful, what a nice thought."

"I couldn't resist. Mother had the same planted all around the house, and well, the purple ribbon represents a little passion."

They stop in a restaurant offering sushi and take a booth near a window where they can catch a glimpse of the impressive bridge. The view is fantastic; he is happy to see her, finally touching her hands and he is compelled to tell her everything, all his little secrets, even the simplest ones. "The first English song I learned was *London Bridge is falling down*, but I'll spare you my own rendition."

"No offense but thanks." She mocks with a giggle.

Playing with a napkin, he folds it to make a swan. Handing it out to her, she happily takes the delicate gift. "How was your week?" She enquires.

"Hard . . . very hard, Lorne and I found eight kids, I think. I lost count. There were a lot more cases to solve but I couldn't go on. The good thing is that five of them were recovered alive and well."

"That's great. You could work in many fields, being a language teacher, an artist and still, you chose an extremely demanding profession. Why?"

"Is it needed for every action to have a reason?"

"I believe so. My past educations lead me to what I'm working on right now. Your flowers reveal a little attachment for my person. The way you place your hands near me, the glare in your eye; everything means something. Doesn't it?"

She stops talking for a second, cornering him into secrecy.

"What I want to get to is why you were interested in working for the police?" She softly adds. "Have you ever been kidnapped?"

"Would you like more tea?" The Japanese waitress politely hushes.

"Please." Josh answers.

"None for me thanks." Charlene replies. The waitress delicately pours the amber beverage into the porcelain cup. He bows, tells her thank you in Japanese and turns to Charlene. He takes another napkin, starts playing with it.

"I'm waiting . . ." She nags.

"Yeah . . . o.k." He sets the folded paper aside.

"How old were you when you first met Lorne?"

"Sixteen . . ."

"Under what circumstances did you meet?"

"He was on duty, I wasn't . . . I was partying with my friends on a hot summer night in Montreal. We had just finished High School and I was pretty high on booze and drugs."

"I thought you never drank."

"I quit shortly after, that and doing drugs. It was one of Taylor's recommendations to enter the Police Force."

"But you were so young, I'm sorry. I keep interrupting."

"That's o.k. There's nothing much more to say. I was as stoned as a rock the first time we were introduced to each other. I found this boy who had been missing and I saw his soul rise above him. Lorne figured it out and saw in me something I never dreamed would be a working asset." Flashes about the boy found raped and violently beaten spark in his mind. Josh bends his head down, unwanting to reveal more, gently rubbing the side of the porcelain cup with the oriental design. "We sort of found reciprocal avenues to work together. That's all. Please, let's talk about you. What made you choose history teaching?" He incites to get a feedback.

"Well, even before my teen years, I used to ask my friends to hide a painted rock and we would play warm and cold getting near or away from it. I wanted to dig up dinosaurs but they seemed to have chosen another resort than this island, to become extinct."

"That's funny."

"I get a sense of accomplishment when I find or understand something. But this, what I'm working on right now, to re-evaluate all the history behind Eilean Donan, is the summum of my dreams. Grandpa took me to the castle almost every day, especially after my father was lost at sea. He would tell me about the history within its walls, some of it very contradictory to what was written at the time. So much was to be said about the bravery of the warriors standing up to the British army. And when I was old enough, he told me about the Book of Kells and the casket which protected it. He wanted to be the one to find the jewels ornating it and bring them back to Ireland."

"So in conclusion, we both like to find something." He reckons.

"Seems like it. Is there anything you've always wanted to do but never had a chance to?"

"Well of course." He retorts.

"What is it?"

"Get into an F-15, a Stealth, or some other jet, climb up to the sky, look over Scotland, fly to Canada, take pictures of the autumn leaves from up there and come back to this country to lie down."

"Only that?"

"That's a wish. That and something else I put down on my will."

She frowns. "But you're so young! How old are you?"

"I'm twenty-six; I'll be twenty-seven in November."

"And you've already made your will?"

He raises his chin up a bit, tilting his head sideways. "I wanted to. Making sure that my family wouldn't be in debts and more than anything, I want to leave a trace behind."

"You already do, you paint."

"That's far from enough, for me anyway. There are much greater things I want to achieve in this life span." Food is finished and the tea pot is now empty. They get up after the bill is paid and start walking down the street toward his apartment, strolling and talking about general things. He keeps turning his head toward her, looking at the finely designed lips and the dancing hair floating above her shoulders, he gently stows a strand away from her pale, pinkish cheek.

Walking up the stairs to his place, he turns the key and places her small bag in the living room. She takes off her coat and he places it on the entrance rack. "Would you like anything to drink?"

"Juste un peu de thé s'il-vous-plaît (A little bit of tea please) and water for these beautiful flowers." She says following him into the kitchen.

"Your French is getting better every day." He complements her approaching a tall glass filled with lukewarm water and setting the tea pot on the oven.

"Well thank you, agent Forge."

"I wish I could get rid of my accent." He admits letting her set the blooming arrangement.

"Are you kidding? It does add up to your charm."

"Seriously?" He exclaims making an odd face. This was the first time he ever heard this comment.

"Very . . . Can I visit your room?" Surprised, he can't avoid widening his eyes.

"Yeah . . . sure, it's upstairs." He lets her walk in first and turns on the light. The mattress that serves as a bed is unmade but everything else is tidy. She looks around, impressed by all the paintings. Standing in front of the creations one at a time, admiring the grace of the bodies and the luminosity of the sceneries, she is in awe of such talent. "Where do you find time to paint so much?" She hushes gently flipping a few that are resting against the wall. "It takes my mind off work. I usually wake in the middle of the night to continue whatever I have already started." He didn't really care about the opinion of others regarding his talent but he could clearly see that she enjoyed his work. "The themes are quite different from one another but the way you render them is the same. I'm no expert on the matter but I can see the emotions you're trying to express." Flattered by her assessment, he decides to reveal something he has never told anyone before. "There is a story behind each and every one of them." She looks back at the artist, analyzing this last sentence while he told it as if it was momentous secret. "I'm sure there is." She approves. A strident whistle is heard from the kitchen so he excuses himself to prepare the concoction. When he comes back up, she is standing at the foot of the bed evaluating the last canvas overheading the place where he sleeps. Just like in his old house, hanging it over the resting place seemed to be the most natural thing to do. "What is he doing?"

"I'm not sure, probably praying. I painted it after seeing him in a dream."

"But he's naked!?" She exclaims. He smirks before answering. "Is there a law preventing you from praying in your simplest apparel?"

"Don't you feel vulnerable when you're naked?" She inquires after sipping on her tea.

"It depends where I am, who I'm with and what I'm doing."

She gets close and words are no longer necessary when their eyes meet and with prudence, she pushes the tea cup over the only piece of furniture that isn't an antique. Ever since his first relationship, he had to cover the inside of his right palm, otherwise his partner felt a very acute tingling that broke the mood. First, he slightly disrobes the cardigan from her soft gracile shoulders.

Then, he caresses her arm with his right hand to make sure that the absence of reaction when she first touched it was not a fluke. To his surprise, she neither jumps nor complains about a burning feeling so he celebrates the moment by voluptuously kissing her like he's never kissed anyone before. She pushes him against the door to close it back on its hinges. Bringing her near the mattress, he takes pleasure at watching the lady sensually dropping the tick sweater from her tender peach chest revealing lace lingerie. Unfastening the skirt, he lets it drop to the floor while she unbuckles the man's Gabardine tailored pants. Soon, his hands gently embrace her hips to lower her body down, caressing her bottom. Pressing her breast against his torso, he kisses her everywhere, worshipping her mortal envelope. As he is feasting on each single part of her body, she arches her back in response to the demand which leaves her craving for more. He almost cries his happiness of finally meeting his equal, his soul mate. Slowly through a dance of sweet surrender, he lets her invade the depth of his whole being until she reaches the far end of his core.

Morning comes and he wakes all alone in bed, the cold air of dawn making his naked body shiver. Was it just a dream that the lady was by his side but soon, an empty tea cup makes him think otherwise. He grabs a pair of jeans and rushes down the stairs. Charlene is sitting in front of Lorne both having a strong and fuming dark beverage. "Bonjour." She expresses jovially.

"Hi." He responds bending down to kiss her. "So I see that you've met my partner."

"Charming man I must say."

Josh pours himself a coffee and sweetens it with honey while he questions his roommate: "What time did you get in?"

"I got in a little after midnight."

"You stayed at the office?"

"Taylor and I went to a restaurant and then to a pub."

"You and him went to a pub? That's got to be a first!"

"He hasn't been in one for years. We had fun and he even met an old friend of his. But being away from the Montreal office bugs him. He wants to leave next week."

"And when are you leaving?" Josh throws taking a croissant and a few berries already set on the table.

"I'll depart whenever we find the right channelers for the group. At the most, six weeks."

Josh continues eating, thinking over that last sentence. He lifts his eyes, looking back at his pal who instantly retorts: "Now, don't give me that look." Charlene turns to the man with dark hair and unshaven beard. His eyes are so bright that it is almost impossible to resist his charisma. He finishes his bite, takes a sip of the strong coffee and gets up. "Jocelyn! Come back I've got something to tell you."

He nonchalantly gets back into the kitchen and leans his shoulder on the doorway, arms crossed. "Taylor and I were out yesterday for a specific reason. We came out with this idea that you may be able to meet the shortfall for the department."

"Getting funds by robbing a bank is against the law and you know it." He reproaches before turning his back to leave again.

"The friend he met yesterday is now a producer at the most watched television station in U.K. and while Taylor was explaining the reason for his stay, his friend proposed an idea. You could say a few lines in front of the camera about the institution. Taylor is in charge of consulting Wilkinson about it."

"You're not serious are you?" Josh supposes from the corridor pivoting back in the kitchen.

"Never been more . . . except when I proposed to my wife. Go and take a shower. I'll tell you the details after."

"Allright, Charlene, I'm leaving you with *mister assistant-producer* now."

She laughs loudly and pours herself another cup.

After listening to Lorne's proposition for a television commercial, Josh takes the lady out to a modest restaurant then a visit to the zoo just as she wished where they watch children play and marvel at the march of the penguins. Unwilling to impress her with lavishly festive places, they stroll around the city, taking time to talk and listen to each other. Being far from the apartment, they decide to turn around when an old lady, carrying a grocery cart filled with bags of clothes and a cat in a woolen leash, stops and grabs him by the arm. Surprised, almost offended by the rude contact, he darts his gaze to her. "You should be careful. Wear your weapon at all times." She advises. Wide-eyed, Josh looks at the arched back lady scavenging the streets looking for some bargain or food for her and feline companion. With her finger crooked by arthritis pointing at him, she almost looked like a bad comparison of a witch before strolling away with her precious belongings. "Wait." Orders Josh who walks back to the homeless and offers her a nut bar taken from his coat pocket. Charlene looks at them from afar, the lady once again touching his arm, this time more firmly as she gives out another recommendation, this time free of charge. "What was that all about?" Charlene asks her lover walking back toward her. "Nothing, don't worry about it."

"But she said . . ." Impatiently, he stops the discussion. "She' just . . . . listen, she probably took me for someone else."

"So why did you run back to her?" It was clear to Charlene that she would not be given the details about this odd conversation so she tries to enjoy his presence even though she feels the young lad is now absent-minded.

That same night when they cuddle up in his bed, although the warmth of her body against his is unsurpassed by anything in the world, all he keeps thinking about is the warning the homeless woman gave him about staying on his guard for a sign of impending danger.

By mid week, part of the team is already at the local television station to record a message for the welfare of the citizens. Charlene wanted to be present and is sitting further away from the set. The short footage in accordance with the police protection board is to issue a sensitization campaign that simply cannot wait. The script is short and takes one minute in each language. Clothing, make-up and hair styling personnel are all buzzing around him. Because of his age and the way he looked, he was the best suited person to address the message to both adult and susceptible adolescent communities. The publicity will be broadcast at the end of the week in Europe and in a few more days in North

America. Two versions will be produced, one in French the other in English both comprising a simultaneous sign language translation. Spanish subtitles will later be added at the bottom of the screen for the South American public therefore reaching a larger audience. His message will be clear and meant to be aired in the evening, so young children will not be disturbed by it.

A hair stylist places his mare while another employee from the station runs some lighting tests. A man, probably a decade older than him, with energetic manners, is endlessly groping the white long sleeve shirt. Shortly after, the young Canadian is entirely groomed and waits on the stool while other lighting tests are being carried out. "Monsieur Forge, can you say a few words for the sound check?"

Sitting on a sturdy metallic bench, he closes his eyes and searches in his memory. "It must have been October or shall we say, the month where all leaves fall from the nesting grounds to whirl around in the sinister skies . . . how's that?" His voice is deep, clear, and very easy to set. "Go on . . ." Adds the sound technician. Slowly, he shuts his eyes again and pursues the poem. "My horse had stopped to be fed but Thee, would Ney be by nothing but the arms from Thy lady miles away, waiting by the shore . . ." A few women and technicians on the set turn to him while Charlene is spellbound by the way he plays with the words displaying charming intonations, pausing when it is important to leave space. ". . . She is my love, my breath, and is as beautiful as the horizon falling at the sea's bed side. I languish for the time when Mo body will be back by her side, to linger into her devotion's cage. Mise is the bird who would sing to wake her in the morning and cover her with my wings at day's end."

Slowly, he opens his eyes again. From the stage, he is looking in her direction, searching for her approval but the violent lighting prevents him from seing her expression. Charlene is stunned, knowing the words he told in front of everyone, were lovely and more than likely intended for her to hear. The sound technician nods appreciating the testing. "That will be just fine. We will now get ready for the real thing."

Lights are dimmed once more and the make-up lady comes up to powder his nose. He frowns, reluctant to be so pampered. The camera takes shots of him from all angles while the script is displayed. Wilkinson is on the upper deck, taking a look at everything that is presented to him. Taylor stands right beside while Lorne makes fun of the situation by placing a towel over his forearm, pretending to be a servant. Josh tries to hide his laughter while the set director gets angry and threatens the comic that he will be thrown out of the studio if he doesn't behave. A unit of thirty people gets ready for action. The scripter comes close, tells the fresh actor details about the message, verifying if some of the words may be too hard for the French speaker to pronounce in English. After a short while, the stage director agrees to the desired intonation and the scripter walks away from the set. The young man raises his back, breathes out, pressing the palm of his hands over his lap.

It was time to address the troops,
Speak of allegiance for those standing in front of Mise.
All were there, but one . . .
KMK

"Are you ready Jocelyn?" He hears from behind the projectors. Nervous about the demanded task, he reaches deep inside to get into the right mood. "I am."

"O.k. people, let's roll." The red light on top of the wide lens goes on. A man with headphones standing by the camera looks at Josh, points three fingers out and retracts them one by one. "There has been lately . . . sorry."

His voice cracks. He lowers his face down, raises it. "Its o.k. Jocelyn, just continue." Encourages the director. The camera is still on. He breathes, adopts a poised, decontracted posture and starts again. "There has been lately an increase in child abductions. This situation has led us to make the population aware about recognizing the signs in which these sad situations could be avoided. The British security department and seventeen other organizations from around the world have set up a toll free line for teens in distress, child abuse programs and a display of fowl play recidivists who could be a threat to society. The government board has issued a world wide action program, asking for your participation which could be a turning point for thousand of children's safety. I'm Jocelyn Laurent Forge former agent for the Canadian Security Department in Montreal now affiliated with the prestigious British Security Office located in London. Thank you for your time and concern."

A toll-free number and a web site then appear and will be the last image viewers will see from the commercial break. Following the English version, Josh translates the message in French. Each commercial is made five times and the best of each will be kept and edited until approved by the producer. His deep voice, unmistakable French accent and uncommonly casual features are an attractive asset that Wilkinson intends to exploit to its limits. The unpretentious but serious speaker looking half-way between a sermon lecturer and a poesy reader uses the same manner in which he would approach children and teens, fairly and respectfully. "Cut!" The producer yells through the microphone, after the third version ends. When all is done, the red light on top of the camera shuts off and the staffs clap their hands. Josh gets up from the bench and applauds the team, turning to all employees around. Charlene comes and joins him while a set employee rids him of his wireless microphone.

"How was I?" He requests to his lady. "It was like you have done this a thousand times before."

"I'm still shaking."

"It never showed." Wilkinson gets down with Taylor. "That was sublime Forge."

"Thank you, sir." The producer gets near, giving a copy of the signed paperwork to Josh. "It will be broadcast over Europe at the end of the week and over in America in nine days. Where shall we send your cheque?"

"Just give it to the organization."

"It's quite a big amount sir."

"I know . . . I may end up having the requested staff after all." Josh looks at Wilkinson with a defiant smile before walking away to the changing room.

"You're so rough with him." Conveys Charlene when they are out of audible range.

"I don't like people who change their minds. I quit my job in Montreal, sold my house and my car to move here and now that he realizes that the department is lacking the substancial funds, we have to find ways to make it efficient. Please . . . give me a break. I'm far from being too rough with him." He replies while taking off the lended shirt and rubbing his face from the itchy make-up with a towel. Cheering and clapping his hands together, Lorne walks in the loge followed by Taylor. "Fantastic. Couldn't have done it better myself. You'd better get your gears sharpened for next week though."

"You're that confident Sir?" Josh proposes.

"Without a doubt . . . it was Lorne's idea for you to be the spokesman. He hardly had to convince me. You wanted a way to save kids? Well, here it is . . . Let's do it for David and all the others o.k.?" In Josh's ears, the name of the child found on the night he met Lorne, bears the same echo of time passed. Both co-workers exchange a comprehensive look, approving Taylor's words.

Peaceful it was to see such a vivid companionship.
Lochland, master of Skye, was the best of man to be at your side.
Protecting without overshadowing, listening more than talking, he
had this friendly humour always near. In front of my castle was his
own island and I am certain that if death would not have been so
present in his life, he would not have cherished it so much knowing
how fragile is was. He was the best confidant, breaking or raising you
at the right moment. Without him, my life would have been a bleak,
austere and immensely meaningless way to grow old . . .
KMK

The rest of the day is for the couple an opportunity to visit the British city, posing beside the Queen's guards and Beefeaters of the court. Visiting Hyde Park, Josh lets the lady see his real self, a very tranquil, less edgy and very pleasant one. She shows him plants on the grounds and tells him what people in Middle Ages would use them for. The soil and the sea provided all the necessary herbs to concoct medicine in those days, she explains with enthusiasm. When they arrive near the London tower, Charlene cannot hide her interest and sweet-sour admiration of the structure.

"Two of my ancestors were jailed in there. I would have liked to see it but I doubt that we would have access to the highest part." She comments.

"What have they done to deserve their punishment?"

"The older of the two brothers killed a British high ranking officer but both were caught to be hanged after starving for a week."

"Were they?"

"No, our mysterious writer tells how he and a few friends went to save them both."

"I tought the Tower was inviolable." Charlene turns to face her lover. Fire was in her eyes as if she was the one who saved the prisoners.

"Not for them."

Father came to greet Mise on Éire after my coming of age. He arrived on the island unnoticed with Fran and Chas, both my siblings. I had left Iona, ready to face the world but somehow, my plan to get back home after my ten years stay on the sacred island took a wildish turn. Gaël and Lochland, forever my friends, were part of this conspiration for me to join in and save the MacRae brothers from the claws of the British Empire. They had been arrested after the oldest brutally attacked one of King George I soldiers, the reason being of a nagging conversation about the Scottish that should have never taken place.

They are now at the top of the monument, in the devil's tower, waiting for their sentence to take place. Father wants me to be part of this insurrection. He says that I am ready to fight. How could he know for it has been a decade that we have not laid eyes on each other? How could he know how I feel, what lingers into Mo mind or does he think that I am his resurrection . . .

Is that what he expects me to be?

KMK

"Go again?" He pleads spinning his head in her direction. "You're not translating a book written by the MacRae's?" The way he stares back reflects his total lack of undersanding. "No of course not, the writer always signs KMK. So he couldn't be a MacRae. I just started translating it from French this past month; I could not understand a word from it before. Still, I have no idea who this man is or his role in the castle but I do know he fought beside them and how his presence was crucial."

"How do you know it's not a lady?"

"Well, it's only a presumption but I believe that it would be hard for a woman to battle with a sword weighing two stones and a half."

"And how much would that be in today's measures?"

"Just about thirthy-five pounds."

Hiding in the deep fields, Mise could smell the water but rising was at the moment the most demanding task to accomplish. Precious blade of mine weighing the common two and a half stones, it was now filthy with the ennemy's blood. The MacRae brothers had insertions at their wrists that would never disappear. They smelled as death had passed its shadow above them. Fleeying away in a slyly borrowed carriage, Chas was inflicted with a bullet in his left arm and the reins just flew in the air. I was on a horse right beside him when it happened. To hear him scream a sharp sound was totally unexpected and I fired back at the Brits with a weapon stolen from one of the guards. Lochland turned as well and sent an arrow right through one of the guard's throat. Thy heart was racing, everything moving much too fast, everything not going the way it was intented.

Reaching my brother Chas by the left side and holding the reins again, I was assaulted and fired at. Kicking back the horseman, he fell to the pavement and got stumped by dozens of hoofs. My oldest sibling barely holding himself was losing blood, too much. I held him back while Lochland raced the carriage like a madman. Gaël was using his sneaky abilities by tying a rope to an arrow and aimed it at a tree. He fired the other end to an opposite tree causing five horsemen to find their life path terminated, falling on top of one another.

My feet are incrusted in mud, face so close to the ground, heart racing like never before, it's beginning to hurt. A robust hand lies on my shoulder, grabbing tight. Turning around with my sword, I am

alleviated at the sight of Father, reaching out, bringing Mise back to
the rightful direction.
"Trobhad gorm sùil féidh" (Come blue-eyed stag), he tells me before
we both grab the MacRae brothers and start to run out of this hell.
KMK

They both enter a candy store where Charlene buys half a pound of dark fudge, a treat she cannot resist and playfully, she tempts her man with it. A store offering old books and maps from the last century attracts his attention. "It must have been some adventure to sail the sea in those days." He deduces admiring the traces of old continents on the parchment. "Got this running through your veins don't you?"

"What?"

"Travel the world."

"I wouldn't say that. I cannot wait until I settle into my own home."

The lady cannot hide her appreciation finally tantalizing him with the sweets.

"Why are you smiling?" He throws.

"For the first time, you are actually saying the word home."

On that special evening where a little rain is damping the unsophisticated clothing of the Englishmen and the wide variety of distinguished ladies felt hats, both feel like strolling. Suddenly, the shining lights on the sign above their heads catch his attention. A play is already underway at the theatre so he tells Charlene to wait a second and tries his best to get a pair of tickets. Explaining to the cashier, an old but romantic woman that he is a visitor desperately trying to please a lady friend, with words only he can think of, she is all ears. Only left with a couple of tickets, she offers them at half price because the spectacle has already begun. They of course, cannot be seated where ladies are wearing gowns covered with spangles and men displaying tailored tuxedos. Still, Josh is overwhelmed by the turn of events and runs back to get his lady.

"Allez Charlene, viens! (Hurry up Charlene, come!)" He spontaneously shouts.

She adored when he spoke his mother tongue. It sounded so different, almost exotic. He grabs her hand and both run all the way up the stairs. They get in the dark theatre where the usher guides them to their seats. From where they are, it is almost like a bird's nest, their vision plunging down the valley of dreams. The setting is flamboyant with an architectural Romanesque period decor, botanical compositions enhancing the stage and fluctuing lights illuminating the scene. The music played by a philharmonic orchestra is lead by a famous unconventional personage with long white hair drawned at the back into a poney tail. His gestures full of power transcending through the musicians, interpret the mannerism passing through their instruments. Dimmed lantern lights are seen from the pit where the refinement of subtle notes emanates from. Two hours later, as the last scene takes place, Charlene takes a quick glance at her companion whose lips are slightly open as to receive the divine bread of Christ. He is not gazing at the scene where the turmoil of the setting escalates from one emotion to another, but at the musicians working together a symphony, performing the lingering score in unison. He doesn't contemplate the stage where actors play their part with deepness, something he could relate to, hindrances, refusals, sadness, betrayal. He is pleased with the voluptuousness of the chords, the nuances of the violin's lament, and the sweetness of the piano's melody. How he loved to see the synchronized movement from an assemblage of players, arching their backs, eyes concentrating on the white pages filled with black notes like a pointillism painting. The young man bends his head in total ecstasy when the rhapsody vibrates just like it should, peacefully like the beauty of a newborn baby sleeping. She cannot get over how this man, so candid, filled with emotions of tenderness and love, is finally close to her. Never in her entire life has she desired someone as much as she does him, to warm, cuddle and embrace. Slowly he turns, thinking she wants to ask something. By the way she looks at him he knows what she's thinking of. "Do you want to make love to me?" He proposes in the lowest voice possible. She fathoms the wording, confesses to the proposal without speaking. Shyly, he approaches his face.

The play is over. People start clapping as the actor lies dead, in the arms of the heroin. "Someday, we will unite in the Highlands and lay in a garden under the blue moon." He whispers to her ear.

"Is that the way you figured it would happen?" She murmurs inquisitively.

"Being with you while having as a back drop the five sisters of Kintail, that's how I see myself one day."

"Wouldn't it be like being on the land facing Eilean Donan?"

"Exactly . . ."

Hunger for Mo, for there is no time to waste.
Tomorrow might never come
and the deep of the night is much too far away.
KMK

Early on the Friday morning, he brings her to the train station instead of the airport now that she has more time to go back to Edinburgh. "Can I call you on Monday?"

"My course finishes at four and I will be in my apartment around a quarter to five. What time do you finish work?"

"Six but sometimes I stay a little longer."

"Like midnight?"

"It does happen." He precises honestly. Touching her hair, he lovingly places it behind her ear just to have an excuse to play with it. The train comes in and soon, a voice on the intercom calls her destination. "I have to go otherwise I'll miss it."

"And that would be sooooo sad." He answers mocking her before they kiss one last time and she hurries to the wagon. Finding a seat near the window she looks out and places her hand against the transluscent panel while he stays behind the fence. He imitates her gesture and the train gives off a last ringing tone before shutting the doors and taking her far away.

Getting out of Victoria station, a limousine approaches him and the front passenger window lowers down, Josh recognizes one of Wilkinson's puppets who is hailing at him: "Agent Forge, won't you please step in? It's a request from my superior." He pleads immediately stepping out of the car to open the door for him. Unable to refuse, Josh takes a seat in the latest luxury model where six passengers can sit comfortably. He realizes that Lorne, Taylor and Wilkinson are already inside. "We are all on our way to the office." A small monitoring television and miniature refrigerator are surrounded by seats of dark mohogany leather.

"How did you know where to find me?"

"Mister Landers said we may find you here."

"This is very kind of you sir." Teases Josh cockily.

"You look pale agent Forge."

"Do I? Sorry to hear about that."

"Anyway, we were just talking about your abilities. I wanted to hear your own version of the last session because we never really discussed it. Can you elaborate on your finding methods?" Because he knew this question was bound to turn up, Josh chooses small words without displaying the complex psychic version. "My body has to be calm and restful in order for my mind to receive impulses that are out there, waiting to be detected. If I have any kind of worries or preoccupations, it just won't work."

"Were you born with your gift?"

"Could be, but my first vision was only at the age of thirteen."

"I saw in your file that you can also see the aura. Please explain."

"Everybody has a light surrounding their body. It comes from the energy each of us possesses and makes our body what it is. Some people are true masters about hiding their feelings and somehow controlling their aura. In some situations, it does happen where I will not be able to discern any immoral value through a human being but most people cannot control their energy field so their aura is as clear as a window. Let's take you for example; I can see that you had an injury in the past on your left knee because there is almost no light around it anymore. Am I right?"

Wilkinson looks surprised and acknowledges the extraneous information. While his college pal reinforces his questioning, Taylor peacefully contemplates the smog dancing over the Thames, a scene reminding him of his childhood. "You can draw and paint, were one of the few to have 98.7 % on your government final Art exam. You're also an accomplished linguist; French, English and sign language have no secrets for you. I'm wondering; you could have been excellent in all those fields so what made you choose the police force?"

"Just like Lorne and Sir Taylor, I thought I could be of use."

"Some people would pay to possess half of your psychic faculties. Never thought about using them to the wrong essence?" Josh pauses a few seconds while Lorne gets offended by the comment and Taylor pivots his eyes further away, ashamed of such an assumption. "God sees everything and I wouldn't mess with Him." He retorts on a peaceful tone but wondering where the Chief Superintendent is leading to until he asks a last question. "Do you consider yourself an angel or maybe a saviour mister Forge?"

Lorne is hissing out his breath, a little louder. Taylor gets a notch above troubled by the superior's inquiry. "Some people rot in drawers, waiting to be utilized and others will be exploited 'till they break. I simply hope that I'm neither."

Wilkinson's attempt to provoke the newest member of his prestigious organization fails and out of good faith, he has to surrender. "I'm not used to having such a conversation or to actually have people with your abilities around me. It just makes me wonder about the legitimacy of it." Pressured, tired and almost intimidated, Josh feels out of breath, his torso starting to hurt. "Do you mind if I pull down the window a bit?" He snaps getting paler by the minute and starts executing himself but Wilkinson stops him. "Those windows are bullet proof and I do prefer to have them up. We can raise the air conditioning if you want. Please let me handle this. If you push the wrong button, the driver will stop sharp and barge in here with a gun."

"And we don't want that, do we?" The young man ironically completes. After some fresh air fills the closed compartment, Wilkinson starts talking with Taylor about political issues concerning world poverty and the connection it has with crime evolution. Earth is a small planet containing the vastness of heartful men and mentally disturbed executors who both think they are right. Just like his superior, it was in Josh's way of thinking to be surrounded by the challenge of the balance, the positioning of two opposed groups who would decide on the fairness of their actions. But, the Canadian agent keeps quiet just like Lorne, letting the two police masters exchange their point of view, the irrelevant conquest for monopolizing a sole strength above all others. Victims and persecutors, good against evil, was a conversation that could certainly last for days if not months. Wilkinson was far from being as profound as Taylor, simply thinking that he was only a human being and there was only so much he could do to prevent crimes. He did not believe in life after death and certainly not in a superior, celestial being that would decide of our path. The pure bred British who seemed heartless, had not set foot in a church nor prayed since he was a teenager and was surely not favorable to people who devoted themselves to a religion. Faith had been ruled out from his language but the lad was not offended by his frankness. Instead, he was glad that the Union Jack security master mind was freely speaking about it but curious as he was, Josh has one question in the back of his mind: "Would it be too abrupt to ask about your family sir?" Wilkinson turns his head to the inquisitor, makes a pause intrigued and then begins revealing his own personal status. "I have a wife. We have been together for thirty years. I have a daughter of twenty-six, married with two children. And of course, you must have heard about my son."

"Not really sir. I only read a brief article about him on your website."

While the atmosphere radically changes, the leader bites his lip and inhales before beginning. "It was a Friday back in October, eleven years ago. It was raining cats and dogs and Andrew was to come home from college. He had called my wife earlier in the day, saying he had to finish homework before coming home. At first, when we saw that he wasn't back at ten, my wife and I thought he'd changed his mind and had gone out with friends. Around midnight, my wife still wasn't sleeping and she came to get me in my home office. In those days, I used to bring files back to our domicile. She . . . had a feeling that something was wrong so she asked me to call the college. We of course had to wake a few people up to seek for our son and the last one to see him alive was the janitor. He remembers him well because he was about to go through the doors a little before ten but seeing the rain pouring, he went back to get his raincoat in his room."

"So he actually saw him leave?"

"Yes he did and he recalls my son telling him that he just had time to catch the last bus."

"Was he alone?"

"He said that my son left the college by himself and nobody ever saw him alive after that. He never made it to the bus stop." Josh lets the man continue at his own pace, revealing the atrocity of the find two weeks later in a deserted area, ten miles away from the college. The young boy had been severely beaten, his body covered with his own blood. The cadaver had started to decompose. "Were there any revealing details found on the scene?"

"DNA expertise wasn't as efficient as today back then and a thorough search was carried out in the vicinity of the find. We finally put him to ground a week after discovering him but the investigation lasted more than a year." Wilkinson was so eager to avoid showing any kind of facial emotion or body language, that Josh knew it was only a facade. "You feel it's your fault?"

"I always did, I could have asked my driver to go and get him and nothing would have happened to him. So many questions turn in your head when these things happen. You know what I'm talking about, don't you?"

"Of course I do. All parents who have lived similar tragedies think the same. Fatal endings make no sense for those who endure them. You have my sympathy over the matter sir. What you and your family have been through is probably the worst experience ever. But it seems to me that «la boucle n'est par bouclée»." He makes a circle with both his hands, starting at the bottom and failing to attach it at the top.

"What is that?"

"The circle path of your life is not yet attached . . . and it will never be, until you are convinced that *you* had nothing to do with your son's horrific last moments. Some people think that only the Lord, Jehovah, Allah, call him as you please, decides of the road our lives take. Angels work as His followers and there will always be a dark source to tempt you, discourage you from following His ways."

"And what do you believe in?"

"I put my trust in endless human possibilities as much as celestial ones."

"And you never had a leap of faith?"

"No, I never did."

To this answer, Taylor's head turns to the lad and gives a discrete approval look. Wilkinson's dark brown eyes, almost the colour of a shark's, contrasting with his salt and pepper coloured hair, stare back impassively and swallows painfully. "Do you think he's well? I mean, wherever he is?"

Lorne having his own theory on the subject gives a cautionary look at his companion wondering what his answer will be. Josh did not want to break the man's half serenity knowing that his way of thinking led him to believe that whoever suffered undesired pain, would linger never knowing the peace he or she was entitled to, until put to ground. Screams of souls begging, pledging for eternal peace, was often heard whenever he connected. "You clearly loved your son and it shows. If you did have the respect of having a mass said in his name, then you have nothing to worry about." Lorne's relief is shared by Taylor as Wilkinson acquiesces and changes the subject. "You solved another case this week-end?"

"I only brought one file, the one from the private school teen, what's his name . . . Tommy, Tommy Sacks. But no, I could not conclude this one so he's probably alive. I did not feel anything dark when I touched the photograph."

"That's good to hear. Anyway, I have another one you could . . ." Wilkinson begins as he extirpates a file from his suitcase, leaning over to hand it to him.

"I could not do it here sir. The car is moving; I'm a bit tired so it just won't work."

"I see."

"Maybe later, with Lorne's help I'll be able to."

Unhiding his deception, Wilkinson takes back the file.

"Anyway mister Forge, I'm glad you accepted to do the commercial and I hear good things about your group. We are on our way to a special meeting concerning it." Josh's face is now turning to a paler colour and his pulse beats like a storming wave rushing against rocks on a sharp cliff. The limousine comes to a stop in front of the grey building where two security agents are standing.

Hockart is already in the conference room with twenty other agents, most of whom Josh already met. Wilkinson politely asks everyone to take a seat while he takes his own place at the far end of the oval table near the wall. Both sit on either side of the polished slab, facing each other. Refreshements are offered and as Josh grabs a glass of water, it gives him time to look around. Men and women are quietly discussing small talk around him. He takes a few sips from the clear beverage and tries his best to have a more regular pulsation. A few seconds later, something strange happens, something beyond his control. Lights above his head seem to dim and his head begins to feel dizzy. Air is rarefied but in the company of so many people, he tries his best to look poised and puts the glass on the table with a shaking limb. Images in front of his eyes change the setting of the place and amazingly, the roofing becomes an arched stone vault. His brain works at the highest speed as he presses his hands together, to dominate the urging encroachment.

Surrounded by seated armoured soldiers, I can feel the weight of my own weapon at my thigh so I put it in front of Mise, on the venerable oak table. Both my brothers, Chas and Fran are by my side. MacRae's oldest son is discussing of the engagement recently deployed in the Grampians. Laid beside the candelabra is a tin buck filled with water. All others but I, share the coarse taste of amber scotch. Black bread rests in the middle of the table with recently picked apples. My right leg hurts. Blood is coming out from my knuckles. My beard is long, dirty and sweaty. The sword I just took out from my side is the one of my late father's, engraved with Celtic knots at the base of the handle and leather is fastened around the hilt for a better grip. It shines with the candle light for there is only one small window in the Billeterie. This is where all important meetings take place, far from any outside light, far from any unwelcomed ear. Facing I is my long time

companion, Lochland MacLeod, master of Skye. Over his shoulders,
a dark coloured cape with a silver fox trimming strengthens the
darkness of his ebony coloured hair. His eyes, green as spring moss
are hard to sustain but not for I. In them I find comfort and peace of
mind. Gaël, soon to be master of Mull is by his side. Ethan, another
of my warriors, comes close to the table and accidentally hits a shield
that violently falls on the floor.
KMK

A sharp sound snaps Josh out of his distant vision and an agent near them excuses himself for dropping a tray on the floor. Lorne creases his eyes and stares at his friend facing him who is trying his best to return to the present era. For the first time in his life, Josh has no control over his mind wandering off a couple of centuries back and then rushing to the present. The vision lasting less than a minute was enough to make him feel disconnected from the world he knows, leaving him immensely disturbed. Suspiciously looking at him, Lorne tries to read the message over his buddy's face but the young man turns his head to Wilkinson who may have said a few sentences while he «was away». He has difficulty breathing, keeping his eyes open and an uncommon paleness covers his face. Lorne cannot help to glimpse back to his partner, disliking the condition in which he is while Wilkinson speaks a little louder to get everyone's attention.

"Over the course of the last ten days, all of you took part in children's searches. Thanks to this group effort, nine of the ten kids have been found, eight of them, alive and well. Triggering actions of the newcomers from Canada really made the difference. Without agent Landers and Forge, I doubt that we would have had such rapid results. I of course, would like to thank my old friend Lieutenant Taylor for making those two men part of our institution."

Wilkinson applauds followed by everybody else in the room. Josh gets annoyed with so much attention shyly saluting, holding tight the chair's arms. Lorne gladly take all the praises he can get, receiving them like a well deserved honour and Wilkinson continues his debriefing: "There will be a special broadcast regarding those finds. In accordance with each parent because they're all minors, the program will show how the incidents happened and mainly what could have been done to prevent them. The need for security has significantly increased over the past ten years. Since some of our effectives are to be centralized to the anti-terrorism group, prevention is the main key. Every head of family is entitled to reach out, grab the information and utilize it to the best of their knowledge. Earlier this week, a commercial was recorded and starting tonight, will air on every television station in the U.K., and the rest of Europe. America will soon follow and South America with a Spanish version. All will be simultaneously be translated in the sign language. There will be a banquet on Saturday night, at the Grand Ball auditorium in the center of London to honor every member of the special force and special units, as well as their reunited families. It will also be proposed to the grand public which will contribute to raising funds for the cause. I hope to see you all there. That concludes our morning meeting. Now if you'll excuse me, the Media are waiting outside for Sergeant Hockart and I to give a speech. You can all go back to work and have a good day." Cheers and applauses are heard through the vast room. Josh gets up with struggle as Lorne can handle more of his share of congratulations and doesn't stop shaking hands. Josh welcomes the thanking, avoiding staring too long with his glazed, grey eyes. The partner finally makes his way near his buddy grabbing his shoulder, making his presence known. The young man turns, as pale as a ghost. "Tell me, tell me something." Whispers Lorne lowering himself in front of him.

"I hate this . . ." He admits out of breath. Lorne steps back, worried about his expression. "What happened?"

"Are you o.k. son?" Taylor begins coming near.

"Certainly sir, Josh is just fine. He and I were both on our way to his office to look up a few more files with the candidates." Interrupts Lorne. But the boss knows that he is lying through his teeth. As Josh is about to leave, Taylor grabs his arm. "Hey lad, I'm right there if you need me." In the young man's eyes, the superior sees distress, torment and even anguish. Still breathing hard and making efforts so that no one can see the state he's in, he believes that nothing can be hidden from his boss. "I know Sir." Josh finally concludes so Taylor lets his grip loose and leaves his man to walk away beside his partner.

Chapter Eighth

In her room near the University, Charlene watches the evening news while folding some freshly washed and dried clothes. "Earlier this week, a vast investigation from the Londonian Security Agency gave a lot of anguished families the surprise of their lives. A dozen families, whose child had been reported missing for months, even years in some cases, were contacted to receive the news they've been longing for. We have footage of the reunions from different parts of the country and even one that took place in France. For the parents contacted and filmed in this segment, there are no words to express the gratitude and exhilaration to finally have their lost ones now back home. Here are some of the declarations." On the screen, police agents are reuniting children with their families who throw themselves in each other's arms. The whole scene is overwhelmed by screams of joy. The head chief makes a brief appearance. "Mister Wilkinson, is this the first of several operations in regards of the child disappearing squad?"

"A task force of more than fifty police officers has been working on the cases for many months and with the help of two Canadians recently joining our unit, we were able to conclude certain files more rapidly."

"Can you give us their names?"

"Certainly, their names are agents Lorne Landers and Jocelyn Laurent Forge." Charlene raises her head up, gets close to the television set to turn the sound up and calls her mother.

"Ma! Turn on the television on the news channel. They're talking about Josh . . . . Tha (Yes) . . . bye." She approaches the set with the cell in her hand and sits on the simple chair of the modest apartment. "Here is a clip filmed a couple of years ago in their homeland Canada, where we can see both agents in action with fellow police officers." Footage of the two men appears on the screen, showing them on a past rescue mission. Immensely touched by the amplitude of the reporting, Charlene's eyes just water incontrolably. Lorne had a little more hair, pulling on the boat that hit a mass of rocks barely seen over the water, while his co-worker is sunken up to his arm pits, extirpating the young boy from it. The « Josh » that appears in the report is no different from the one she left the night before. Holding him tightly by the neck, the child is crying over the turmoil of a dark, cold night spent beside his father's corpse. Josh's wet shirt is molding the upper part of his body and the soaking of his jeans by algaes and mud makes it hard for him to climb up the river bank. His face and both his arms are scraped from sharp brambles as if he had been whipped. She stares at the image of the dark haired, bearded faced; grey-blue eyed young man, stroking the back of the child weeping in his arms. Protecting and consoling the fragile four-year-old while his dad is being carried away in a black morgue bag is an almost unbearable scene to watch.

"What makes their finding method different from the ones used before?" The reporter inquires to Sergeant Hockart. Discrete and rigorous of the privacy involving the police department, he answers with the sharpness of a knive. "As you probably know, this is classified information but a gala will be held Saturday night in a week from now at the Grand Ball auditorium where children will come and speak about their more than appraised homecoming. Tickets can be bought on the web site that will appear at the bottom of the screen and benefits from the evening will go toward the prevention of these crimes. Agent Forge also did a commercial that will follow. As you can see, he and his group are very dedicated to the cause."

"Thank you for your comments Mister Wilkinson and Mister Hockart."

"It was my pleasure." The camera turns to the anchorwoman in the studio. "That was our correspondent from central London, talking to the Chief Superintendent of the London Police Headquarters, Mister Donovan Wilkinson and Sergeant Hockart, the person responsible for the child recovery section. And now, let's go to the sport segment . . ."

The following Monday in the office located on the 11th floor, Josh has open files all over his desk, including the one of Wilkinson's son. His white porcelain cup has a lingering rim of darkened coffee and half a bagel stares back knowing it will be neglected. Both his partner and secretary are discussing a case when his cell rings. "Forge." He answers still reading the file. "Hi, it's Charlene."

"Hi love." He exclaims as he takes another file from the cabinet.

"I saw you on television last Friday."

"Oh, did you. How was I?"

"You haven't changed much over the years and you looked very brave with that child in your arms."

He blushes and rapidly wants to change the subject. "Thanks. Listen, there's going to be a gala this Saturday to raise funds. Will you be able to come with me?"

"What will you wear?"

"You, of course." He whispers placing the file above the drawer.

"Seriously, you have a suit for the occasion?"

"Don't worry about that. Will you be there to hold my hand?"

"I will."

"Then nothing else matters." Looking out, he sees on the streets smog gently rolling under the freshly lit lanterns, conferring to London its most reputed atmosphere. The sun setting in a brushed tint of pinks and yellows is worth the mastering palette of a certain painter named WilliamTurner. "I miss you." He continues.

"I miss you too. I'll confirm you the time of my arrival on Friday evening."

"I'll be there, I love you."

"I love you too." He hangs up first before loosing his head otherwise, he would have asked her to come home to his arms right this minute.

Who was I to think that I could be above anything because of my young age?

I had travelled many shores and helped children get back home,
respected my parents, worshiped God, angels and archangels above,
but even that could not save me from being drawn to the fires of
loneliness.
KMK

She sits at the table and staring back at her are the notes she
just translated. They fill her thoughts realizing that the writer of
the long gone era had more and more similarities with the man
she was dating.

Hours later, still working at his office desk, piled up notes
are placed in front of him in seven stacks. He lifts one up in front
of the light when there is a knock on the door. "Who is it?"

"Taylor." Josh gets up, unlocks the door. The tall man is
standing by the edge of the doorway. "Can I come in?"

"Yes, of course . . . Why aren't you home?"

"I was just about to ask you the same question."

Josh picks up the sheets and places them in a folder before
sinking them in the filing cabinet. It immediately locks itself
as soon as the drawer is shut. "Now, will you tell me what
happened last Friday in the conference room? It was as if you
were a thousand miles away." Taylor snaps as Josh exhales and
clenches his fingers through his hair. He rapidly strikes his chin
up to face his boss. "I have no freaking idea. I was suddenly
wrapped in some medieval castle set in the Highlands, about to
address my soldiers."

Awfully disoriented, Taylor's stare is somewhat new to the
agent who obviously was waiting for some lucid reply. "And
you provoked it?"

"Of course not, I used to draw him, and the castle is the one
that lies in front of Charlene's mother's place but what happened
was so awkward. I was the warrior, this was my castle. I could
feel the weight of the sword on my side, I could smell the scotch
those men were drinking but mainly, I could feel the burning
sting of a gash on my body and the tiredness after a long battle.
Am I going nuts?"

Without reserve, Taylor finds the comment quite ironic and about to leave, gives his reply. "You've been under a lot a pressure and you're quite imaginative. I wouldn't worry about it because you can tell the difference between the real world and your fantasies."

"You don't get it, do you? I could not control it."

Taylor stands and rigidly looks back at his employee. "You came back, didn't you?"

"Yes, but . . ."

"So you still have control over your mind and it's not because you had a brief daydream that you should be anxious or even disturbed about it. You said it yourself, you were tired. It's now close to eight and you're still working. Just go home, get some rest, or go out, have a fine meal and for God's sake, **sleep**. If you do have more of these sudden flashes, then I will have you psychoanalyzed. Now C'mon, get up, close the cabinets and shoo."

"Fine, I'll take your advice." As he gets up, another incoming message from Sergeant Hockart's department beeps on his computer but Taylor reprehensively looks back at Josh. That convices him to shut it off and he then locks the files before closing the door behind him.

On Thursday morning he realizes that even working ten hours a day is not sufficient to bring their head above water in this sea of documents. The weather, unusually warm for this part of the continent, makes everyone happy to shed off a few layers of clothing. The gala planned by the London Police Force was the event of the week and on everyone's lips. For the occasion Lorne has his family flown in. Marie is so excited to see her father and her uncle again. At Heathrow, warm poignant embraces seem to be all that matters until Lorne realizes that his wife has gained weight.

"You're pregnant?" He shouts with surprise written all over his face.

"Four months now. Josh knew just by looking at my face when I drove you to the airport."

"Why didn't you tell me?" He pleads to his wife. "I was afraid you'd refuse to work in London. Josh needed you and deserved your help."

Sylvia is all smiles when Lorne kisses her a few hundred times more.

After walking in the modest apartment, plans are made for the kids to sleep in the living room while Sylvia opens the refrigerator and shakes her head in despair. "Dearest husband of mine, where is the closest market?"

"Two blocks away. I know we have to get some more food. Kids, you want to stay with Josh or come with us?"

"I want to stay." Marie warns tagging Josh.

"Have you got any bike magazine?" Bryan requests.

"Tons." He replies pointing at the coffee table.

"O.k. so we'll be back in an hour or so." When Lorne leaves with his wife, he doesn't even bother to lock back knowing Josh is there.

"Are you guys thirsty?"

"Milk for me." Advises the little lady taking her hat off.

"Soda if you have any." Shouts the teen his head plunged in a magazine.

"Is anyone hungry for lunch?"

"We all had breakfast on the plane Uncle Josh." Confirms the teen. After bringing them their beverages, Josh climbs the stairs to his room and, as he is looking for some crayons and paper for Marie to draw with, he turns around and sees the little girl standing in the doorway. When she descries all the paintings aligned around, her mouth opens in amazement at the execution of each of them. "I want to be as good as you. Can you teach me how to paint?"

"Well sure, I didn't think you were ready for that yet." He puts back the drawing materials in the portfolio and takes his wooden paint box beside the easel. "I don't have any new canvases though. You don't mind painting over cardboard, do you?"

"As long as you teach me how to paint, I don't care." She declares with her happy, high-pitch voice. She sees Charlene's book on his desk turns it around and examines her picture on the back cover. "She's pretty, you know her?" Josh smiles, bringing out a few paint brushes and linseed oil. "We are dating."

"Daddy told me that your girlfriends don't go out with you for long." He bends down to her height to catch an eraser that fell on the floor. "She and I are seeing each other but that doesn't mean that we will spend the rest of our lives together. I know I have feelings for her and I believe she does for me but that's it Marie. If you put too much pressure on a person, she's just going to run away."

"Is that what happened with your last girlfriend?"

He opens his mouth but then shuts it right back to choose the right words.

"She got frightened."

"She left you because you're different?"

"That and she also said I worked too much." She places her small hands over his cheeks and her gesture takes him by surprise. "I wouldn't change you for anything in the world and I hope your new lady is feeling that way."

Innocence and thruthfulness emanate from the child which brings a rush of emotion to his heart. Opening his arms to invite her over to be snuggled, he makes sure his right hand is clenched.

When Lorne comes back to the apartment with Sylvia, Marie is intensely caressing the thick carboard with a brush filled with crimson and a touch of magenta oil paint while Bryan is asking about the latest British motorcycles. Josh is seated between them having homemade lemonade.

"Sorry it took so long. I probably lost my wallet at the grocery store. Do you have any money to pay for the fare?" Lorne begins dropping the grocery bag at the door.

"Sure." Josh answers heading out but as both reach the sidewalk, the taxi driver hands Lorne's leather purse to him. "I believe this belongs to you sir, it fell underneath the seat." The driver explains. "Oh, thank you. I tought I forgot it at the store. Here is what I owe you and a little extra for being honest."

"Don't mention it. It's my pleasure." The driver tips his hat and as Josh puts away his own money, he has this funny feeling that the driver isn't telling the truth. Maybe he had been working too much and everyone seemed not as sincere as he hoped they would be so he shakes his head and follows Lorne in. Marie is still concentrated on her creation and cannot wait to get her uncle's attention. "What do I have to do after I have placed my main character at the focal point?"

Around six the food is set on the table and just like in the old days, Josh is enjoying the feast with his second family. Everyone has their turn at telling stories, sharing a conversation and bringing water to the mill of knowledge. When Marie's turn to speak comes, Lorne cannot believe how fast his little lady had grown mentally over these last few months. She kisses her mother's belly before going to bed. "Good night sweetheart." Lorne murmurs to his daughter before getting to the improvised bed over on the sofa. Josh gets up, picks up the dishes and puts them in the dishwasher. "Do you have a suit for Saturday night?" Lorne requests to his partner who is annoyed by the question. "Why is everyone worried about that? Charlene asked me the same thing."

"We just don't want you to wear jeans."

"I have something, don't worry." After turning on the machine on heavy cycle, he picks up a cigar and his lighter to leave the house. Sitting on the apartment's front stairs, he lights the defended stick and dials Charlene's number. "Hi, it's me. What are you doing?"

"Correcting papers again, what about you?"

"I just finished supper. Sylvia arrived this morning with the kids."

"I can't wait to meet them tomorrow."

"So my lady; what shall you wear at the gala?"

"It's a surprise monsieur."

"Oh c'mon, just tell me the colour."

"I won't give you any details but I think you'll like it. What about you?"

"I rented a black tuxedo."

"Will you have a bow tie?"

"I don't like those, they make me feel strangled."

She laughs. "I have to go. I've had a long day. I'll be at the train station at eight fifteen tomorrow night."

"I can't wait. I love you."

"I love you too." He hangs up and places the cell in his back pocket. The night is clear, humid and a feeling of loneliness invades his entire body, taking him back to his childhood when the suffocating August weather would keep him from sleeping. He was about thirteen and the evening was exactly the same, all the neighbourhood windows were open in this heat wave and alone, he sat on the stairs of his parents' home. Facing the house, right behind la Rivière aux Chiens (Dog's River) there was this factory where wood was transformed. Huge logs were piled in different stacks and all night, water was sprayed over them so no fire would ignite a blaze. There he sat and looked at the logs being sprayed over and over again mainly because there was nothing else to do so late in the night. He kept staring at the wood piles and there he imagined a monster just like in Goya's painting coming from behind the logs. A tall, rustic man with strong arms and beard, walked so loud that the earth trembled. "I'll defy you!" He told the giant grinding his teeth.

"Jocelyn! Viens te coucher (Come to bed)." Ordered his mother.

At the thought of the recollection, he doesn't laugh. He simply recalls it as being a memory he will never forget. The giant was the materialization of nightmares that foretold real events. At that age, he didn't know how to control his gift and it scared the hell out of him. Now, a decade and a half later, he was seeing other atrocities, monsters made of flesh and blood who were terrorizing children but this time, he was not going to hide under a blanket to ignore their existance.

Saturday evening, night of the Gala.

Charlene walks out of the limousine in a beautiful taffeta gown of deep green beside her lover. Her hair is up with exquisite taste, and the young man simply cannot get over how beautiful his lady is. It was the first time he wore a tuxedo, but no bow completed the look. Introductions to co-workers undergo in the lobby, cocktails and amuse-gueules are offered while a leaflet describing the course of the evening is handed out to guests. Josh takes his and slips it in his back pocket so he can discretely play hide and seek with Marie behind the pillars of the majestic entrance. Soon after, everyone is asked to enter and take their assigned seat. A tall and slim man comes up to the microphone at the edge of the stage. Near him a lady does simultaneous translation in the sign language something which pleases Josh. The lights are dimmed and the clamour from the audience becomes a hush.

"Ladies, gentlemen and children, good evening; we are gathered tonight to . . ." The representatives of the British security agency as well as those of the seventeen other organizations are present. Policemen in their uniforms come to talk, declaring how hard their task is; parents of lost ones, families of the lucky ones who came back to their nest are either listening or giving their own version of the dreadful events. The emotion is palpable, the bond tightened between the police task force and the children who were saved from the pornography network operating from the underground, is tremendous. Lorne lurks in his pal's direction to observe his gesture, afraid that whatever happened in the meeting room last week will repeat itself. Josh looks relaxed, and with the help of the clement weather, the contrast of his tanned face with his eyes is now more striking. Reassured, the blond man then turns his gaze back to the master of ceremony in center stage, continuing his speech. "Recently, the central London station received a happy turn of events with a young teenager. She asked to be part of this celebration and of course, we simply could not refuse. Please welcome Miss Mandy Simms." The entire audience claps their hands as the young girl wearing a long light blue gown approaches. The presentator lowers the microphone to her level and Mandy places a sheet on the lectern in front of her. She turns to the man in the elegant suit who asks her a question to which she nods approvingly and looks down on her sheet. The man wearing a tuxedo and a bow tie then walks to the side, to wait in the dark while Mandy faces the crowd with assurance. "Good evening, buenas tardes, guten tag, bonsoir. A short while ago, I decided to run away from my parents' place. With the influence of a friend, I managed to succeed. My reasons were not so different from the thousands of teenagers who do it every year. I know I caused my family torment with my decision and thankfully, remorse came over me. With the help from the police, I was able to return home unharmed. Some of us unfortunately don't make it back and tonight, we are here to make people aware of the signs; how parents and children can learn from my experience and that of so many others. Please greet from the London police task force, Chief Superintendent Donovan Wilkinson, and from the highest authority of the Canadian Security Services in Montreal, Lieutenant John Jacob Taylor." Wilkinson comes forward to speak in the microphone while Taylor waits on his left.

"Thank you Mandy. Luckily, our institution gets rewarded by perfect endings. Mandy's case is one of them."

Lorne deliberately drops his leaflet to take a peak at his co-worker's expression. Josh's stare is one of concern, not of anger but of revolt probably thinking that if they had waited longer to start a search, the result wouldn't have been the same. The robust agent leans back on his seat, thinking how much his partner's involvement was superior to his. When the applauses cease, Wilkinson continues his speech.

"When her parents came to us, her situation seemed as desperate as the hundreds of others we get every year. Over the world, thousands of disappearances don't have such happy endings. When they do, it's with joy and delight that we celebrate our involvement, our decision to pursue the most demanding task a human can accomplish, which is to save people. It is a harsh and a cruel demand to be confronted with telling the parents of those who disappeared that their child has been found but not in the way they wished he or she would have been. My own son was found dead in a vacant lot years ago. He wasn't the only victim, his entire family was. Since that day, I promised myself not to find the murderer but to help prevent that kind of situation and take anti-terrorist security measures for the entire nation. Finally, the time has come for our project to be concretized. My son is my force, an unbreakable link to the survival of others. When I meet women and men carrying the same torch, I can only thank them to have crossed my path, because I could never do it alone. Many of you know that our police department will specialize in terrorist prevention but there is also a great demand for child protection. This evening is dedicated to recognize those who fulfilled their duties to the limit and will be presented with a specially designed medal, a reward known as Saint Joseph's embrace. On it you can see the Saint patron bearing on his shoulder his own son, crossing a brook with the help of a cane. We added our own touch by ornating it with a ribbon in the colours of the Union Jack. Tonight, we are proudly presenting this special award to two Canadian agents who played a major role into Mandy's epic and so many others'. Please welcome agents Lorne Landers and Jocelyn Laurent Forge." As everyone starts clapping, Josh turns to Lorne. "You knew!"

"Sorry. I had to keep it a secret." One after the other, they get up the stairs and approach sir Wilkinson. Small talk is exchanged while receiving the honouring medal, pinned on the heart side. "This is a real surprise. Thank you very much sir." Admits Josh.

"My pleasure, you deserve it." Taylor steps in to congratulate both his men and soon after, young Mandy draws near as well, thanking Lorne politely with a timid hand shake. When she gets to Josh, both exchange a long, meaningful look. Unafraid to show their emotions toward each other, they can't repress the intense hug they need to share despite the audience watching them. Her family gets up to cheer and so does everyone else. Josh smiles avidly after kissing her on the head, just like a protective seal.

All I could hear was the clapping of birds's wings, flying off to a distant land . . .

He steps backward near Lorne and both respectfully congratulate each other with a warm open palm on the shoulder. Once more, Wilkinson approaches the microphone.

"Mister Landers has joined the force a little over twenty-two years ago and mister Forge just celebrated his tenth year. Their team has solved more than a hundread and fifty cases of missing children." A pause is observed by the security mastermind to let people give another round of applause. "We will now present to you the short footage made earlier this week."

The lights dim while a huge screen is pulled down. The movie begins with the screening of a wood, a shopping center, an amusement park. A voice is heard. "We don't want to frighten people. We only want to make them aware . . ."

Josh recognizes Lucy's crisp British accent then another voice that of Taylor is heard. "To serve and protect, to be careful and foresee danger. We, agents of the British security office with their affiliates, have been mandated to protect civilians and bring back home their children." Pictures of kids saved by the Canadian duo and their colleagues in action appear on the screen. Lastly, a very young girl's voice tenderly gives her own message. "Stay close to your mom and dad and if you get lost, go to a police officer to get help. Don't go with anybody else." Josh is undeniably listening, so is everyone in the audience but the emotion he feels is almost too much. The weight of the building seems to put pressure on his shoulders and makes his heart race. Afraid to crack, break, scream his lungs out, he keeps breathing discretely, trying to concentrate by slowly counting in his head. Having Lorne beside him makes the burden of being in a closed area a little easier and, right when he thought he couldn't take it anymore, the film ends, the lights go on and the screen is rolled back up. Wilkinson comes forward, once again accompanied by Taylor. "Let us now present to you all the other agents that helped with the most recent operations." More than fifty security and police agents from England, Scotland, Ireland and France take place around the two Canadians. One by one, they are called by their names and thanked for their contribution to society with an honorary medal. "With the approval of their parents, let us now welcome the children that came back home with the help of these agents." A little more than a dozen children, ranging from teens to young adults come forward, shaking hands with each person in uniform. Every child takes place in front of an agent, all except for Josh. "We seem to be missing one, Wilkinson notices. Aïsha, you can come out now."

The child of four, with a doll under her arm, comes on stage wearing a beautiful pink dress concealing a fluffy petticoat. She thanks all agents one after the other, starting with sirs Wilkinson and Taylor. People in the audience just cheer at the little lady's attitude, assertive walk and firm handshake. Her long blond hair decorated by a pink bow at the back of her head enhances the tenderness of her youth. Being the last person to be thanked, Josh can barely keep a straight face until she arrives in front of him. He is already crying through a vibrant smile. She lifts her arms wide open. He pulls her up, embraces the child hiding his head near the tender neck, holding her so tight and gently starts rocking her. People in the audience get up to cheer even louder. "I dreamed of you." She confirms holding the doll under one arm. "Right before the police came to get me back home, I dreamed of you. Isn't that funny?"

"Yes it is sweetheart." He replies with effort.

"I'll never forget you." She ends before placing her little hand on the man's cheek. Like thunder, the words she uses, same as the ones he told the piper so many years ago back in his hometown, make his heart skip a beat.

"Neither will I." He whispers through a broken voice.

Putting her back on the stage, she turns to the audience, all smiles. A sweet, sweet déjà vu experience, so warm, filled with love, he thinks. There was no way he could not get emotional with this reunion. Lorne looks at his friend with pride, touched by the scene unfolding before him. Wilkinson takes the stand once more, politely asking people to sit. "If it hadn't been for Lieutenant Taylor, this operation would not have been a success. Without the involvment of the French security, two of these children would not be here tonight. The police force from Ireland also concretized three really hard cases of abduction. And what is there to say about the Scottish Bobbies, nothing but the best. Ladies and gentleman from the police force in Europe, please receive from the bottom of my heart, my deepest gratitude." All agents as well as the children, head for their seats under continuous applause from parents and friends. Back near Charlene, Josh is simply overwhelmed by the honour that he now wears on his jacket. His chin trembles and his Adam's apple keeps going up and down choking under swallowed tears. "This is as good as my black karate belt." He assures her easing up the mood of pure emotion while she just bursts out laughing at the comment.

The evening goes on displaying theatrical and humoristic scenes related to teenagers having troubled times. Later in the show, other law representatives get thanked for services rendered in the city of London, pinning down drug dealers and helping children on the streets. Chorus lines are presented, strong hearted poems filled with deep thoughts and lastly, a solo singer who fills the scene with profound lyrics. The fund raising event is a success and halfway after the ninth hour, the closing ceremony brings back Wilkinson who thanks everyone for being present.

Along with Charlene, Josh follows Lorne and his family out to the lobby where he decides to detach the medal and put it safely inside his wallet.

"Hey MacKenzie!" As if he had been called, Josh turns in the direction of the voice. Right beside him, a man whose golden age left traces on his face walks forward to the one who shouted and both shake hands with vigour. The young agent turns back to the group, eyed by Charlene who just finds his reaction rather troubling. Accompanied by two bodyguards, Wilkinson and his spouse approach them. "Everyone, I would like you to meet my wife Edith."

"How nice to finally meet you Mrs Wilkinson. Did you enjoy the show?" Lorne assures taking her hand. "It was perfect." Charlene follows paying her respect and Josh politely bows to the lady in her early fifties with hair coifed in a traditional manner. "Could I treat you all to a late supper? Jacob?" Wilkinson offers.

"It will be my pleasure Donovan."

"Mister Forge?"

"How about it Charlene would you like to go?"

"That would be great."

"Then the answer is yes sir." After consulting with his wife, Lorne gives his answer to Wilkinson: "I think we'll just head back to the apartment, it's getting a little too late for the kids."

"No problem Mr. Landers." Wilkinson concludes.

"Good night Uncle Josh." Josh bends down to young Marie. "Good night sweetie."

"Can we paint together tomorrow?"

"We're just off to have a late supper. Tomorrow morning, I'll be the one tickling your toes to wake you and then, if Miss MacRae wants, we could go to the Zoo and watch the pengouins performing their march."

"Is that a promise?" She enquires her eyes wide with excitement.

"Of course it is. I have never broken one, have I?"

"No, never." Josh smiles and cuddles her near. With an appreciative glare, Sylvia waits for her daughter to let go of the « uncle » who now turns to Bryan. "What would you say if you and I went for a little bike ride this week?"

Josh takes out an envelope from his coat pocket. When the teen looks inside, a subscription to a motorcycle driver's course with his name on is revealed.

"It's not even my birthday!"

"So? Are there any laws against gift giving in the odd season? Anyway, both your parents agreed." Bryan « jumps » over his uncle's body and hugs him like never before. "Oh man, this is great! Thank you."

"You're welcome."

"You're spoiling them." Reproaches Sylvia.

"I would never do that." He cuts short to his partner's wife. She was happy to see him like that, back to a cheerful giving person and not to a shaky and troubled man on the verge of a nervous breakdown. He smirk a happy grin in her direction before turning away from the rest of the group.

"I'll see you tomorrow." Exclaims Lorne before holding close his family and haling a taxi.

A few minutes later, right by Trafalgar Square, they arrive with a limousine at a place so luxurious that Charlene is unfortunately very uncomfortable. Far from being impressed, Josh is as nonchalant as always toward the setting. When they enter, Wilkinson is greeted by the maître-d'hôtel who obviously knows him. Two bodyguards inspect the place before letting him in. The cloakroom attendant lends a tie to Josh, a mandatory item to enter the restaurant. Delighted, Charlene takes great pleasure in helping at the finishing touches of placing the bow tie. "Don't put it too tight please."

"Don't worry. I have no intention of strangling you." The windows are huge, covered with pale golden tulle panels and velvet sidings. All tables are lighted with oil lamps, gracious cutlery shining on a dark blue embroided cloth napkin. Masters' reproductions are all around, representing the so numerous battles English military fought overseas. When they sit, they are asked for their favorite beverages and start conversing. "The trout is simply splendid here." Wilkinson comments opening up the menu. "Isn't it darling?"

"Of course, I'll have this and a « salade du chef »."

"Vous parlez Français? (You speak French?)" » Josh lets out after noticing the perfect diction.

"Un peu seulement (only a little bit)." Mrs. Wilkinson precises.

"Votre accent est impeccable, où avez-vous appris? (Your accent is impeccable, where did you learn?)"

"J'ai fait mes études en France pour obtenir un *master* en arts, plus spécifiquement, en orfèverie. (I studied in France to obtain a Master's degree in Art, specifically as a goldsmith.)"

"Vous peignez? (You paint?)"

"J'ai enseigné l'histoire de la peinture (I teached Art history)."

"Quel grade? (What grade?)"

"Majeure, deuxième (Second, major)."

"C'est très impressionant (Very impressive)."

"Ce le serait plus si je n'éprouvais aucune passion pour le sujet (It would be if I wouldn't be so interested in the subject)."

"Dear?" Wilkinson interrupts.

"I'm sorry. My husband doesn't understand a single word of French and gets a *little* frustrated when I use that language." Josh finds the comment amusing and turns back to the succulent menu, conversing again in English. The music from a duo of violinists is gently filling the background.

The meal is a perpetuous gastronomy of the best vegetables, finest trout, partridges and poached salmon with a thick white sauce, composed with at least seven fine herbs. The entire group but Josh, shares two bottles of the best French white wine of the establishment. As usual, no desert for him but the rest of them get tempted with a decadent « oiseau en cage », a clever pastry with a fine marzipan filling covered with a coulis of fresh berries. Throughout the meal, conversations are going well and all are enjoying themselves when suddenly a vivid outburst accentuates behind Taylor. "Bloody h . . ." The white-haired begins.

A couple seems to have insufficient funds for the meal taken and is arguing with a waiter. The security guards look around, finding the diversion rather suspicious, and rapidly see two other men standing in opposite directions, guns are flaring out. Both of Wilkinson's guards are shot in the rip of a second and at the recognizable sound, people start screaming. The first one dies instantly while the second is destabilized by a neck wound. Taylor pulls out his gun fearing that the security master is now becoming their target.

"Get down!" He orders Wilkinson while Josh stands up and runs toward the nearest of the two assailants. Using all his strength, he forcefully kicks his chin with his right foot, pushes him to the ground and starts fighting with him. The second hitman approaches to fire at Wilkinson, misses his target by an inch but strikes Taylor with a bullet on his right hand which makes his gun drop to the floor. After knocking down the first man, Josh turns to see where the second one is aiming and stunned, realizes he's the next target. The striker smiles and with uncommon ease, shoots him twice. Screams are heard again as Josh is hit on his right clavicle then in the right thigh, propelling him backwards to the surface of a table. His body yieldingly collapses to the floor. The second gunman helps his partner up and both men get away through the kitchen door, forcing everybody out of their way with his pistol still aiming. During the rampage, the lady accomplice sitting with the second gunman takes the opportunity to leave by the front door, blending in with the rest of the clients evacuating the premises. The entire attack lasted less than three minutes. With his right hand full of blood, Taylor is on alert crawling to seek other threats. He gets to the first security agent laid on the floor where obviously, nothing can be done, he hurries to the second and sees that his injury is serious but not life threatening. He asks one of the clients to rip a piece of cloth to improvise a bandage and put pressure on the wound. Ducked under a table, Charlene looks around and soon hurries close to a body resting on its side, in the western part of the dining area. Reaching then to Wilkinson, Taylor asks if he and his spouse are fine. Mrs. Wilkinson is trembling, her ears half deaf from the loud sound but she nods a couple of times, reassuring the Lieutenant. The restaurant personnel peek out the kitchen like little mice out of their holes. A few of them, just like the clients, are in a state of shock, either screaming their anguish or crying. Two of them fainted and one man suffers from chess pains. Dishes, food, flower arrangements and a few oil lamps are discarted on the floor with two broken violins. Remaining customers start putting the flames out using water pitchers. Blood is all over the overturned table and slowly runs to a deeper shade over the carpet. Afraid to move or touch the body, Charlene keeps calling his name more insistantly. The maître-d'hôtel tries his best to calm the clients, asking them to wait for the police before leaving but gets pushed away, some people not even bothering to take their coats, running out of the place. In the cacophony of screams and orders, the white-haired British gets up and from his loudest voice, asks if anybody else is hurt. Taylor starts looking around, searching for his employee and soon sees the red-haired leaning over someone on the floor.

"Oh please God, no . . ." Recognizing the rented tuxedo, he runs toward them both. Taylor gently turns the body on its back feeling dampness in his left hand. "Ask someone to turn on the lights." He pleads to Charlene. The demand is neither heard nor understood. "Charlene! Tell someone to turn on the lights please!" He advises again, insisting with eyes locked on her. For an instant, she is scared by the request, fearing what she might discover, but then gets up and complies with his supplication. Dark ruby fluid covers the upper right side of the young man's body. Taylor detaches the borrowed tie in a rush, rips out the shirt that used to be white, and brutally opens the coat. A bullet has hit through at the base of his right shoulder. The boss soon realizes that a second projectile hit his right thigh, in the center of the muscle and is probably still stuck inside, stopped by the femur. "Can somebody call emergency services?" Taylor impatiently shouts after overlooking the situation. "It has already been taken care of mister." Says an employee coming through the corridor. "How many ambulances did you say you needed?"

"I did not mention the number sir. I told them that there had been a lot of shootings."

"Call them back and make sure there are at least four."

"Yes sir." The employee pushes his way through until he reaches the telephone at the reception desk. Josh's eyes open a bit while Taylor rips the sleeve away from his man's shoulder as delicately as he can with a steak knife. Grabbing a silk ribbon used for the curtains, he ties it to his leg to restrain blood from spurting out from his body. Josh is fighting not to lose perspective, his face turning livid. "Did I get him?" He articulates his voice getting hoarse.

"Don't worry about it son." Trying to get up, something even more important flares in Josh's mind: "Charlene, where is she, is she alright?"

"I'm right here, I'm fine."

"Stop asking questions son and don't move." Without listening to his boss, Josh still tries to raise his head, his right hand trying to reach something, anything. Charlene inserts her hand into his but it's all frail and unwilling to close. "Dia (God)", he lets out vaguely while his neck draws backward making the air flow into his lungs more easily.

"Josh, look at me. The ambulance is on its way, just hang in there. Don't talk . . . just stay put o.k.?" Taylor says trying his best to stop the blood from gushing out from his shoulder.

"Soitheach, an soitheach (Boat, the boat). Tha mi faighinn air falbh . . . (It's getting away . . .)" Taylor squints at the words that make no sense to him. "What is he saying?"

"He's talking Gaelic, he's asking why the boat is slipping away!?!" Charlene reveals bearing the same puzzled stare.

*We were still trying to escape the militants of the British Monarchy.
Our boat was moored one nautical mile from the English shore,
protected by a dense fog. My oldest sibling had been shot in the arm
and we were to raise him up to the deck. The MacRae brothers, still
too weak from their detention in the upper tower, needed all the help
we could provide. I was the last to embark and in the turmoil, gave
in a rush my two sided blade to Chas for him to take on the vessel. I
was about to forget of my memoirs from the Abbey which I brought
for protection so I grabbed the sack in which they lingered and a
furious explosion broke the silence. The oar shattered into hundreds
of pieces, letting the nail that was holding it, piercing my right thigh.
My body jolted back with uncommon violence in the row boat and
my right shoulder was punctured by a piece of wood so sharp, it went
right through. Then, a second explosion, this one more precise, flashed
into the huge boat that was to bring us back to Caledonia. Part of
the upper deck was no more. The exact place where Father stood a
moment earlier, his mouth trembling from seing I vanish away unto
the ocean . . .*

KMK

Charlene frowns, salty pearls rolling down her cheeks,
caressing Josh's numb hand. The ambulance personnel rush in
a few minutes later, placing the stretchers near both wounded
bodies and the man suffering from chess pains. A fourth one is
in the lobby, waiting to get near the security agent who already
trespassed. Trying his best to stay poised, the boss moves
further away to let the medical staff work. Charlene has never
had so much action in her entire life and she certainly would
have done without it. Taylor grimaces at the sadness of the event
but tries his best to keep calm. "Who will accompany him?" The
paramedic questions putting thick gauzes over both wounds.
"Can she leave?" Taylor snaps to the police officer who just
came in.

"Yes she may. We just need a telephone number where she
can be reached."

Taylor turns his head to one of the paramedics. "Where are
you taking him?"

"We'll take him to Queen's Memorial." Totally uncomprehending what just happened, Taylor looks at Charlene. No words are needed while their eyes meet. Swiftly, she grabs her coat and follows the stretcher out from the crime scene.

Josh is embarked in a fluorescent vehicle with Charlene riding up front. All other ambulances follow with the injured bodyguard and clients. As soon as the ambulance doors close, the paramedic looks for a medaillion or a bracelet that will attest of a medical condition. Then, compressing both bandages, he takes Josh's pulse to seek any dramatic change. It doesn't take long for him to realize that too much of the vital liquid has been lost and he is fainting his way to death. The pulse rate is much too low and his head slowly drops to the side. "Hey buddy, don't do this to me. Wake up!" He urges the words gently tapping his face and putting an ice pack on the back of his neck. The grey eyes open to discover an unfamiliar face but soon a pain so vivid in his abdomen makes him squeeze his eyelids tight. Vital signs are beginning to go up and down like a roller coaster. All indications are leading to the conclusion of a heart failure while they arrive at the hospital ward. The vehicle is stopped in its haste and the paramedic hurries to signal to his colleagues the "red code" while the stretcher is pushed inside the hospital. Following her boyfriend, Charlene races in but is stopped by a nurse offering a place for her to sit as the doors of the operating room shut in her face.

There must have been a dozen police officers in and out of the restaurant. A restrictive yellow ribbon at the main entrance sets back the vultures with cameras while investigators begin taking notes and prints. After only a few testimonies, it is understood that two shooters were involved. A huge white line is drawn around the corpse of the bodyguard on the burgundy carpet and endless pictures are taken before his body is removed. The curtains are drawn from the sight of opportunists who rush out to sell pictures taken with their cells to the most offering newspaper agency. Inside, Wilkinson takes a sip and still shaking, puts the glass of water back on the table while his wife looks exhausted. He takes her hand, trying to comfort her but all of a sudden she thinks about her daughter and wants to make a phone call before the shooting makes the evening news. "Lieutenant Taylor?"

"Yes?" He answers abruptly whilst the cuts on his face are being treated, as was his palm.

"I'm Chief Inspector Arkin from the squad. We will need your version of the events." He sits back at the table where an hour and a half earlier, he was enjoying a succulent feast. Everything happened so fast, he keeps thinking but now, the interrogation was taking forever. Arkin is listening, writing all the details down, flipping back a few pages, repeating his question through different modus operandi. Taylor's version is somehow different from the others' when it comes to telling about the outburst preceding the shooting. "So in fact, you think that they were more than two?"

"This is what I believe. Maybe more evidence can be found on the surveillance cameras."

"The films have already been brought down to the station. Now let's go over the incident once more . . ." Even though Taylor knew exactly the reason behind the relentless questioning, to verify the exactitude of the replies, the white-haired British is without a doubt, getting annoyed by the insistance of being cross-examined by a fellow policeman. "During the exchange of fire, you mentioned that mister Forge replied physically but with no weapon am I right?"

"That's correct."

"Why?"

"Being on British soil, his license to kill needed to be re-issued but he declined it."

"Can you be more specific?"

Wilkinson turns his eyes to Taylor. All the British born Lieutenant could do was to look at Arkin, annoyed by the trail the investigation was leading them to. The Inspector approaches his face.

"I could call head office and have the answer in a few minutes but, I'm going to ask you once more. What made your agent decline his weapon permit? Arkin repeats insisting a little more.

"He went into a depressive state last year which provoked a partial loss of sight of his right eye. He didn't want to take any chances using a weapon. Does that answer your question?"

"That makes part of it clear." The Inspector writes again while Taylor looks away, grinding his teeth. Arkin gives Wilkinson, who is simply overwhelmed by the events, the right to go back home with his spouse. Two policemen will stand guard at his house for the entire night and other security procedures will eventually follow. Arkin then turns to Taylor and adds on the coldest of intonations: "You can take a little break but don't leave before I tell you so. I'm not done with you."

Taylor gets up, furious with the lengthy procedure and violently pushes the kitchen door that leads to the back alley, in front of a few whispering members of the staff still there. Rain is now pouring hard. Taylor screams his madness, kicks the garbage bins and then drops his back against the restaurant brick wall. Shattered, he bends his head down, hiding his face in the palms of his hands. Feeling the stare of someone, he lifts his eyes. A homeless person is there, in front of him, beside the garbage container and for the first time since his wife died, the Lieutenant badly needs someone to talk to. The homeless man, hands out a half-filled bottle which Taylor politely declines. He rubs his eyes, swallowing back his anger. "Lots of noises were coming from the restaurant tonight." The beggar lets out. "Three people were shot, including one of my men."

"Sorry to hear that. You care for a fag?" The man mocks lighting up a broken cigarette with a wood match and offering it. "No thank you . . . Why don't you go to a shelter?"

"Those jerks don't allow drinking and smoking." He replies with a smile that looks like a piano keyboard. Taylor takes off his coat and gives it to the man sitting in front of him. The pauper covers his shoulders with it as if it were priceless. "Are you hungry? I could get you something." Taylor offers.

"Don't bother . . . plenty of it in this alley." He admits pointing his chin to the waste container beside him. Taylor returns to his initial position, raises his neck and closes his eyes, catching every glimpse of rain he can as to wash his mind off from what just happened. "Angels are everywhere." Taylor hears coming from the improvised shelter. "I beg your pardon?" He demands lowering his face back to the stranger. Somehow, the homeless' voice suddenly sounds clearer, deeper and much more articulate.

"You seem to be disturbed by your man's challenges . . . did you ever wonder why some people suffer and others don't? You must understand it, haven't you been there yourself?"

Taken aback, Taylor shivers and now directly addresses the man who stepped forward from his lair. "My employee is a good man. He doesn't deserve anything like that happening to him." The British replies almost mad.

"Says who? You do? You think you have the kind of power that decides upon the fate of somebody's path just because you're his mentor?"

"No that's not it, he . . ."

"There are always reasons for events to happen. If you say that he's a good man, he will come out of it only for the better. God sees everything; your protégé said it himself."

"How would you know what he said? You know him?" Taylor supposes confused. The destitute pauses a few seconds, tilts his head just a bit, enough to make him have a more conciliatory appearance.

"Through our eyes, God sees everything. Your man has been *so* deaf to the call and « voices » are making him aware. Maybe he has one last person to lend a hand to before he walks on. Don't you think Jacob?"

Taylor shuts his eyes, poignantly compressing his arms around his stomach. His man was hurting, he could feel it. Realizing that the stranger was the closest thing to the truth right now, he finds the strength to raise himself back up, opening his eyes filled with tears of pain. The cardboard box is now empty. There is no trace of a cigarette butt or a half-filled bottle of booze. All he sees is his heavy coat neatly placed in the middle of it. The London born looks at both ends of the deserted back street. Delusion or hallucination, the large shouldered man thinks that his mind is in a state of shock, and escaped to a comfort zone, searching for some kind of answer. He walks over to the improvised shelter, grabs the woolen jacket to put it back on his damp shoulders. With a decisive pace, he walks through the restaurant's kitchen and approaches Arkin, still in the dining room. Bluntly, he snatches the pen from the Inspector's hand and starts writing on a sheet from the menu. "Here is my cell number and the telephone at the office. I can't answer anything anymore and I need to see how my agent is doing. So if there is anything that you haven't asked me at least a dozen times, just call me tomorrow."

He rips the page out and pushes it into his hands with the pen before aiming toward the exit. Before the Inspector has time to nod or reply, Taylor is already hurrying to catch a cab.

My body is weak, injured. The blast from the oar left such an immense
hole and the pain is beyond imagination . . . I'm trying to speak, get
up but, simply cannot. The water is slowly getting the tint of my own
blood inside the boat. The waves are bringing me closer to a land I do
not recognize. The rocks on the beach are round. The steep hill does
not bear the same grass as on the Saxon territory. I am afraid, restless
and cold but I have knowledge that I am alive . . .
I want to live, I want to live.
KMK

Adequately prepaired to receive the wounded, the closest hospital's personnel are already divided into groups. Through waves of sounds; Josh can hear someone telling him to keep still. The lights above his head in the corridor are atrociously bright, forcing him to battle to keep his eyes open and see what's going on. The paramedic from the ambulance tells the staff about the inscription on his medical bracelet and a probable heart failure. The monitoring system gives a positive cardiac tracking and immediately, adequate procedure is being launched. While all his clothes are being ripped with scisors that not even his leather belt can resist, his eyelids twitch and barely stay open. Someone uses a pair of sharp cutters to rip off the chain on his neck and takes off his earring in a flash. Horrifyingly, the smell of blood, his blood, fills in the room. At the far end of the room, a man of small stature is waiting; his skin is dark and his hair, partially grey. It's his father.

"His blood type is O Negative and he's got a strong allergy to penicillin. Verify if he has any kind of identification card that could tell us more." The traumatologist orders while checking the reaction of his pupils with a miniature flashlight. Knowing all those answers but somehow, being unable to respond, Josh lets two male nurses search for his identification and driver's license.

"I got it!"

"What's his name?"

"Here, read it. I think he's French." The doctor takes the cards, flips one after the other and finally finds the police force Identification card. After every pocket of his clothes has been turned over, everything is tossed cavalierly in a corner of the room. His nakedness makes him feel abandoned at the mercy of the strangers he has to place all his trust in. At the foot of the bed, Josh still sees his father. "Ne m'amène pas avec toi papa, pas tout de suite s'il-te-plaît (Don't bring me with you dad, not yet please)." He slowly begs mentally. The man hears the silent reply, and even though he has nothing to do with that fateful decision, brings down his chin in agreement and vanishes away.

Everything is an effort. Losing consciousness would be less of a hassle than trying to fight this compelling pain. I do not know these busy people around me, speaking not to me but about me in a language I cannot comprehend. Just as my clothes are getting ripped, I can smell something strong like metal burning. I can feel the strap attaching my leg to something, preventing it from moving or jumping. Someone just touched my face, fingers as delicate as petals of hydrangeas. She pulls back the blood thickened hair from the silver earring on my left ear, caresses my forehead. For an instant, eyelids open upon the vision of a muse, hair of gold and autumn sunset. The pillars on the ceiling are crossed and the morning light has barely begun. A rooster screams his welcoming sound near by. My breath is shortened before this man with an Irish intonation who places a wooden stick athwart my lips, right before a blazing weapon dips into my thigh to retrieve the oar's nail stuck into it.

After a suffocated scream of pain, everything becomes quiet and dark . . .

KMK

"Mister Forge, you have been transfered to a hospital. You have received two gun shots but they are not life threatening. I see on your bracelet that your blood type is O negative and that you have no other allergy than penicillin. We need to know if you have a medical condition before we operate." Covered by an oxygen mask, Josh's mouth opens and he tries to lift his neck up.

"No, don't move; just shut your eyes once for no and twice for yes."

Eyelids fall once, then another time.

"Contact the security agency where he works in London. Try to find if anything is written with his medical record and ask the reception desk if anyone accompanied him."

"The agency is probably closed at this time. It's after eleven."

"Try it first! He certainly had tests to undergo before being hired. I need to have the answer in less than five minutes."

"Yes doctor."

"And bring me back his hometown medical record also." He advises another nurse who rushes out the trauma room.

"I found this in his coat pocket." A nurse announces presenting a medication bottle to the doctor. Looking at the prescription, he believes the patient to have anxiety and claustrophobic attacks. Paralyzed by the shock, the victim opens his mouth but no sound comes out and his warm breath forms a mist of fumes within the mask. His eyes are swollen from tears, his torso is painfully rising with every heartbeat and, even in this turmoil, he still wants to know if anyone else has been hurt and tries to catch the nurse's attention. His entire body seems to be glued to the stretcher, immobilized while total strangers are working around him. After what seems like an eternity, a nurse comes back papers in hand and approaches the doctor. "I got his Canadian medical record."

The intern swarms in the observation room bringing the other requested record. The traumatologist reads both reports as fast as he can, then stops his finger on the last paragraph. "We have a male patient of twenty-six who had a nervous breakdown last year, lost some hair and partial sight of his right eye. His blood type is O negative and he's under regular medication for claustrophobic and panic attacks. Investigation from his present employer was about to be underway for a head scanner so we may as well do it now. Harry, prepare the room for a head test after the gun wounds surgery. I want the cardiac monitoring system to be on at all times, if he skips one single heartbeat, I want to know about it." He then turns his gaze to face the patient. "Mister Forge, don't worry, you'll make it." Josh flicks his eyes twice meaning he understands and closes them with relief. A stupid tear of pain runs down the side of his cheek bone, which is filled with splinters of shattered glass. Then a nurse inserts in his vein a clear fluid that sends him ten seconds later in Morpheus' arms.

Fourteen hours have slowly gone by since his admission. A nurse is checking up on the insulin and the blood transfusion pouch. The monitor tracking device displays a more regular movement of his heartbeat and gradually he opens his eyes.

"Hello mister Forge, welcome back." She teases to the man lying in bed. His head has been shaved and traces of crayon lines are visible. Only his goatee has been left untouched, like a solemn emblem of what he used to be before the shooting. Under surgery, the bullet in his thigh has been retrieved and both gun wounds have been cleansed and sewn. He has been strapped like a mummified relic, his limbs immobilized so they can heal faster. "Is my girlfriend here?" He questions with a feeble voice. "Yes, she's down the hall with two men. I'll go and get them for you." The nurse leaves the room and walks near a trio that has patiently been waiting. "He's awake, but still sedated. Each of you can see him but one at a time and only a few minutes." Charlene, Lorne and Taylor enter the room one after the other, each unknowing what to expect. Weak as a chick, Josh can't even tell Lorne how happy he is to be alive, make a joke about his boss' long beard or ask Charlene to stop crying.

That night, either the pain or the large dose of morphine gives birth to a strange nightmare that infringes his rest. Walking in the Ste-Thérèse cemetery, he stops in front of his parent's grave. Taylor pulls his own gun out and calmly inserts bullets into the slots. He flashes back the barrel in and places the gun over the funeral stone. Josh stares at the weapon, then takes it with his left hand and, very slowly, brings it up against his brain. The American piece is heavy and cold. He can feel the negative power emanating from it, how in an instant, a life' thread could be fatally terminated. Pulling the trigger, he wakes just before the bullet fires out. The thought of the revolver against his own temple makes him shiver and for an instant, he is totally disoriented.

Lying in the hospital bed, he realizes the reason for his being there and recaptures the memory of how he got the deserved right for the possession of a weapon at the tender age of twenty-one. He was a perfect shooter blowing cards out from the furthest point. He remembers the posture of the legs, a little apart, the straightness of the spine, the stiffness of the elbows, one hand supporting the other one.

He also recalls the stories of gun holes at the bank where his father worked. Through an unclear state, he recollects the tale about the nice lady cashier having a nervous breakdown and the reality about the mercy his father asked. Stories he heard from his bedroom late at night, when his father got drunk and told his Uncle Gerard, still come to his mind like a hammering of guilt. The young man's recollection of the sixteen hold-ups his father survived in thirthy-two years of service did not benefit anyone. Whenever the employees survived a robbery, they never received compensation or get an extra day off. Only once did his father receive a congratulation letter for his years of service from the Bank's administration office.

The young man remembers one hold-up more vividly than the others; the thirteenth was the most awful, violent, unexpected crystallization of one's worst nightmare. Josh, who was eleven at the time, knew that something had gone very wrong when the black limousine pulled up in the driveway with two security guards helping his father out. It was a Friday; he knows that for sure because they always had fish on Fridays, a

Catholic tradition. When his father entered the house crying, he fell into his wife's arms. She did not put her hands around him. His mother did not reply to her husband begging for comfort and sympathy. She was fed up and tired of this nonsense and knew it was to kill her spouse one way or another. His sister Francine, who was sitting on his right, got up, took the chair she was sitting on and threw it in the air. The security agent that brought the small statured man back to his nest, the one sitting next to Josh, raised his arm up so the chair would not fall on his head. The sibling went to her room, crying and slammed the door so hard that a framed picture fell off the wall. His oldest sister Carole having been called at work, rushed into the house. An expression of fear was written all over her face as she came near her father to console him. Josh just stood there, in front of his plate, not crying, perfectly still, this scene frozen into a time warp that would last until his dying days. The security agent asked him to eat and all he said was « no » on a very peaceful tone. The man that was twice the size of his father asked him again so the child replied: I won't eat it; I hate this kind of fish. The child did not show any emotion and took advantage of the situation to skip the disgusting meal. Everything was so unreal; it felt just like those black and white gangster movies. The child just stared at the two huge security men that brought his father back from one of the most intense situations a person could go through. Four men rushing inside the bank screaming, their face covered with panty hoses, shooting at anything that moved. The bank security guard standing at the doorstep of the edifice was the first to be shot. A father of four children, the man ever so proud to wear the black uniform and shiny badge died instantly. Shots were aimed at the ceiling to get everyone's attention. Clients and employees were asked to lie on the floor but a child of about four would not stay quiet. The robber turned around, aiming at him. Josh's father flew from his office and covered the child with his own body. The gunman pointed at his head but timing was getting out of hand. A « good » hold-up, as his father used to say, usually takes under two minutes. After that, the criminals get blood rushes and excited since they most commonly never act sobre. The robber cursed to his father that he was lucky they ran out of time. The police busted in and the amazing sounds of long rifles mixed with six shooters seemed endless. Two robbers were shot on their way out. Even when everything was over, his father was asked to rise on his feet but the sound of bullets still resonated in his ears. He could not understand the police asking if he was fine and the child he was protecting was brought back to his mother. The blood on the wall from the security agent and the robbers looked the same, red and deep, a brotherhood of fluids so far apart in their genes. One couldn't tell them apart.

A fortuitous ally, a youngster of fourteen saw the robbery before getting inside the bank and hid in the telephone booth near by, writing down the licence plate number of the getaway car which led to the perpetrators' arrest. The next day, headlines could depict the event with all the appeal of a writer's dramatization. Pictures of the bodies lying in a pool of blood were self-explanatory. Josh's father's name was not mentioned in the article but the location of the bank and the identity of the deceased security guard were divulged. An estimated amount of $200,000.00 was stolen during the robbery, a fortune in those days. "Un hold-up qui tourne mal (A hold-up gone wrong)." Could be read in the local newspaper designed to captivate a blood thirsty and sensationalism junkie population. The following Saturday, a week after the event, sitting in the backyard, his dad was still looking at the pictures, reading over and over again the article of a page and a half. "What happened to the kid who got the licence plate number, dad?"

"Thanks to him, they caught the robbers that ran away. As a reward, I asked him if there was something he would like and without hesitation, he said a bike."

"The bank bought him the bike?"

"They did not want to. They said that he was only doing his civil duty so I took him to the store let him choose the one he wanted and put it on my expense account."

Josh's father keeps his eyes on the newspaper while he frowns, disappointed by the bank's Head office ungratefulness. The man's hands are shaking while he tries to keep a cool face.

"You did good dad." Josh replies smiling at his father.

"I know . . ." He answers avoiding looking back at his only son, his third child.

While it was forbidden for a man to shed tears in those years, Josh just knew it was uncomfortable for his father to talk about the event so he gets up, leaving the man he placed on a pedestal to himself, underneath the gorgeous maple tree in full bloom. When he turned the corner of the house, he looked back at his father. The dark skinned man had placed his hands in front of his forehead as if to pray, his shoulders starting to quiver from sorrow. Despite his effort to hide his emotions, Josh just knew his father incapable of holding back his grief.

Exhausted mainly from keeping still in his hospital bed, the young agent welcomes the distraction of an incoming visitor, towards whom he pivots his tired eyes. The man with strong shoulders lets out a single brisk clearing of the throat and embraces his employee in the large circle of his arms. Charlene is right behind, her eyes red and her face paler than usual due to insomnia. "Wilkinson is grateful that you saved him and his wife. He's sending his best wishes but he's still in shock so he won't come and visit you for the moment." Josh's eyes glare back without answering. His body is placed in an awkward position because of the two bullet wounds, his right leg sticking out of the sheets supported by a metallic brace. The right part of his face still bears traces of the splinters made by shattered glasses that exploded when he fell over the table with all his weight. The beard covering is chin is somewhat longer but his shaved head gives him a fragility that no one is accustomed to. "How are Wilkinson's security guards?"

"The one who was shot in the neck is getting out this afternoon."

"What about the other one?" Taylor's silence doesn't need any precision.

He turns his head away, mad as hell when suddenly a sound catches his attention. "Knock, knock!" Lorne teases entering the room with his entire family.

Cheers and laughter are heard while Marie grabs her uncle by the neck, showing him a handmade get-well card. Bryan places an enormous fruit basket on the window ledge while Josh tries his best to open Marie's card, in vain. Seeing he cannot manage such a simple task with only one hand, she takes it back, opens it and starts reading it.

"Guéris vite, tout le monde t'attend (Get well soon, everybody is waiting for you)." Josh can't help to smile at the frankness of the eight-year-old and thanks her for the nice drawing of a cat sitting in front of a three-storey house. He has no idea why the drawing is comprised of a cat and a disproportioned building, but it's a sweet gesture. Charlene is far in the back of the room, trying her best to stop the tears from brimming over the edge of her eyes so he asks her over. "It won't be long before I'm out of here Marie, I promise." He reveals slowly and almost inaudibly before holding on to Charlene's hand.

"I sure hope so. I still want to go to the zoo with you." Swallowing laboriously, he feels so tired and dazed from the drugs that even though he loves them all more than anything in the world, he wishes they would all leave, all but his lady. His pulse is slow, as registered on the monitor behind him. The serum attached to his left arm drips like the rain tearing from the Londonian skies. Exasperated and hurt, he feels as demolished as the shards he inadvertently sank his hand into when trying to get up after the shooting. Even though he tries hard to focus on Lorne and his comical way to ease out any situation, all he can think of is the split second when the gunman looked up at Wilkinson, fired and then aimed back at him. He recalls the determined stare of the opponent looking at him straight in the eyes which keeps haunting his hippocampus. He knew him, he had seen his face before but couldn't recall where. The offender raised the corner of his upper lip before he shot twice with the precise intention to wound and not to kill. He recollects the burning pain in his thigh and shoulder propelling him backwards. The scene plays over and over again in slow motion in his mind like some defective movie clip that runs endlessly.

"So anyway, that's how we got the last tickets to the show." Lorne concludes as demonstrative as ever. Josh lifts his head, looks at his partner, drifting slowly from a cloud. "That's good."

The patient replies not knowing what the conversation was all about. "What hurts the most Uncle Josh?"

"Marie!" Sylvia cuts in.

"Its o.k." Replies Josh easing things down for the mother. "Come here." The child approaches the bedside where Josh can pull his left hand out to reach her.

"I won't be able to eat fudge popsicles anymore."

"Oh! Why?" Marie pleads wide-eyed.

"Because it will gush from the hole in my leg." Marie's mouth opens but when Josh weakly smiles, she realizes she's been had and playfully begins to laugh.

"Visits are over." The nurse claims after an hour, entering with a tray full of medicine and bandages. Josh makes a sign for Lorne to approach. "How many employees did you find so far?"

"Until now, seven people demonstrate abilities." Josh's eyelids are open but somehow, Lorne knows that behind that foggy glare of weakness, his mind is thinking up a plan.

"Listen, I met someone in a bar a few weeks ago, her name is . . ."

"Visits are over sir." The nurse repeats insisting on them ending their conversation.

"Yes, yes, I'm leaving!" Lorne agrees but immediately turns to Josh.

"The bar's name is Ladder's refuge and her name is Shadow. Contact her, she'll be good, I know it."

"I'll keep you posted." Replying with a single nod of the head, Josh then looks at Taylor who hides his worried feeling behind his intrinsic mask of control.

"Chief Inspector Arkin is the person in charge of investigating the shooting and watch the camera excerpts from the restaurant. He will be back tomorrow with pictures if the doctor allows him to."

"Sure." He replies to his boss, weakly lifting his hand for him to hold. Their grip, a sincere and trustful one, lasts a few seconds but the energy irradiated by Taylor keeps reminding the broken one the importance of friendship in such moments. The nursing staffs are aware that Charlene is their patient's girlfriend. As such, she is entitled to the privilege of staying as long as she wants and keep vigil. The nurse pulls out the invalid's left arm to take his pressure and counts the heartbeats looking at her watch. The red-haired lady is near the wall, looking at her maneuvres, checking her reaction to the vital signs. The plump nurse all dressed in white verifies the flux of the insulin and records the results on her sheet. She then asks an intern to move the patient to another position to avoid bed bruises. The pillows are moved and the sheets fixed with care and a little humour is told when the male nurse takes Josh in his arms.

"I bet you'll never be carried like this, not even on your wedding day."

For a moment, the tension is eased out until the sumo look-alike nurse brings them back to reality.

"Do you need anything else mister Forge?" She questions placing her hand upon his forearm.

"No, thank you, I'm fine." He barely whispers.

Charlene thanks them both before they leave and shut the door behind them. She contemplates her man while he keeps looking through the window, undeniably avoiding any conversation. His eyes have never been as pale as if their colour drained away with all the blood that spilled on the carpet of the restaurant. His lips are shut tight and his fingers sticking out from the cast tremble like the leaves under the cold rain again bathing the Londonian city. With the grace of a ballet dancer, she approaches and brings a chair to sit close to him. As he keeps staring into deep space, she gently takes his shivering fingers into her hands, hoping this contact will make him open up.

"When will they operate?" She inquires after clearing her voice.

"In two days." He replies after a while, surprised at the fact that she already knows.

"So that means that your strong enough . . . that's good." His eyes slowly turn to her but she couldn't see in them what she had fallen in love with. "If something happens . . ." He begins.

"Nothing will happen!" She almost shouts.

"Écoute-moi (Listen to me)." He pleads with an imposing tone of voice. "If something happens, Taylor or Lorne will get in touch with your regarding my last wishes."

She is now the one with tight lips but tears are on the verge of dripping from her warm brown eyes. "I love you so much." She admits between sobs.

"And I crossed the ocean to find the companion that is my equal. Someone I wish to grow old with so you really think that I'm going to give up without a fight?" Tears are tumbling on her pale pink sweater and her hand is in the one that tries so hard to squeeze back. Candidly, he pulls her toward his own body, both their lips savouring a paramount essence and will to survive.

Will you be there for me?
Would you stand the grounds that I walk on, raise your feet in mud
and water up to your chin to save a human being?
Would you put your life at risk for a total stranger?
Someone you never heard of before or have any idea if this person
would be worthy?
Would you plunge into darkness?
Sleep in the woods when insects would devour you, bit by bit?
Would you spend time calling me?
Screaming my name from the top of your lungs, knowing it might be
days before I would answer back. Would you endure sleepless nights,
searching, waiting, and hoping for me?
Would you?
Because for you; I would . . .
KMK

As promised, Taylor is back the next day with Inspector Arkin and a laptop showing all criminals still at large or individuals with a dark past. Nowhere on the film from the restaurant did they get a good still of the shooters. As if rehearsed a thousand times, both knew where to look so their faces would not show. "The first guy was taller than me. I may have broken his jaw and his right arm." Arkin starts asking questions about the incident but moderately not to perturb the patient any further.

"When we looked at the tape, we took note of the injuries you must have inflicted on him and a search in every hospital in the country has been going on but until now, there is no match found. The camera angle would not give any clues about the second gunman. Can you give me any details?"

"He was white, in his late thirties, but too far for me to see the colour of his eyes. He was also taller than me with a strong build and his hair was dark brown."

"We'll look at the tape again and enlarge his features. Anyway, enough for today, we'll let you sleep now." Arkin and Taylor are putting away the file and laptop but all of a sudden, Josh recalls one last detail.

"He smiled."

"What did you say?" Arkin throws coming back toward him.

"Just before he fired, he smiled. Maybe it doesn't mean anything but I find it odd. I wish Diane was here, she would draw him."

"Who's Diane?" Arkin claims intrigued.

"She's a colleague from the Montreal office." Adds Taylor. "She draws people's features with unbelievable accuracy."

"We could put her on the webcam so she and Josh could have a live conversation. She could draw and make modifications as they talk to each another."

"That's a bright idea; we'll be back tomorrow otherwise Head nurse Bertha will throw us out the window."

Taylor approaches and gives a hug to his employee. "Everything will be just fine." His hand was warming his shoulder and immediately, Josh couldn't let go of it wanting more from his boss; he felt weak, defenceless and needed him so bad. Josh's jaw hardens and he closes his eyes before releasing the man that hadn't slept for days.

On this boring, monotonous afternoon, Josh is lying in what feels like a mortuary casket, his eyes half-closed to the present world. The female goddess with such a sweet accent is right beside him, as she has been for the last six hours. How beautiful she stood in the light against the dimming grey sky that let a last ray of sun pass through stills of a nebulous formation. With her locks the colour of an autumn sunset and the warmth of her eyes she was the most desirable woman he'd ever met in his entire life.

"Parle-moi, je ne veux pas dormir (Talk to me, I don't want to sleep)." He pleads in a tone so low that he seemed on the verge of fainting. Charlene looks at her man thinking that the drug injected to relieve his pain is so strong that delirium is invading his thoughts. "Why don't you just close your eyes?"

"I'm scared, what if I can't open them anymore?" He expresses for the first time in his life. "Just let go. I'll stay right beside you and chase the monsters away." She softly murmurs. With the infantile presumption, he contemplates the effortless compassionate glance. "Stand guard for me." He lets out. To rid him of as much discomfort as possible, she takes out from her purse a small translucid vial containing a yellowish vitamin E ointment. Placing a thin layer on her index finger, she then rubs it gently in a sensuous back and forth motion against his dried lips. The soothing attention relaxes him as he stops fighting the fatigue and allows his eyelids to close toward a distant time.

A Scottish Highlander is resting in a hay bed being cared by a beautiful French lady with reddish hair down to her waist. The room is simple, a lavender smell floating about, a black rooster standing up on the fence near by, reverencing the day's dawn. Sounds of chickens and goats are heard in the backyard while she wraps his wounds.

"Je vous fais mal? (Am I hurting you?)" She supposes to the man who landed on the shores of her country. From his grey eyes, the Scot takes a moment to realize that he is not home. Desoriented, he looks at her trying to compose with what she just said. "I'm sorry. I'm afraid I cannot speak your tongue."

"Attendez un instant (Wait a moment)." She replies pointing one finger up and then leaving the room.

The warrior recollects the last events before arriving into this stranger's bed. It was improbable that the ship had turned back only for him and he was afraid that soldiers from King George I would hunt him down, even in this part of the world. The hole in his thigh started to get infected by a nail piece, wedged in rather deep. His right shoulder is excruciatingly painful, more than likely broken from the impact of the cannon blow he got when thrust backward in the small boat. A man wearing leather, hands as wide as a bread palette enters the room. Talking very calmly to the young woman, he then comes near the injured.

"I will heat up tools so they will be desinfected. Then, I will snatch the nail out of your leg." He explains with a strong Irish accent. "Are you a doctor?"

"No, I'm only the iron welder for this family. Your wounds look very peculiar and I doubt that the village doctor would keep his mouth shut about it. How did it happen?" The soldier hesitates before revealing anything.

"I helped save friends of mine that were in the London Tower and when we escaped, I was still in the row boat when a cannonball hit the oar."

"Nobody comes out of that tower alive." While they talk, the lady comes near with lukewarm water smelling of coriander. "I must have been rocked by the waves before landing on your shore. What is this place that I reached?"

"You are in France dear Lord." The fired tools are brought in a tray by another man and the owner of the house follows. "I know you will curse and hate me for what I'm about to do but one day; you will thank me."

"Tell me one thing before you cut my leg open. What is an Irish man doing so far from his homeland Éire?"

"It's a long story and I will tell you when you feel better. Just remember that my name is Doray." The warrior stares back at the modest man while three others attach him to the bed with horse's leather reins. The blacksmith brings up the hot red tools close to the bed side, looking straight into the traveller's eyes. "Are you ready?"

"All my confidence is in you." It was hard to believe such words when all I wanted to do, was scream. Right after a piece of wood is placed in the traverse of my mouth, the curve of the knife dips right into the limb, making all my muscles tense and forcing me to sink my teeth in until it breaks in half."

Josh opens his eyes in a flash. The nurse had unvoluntarily pinched his skin when she tried to get the brace off his leg. The patient's abrupt and jerky motion startles Charlene.

"I'm sorry about that Monsieur Forge, here is your medication."

There is compassion in her words but he was just another patient, one too many and because of his young age, she probably figured he had more chances of healing faster than others. Raising his left hand, he takes the small paper cup containing two pills, puts them in his mouth and hands back the empty container to drink some water. With a rigid face and her lack of sympathy, the nurse walks out and totally scandilized, the red-haired follows her with her eyes. As soon as the lady in the white uniform leaves the room, Josh spits out the pills and hides them in the flower pot beside the fruit basket. "What are you doing?"

"I'm barely touching ground with their pain killer injection. Last time I was this high, I was in my teens."

"Doesn't it hurt?"

"Like hell."

"So why don't you take them?"

"I'd rather feel something than be numb." Charlene cannot hide her worries while his head reaches back the pillow. "Just come here and hold me tight, this is what I really need." He softly begs. She brings herself closer, resting her head on his torso, her arms around his waist. With delicacy, he places his feeble fingers on her hair and kisses her forehead.

After two months of being cared for by the French lady and the Irish iron welder, I knew it was time to go back home. She was only sixteen and her father died in the previous winter of a lung disease. Knowing she was still a virgin, the Irish welder never had the intention of proclaiming her his wife to be. Now, since nothing ever happens without reason, I asked him to come and join me into the castle that served as a bastion for my family and the MacRae clan since there would always be work for such a man but he refused. The French youngster named Sarah was without a doubt the most desirable lady I ever met and plans had been made for her to marry a young apprentice in a neighbouring village. On the eve of my departure, I was walking along the shore, contemplating the waves when she appeared from nowhere and without further thought, I kissed her like I'd never kissed any lady before. After a sleepless night, Doray shaved

my head and disguised me with a monk's robe, after which I embarked
on a vessel meant to reach first the Irish coast and from there, board
another to follow the Hebride Isles to get back up circle around Skye to
the narrowing Kyle of LochAlsh. From there, I walked until reaching
Eilean Donan late one evening. There was weariness around me, a
ring in the back of my ear; a distant setting of clouds standing still
all around. Something I could not quite make out but knew of it to
be disturbing, my inner senses telling me to beware, be on guard. At
the turn of the road, I was greeted by a huge and undestroyable rock
which I carved with the emblem of the rampant lion, noble sign of the
Scottish independence. As I crossed the three-arched bridge, I silently
stood waiting for the guards to discern me from the fog.
"Who goes there? State your name and rank stranger?" A voice
shouts from the southern rampart of the castle while ten men aim
Mise with their crossbows.
"MacKenzie! MacKenzie of Kintail!" I replied pulling down the hood
from over Mo head.
"He's dead stranger, go away before my bow rides through your
cage!" He shouts furiously pulling the cord a little further back.
"He is not dead because he has come to hold his two sided blade that
his brother Chas brought into the vessel before being attacked by the
British."
"Anyone could have heard the story; you're a fairy tale raconteur!"
"Not if I'm the one with the six-legged star in the palm of my right
hand!"
I shouted out as I raised my arm out in the air and stared back at the
archer without blinking. At these words, the archers lowered their aim
and kilted soldiers appeared prudently from the heaviest oak door of
the western wall.
Chas, my oldest brother was the first to entwine his arms around me
and then followed Fran.
"Where is Father? I asked but by the look upon their faces, no words
dared be spoken so I closed my eyes for a moment before being
welcomed back home.

MacRae the eldest, Lord of the castle was the one closest to my father
Kenneth. When I approached him, he had almost lost all faith of ever
seeing me alive again and we both wept upon the loss of the master of

the garrison. Both his sons were too weak to ever gain back confidence into holding the fort so, with a document signed by them and himself, he designated my person to be the Seigneurial master of Eilean Donan over my own brothers Chas and Fran. Who was I to reign at the tender age of twenty-six when so many warriors envied the appeal of Masterhood? The old Seigneur-des-lieux handed me the sword of my fatherly predecessor, slashed at many places from the running of metal on its edges. Engraved at the handle were his initials, KMK same as mine. At the ceremony, MacRae insisted on the fact that my name had something to do with his choice of successor, something that will probably make covetous people think of him as irrational to have a different point of view.

The blade is heavy and the grip had to be adjusted so I could maneuvre with both hands. To be its next holder meant exaltation. To now be the one guarding the castle he preserved, symbolized the world to me.
My breath is his breath.
Your weapon in my hands will be less than the light that emanates from it.
To be the guardian of such a castle involves passion.
And passion can only be revealed with action, for words are nothing unless action is taken . . .
KMK

She lets her hand turn the paper over, places the pencil back in the cheap cotton case and closes her twin-pocket binder filled with the photocopies. So his name was MacKenzie but still, she has no clue of what is first name was and somehow, she knows in the depths of her soul that this man played a vital role in his time.

The second her translation mode leaves her mind, her thoughts turn to the man who crossed the ocean to end up in the hospital recovering from a double surgery and who just discovered he has a brain tumor. Half of a sigh comes out from her trembling mouth where words of anger and injustice yearn to be freed. Sitting close to the bed, her mind wanders off looking at the man who connected with Diane at the Montreal office in the morning to draw the portraits of Wilkinson's assailants.

After Inspector Arkin left, he thanked his boss and partner. Waiting in the corridor, she heard him say words like grateful, friendship and honour with a voice so weak, the profoundness she was accustomed to was even more amplified.

"Would you really consider it sheer luck for me to have been there, that precise evening, ten years ago on Mont Royal? It changed my entire life path because I met you both that night. When you brought me back home, you were trying to convince me that I was needed but I had doubts. As confidence grew in me, I vowed to God to save as many children as I could to repay Him and you for not letting me be one of the missing. I want to thank you both for being there."

Lorne tries to agree to the genuine revelation. Taylor looks at the wounded persistant man lying a foot from him. Pride replaces sympathy in his thoughts and Charlene, still out in the hallway, raises her eyes up to heaven, beseeching for someone to hear her supplication for a prompt recovery.

A few days after the shooting, under the pale light hanging over the bed, Josh seems peaceful. When his eyes are closed and the sheets are high enough to hide the shoulder blade covered with the thick bandage, he doesn't look sick. Under other circumstances, his exposed scalp could have been a new trend and the length of his beard the result of partying too late with friends. Pale crayon lines can still be seen on the bare skin of his head like a memorandum of the harsh reality. She stares at the man met a few weeks ago, the visitor who entered her life, the one who jostled with a different concept of wisdom and understanding. His lips are open, exhaling a brief and irregular breath. No one could have foreseen the outcome of the scanner he went under seven months ago in his hometown but the insistance of the British doctor of having a second examination only days ago proved him wrong. Charlene glances toward Josh's sleeping face and opens her book once again to read and translate in silence.

Angels, where are you now . . .

If I could, I would make you understand but forces in this universe constrain me to be silent rather than unveiling my position on a land that closed minds would never understand.
Only a few know, and fewer accept . . .
I languish for your arms to savour the rising of my spirit.
For your lips to reconcile with mine, for your hair to surround and wind around me.
Lie against Mo body, like the setting sun does with the vast ocean, Near me, feel me.
Don't ever let go of Mo sight, for I without you, cannot breathe, smile, nor live.
KMK

Exhausted by the qualms, she finally falls asleep and in the morning is waken by the Head nurse. "Miss MacRae, we have to prepare mister Forge for the operation."

She lifts her head and her hand releases his, which she has been holding all night. Opening his eyes, he recalls what is scheduled for him and has a moment of panick. Frightfully, he brings his left hand to his mouth and begins to tremble. Charlene steps out from the room to let the personnel bring him out. No one but the head nurse dares to talk, trying her best to put him at ease with reassuring words.

Before long, Josh is being pushed in the corridor of the well known hospital while Charlene walks besides him, holding his hand to infuse him with courage. When they arrive at the doors where two doctors and numerous assistants are waiting, he asks the male nurse to stop pushing his bed and turns his head to Charlene. "Please kiss me." He begs the sweet lady. She bends to reach for his lips and with effort, he places his trembling fingers upon her cheek. He then pulls her slowly so their foreheads touch one another as he whispers "Je t'aime tellement (I love you so much)." The trembling of his hands disappears and with determination, he can now face what he's been dreading. "I'm ready." He announces to the male nurse, who immediately pushes the stretcher to the sanitizing station, forcing Charlene to let go. A classical music tape is put on and Josh asks the nurse beside him to place both his crosses near him. Complying with his request, she seizes the disinfected items to rest them in a metallic tray beside the operating table. Two brain surgeons and their team of assistants are scheduled to perform the operation that will take at least half of the day. Charlene looks at the doors shut tight without moving, barely breathing. A touch on her shoulder makes her turn around. "You need company?" Enquires a familiar voice.

"Do I ever!"

"Let's grab a coffee and after we'll go home."

"What about your wife and kids?" She warns to Lorne.

"They won't mind. Let's get out of this place."

Chapter Ninth

*It is rare for humans to have no fears. Some of them might be vile,
others intense and paralizing, even diminishing one's quality of life.
Experiences, false moves, bad incidents get into life paths to seek what
we can accomplish and what we can overcome. My worst affliction
was to be considered a coward. Kenneth, my father never used those
words but they are the ones he heard from people who would laugh
at warriors when they spoke of the coldness of the blade on their
throat. Their mockery only enhanced his desire to retreat into a world
where he would live a normal life, where his spouse and three sons
would consider him a decent provider and not a victim. But first, he
had to find the jewels and bring them back home. Now that he was
gone, MacRae father spoke of him like a man whose journey had to be
undertaken by his legal follower, me.*
KMK

Charlene takes on Lorne's proposal to take a shower and some
time off at Josh's apartment. When she comes in, Marie welcomes
her with a ton of questions.

"Will they sew him back?"

"Yes they will."

"Is it going to hurt?"

"He will be under medication so it won't hurt so much."

"When will he wake up?"

"Not today, that's for sure."

"Marie, why don't you leave Charlene alone just a bit?" Her
father begs.

"That's o.k. I don't mind." The red-haired lady replies to the
curious child.

"Charlene really, you look frazzled. Why don't you go and
sleep for few hours?" Sylvia proposes touching her shoulder.
Seeing her hesitation about which room to take, Sylvia forestalls

her doubts and proposes: "You can take Josh's room. I'm sure he would be pleased."

Approving, she climbs the stairs to his refuge and closes the door. Her hair is still wet and she swirls it around just so it won't touch her sweater. Fatigue makes her shiver so she takes his police jacket laid over the back of a chair. Gently, she rests her body over the bed spread while her hand reaches for a cushion. There are no pillows on the hard mattress but seven cushions decorate the bed, each with a rainbow ray. She takes the mauve one, his favorite colour and with the movement, brings the colar of his police coat to her nose. Made with wool lining, it induces an aroma filled with nostalgia. His smell is there, a soft, demure personal fragrance that she can't really describe, maybe a little musk or sandalwood. Faithfully, the paintings are waiting around the room for their master to come back. Huge, wonderful, rendered with a sublime precision and yet, a vague halo of cobalt hues makes most of the background. The one with the nude man seen from the back is so different from all others. Executed in the Prussian's tints, like Picasso's blue period, the sombre almost mournful illustration brings a feeling of despair. The personage seems humble; both arms open, being at the mercy of a superior diety. His nape bended to receive an above light waits for something invisible at its source yet so present. Same back as her lover, strong shoulders, showing a paler fragment of the scar on his left side of his waist is shown. Did Josh forecast his vulnerablity in this composition, or was he praying, offering his own body and soul to a cause, she asks herself. A tear of loneliness finds a nest in the woolen piece of fabric which is brought even closer to her face. With abandon, she seals her eyelids and hopes that sleep will find her soon.

Under anesthesia, Josh has the weirdest dream. With the two shots already in his body, he sees himself in a Londonian pub with all his friends. Limping to the bar to get a lagger for Charlene and a mineral water for himself, he waits at the end of the counter to ask the barman for the drinks.

"So, how does it feel to have holes in your body MacKenzie?" Josh turns around to the voice of someone sitting near. "I'm sorry? Are you talking to me?"

The man hands out his open palm to the newcomer. "Oh . . . I'm sorry." He continues, drawing back the large fingers and bowing. "You would lose your ability to link, wouldn't you?" Josh frowns, suspecting a monstruous prank upon him. The man grabs his dark ale and moves one stool closer. On his guard, Josh tightens his metallic cane, maintaining his eyes on the strangely behaving man. "What do you want from me?" Josh frowns.

"People are out to get you. You shouldn't use your precious gift anymore. You've done enough." He adds rolling his « R's ». The man keeps silent for a second. "You always have been attracted to mountains all over the world and now you have come to Caledonia to get answers. It's only been a few centuries that your family and mine mingle. The Tower, the MacRae brothers, your gift . . . C'mon Mackie; don't tell me you've already forgotten about us?"

"My name is Forge; I'm sure you're mistaken."

"Yeah . . . sure gorm sùil féidh (blue-eyed stag) . . . , you can't fool me with a French name. You know who you are and the real reason of your being here. Why don't you finish it once and for all? Find the jewels so you can finally rest."

The deep red-haired man brings up his left arm and tilts to the side of his head showing the inside of his wrist where a dragon is tattooed. Like thunder, Josh recalls the man tripping over him at his arrival at Heathrow, and with a different hair colour, one of the two gunmen from the restaurant. Josh speechlessly looks at the man disappearing in the crowd as if nothing bothered him. The music is loud, smoke is dense. With the same nebulous mind as when he smoked dope, without touching ground; it takes him a minute before he realizes he has to go back to the table where friends are waiting. "You forgot my drink Josh?" Charlene reproaches. He peaks at his own glass, smells it, thinking somebody placed drugs in it and slowly pushes it away with his index. Seing Josh staring out in deep space, Taylor ceases talking to Lucy, right in the middle of his sentence.

"You don't seem to be with us. What happened?" Josh raises his head to him, looking very disturbed and answers: "I just met my shooter's accomplice."

A clear and acute alarm loudly reverberates in the operating room, taking everyone by surprise. All heads turn to the device which lets them know the patient's main vital organ stopped. Equipped for any eventualities, the operating room is also provided with a resuscitation apparatus. Two metallic plates are anointed with gel in a rapid movement. "Clear!" The assistant orders before placing them upon his torso. The electric discharge makes his body rise above the stretcher and the doctor looks at the line on the monitor. Unpatiently he waits for thirthy seconds to glide down the streak of time.

In his mind, Josh sees himself back on the island of Iona, stepping out from the Abbey. Very little clothes are covering his body, a mere pair of jeans, his favorite ones and a kurta made of white linen. His wounds are both there but they do not bleed and hair covers his head like it used to. Barefoot, he glides from the Abbey to the house that sheltered Charlene and him only a few weeks ago. Her voice is calling him over, sweetly, just like in a song. Snow is covering the entire island and with struggle, he strives to reach his destination facing the strongest winds he ever encountered. Battling against nature's will, his body cannot compose against the elements and loudly falls to the snowy ground.

"Clear!" Repeats the doctor, this time a little louder.

Laid at the foot of the Celtic cross against the frozen surface, the white iced droplets pile up against his face and side. "I can't give up." He convinces himself but weakness prevents him from moving. Then, when all his hopes are gone, he finds himself being lifted by someone so strong that no efforts seem to be needed. Like a baby, Josh is drawn in the arms of his saviour to the shelter of the Abbey, at the birth of the stairs before the altar. A thousand candles provide warmth and peace of mind. Opening his eyes, he finds a man about his age, with arms the size of tree trunks, wearing a kilt in the tartan colours of blue, green and black. The bearded man looks so much like Josh but in a boor version.

"Dèan finealta (You'll be fine)." There is no tenderness in his gestures but by sheltering the injured body, it is clear that the stranger saved his life.

Seconds later in the operating room, a jitter appears on the monitor, unstable but strong enough to indicate that the patient will survive. The surgeons look at each other and rapid instructions follow to re-direct their efforts to the new priority.

The operation was almost over before the untimely cardiac arrest occurred, which was the one thing the doctors feared the most and could not predict what eventuality would result from it. After the incision on his head has been cleaned and wrapped in thick bandages, Josh is cautiously brought to an intensive care room along with the cardiac monitoring system. It took the surgeons and their staff fourteen hours instead of twelve to remove the malignant mass, which was the size of a prune. A few hours after his transfer to the isolated room, Charlene sits facing a window to be the first person his eyes will open to.

If life was meant to live with someone,
I would choose a companion who day after day, would make me grow,
enhance my abilities, and uplift me in wonder.
Like valleys and hills make the best of the surroundings, Mo life
without you would be nothing but a bleak and plain existance.
Day after day, you would be the mate who I could look into, straight
in the eyes until I reached your soul.
I need someone unafraid of road mishaps, deep ravins and sharp cliffs
to climb.
Day after day, I would praise your company, because of your unselfish
endearing, and would then become more than twice myself.
KMK

In the middle of the second night following his operation, Josh's cardiac rhythm changes drastically and soon, a nurse hurries into the room with an assistant, donning gloves, masks and smocks. From her chair, Charlene wakes and gets up in a flash. A doctor is called in; he arrives a few seconds later, also putting on the protective apparel, and enters the room rapidly.

Agitated like a swarm of bees, the medical staff commence some emergency procedures while the lady tries to peak through to see what is happening. The nurse pulls down the blinds on the window separating her from the alcove, thus cutting her from the commotion. Charlene's hands are magnetized to the glass panel.

"What's going on?" She asks another nurse outside of the room, eyes filled with fear.

"Miss MacRae please calm down."

"No! I want to know! Can someone tell me why he hasn't woken up yet?"

"Please, just sit and be quiet. The doctor will come and see you soon."

"No I won't! I need to know now!" She yells once more while being taken away into a quieter waiting room.

Taylor and Lorne arrive after being called by Charlene. Her face is white, almost glowing in the dark and with compassion; Taylor sits beside the lady to take her hand.

"The doctor has something to tell me and I don't want to be alone. I hope you don't mind."

"It was the right thing to do." Assures Taylor while Lorne approves by nodding while only a vague sound resounds from her throat. The doctor comes in and brings a chair near, facing Charlene.

"What I have to tell you is not easy for me . . ."

Like in a blur, they listen but don't believe the words from one of the two specialists responsible for the intervention. Taylor is listening as well and while holding Charlene's hand, his chin starts to tremble under the solemnity of the condition. Lorne's face becomes as rigid as a cement wall, his hands grasping at the chair. When the doctor is done, she gets up, leaving the comforting hand behind, and runs toward Josh's unit until she is stopped from entering by a nurse. Uncontrollably, she starts weeping, spluttering incoherent words while Lorne rushes to her side, just in time to catch her fall before she hits the ground.

A week after the intervention, Charlene is beside her man lying in bed, still in a coma. The transcriptions are laid over her lap while her left hand is holding Josh's numb fingers. His eyes are closed, his lips half-open. The movement of his heartbeat is weak but now regular. His eyelids twitch, a normal reaction and a proof of a certain brain activity. Seconds tick away in silence on the wall while she counts the graphic peaks, wondering if this tragedy could have been prevented from happening.

Such a simple gesture can be found in the kiss of protection, sealing what Mise felt to be the most valuable asset of knighthood, the power of belief . . .
A million miles away is where Mo mind is.
So far but yet so close beside the Love I have been longing for.
What more could one ask for?
The wind is brisk, Skye is covered with a carpet of snow, eagles are flying out to return to their nests, the fine line on the horizon, guiding to the sun, the entrance to rest. Bushes of mauve heather stopped at their growth, surrounded by wreaths of hollies clinging to the rocky walls. We had to get back home after another battle and knowing that the castle was near made it easy.
Like a friend always opening his door to welcome you back, Eilean Donan was there.
She, the one who saved me, was a million miles away, still in France. Every single note since my childhood is, with the help of Father Caspian from Iona, translated in the French tongue in fear of the British to stumble upon them.
As pages are showing a different face, the original is being burned just like the flame of her absence is consuming me.
KMK

Lorne enters the patient's room, his eyes as red as the Canadian flag. Charlene puts down her papers to greet him in. Their embrace, pure, strong and reciprocal of their common friendship, lasts a long minute. "Are there any changes in his condition?" He demands with a cracked voice.

"No . . . he seems to be dreaming though. They tell me that he hears everything and might smell too. You want to tell him something?" Lorne makes a head movement approving. "I'll be back in a few minutes." She proposes making an excuse for them to be alone. The door is closed and painfully, Lorne approaches his partner lying in bed while his face wears a tint of grey. The respiratory tube sticking from one of his nostrils, the serum hanging over his head, the cardiac monitoring wire plugged on his chest and the bandages around his head, shoulder and leg make him look frail, vulnerable but still, the partner takes a deep breath and approaches his long time companion.

"Hey Josh, it's me Lorne. I know you can hear me. I'm just back from the office. Everybody is saying hello, wishing you well and knowing that you're in the best hospital around. They also believe that you will be back on your feet very soon. The group is doing well and a few cases have been solved. Taylor is supervising the staff with his own methods but he came across some notes you wrote. He has trouble understanding most passages or maybe . . . was it intentional. Maybe you thought it would be dangerous for them to be stolen. He wished he knew what was on your mind at that time."

Lorne stops talking, bites his lips, pulls his chin up not to cry or let any sound of madness slip from his mouth. The scar above his left eyebrow seems deeper, like all those lines that recently appeared on his forehead.

"Despite all my efforts to stay, I've got to get back to Montreal and take over the office because the guy that replaced you just quit. Taylor will stay here in London and take over the group. Everything has been fixed with Wilkinson . . . I won't bring back the kids to the hospital. I want them to have a good lasting image of you. Sylvia is sending her best but cannot . . . (Tears are now shedding over his cheeks) see you like this. I know it sounds awfully selfish but please, don't hold any grudge against her. She's tremendously sensitive when she's pregnant."

Josh's body, inert and barely breathing, is laid in front of the partner who for the moment can only keep a minute of silence. Charlene enters back in the room.

"Am I too early?"

"No, no . . . I have to go." He indicates her still standing up, quickly wiping a tear away from his cheek. She puts down her coffee on the table and comes close to give him a hug. "I'm leaving for Montreal in a few hours." He announces his voice cracking up again. She nods twice. "O.k . . . ."

"I'll call you."

"Fine." She confirms with a smile. While his silhouette fades away in the corridor, his hand lifts up to take other tears away.

Lochland MacLeod, Master of Skye,
Irreproachable warrior he is, a true companion whom I fought
memorable battles with. Hair like a raven's and deep green eyes,
He was always the one to be beside me, argue with me or approve of me.
When I was hurt by the splinters of the oar that broke under the
cannonball, he felt it and screamed at the sight of my body thrown in
the back of the boat, slowly fading away in the fog.
Chas and Fran had to hold him from jumping into the water at my
rescue.
And when the second cannonball hit the ship exactly where Father
stood,
I knew it was best for him to stay on board.

Surviving to such a blow would have been nothing but a pure
miracle.
As I laid wounded inside the boat, rocked by the waves,
I could vaguely hear Lochland screaming my name, being held against
his will to come to my aid.
Without a doubt, I would have done the same.
KMK

"When a person enters a coma, most senses still function but are so dimmed that they do not respond. In mister Forge's case, it was provoked by a heart failure and the trauma of the operation but we could not foretell such an outcome and not taking out the mass would have been suicidal. Like an automatic defense, his body simply shut off under the pressure. Like I told Miss MacRae, it may take a while for him to come back to how we knew him and again, he may never be his old self again. Only time will tell."

Taylor listens without really hearing the doctor's voice and replies by an evasive thank you before heading to his wounded agent's room. The corridor is quiet in this aisle except for a sweet humming classical music. Nurses politely say hello to the British but his hardened face dissuades them from starting or holding a conversation with him. As he steps in the room, a CD device plays a more rhythmic music and a bouquet of flowers deploys a light scent.

"Hello sir." Charlene breathes out with a smile turning to Taylor as he enters. The Lieutenant kisses her on the cheek and brings a chair on the other side of the bed. "Good day. How are you?"

"Better . . . I guess. I have hope. Grandma and mother are praying every day for his recovery and so am I." He clears his throat, leans forward and joins his hands. "Jocelyn, this is Jacob. I'm just back from the office and your group is doing pretty good. We are up to eleven candidates but most of the notes you left behind cannot be understood, nothing seems to be in English or French so I have no idea what you wrote. Your document is quite heavy and I would really like you to wake up and show me how to comprehend it."

Charlene gives the boss a side look and then turns back to her boyfriend to seek any kind of reaction. A deep breath comes out like the sign of an effort.

"That's it Josh, concentrate, hear my voice."

Taylor inserts his hand into his, waiting to feel any squeezing. He then brings his body closer, touching his forearm. "Ask your guide to pull you out of this one. He can help." Charlene sees in this last sentence an opportunity she never considered.

In his mind, the young man is all alone in a dark tunnel, naked and cold. A light is beaming down over his head. All he is wearing is the cross on his neck and the smaller one with marcasite stones suspended on his left ear.

"Can someone hear me? Can somebody please tell me where I am?" He shouts.

A shadow comes over the beam of light. "Hey! Come back! Help me out! Aidez-moi quelqu'un! (Somebody help me!), Cobhair! (Help!)" He screams at the top of his lungs. He starts banging the floor because no walls are around, only a wet, damp surface and a hole in the ceiling is letting through a pale light.

"Tell me what I have to do to get out of here!" A faint voice is heard from above so he keeps quiet a second and recognizes his boss.

"Taylor Sir! Tell me how to get out, how to get away from this place. I need you!" He pleads.

All his muscles are tense. His body bleeds from so many places that it's almost impossible to seek where the wounds are. Still standing, he pulls his neck up, letting the frail light brighten his face and the upper part of his body.

"Help me . . . someone please help me." He whispers but then, his rage takes over and he begins screaming but this time with such violence, battling whatever is surrounding him. Fighting against the invisible, he soon realizes that getting mad is not the solution, so he drops to the floor, wraps his arms around his legs to warm his shivering body and starts to rock himself.

"Angels and Archangels where are you? My guide, please come forward and lean your hands over my shoulders. Rescue me from this torpor."

So many efforts yet, Taylor does not feel anything into the palm of his hand. The cast over his arm must be too heavy he thinks but Charlene is holding his other hand and nothing is felt on her side either.

"Son, I have to go back to work but I'll soon return. Everyday I'll be back and we are going to pull you out of this." Seeing the inert body covered in the impeccable white sheets hurts Taylor more than if a dozen of upper cuts hit him. The tall man rises, gives a quick kiss on Charlene's cheek and vanishes out of the room. He felt like punching, screaming his madness but none of that would have changed his employee's fate and he knew it well.

The dream continues into the young man's brain like an endless film. He gets up; running the best he can to what he feels is the north, seeking for other holes into this weird prison but soon, finds himself confronted to a wall of flexible matter. He punches it but the obstacle simply turns to its initial position.

"Let me see on the other side!" He implores as loud as he possibly can. Nothing moves so he pauses and adopts another attitude.

"Please, my Guide let me see on the other side."

Using both his hands, he forcefully pushes against the division and finally makes an incision. Pulling the opening down to the ground, he frees himself out of it. Amazed and totally desoriented, he lets one leg out and falls in a wet field. His body turns around to see what his confinement looked like but nothing is there anymore, no dark, flexible matter is behind, only five mountains with peaks filled with eternal snow. He pivots his naked body back to the north where lying at his feet are a pair of jeans and a white shirt. He picks them up, puts them on and barefoot, starts running away from the place that held him captive, going faster and faster until he reaches the cliff. Down below is a castle, gorgeous, preceded by a three-arched bridge. He recognizes the bastion he drew all his life and without hesitation, like a hunted hare, dashes even faster toward it. As if time stood still, he enters the fortification a second later. The whistling winds diminish and barely echo inside the thick stone walls. The entrance is quiet, lonesome, and almost scary. Climbing the stairs to the second floor, he enters the room where tall windows shed a light with the colours of the prism. His heartbeat starts pacing stronger; something intrigues him. The air inside isn't the same. The warmth of it is peculiar. Listening only to his inner feeling, he rests on the floor, exactly in the middle of the room. Crossing himself on his forehead, heart and third plexus, he breathes out. There is no hesitation in his movements. He knows exactly what he's doing, like a hundred times before. The left hand, the one which receives, is pulled out. His right one covers the silver cross suspended on his neck. Hushing air out of his lungs, the young man immediately deepends into a soothing state.

It was hard to search out for the children on this never-ending day, my mind wandering off to a swirling inferno. The dark entity scaring me off was again placing itself on my path but stubborn like people knew me to be, I again confronted it. My guide was there, not even asking to get involved, only staring at how I was to manage the situation. At one point, the sad, dark image of my fears got so huge, bigger and more powerful than I have never seen it before; I could only use what was

left into me to fight back, Mo faith. I ask my guide to stand beside the
three archangels, silent buystanders while I get rid of it. The sad ombre
letting me know that everything would be so easy if I were to follow
it, no more pain, feeding it with young souls. It was merely a fight
between good and bad, my beliefs and integrity against his.
I had to take it alone, do it on my grounds.
I set myself in front of it, closing my eyes, asking Father for mercy, for
all the anger I felt toward him but that was not enough. The shadow
asked if I wanted not to suffer anymore by letting go of my search for
the children. My answer was clear as the livid water of the
streams: Never.
KMK

Within the nebulosity of the linking state, his body slowly gets up and stares at the lettering over the mantle. So harsh in wording, as sharp as a knife, it was almost a throat slitting phrase: « Candide secure nec curo, nec careo » (**I without a doubt will not tear or remorse, no longer caring for you**.). Was it the end of a love affair or the declaration of a warrior to another? No signature is left at the bottom of the carved message. The words make him think about his own life, how he was the avid one regarding truthfullness as a main drive, being implacable with the scrutiny of treason. Being faithful to those who believed in him was probably his major personality trait. Slowly, his head falls to the left side, dozing off where his mind captures visions of warriors back from battle that resolved in many losses, grief and pain. His soul rises up near the window and as always, is followed by the silver thread. The season is the one filled with orange and carmine coloured leaves and dusk is the time of the day. In the courtyard, a warrior with a dark blue and green kilt is helping another man getting off his horse, injured by the sharp cut from a blade over the left eyebrow. Blood is shedding down his face. Both men walk in the arched room, followed by half a dozen other soldiers, survivors of an attack from the British. The young goatee bearded warrior isn't as tall as his friend, but his strength is as great. Soon, another man enters the room, the Irish iron welder. His hands bring in a bucket of warm water and clean cloths to take care of the soldier's wounds. Josh has his back against the wall near the panelled window, listening, without being seen as the spectator from another dimension that he is. The discussion is loud, the gruel sound of the weapons being hurled on the table and the traces of sweat and blood make for an everyday scene. The astonishing view of the brave warrior's weapons eclipse the conversation in his mind. The tall dark combatant being taken care of by the iron welder is silent, trying his best to concentrate on anything but the pain of the wound; he is listening to the present master of the castle. One warrior leaves his chair, certainly too high-strung to be a strategic leader. Excitement is making the flow of his words race. Trying to convince the audience to set up troops and invade England, all frantically engage in the conversation, all except the man with the wound over his eye and the one with the dark blue plaid, jaw forcefully shut. A lady with locks the colour of autumn leaves comes in. The French demoiselle that arrived with the iron welder six months ago, leaving her homeland and following the instructions of the Scottish man to find his castle in the Highlands is now here, in the same room. A rock, a simple rock with the carving of the rampant lion was to guide her to him. Everybody gets up, paying their respect and the leader turns toward his life companion. Her beauty is as ravishing as any sun bound day caressing over the heather hills of this country.

"Lève ta manche mon Seigneur." She assures him.

The wife, now pregnant, demands to the quietest of them all to lift up his woolen weaved sleeve. When she pulls out a piece of iron from under the skin of his forearm, he jumps. Turning to her like a whip, closing his mouth tight before any harsh words could be spoken, he turns to his companions of arms and listens once again to their complaints or comments. One warrior with a plaid of orangine colours takes out from the cabinet a bottle filled with amber liquid, fills thirteen glasses and brings the bottle back in the furniture so it wouldn't be exposed to any light. The atmosphere is dense as the in-between season weather outside, the Brits again took advantage of the mist; the battalion had once more been deposessed of other souls. The lady with braded red-blondish hair is about to leave. The man she took care of thanks her in French, looking back at her only like a lover would. She grabs the dirty cloths at the foot of the iron welder and inaudibly closes the door behind her. Somehow, Josh knows that the one keeping silent is the leader, the same man who raised him from the snow on Iona. Obviously mad as hell, he sits still avidly listening to his warriors hardening his jaw, while the youngest is expressing himself with too much arrogance. Still, the man in his late twenties keeps his serenity. The proposed idea of an offensive isn't realistic, the calm Seigneur tells the others as he gets up from his hunting scene carved chair. Wording from the juvenile Highlander toward the protector of the castle are harsh, ruthless, mean. "We have lost too many soldiers." The leader replies in Gaelic: "Do you want to send in women and children now?" Still, the youngest who answers by the name of Gaël insists and challenges, standing much too close to the leader. A single word comes out: "cladhaire (coward)". The one with the injury above his eye, Lochland, gets up and with a simple stroke of his elbow, pushes the presumptuous owner of Mull back into his seat.

"He's scared to touch me!" Gaël replies looking at the leader.

"Mise is not scared (I am not scared), I just don't want to be responsible for your death!" He claims with eyes of firing greyish blue.

The discussion is turning sour. All are hurt, tired and certainly hungry.

Gaël unrealistically wanted to defy the entire British fleet with troops that no longer existed. His words toward me were cruel, maybe painfully true. Still, Mise knew our stronghold could not be left to meet other companions near the Adrian wall. It would have left the door wide open for the Saxons to penetrate. Mise told him not to provoke another assault by teasing their grace. Lochland stepped in, concuring his voice with mine. The owner of Mull, young Gaël MacLean, could not be deterred so he left, furious.

KMK

It was not the first time that Gaël crossed the arched bridge with arrogance but it was the first time that the word "coward" escaped from his lips. The warriors were at a turning point for a reply but from two different points of views. The protector of the castle asks all his allies to leave and would seek each of them for another meeting, evaluating what could be permitted, if Gaël's idea was pure greed or not.

When all are gone and the oak door is closed on its hinges, only he and the iron welder are left in the room. Both face each other and the place becomes silent again, only the crackling of wood blazing in the fireplace is heard.

"Should anything happen to me, I wish you to be the one to take care of my wife. You can ask Lochland to guide you out of the country. He will know the way."

"On my honour, I swear I will bring her to safety." The iron welder promises before bowing and walking out, letting the leader to himself and his shadow. Very muscular and blessed with the torso of a powerful warrior, the man with the sculpted cheek bones approaches the light of the fireplace holding his tin cup filled with Scotch. He removes his woolen shirt revealing a black leather cord from which hangs a cross made of two horse shoe nails spliced together, embellished by bright incrusted marcasite stones. His head tilts down as he looks at another injury he hid from his soldiers and wife. Badly inflicted on his left rib cage, almost piercing through to the back, the wound is flooded by the flow of the amber liquid. The burning feeling of alcohol on the torn flesh makes him jerk from pain and breathe rapidly. His muscles tense up and without warning he walks back to the table and hits it so hard that the heavy chandelier falls on its side, breaking most of the beeswax candles. Josh lifts his sweater to see the scar he was born with; same length, same position. The warrior sits back in the engraved wooden chair and joins his hands together, sweat pearling on his forehead. Elbows resting on the thick surface, he bends down his head upon his blood scuffled knuckles. Through his linking, Josh approaches the table and sits in front of him. The warrior pulls his head up and for a second, gazes into the invisible. The castle master's eyes are as ice blue as can be. Sharp, revealing a lot, same as the young Canadian. The warrior moves his right hand forward, presenting it to the one almost three centuries younger than he is. "Cumhachd an bileag-fheòir troimh an beothaich, Luceo non uro." (Reach the blade through the fire. I shine thus not burn)."

"What is your name?" Josh begins tempting the vision.

"I wear many: Blue-eyed stag is one of them. My friends call me Kreg which means rock and to the British, I'm the most arrogant . . . I'm MacKenzie of Kintail."

The leader's features are the same as his. Hair dark and weavy, jaw cut with a sharp edge, lips as full and sensual as can be. Across the thick oak table, both link to one another, to the grasp of confidence and belief in infinite protection. The warrior's insisting stare is penetrating through Josh's soul. The young man looks down at the pendant around his neck, in the middle lays the cross given by his mother. He instinctively touches his left ear now bare.

When his eyes glared into mine, Mise knew something fantastic
happened, an unprecedented event. He and I finally met.
KMK

The inside of Josh's head swirls like the outside wind, whipping hard its madness against the windows. For the first time since the operation, he opens his eyes with ease and sees Charlene sleeping beside the bed, her head gently resting upon the sheets beside his leg. He tries to make a sound but nothing seems to come out so he moves his hand toward her and with unparalleled pleasure caresses the softness of her face. For a second, Charlene savours the stroke before waking up "Oh Lord, you're back!" She exclaims with joy but as her sentence ends, his head abruptly falls back against the pillow and the limbs become numb once more. "Josh, wake up! Please my love, please . . ." She pleads crying, pushing the alarm button to advise the personnel of the brief coma interruption.

I will not capitulate . . . I will never surrender . . .
Those words are not the ones engraved on the fireplace mantel, but
Mise will observe and set the example.
If God would not have wanted me to recover the stones,
He surely would not have given me the « sight ».

Mise will stretch my hand toward them, all thirteen of them, the
young and the old ones.
Mise will, always.
KMK

After this brief awakening, he finds himself back in the fields at sunset. Someone is on the bridge, a Highlander standing tall on his horse, his shoulders enduring the skies' fierce blow without complaint. Josh blinks and with respect, lifts his right hand up to the warrior's reply, assuring him of his will to be faithful, no matter what.

Don't ever turn your sight from the past if not to learn from it . . .
Watch over Mise, bring my body closer and hold my hand.
Guide my path so I will not fall or tremble in front of shadows.
Let the wind bring my flesh to the vast cities over the continents, over
the blue hair of the deep seas, around the mountain tops and
under the clouds.
Never quit; never abandon.

Should I ever cease to find my way home, please let it be you that I see
at the end of the tunnel, guiding mo soul, reaching for your fingers,
making mo sword a useless ornament that should linger and collect
dust on a stone wall.
Mo blade should be waiting inside an empty castle that no longer
needs soldiers to protect it from the enemy . . .
KMK

The next day, Josh's pulse is again very low as if the strain he put into waking a few seconds took all his energy. He feels his mind being drawned back to Iona. Gliding above the ground, he enters the Abbcy and closes the door behind him. Snow is hailing on the side windows. Over his shoulders, a light white shirt is opened a few notches. Suspended on his neck, the silver cross can be seen and on his left ear, the smaller cross is hung. Wearing an old pair of jeans with holes at the knees, he walks toward the altar. No parts of his body hurt anymore, steps are light, effortless. His breath sends misty puffs in the humid air; no one is inside the sanctuary but him. Closing his eyes, he spreads his arms and begins praying. A simple invocation containing one single verse asking redemption for all his past faults, whatever they might be. For a second, he could have sworn that a tearing, metallic sound had broken the silence so he opens his eyes. The stained glass window bearing the image of Saint George killing the dragon beast appears. Curious as always, he approaches one step at a time. Much to his surprise, the art work turns to him, the Saint pulls the heavy lance out from the monster who gives a last breath of life. Weapon aimed at the young man, the armoured representation pulls his arm back, and with an uncommon force, throws it right into his sternum. Violent sparks of flames gush from it and through a scream, propels with rage the mortal penitent backwards on the floor. In his life, many times did the young agent get scared; rubbing elbows with death but this was another experience all together. It was the incomprehensible, something like standing at the edge of the universe, looking at boats sinking down into a long flat precipice like people figured the edge of the world would be. Saint George is still attempting to his life by throwing spheres of fire in his direction. Having nothing to protect himself from the menace, he dashes out of the Abbey in the damp Scottish winter to seek refuge with the huge Celtic cross and breathe a little easier. Because of the blistering wind, his hair is being tormented as much as the nude branches from the rare bushes. The light white shirt over his body is waving like a flag on the main mast of a vessel. The day is dark and the culminent murmuring of the Hebridean airstream is silencing all other sounds. He knows he had gone too far when Lorne warned him so many times not to drift as a solitaire into that dimension but, like a child at the candy store, never could he get enough. His rib cage holding the precious organ hurts like crazy. With his arms, he tries to pull himself up again but falls right back, both hands and knees sunk in the snow but awkwardly, his body doesn't feel the cold anymore. Only his heartbeat diminishes in his ears, like the dying pounding of a drum, slowly distancing itself with the sound of the waves crashing on Marthyr's Bay. Without resistance, he abandons himself down, unable to fight anymore. Then a hand, rugged and strong, places itself under his body lifting him up once again from the frozen ground.

"The heartbeat is back to normal." Confirms the nurse looking at the monitor.

The patient can't talk, he's too weak and both his eyes are tightly shut. Charlene hushes words of encouragement. "C'mon Josh, fight back, you can do it." Her hands are joined before her lips so no one can hear what she's saying. Seven months have gone by since the shooting and spending her time between the University and the hospital, she knew that this was the first of many steps for him to come back.

Be my love, for there is nothing else in the world that I cherish more.
Before you, I was only surviving.
With you, I am living.
After you,
I will be fading.
KMK

The following day, late in the evening, the telephone rings in the Montreal suburb. Lorne answers and cheerfully talks to Taylor when suddenly, his expression changes and his legs become so weak that he has to sit. The children raise their heads, Sylvia stops cutting paper dolls with her daughter. "Yes sir . . . . of course sir. Thank you for calling." With difficulty he hangs up and turns to face his family. His lips start to tremble.

"What is it?" Sylvia demands.

"It's Josh . . . he woke up. I'm taking the next plane for London."

Two o'clock in the morning, Queen Memorial Hospital, central London. Taylor is hanging up the telephone and coming back to the patient's room. Charlene is silently translating the verses one after the other while caressing her lover's arm.

May your hand glide into mine for I shall be greeting you in a castle
where Love will for always be our companion.

Passion, passion, for you I will conquer all,
For you I shall breathe and only for you.
Lift me up for only in your arms that I feel welcomed.
Right between the mist at dusk and the clouds at sunset,
Kintail is where I will love you, make you my equal.
Forever and always, I shall be beside you in faith and trust. You shall
be the reason for Mo breath to compose of life. I shall be the one to
protect and never console, for I shall never willingly make you cry.
You will be my sole and unique lover and this I promise.
Mise shall bare the shoulder you rest your head on, when the sun
vanishes and lies down with the earth, when the stars fill the vastness
of eternity, when the waves become silent and all you hear is Mo heart
beating.
KMK

Charlene lifts her head from the delicate pages, recalling a conversation that took place months ago about that precise paragraph she asked Josh to translate just to see how much time it would take him. "Now, this guy was deep."

"He also killed without mercy." She assures verifying another page.

"Well maybe he had something to protect." He adds without lifting his eyes from his own sheet of paper. "You mean the jewels?" She suggests.

"I'm talking about his lover. Nothing else moved him as much and that's how life should be when you're in symbiosis with someone. I believe that only once in your life will you meet your soulmate."

It seemed like only yesterday he gave her that reply. Without any fuss, he simply sat on the floor, taking the sheet, not even using any dictionaries. It took him a quarter of an hour to do the paragraph, fifteen . . . simple . . . minutes. Whenever she worked on it, even the simplest of sentences, all her surroundings had to be silent, the door had to be shut and no one could speak to her. When her man did it, music was on, one hand writing and the other playing with his beard and he didn't mind being interrupted by incessant questions she would ask. Paintings were all around him like silent by-standers protecting their creator.

He gave back the translation wearing nothing but his favorite jeans and two crosses with a smile she could not forget. Hair messed up from just waking up, the rebel look of an unshaved beard and a coffee cup half empty at the side of the bed, she thanked him with a kiss and he pulled the sheet back from her hands to wrap her into his arms and make love again.

Taylor enters the hospital room and walks to the patient's bed. Without blinking, Josh turns his eyes to him with fright. "Lorne will take the next plane in; he's going to be here tomorrow."

Charlene places her work away and wraps her hand above his forearm where the cast has been removed. Just like the metallic bars over the length of his leg, the bandages on his head have been removed and patches of hair started to cover his cranium. Josh lifts his left index up and closes his eyes repeatedly. Charlene smiles back but cannot avoid seeing her man from a different point of view. The Christmas tree behind her intrigues him as all the wishing well cards and the numerous drawings from Marie. How long has he been there and what brought him to this place? He couldn't remember and by his stare, she felt he had every right to know. With well chosen words, the doctor explains the situation to the patient. All he wants to do is scream, get up, get out or run away. For the present, no part of his body is obeying his thoughts to full strength and only one thing is clear in his mind each time he dreams: a stronghold with an arched bridge and a warrior wearing a dark blue and green tartan welcomes him inside a picturesque castle.

The next day, at ten in the morning, Lorne comes in the room and rushes to Josh's bedside. He carefully hugs his friend, placing his cheek close to his.

He was like a magnet. People would cling to him like wet sand
over a rock.
That rock being me, also the meaning of my name, one that would
forever bear the rampant lion in his core.
KMK

"Oh Josh, I'm so happy you're back!" Lorne shouts enthusiastically but the one sitting in the reclined bed shuts his eyelids slowly, barely responding to the demonstration of happiness, even scowling to it. The blond agent realizes that Taylor did not exagerate when he told him that he had wakened but was crippled, something that may happen after months in a coma. On his way into the British city, Lorne couldn't believe that his partner was the vulnerable kind and that such a tragedy could never happen to him. His friend was a fighter, he had always been. Now facing the lad with dark circles under his vein punctured eyes, barely being able to lift one finger, he thinks otherwise. He smiles, taps him on the forearm and gets out the room in a rush as Charlene hurries to follow him out.

"I'll be back." She hushes to her man whose challenge is to move a single limb. Out in the corridor, she looks around. Lorne appears holding a ramp before the window at the end of the hallway. Approaching, she places her fingers on his shoulder. Lorne turns to her with sorrow in his eyes. "How could this happen? This is not waking up . . . this is worse than dying!" He snaps through tears of rage. Charlene grabs his arm a little stronger but Lorne talks again.

"He doesn't even seem to recognize me. I've never seen this look on his face before. I want to see his doctor!"

"He'll be here this afternoon. Now calm down. Josh is in a state of fragility. If you rush back in his room with this attitude, I'll be the one to stop you from being close to him." Lorne's eyebrows almost come together and his lips seal but keep trembling. Tears are running down his cheeks.

"Is he going to stay like that? Is he aware that he's totally paralized? Does his brain function?"

"I'm afraid that he is fully conscious of his condition." The red-haired replies truthfully. The long time partner brings up his hands only to let them fall down, demonstrating the inability to face such a tragic outcome. He shakes his head negatively and starts circling around. Charlene lets him engulf the verdict before moving close back to Lorne. "What am I supposed to do?"

"Give him hope, that's all he needs for the moment." She suggests with sincerity.

After being a few hours at the hospital talking to his pal, Lorne sits in a chair at the Londonian apartment of which he kept the key, gazing out the window, turning over and over a pen between his fingers. Oscillating between a shy sun and a pile of low clouds, the day goes by. A stack of work is waiting in front of him. One huge yellow envelope tops everything, the computer pivots a cubic screen saver while the phone flashes a red light beside DND (do not distub), automatically transfering all in-coming calls to his voice-mail. Back home, the kids are already in school after the Christmas holidays. Taylor walks in the room and out of the blue, Lorne gets some things off his chest. "All these years that I've been working with him, I never realized how much he's grown. I still think of him as a teen with peach fuzz, crashing his motorbike in a ditch, smoking joints and drawing on any damn sheet of paper available." Lorne's voice ceases, time enough for him to swallow tears while Taylor listens. He lets the pen touch the desk beside the pile of reports and then lifts his eyes to speak again.

"You asked me to teach him all I knew and a while ago it hit me. Just like a painter and his apprentice, I believe the student surpassed his teacher."

"In what way?" Taylor articulates deepening the conversation.

"I'm sure he knew something terrible was to happen because he planned everything as if he would not be there anymore." Taylor's eyes crease and enigma can be read all over his face. "I don't get you."

Lorne presents a thick notebook with a frayed cover and curled up pages, as if they'd been consulted and flipped through a thousand times. "This was on his his desk upstairs laid over everything else. All his notes about getting the kids back are in it, notes that you can understand. The USB flash drive he gave you was only a lure so I believe he feared it would fall into undeserving hands. I found this in his stack of documents as well. He shows his boss a huge yellow envelope with the word "WILL" written on it.

In the hospital, a small evergreen stuck in a clay pot covered with a red ribbon looks expired, tired and unhappy to be captured and isolated, just like the man looking at it. Winter had never been so bitter in this country and from out the hospital's window of the metropolitan city, the snow is piling up on the cement ledge. A bird, a common sparrow, tries its best to hide from the cold. Eyelids still heavy from mass injection of pain reliever, Josh turns his gaze to it. His beard is long, the skin is pale, the stupid smock is nothing but warm and lets part of his butt uncovered. His gaze wanders off to the surroundings. Wishing well cards from the Montreal's office and the co-workers in London stand side by side like a huge and affectionate family. A picture of him with his sisters in a winter setting is pinned to the wall. Another one of him proudly sitting on his motorcycle is next to it. Last spring's pictures in the Highlands with his sweetheart seem so far away but it was such a gorgeous day, you could almost hear in the distance, the capercaillie calling his mate under bushes of mauve heather. Another photograph gets his attention. Wearing his torn jogging pants, he is seated barefoot and shirtless. His glasses rest on the tip of his nose while working on his laptop. The huge painting of the three archangels is hung in the distance while the sun rays illuminate his shoulders. There, on this seized moment, he looked so natural and casual with his hair disheveled and his one-day-old beard. The picture was taken by his lady while most of the world was still asleep. In the hospital bed, he recalls the time when a splendid red-haired took the picture, still on the floor mattress, part of her breast uncovered. When he heard the click of the camera, he turned to her.

"What's that for?"

"I'm taking it for posterity."

"Isn't this picture a bit too indecent to appear in your family album?"

"I'm the master and you're my slave." She could have answered with a thousand other replies but the words she used caught him off guard. With the most amazed look, he stowed his laptop away, crept up to her with panther like steps, and jumped over the lady to tickle her until their embrace got warmer.

On the hospital bed, staring out to the memory that is slowly coming back to him, the off-colour eyes gaze in deep space. They don't shed tears and as a last resort, he swallows back a pain that escalades in his throat.

"Hi Josh." Exclaims a familiar voice coming near, placing back the blanket to hide the lower part of his back. Without moving a single limb, he pivots his eyes to the cheerful sound. "You received another card. This one is from a guy called Daniel from Montreal. I'll show it to you so you can read it."

She places the greeting card in front of him but immediately, his eyes turns away. Hardly able to fake it, she endures the rejection and places it on the table near the fading Christmas tree. "Maybe later . . ." She proposes while he stares at the volatile on the ledge.

"Someone is here to see you Josh. He's a very busy man so I think you should be nice to him and not roll your eyes." Josh shuts his eyes, opens them again without any concern for the last sentence. Certainly, he knew who was about to enter.

"Please Josh. He really wants to see you." She walks to the door and brings in Wilkinson. "Good day agent Forge." The British man says as if walking on hot coals. Only Josh's eyes turn to meet his. Wilkinson approaches his hand to the patient's fingers laid over the pillow, preventing him from hurting his skin with the protective bars of the bed. The man's cracked voice can barely stand the vision of the young paralysed patient. Charlene is at the far end of the room, mute.

"I came to see you a couple of times but you were always asleep. My wife sends some art books so you can read while you're here."

Choosing his words the best he can, Wilkinson places the volumes on the ledge, hiding Josh's view of the bird. How he wanted to tell him to move them away, ordering the guy to leave. Screaming that he did not desire any of his pity, to be seen like this, but he just couldn't. He blinks twice. "I think he wants to tell me something."

"That means a « yes » or approval."

"Oh, good, she'll be so happy." Wilkinson tries hard to smile, putting his hand on Josh's forearm still plugged in with insulin. "Just hang in there agent Forge. I'm certain you will make it." Wilkinson swallows and looks down before continuing. "You saved my wife and me. You placed your own body like a shield in front of us and we are both so thankful." Wilkinson stops talking a bit, lowers his neck, looking back at the staring pale eyes, two windows with a glazed reflection so thick that no noise could be heard from the inside of « his house ».

"You are one of the most determined individuals I ever met. Your stubbornness made you who you are and I know you will come out of this, I'm certain. Please hang on."

The young man fiercely sustains his stare but then, shuts his eyes trembling, knowing that the superior had nothing to do with the predicament in which he was now plunged. Hearing such a declaration makes the patient think twice about his feelings toward him. "I will see you soon agent Forge." Wilkinson concludes before leaving.

Out in the corridor, he mentions to Charlene that whatever the patient needs, or will be confronted with, efforts will be provided to render them feasible.

"Certainly sir, thank you for your visit."

Without any last word and truly shaken, Wilkinson steps away with his bodyguards. The lady turns around, takes a few steps to be beside her man once more. As if she was sensitive to his emotional state, she moves the book to clear the view of the window ledge. Approaching, she bends to kiss his lukewarm cheek, and a faint relief can be seen in his expression. The bird is still there, ducked behind a metallic pipe, dipping in his neck, shutting his eyes to sleep. Josh's eyelids close as well, sharing with the sparrow a stupid and imposed fight. The sky had turned from a pinkish beige tint to a somewhat cyan glaze in this January evening. It wasn't as cold here as his native country, where this would be the month when he would be skiing. In this part of the world, the weather was brisk but tolerable. Mountains would still be covered with a carpet of moss, rounded bushes designed with orange leaves, liatrids sticking up in the air searching for some warmth. Seagulls randomly fly over the city searching for discarded bread left from the urban society. How he missed the V-shaped flight of the Canadian geese, their wailing call, their unity, their grace. The sole thought that he missed the fall colours of the Indian summer leaves a bitter taste in his dry mouth.

After six more weeks, Josh's condition does not improve. The « locked-in » syndrome, triggered by a small blood clog running from the vein on the right side of his neck to the brain's nervous system, has become a burden for everyone close to him. The birth of Sylvia's third child is a happy event but still, sadness is taking over most of the family members. Back in Montreal, Lorne can barely concentrate on new issues and often retreats himself in his office, looking over the report of the shooting and pictures of the event he begged Arkin to give him copies of.

Taylor would often be going to Josh's Londonian office and the group would be called in for a meeting and a searching period. The results often differed from the preconized expectations and in despair, after thanking Mrs Long and the new staff, Taylor almost cursed toward the heavens for ravishing the abilities of his protégé.

Right down in Piccadilly Circus, the restaurant where Taylor chooses to meet Charlene is considered the perfect spot for a quiet conversation. When she approaches, he rises from his chair and welcomes her. "I'm glad you could come."

"It's nice to get out once in a while. Apart from the time I spend in my classes and at the hospital, I don't go out much."

"How are your courses?"

"Keeps my mind off Josh a bit but as soon as I leave the University, my thoughts sink back to him." A brief smile rises from his lips but at the same time, she shakes her head in despair. The waiter comes close presenting the menu.

"Would you like an aperitif?"

"A glass of white wine would be excellent."

"Bring us a bottle of Chardonnay please."

"Yes sir." As soon as the waiter walks away, Taylor turns to the lady. "So what will you have for dinner?" She wasn't really hungry but she could not be rude to the one inviting her. "Chicken and salad will be fine."

The waiter comes back, opens the bottle and serves a swig of wine to the tall man. After tasting it, Taylor approves and the waiter serves the lady by filling her glass and then the gentleman's. He then takes their order to soon walk away to the kitchen. "So . . . tell me what's new." He asks.

"Every day, they try to pinpoint anything that would bring him out of this state. Exercises, swimming, films, books, even provoking him mad but nothing seems to work. Some music has a relaxing effect on him."

"Let me guess, classical with violins and good old rock."

"Exactly . . . The doctor even asked me to get a little more affectionate, to see if he would react but that only made him sad. He keeps losing weight and I'm afraid that . . ." She swallows, unable to talk anymore. How she hated to be vulnerable, not up for this kind of turmoil, slowly diminishing her energy to concentrate on anything else. Gradually, she begins smiling, covering herself with an armour.

"Listen, I'm going to take over." He offers placing his hand over hers.

"What do you mean?"

"With all the vacation time that I have accumulated over the years, I'm entitled to a few weeks off work."

"I don't get it."

"I'll be by his side everyday, encouraging him, planning exercises, taking him out." Mouth open, she listens.

"I believe that what he needs is constant surveillance and I'm willing to do it for as long as it takes." Jumping from her chair, she wraps her arms around his neck, something that clearly catches him off guard. Surprised, he lets his hand tap her back comforting her.

"Thank you." She expresses through tears of joy but Taylor rapidly sets the record straight. "No . . . thank you for standing beside him for so many months. It's my turn now. Hopefully, whatever we have done and will do, will eventually shed a light of hope on his health."

For such a long time, Charlene hadn't smiled. Now, with this well-timed proposition, she was confident that the man sitting in front of her was the right one to pass the torch of continuity.

After the restaurant, Charlene walks back to Josh's apartment and, as she's been doing on and off for the last eight months, she takes a shower and does some cleaning before going to sleep. Moving the exercise mattress, a small piece of paper that was stuck between two planks, flies off to the corner of the room and she crouches to get it. Written in a hurry, the note composed of four Gaelic words peek her curiosity: An toirt cho trobhad (The giving has come). Was he trying to learn the language? She asks herself. Interesting, peculiar . . . that's the least she could say about her lover. His thirst to enlarge his vision and knowledge about so many things impressed her. All of his paintings are still aligned on the walls, so many masterpieces filled with enigmatic personages. Their faces bear expressions as if they were real and their hands show tension. Muscles are stretched and sweat can almost be felt. He was an artist in every sense of the term. How she missed him and would have done anything to be sleeping beside his warmth at that very instant. Tears fall over the police jacket she brings near and slowly, her head sinks before falling asleep.

Look at Mise; find in Mo reflection the warmth of truth . . .
KMK

Lying in the unwelcoming hospital bed, covered with the cotton sheets and weaved plaid brought by Charlene, he contemplates the stars, waiting for his body to wake. Realizing that he can not even end his own life, struggling to make some sense of this new challenge, his mind has time to think, evaluate what is now left of his priorities and take a step back at what had been done in his life, the worth of people's friendship and the epitome of his own accomplishments. Was there something to understand behind this immobility, a curve in space and time, like a worm hole diminishing itself through another dimension? If this was a higher calling, he certainly was not going to let the beast win, not before he confronted *it* again. The salvation of his soul was the culminating point. What was life all about? The depth of actions, most of them usually taken for granted, were now so important. He never sang his happiness, always thinking that doing his duty was never enough. Doubting that he had slipped in the wrong direction, he was now questioning his achievements. Maybe he was too shallow to accept other people's conception of life. Maybe, just maybe . . . Could he have been stepping too far and yet, not deep enough? At twenty-seven, he was at his own life's turning point, getting the wake-up call when most people died without ever getting it.

Drops of rain freeze on the window.
Only their outline can be seen because, just like people,
an aura circles them.
Surrounding me is life,
Just like the rocks that linger on the verdant hills, everything is part
of something else.
Just like any action triggers another, we are all connected, each having
an impact on something or someone else.
KMK

In the deep of the night, footsteps are heard in the corridor. He usually knew who they belonged to just by listening to their pounding. It was either Martha, the plump black lady with the most vivid sense of humor, big Jim, the ex-mason who was working part-time as a volunteer or sweet Agnes who always spoke too low. But the footsteps he was hearing now could not be recognized. The silence in his room is tense, heavy. Laid on his left side, he tries to make out the silhouette that's pushing the door. From the shadow on the wall, he realizes that it is a man. The large shoulders disrobe a heavy jacket, splattered with melted snow. The intruder places the wet coat on the arm of the chair silently waiting in the corner. Josh's pulse accelerates for he knows that this is not an intern. The personage takes the chair and approaches it closer to the side of the bed, near the window and slowly brings his hand toward the lamp to turn it on. The patient is following his every move, scared of his incapacity to scream for help when the man approaches his bed. "Hi Jocelyn." Taylor whispers wearing new boots. The invalid closes his eyes with relief, and then opens them to connect with his boss'. "The staff was nice enough to let me in after visiting hours. I went to the Montreal office this week to see the rest of the group. Everybody says hello and wishes you well . . . I brought something you forgot over there."

Reaching into the inside pocket of his jacket, he takes out a black karate belt with three purple lines. The white-haired Lieutenant knots it on the protective side bar of the bed.

"Do you remember how hard you worked to earn this? How many times you doubted your strength and then hung on just to get to the next level?"

The patient looks at the long piece of clothing then turns his eyes to the one speaking to him.

"You got over your fear of failing. You got over so many injuries and still, I only had to listen to your complaints for you to take on the next challenge. You won your orange belt with three strapped broken toes and when you had the blue belt to pass, blood was on the face of your opponent and it's only at the end of your exam that you realized it was the one running from your own knuckles. I was there. I was there every time you had a belt to pass, right beside your mother. I wanted to know how far you could go and never, ever, have you deceived me but mainly and most importantly, you did it for you . . ." Taylor bends his head, joins his hands, rubbing, squeezing his tumbs together. Josh examines the body language of nervousness and then, meets his superior's eyes.

"Your lady is up to her wits with pressure from the Council to go back teaching full time. So, I closed down the most urgent files in Montreal and I'll supervise the group in London only a couples of hours a week and name Wilfrid in charge. The rest of the time I will spend with you. I've got a couple of weeks of vacation ahead. If it takes longer for you to get better, well, I'll see what my options are. We're going to get through this just like everything else . . . together, you and I."

Taylor sustains his stare while Josh breathes hard, surprised at the proposal, unable to respond. "Do you remember the day you rushed into my office and showed me your first trophee? Do you recall your first words?"

Josh's jaw tries to articulate so hard without success.

"You said: *I did it* . . . It's as simple as this; three little words that can make all the difference in the world." A long silence settles, overpowering the density of the room. "I'm going to leave you now but, I'll be back tomorrow, and the day after, and the next . . . just so we can work together on this. I love you like a son, the one I didn't get the chance to watch growing and I won't let go until you get better."

Taylor places the warmth of his hand on the patient's cheek then turns off the light.

"Good night Jocelyn. Sweet dreams."

He grabs his police leather coat and leaves, quietly shutting the gloomy door behind him.

Chapter Tenth

From that day on, Taylor comes to the hospital every day, working out on his agent's physical condition with another therapist. He dips into the pool, holding in his arms the now frail body that lost over thirty pounds of muscles. Shaving him, constantly talking about good things in life, little things that the patient could relate to, the sun rays, the chirping of the birds, children laughing loud in a near-by park, day after day he accompanies him, hoping his presence can make a difference. Often Taylor brings the patient to a relaxing state, speaking to him softly about his business trips and remembering the most inspiring one, Tibet first comes to mind. With determination, he toiled to climb up the mountains and when he arrived on top, the view brought a flow of tears to his eyes. He had questions to ask, a thirst for answers about his faith and what he had to learn in this life. Only the Lieutenant had this way of reminiscing the past, making it sound like a feat, an incentive that could help you surpass yourself. Taylor looks at the monitoring system where the heart wave takes a more regular pattern and the weak man peacefully plunges into sleep. Taylor leaves Josh's bony hand to rest over his stomach and with a last caring look, takes his coat and leaves.

A week later, after a long and strenuous session at the gym, the white-haired care giver lays the young man in bed, tucks him in and wishes him good night once more with his regular Saxon intonation.

"You know Josh, apart from my late wife I don't think I've ever spent so much time with one single person. I intend to invest all my energy toward your rehabilitation because I would really like you to walk and talk again . . . It's really nice to have goals in life."

The young man stares back, wondering if the last sentence was meant for him or the person who said it.

As winter is slowly turning toward spring, rain becomes constant. If the farmer's almamach is to be right, it will rain more than two-hundred-and-eighty-days this year, on this part of the continent. Taylor turns pages of one of the art books donated by Mrs. Wilkinson so Josh can read on his own. Of course, he knew and recognized each painting but just like a memory book, it was nice to peak at it once more. Also being the connection between the outside world and the caged-in brain, Taylor gives out information on what they both achieve to fellow workers or family. Charlene comes to visit every week-end, giving Taylor a break, always bringing something, flowers, pictures, news, and of course, her everlasting smile. With time, she learns that talking is not always an alternative so she hops in bed close to him, holding him near and sometimes falling asleep hand in hand. In these moments, she feels that everything is back to normal but as soon as she wakes, the blistering reality bites. Nothing was ever going to be the same if her man was to stay like this forever. Yet, her motivation to stand by him is driven by love, not pity or duty.

If I were to invent a world,
It would have lavish hills the colour of your eyes,
fields drenched by a fall sunset, close to the colour of your hair.
At night, a milky way bearing the softness and hues of your skin,
would be swirled in by a spring wind and
unseal all bloomings just like your lips.
Just so I could taste you . . .
KMK

The bird outside the window is still captivating the patient so Taylor makes sure that nothing is ever blocking the view. "I think that Pee-wee here found a Pee-wee-ette!"
The common brown and white bird sympatizing with a female was now building a nest. The volatiles worked so hard utilizing the environment of the ledge and twigs, both hiding

from the wind. With the clement weather of April, nature awakens with buds on the tree branches, blooming flowers in a rainbow of colours and birds singing merrily.

"We'll go out today Josh!" Exclaims a cheerful Taylor. The sidewalks are cleared from snow and it's not raining. Let's bundle you up and paint the town red."

Josh raises his eyebrows, and double flickers his eyelids, approving. The older man bends, takes him from underneath the sheets and starts dressing him up. The veins of his upper arms are more evident than before, constantly being filled with transfusions. The overall skin is now saggy and pale, as if the patient is now twenty years older. His back is bruised from being in the same lying position too long and both his gun wounds are not healing up as fast as the doctor wished they would. Taylor tries not to pay attention to these changes that simply rip his heart out. After putting on his jacket, he gets help from an intern to place the invalid on the specially designed chair that traps his head between two heavy metallic poles. For security reasons, his upper body is also strapped at the hips and chest. Taylor places his legs on the foot rests, binds the woolen plaid around his hips and after all precautions have been observed, drives him out from the chilling place. They walk through the park, enjoying the sight of new leaves and green grass surrounding the pathway. Black iron fences surmounted by pointy tips, circle the area and for a moment, the vision of Saint-George and his fierce lance seen in a nightmare, cross Josh's mind. His heart starts beating faster, screams are right at the edge of his lips, so close.

"There we are." Affirms Taylor. Josh's dark thoughts vanish away observing his boss placing his fingertip on the door bell of a house converted into a store.

"Hello again, please come in." Claims an old man with a wide belly and glasses resting on his nose. A thick metal plate separates the sidewalk from the door step. The door, a double entrance with full hinged panels opens wide, making it easy for the wheelchair to roll in. Josh's eyes grow bigger as the store is filled with artist material. Bristle paint brushes, canvases, brownish clay bags, the smell of linseed oil mixed with candle wax. It was like entering Ali Baba's cavern. Taylor begins chatting with the owner while Josh circles his eyes around, thrilled like he hasn't been for so many months.

"Jocelyn, this is Mister Sutherland. I ran into him and talked about you. He says that he's got what you need to start painting again."

Listening but not understanding how that could be attainable, the one in the wheelchair waits and pays attention.

"We have a band that can be attached to the head, the hand, the toe or the mouth. At the other end, a paint brush or a pencil is fixed. The canvas is going to be on an easel in front of you. All you have to do is move whatever part of your body this thing is fixed to. Isn't that wonderful?" The salesman explains with joy.

The owner's conviction about his product is sincere since he had to go through the same with his own son, paralysed after a car accident. Josh's eyes are as those of a ten-year-old in front of a new toy. Taylor buys a canvas wide enough so that it won't restrain his agent's capacity, an easel, the band, paint brushes, paint and crayons. He thanks the store owner and just before they walk through the door again, the old man bends to the one sitting in the wheelchair. "Art is the door to the soul . . . but, I'm sure you already know that."

Josh liked the man, a little odd, but very charismatic. He wasn't just a salesman. He was a good listener, engaging to satisfy the client's need to the fullest. The shopping bags filled with the artist's material are secured to the back of the chair and Taylor pushes it back on the sidewalk.

"I found this store last Friday after dinner but it was closed, so I went to meet the owner yesterday. I hope you don't mind if we're to try this way to wake your senses." Speaking his mind out, Taylor pushes his employee back through the park until they reach the hospital where they drop off the packages and then head out again. He takes him to the Fine Arts museum near the train station. The access to the building is convenient for disabled visitors and quite welcomed for Taylor. Arriving at the booth, he inquires about the entrance fee.

"That will be fifteen pound fifty for the young man and, ten pounds for you."

"Sorry? Why is it more expensive for him?"

"Well you're over sixty so you're entitled to a discount."

"I'm not even fifty Madam . . ."

"Oh . . . I'm sorry about that. In that case, it's thirty pounds all together."

He hands a fifty pound note, gets back the change growling and places it back in his wallet. Hushing complaints about the lady's comment, Taylor soon stops to listen to Josh making odd sounds and walks up to face him. "Are you o.k.?"

Josh still makes sounds with his throat so Taylor creases his eyes.

"You're laughing aren't you?" The boss can't believe his ears. The sound ressembles a choke but still, it is indeed a sound. He widely smiles at the young man, caresses his hair that has now grown a little and walks to the back of the wheelchair to push it again.

The London Museum of Fine Arts, one of the finest Europe, is proposing a display of masterpieces from around the world. A special section is designated to represent the Scottish masters. Shipwrecks, storms caught at their highest strength, lavish colourful mountains underneath dense clouds letting the sun pass through and probably the most famous of all, Monarch of the Glen, a huge male deer painted by Sir Landseer. Taylor stops a little longer in front of this one.

"Isn't it beautiful? It wouldn't surprise me to think that the artist saw him, high above the mountains, scenting the wind for hunters. Aware of his luck to be on top, so close to heaven . . ."

Josh looks at it and in a flash, an image ignites the memory of when he was on his motorbike and almost hit one in the Highlands. Magnificence transpired in its every muscle and its gracious walk. Yet, it was sheer luck he didn't hit it, destroying such a noble animal's life and thus his own.

We were at the top of Ben Nevis enjoying a last moment of peace. The air was warm, laughter was in the air, good company was by my side and then it happened . . .

My companions of arms stood and stared behind me as a wonderful,
majestic and noble stag waited. I got up and approached quietly.
It would eject air out of its muzzle and stump its foot unto the rock to
impress me but I would not budge.
Instead, I placed my arm forward to provoke an acquaintance.
It backed up, raised its head and pretended to charge but I offered the
palm of my hand for it to smell, speaking words of friendship and then
it happened . . .
The beast licked my skin so then, I petted its forehead.
After a moment, it simply turned and went off to a further cliff.
Amazed and bewildered, I watched it wander into the clearing when
from behind, Lochland repeated to my companions the sobriquet
Father used to call me:
Gorm sùil féidh, Blue-eyed stag . . .
KMK

Charlene finishes the translation of her sentence, and looks out the University window. She had to go out, get some food but the appetite she felt was for something else than poultry or vegetables. She places the palm of her hand on her chin and sighs. His lips on her were missing. His kiss, sublime, soft, tender like nothing she ever felt before was what she deeply yearned for. "My Blue-eyed stag, where are you now?" She whispers, talking to herself.

After the thirteenth hour, Taylor walks in the cafetaria of the museum to grab a bite while Josh closes his eyes to rest. Unable to eat by himself, he had to be force-fed intravenously when they would get back in an hour or so. A lady approaches the quiet man reading the newspaper, sinking his teeth into a roast beef sandwich. "Sir Taylor?"

"Lucy! What a pleasant surprise. How are you?" He exclaims wiping his mouth with a napkin and rising to offer her a chair.

"I'm doing just great."

"What are you doing here?"

"I came to see the exhibit of the old sea masters."

"I had no idea you were interested in art."

"I would be lying if the answer was yes. I'm interested in the sea."

"Oh, how come?"

"Most of the men in my family were fishermen."

"That's very interesting. Would you care for a coffee?"

"No, thank you. I was on my way out and only came here to grab some juice for the road. How is Josh doing?"

"No major changes but on the way in, he laughed."

"Did he?"

"Well, it was mainly a chuckle from a comment the lady at the reception desk said."

"It must have been a good one!"

"She thought I was over sixty and wanted to offer me a discount."

Without hesitation, Lucy starts to laugh. Taylor raises his eyebrows at her reaction. "Sorry . . . that's quite funny. It must be the colour of your hair."

"You think I should change it?"

"No way! You're quite a good looking . . . sorry." She concludes blushing like a rose. Taylor enjoys the sparkling comment. "Would you mind joining me to take Josh back to the hospital?"

"I would be delighted." Taylor takes his tray back and the initial push of the wheelchair wakes its occupant.

"Hi!" Lucy begins bending down. He squints, and then shuts his eyes to open them to their fullest. "Nice exhibit isn't it?" She indicates to Josh.

He shuts his eyes twice. She rubs his shoulder in a friendly manner then starts conversing with the older one. "What have you been doing lately?"

"Right before coming to the museum, we got some art material."

"You got them for you?"

"No, for Josh, he used to paint a lot. I'm going to strap a device that ends with a pencil or a paintbrush. It can be attached to different parts of his body, forehead, arm, foot."

"And you think that it might trigger a change?"

"No harm in trying."

"You're definitely right. I like your optimism."

All the way to the hospital, Taylor and Lucy talk about various things, including work and personal matters. As the insipid edifice of the hospital gets closer, the high rank officer turns to the secretary. "You are aware that I'm going to be off work most of the time to be with him?"

"Sergeant Hockart told me. It's a very sad situation."

"Then you must know that agent Wilfrid Armstrong will take over the class and continue with the project. If . . . anyway, for the moment this seems to be where we are at."

The mature and responsible man was falling to pieces in front of her but still had the guts to ask her something that had been longing for some time.

"Would you like to go out with me when Josh starts feeling better again?" Lucy smiles before replying. "Of course I would like that."

"I don't know when that will be; maybe weeks and then again, it could take months."

"It's o.k. It's quite comforting to see caring people."

"So you wouldn't mind going out with an elderly?"

"Never." She smiles again now wider. She then bends down to kiss the young man's cheek.

"See you Josh. Good bye sir Taylor."

"Jacob." He precises.

"Good bye Jacob." Taylor waits until the lady's silhouette is no longer in view and enters back the too quiet surroundings of the hospital.

Putting the invalid back to bed was always problematical. Not so much because of his weight but because Taylor was afraid to hurt him with the fluid injection needle so, he asks for an intern to help him out mentioning that the patient didn't have lunch.

"Are you comfortable?" Josh blinks twice.

"Good night son." He concludes sliding the karate belt nearer. But that wasn't enough and as soon as the intern leaves the room, Taylor bends, kisses the young man's forehead, and caresses his cheek with his strong hand looking him straight in the eyes.

"Hang on lad; there are a lot of people counting on you." Taylor admits before slipping away. Josh closes his eyes and opens them only when the footsteps are fading in the distance.

My Father, you are such a dearest man with countless qualities. You sent me to Iona for my own protection and education but for so long did I miss your words filled with sapience. To the Britons, you seem heartless and to your peers, you are the fairest.
Even if fate separated us in this life, I long for another where we shall meet again . . .
KMK

For weeks, included in his daily exercise routine, Taylor places the band attached with a brush to Josh's forehead, hands or feet. Nothing was more horrible than to be standing near him, staring at the off-white linen canvas and even though the young man gets furious, raging his madness with a deep growling sound, none of his limbs obey his mind. Exhausted, he shuts his eyes trying to bang his head but even this is impossible.

"We'll try again tomorrow." Assures Taylor drained by the scene imprinted of sadness. Taking the strap off from the young man's head, he reclines the mattress back to its original position. Hands and feet are cold again due to the immobility so the boss rubs the chilled limbs. Josh follows the man's face while getting the warming massage. The words about his past are running like free water while bringing the sheets around the cold body and the woolen fleece of dark colours under the young man's arms.

"When I was in the army, I learned a lot about companionship, about tightening bonds, not letting go of a relationship. If something happened to a member of the battalion, it happened to all others. No one was to be left behind. When we were in a combat zone, many times did I think that I wouldn't wake the next day. On a mission when I was twenty-four, I hurt my back and was transferred to a more secure zone. That's where I met my wife. She was also an officer. I fell in love the second I saw her. Four months later we were married. It was a simple ceremony on the base with a few of our friends as witnesses.

When I finished my service, I was offered a job at the London Police Headquarters by Wilkinson. We knew each other from years back at the University. My army experience helped me to get it and he simply said that I was the first on his list of candidates. Everything was going great, my wife loved me, and we had a splendid son, intelligent and witty. But then, there was this car accident. He was so young."

Listening to each word, Josh's eyes are a little more blue than grey, today. Taylor tries not to get too emotional but somehow cannot remain indifferent to the subject.

"When they died, I couldn't work, couldn't think about anything else. Walking into our house was scorching my heart out so Wilkinson called me to meet with him, proposed to sell the house and work in Canada saying there was an opening. He gave me a week to think about it. Leaving London was not easy but I saw this as an opportunity to start anew. The first time I met Lorne; he was a police agent on the road and clearly hated his job. I felt in him something so powerful just like I did when I saw you. I had some reluctance about your young age but Lorne convinced me and thank God I did listen to him. You have something so few people would stand a chance to develop or use wisely. The three of us have gifts that we cannot dare pass under silence. Whenever I have visions again, I think of the day when you were sitting at the station, and you were thinking that seeing people's aura was due to the fact that you had a little too much dope . . ."

Taylor starts smiling. Sitting by the side of the bed, he really looked awesome. Shoulders never bending, his strong and rigid features making him a person you could really trust.

". . . How far have we gone you and me? What if we never moved each other to go forward? Do you have any idea of the impact you had on *my* life?"

Josh's eyes look back, his brain capturing the substance of the testimony. Never did his own father talk to him this way. Never, did he tell him that he was important in his life, never did he feel so responsible for the rising of a man's uniqueness. Taylor holds Josh's hand now almost skeletal.

"You saved me and I want to thank you for it." The white-haired man indicates.

If there was a moment when Josh wanted to smile, this surely was one.

I never could have been the person I am now if I had not been surrounded by Father, MacRae elder, MacRae sons, Lochland, Gaël and so many others.
Brothers Chas and Fran appeared in my life as a challenge, last but not least, the iron welder who saved me from poisoning myself when injured and eventually brought Sarah, my wife to be.
Even if I am unique, I am composed of many.
KMK

On that same evening, Josh is sound asleep when a furious storm breaks and rain starts pouring down madly against the window. Thunder strikes near making the ground shake, waking him in a jump. All of a sudden, a burning feeling rises from his toes, slowly ascending to his thighs. Like a fire within, it catches up to his stomach making his body heat rise up fast, then reaches his arms, his fingers, his throat. He jerks his head backward in a sudden reflex, opens his mouth and stares around him with frightened eyes. Unintentionally, he lets out a sound of surprise, almost of fear. A strong shiver races through his spine, along the heat sensation that leaves him breathless. Lifting his neck from the inclined mattress, he looks at both his fists clenching the woolen plaid. Lightning is projecting its blinding power into the quiet room. Slowly pulling his legs to the side of the bed, he looks at the monitoring system and knows that by shutting it, an alarm will go off. He decides to bring it along with the insulin. One foot after the other, he painfully hooks himself to the pole, his walk unsteady and gets to the corridor to walk up to the nurse's desk. Only a few people work on the night shift. Big Jim has his eyes plunged over papers and sweet Amanda is coming out of a room. When she sees Josh standing near the counter, she drops her tray. When the noise is heard, Jim rises up his eyes toward the sound and turns to where Amanda is looking. He comes up face to face with Josh, standing a foot away from his counter. "Hi . . . I'm back."

Stupefied and mouth open, Jim gets from behind the counter to meet with him and holds the patient tight with a sincere laughter. Amanda comes close as well, laughing and crying all together. Taylor is called and arrives at the hospital thirthy minutes later, wearing pants and the upper part of his pyjamas. Sitting on the side of the bed, chatting with a couple of nurses, Jim and his doctor, Josh is sipping an orange juice, still unable to eat normally. When the older one rushes into the room, the young man gets up and both fall in each other's arms. Never in his life has the air been sweeter or the bond of another human being felt like a marvel. Other nurses and interns come in one after the other and soon, the entire hospital crew learns about the « miracle », turning his room almost into a party house.

"What was it like when you were in a coma?"

"It was frightening. I often dreamed that I was in a dark tunnel and a light would be above my head, out of reach. I could hear all of your voices and the perception of all your movements."

"You mean when we touched you?"

"More than that, the moves of your thoughts, I could feel them. Whenever you were anxious or feared for my life, I could feel it. I don't know if it was because of my immobility but . . . it was pretty sensational."

His doctor avidly listens, no sense in him taking notes because he will remember that day for the rest of his life. "In those past ten months, did you ever feel you wouldn't make it?" He snaps. Opening his mouth to speak, Josh makes a pause and then offers this comment: "I owed it to too many people and heard each of your prayers. All the efforts you made for me to wake, I just couldn't let you down."

Lorne is called and, things being quiet in Montreal, he is given permission to take the next flight to London and celebrate the true revival of his partner. Because he wanted to get better before seeing Charlene, Josh asked Taylor to keep it a secret from his lady and had to have everybody else's word that they would not reveal the magnificence of the healing. He also had to find a way to prevent her from visiting so, with all the conviction he could express, he tells her that her lover caught an infectuous disease and is quarantined for a few weeks. Hanging up the telephone, he turns to the lad. "You think she bought it?" The British man demands.

"I couldn't have done it better myself."

"But you're the worst liar!!!"

"I know." Josh replies, amused.

"I almost forgot." Throws Lorne reaching in his coat pocket for an envelope. "Someone is sending you a special card."

When he opens the small beveled card, he finds a picture of Diane and Robert wearing a gown and a tuxedo. Their arms are entwined, sharing a flute of champagne.

"When did they get married?"

"Last month. They're sending you their best wishes of recovery."

"I'm glad for the both of them . . . What happened to the drawing she made of the man who assaulted me?"

"She sent it to Arkin but it didn't lead to a portrait ressembling any known convict. Don't you think I wouldn't have told you?"

Josh nods, placing the card on his tray.

Suitcase in hand, Josh gives the room a last long look with mixed emotions. He is grateful for the compassionate and skillful care he received and can't leave without thanking all the personnel. On the other hand, he's eager to reconnect with his own surroundings. Lorne leads Josh in a wheelchair to the taxi waiting that will bring them to their apartment. When seated, Lorne fraternally places his hand over the ex-patient, who is quietly savouring the moment of the long awaited freedom and responds to the contact by squeezing his knuckles over his. A wave of emotions washes him as he keeps staring out the window, with his right hand pressed against his mouth to keep the dam from breaking. Once in from of the apartment, Josh struggles to get out of the car. Harassed by all this pain, he clings on the cement ledge to climb to the balcony.

"Can I help you?" Lorne suggests.

"No thanks. I have to get used to it." Without thinking too much about the number of steps he needs to climb to get to his room on the second floor, he jubilates at the idea of lying in his own bed.

"Do you want to sleep in the living room tonight?"

"I dreamed about sleeping in my own alcove."

Lorne makes sure to follow him all the way up so he doesn't fall from behind. His room is intact, just the way he left it except for the sheets that have been cleared away. All his paintings have been waiting and he looks at them with sorrow, uncertain about ever being able to paint again. Something has died inside him, leaving emptiness, a hollow feeling that he could never retrieve. After placing a fresh pair of sheets on the mattress, Lorne stands near the door and clears his throat.

"Can I help you with anything?"

Turning around, his eyes are filled with tears and soon, he falls into his buddy's arms.

"Thank you." The younger one says with sincerity.

"I didn't do anything. I just waited for you to come back."

"You did more than you'll ever know."

When they part from each other, Lorne doesn't slap or amicably hit Josh's shoulder like he used to. Their relationship has changed, Josh growing old before his time and Lorne barely adjusting himself to that reality. Probably to compensate for the lack of motricity, the young man's conversation and judgment has grown wiser and more mature during the period his body was in idleness. Lorne isn't sure to like this new personage but it was the one he was left with. He walks away to the door and begins to close it. "Please don't, leave it open." Josh begs.

Lorne pulls the door back wide open, clearly seeing that his partner is still afraid to have a claustrophobic attack.

"I'll leave mine open as well so if you need anything I'll be right by." He precises without making big fuss about it.

Disrobing his body from the protective layers of his clothes, he looks at the naked limbs in front of the miror. The two gun wounds left scars that forever would remind him of the dreadful night of last June and his body showed a lack of muscle tone from the rapid weight loss. "Would she love me again?" He doubts. A lump escalades his throat before he slides between the sheets.

Close to his head rests his police coat. As he pulls it away, a hair clip falls from under it, proof that his lady was there, sharing the same nest. A hint of her fragrance in the woolen collar is tickling his nostrils, so he pulls it closer to his nose, shuts his eyes and wishes the rest of her was here with him, right now.

Five days later, the 12th of April, London Police Headquarters.

Taylor and Lorne are keeping the slow pace of Josh, who is temporarily using a cane. Upon their arrival at their Londonian office, they are greeted by cheers and laughter. The unexpected commotion makes Wilkinson and Sergeant Hockart leave their meeting and rush to join the rest of the group welcoming the survivor. All this attention makes him feel uncomfortable and asks to go to his office. After a brief hesitation, he takes out his reactivated security card, punches in the eight digit code into the slot and turns the knob. The view of the park is still as impressive as ever, although the weather is as foggy as the first time he visited the room but something has drastically changed. He now knew that because of his wounds and operation, his life would never be the same.

"How many are they now in the group?"

"Still eleven but it works fine. Five of them are mainly helping out with the terrorist intervention squad. Since . . . last June, twenty-five cases involving children have been solved." Lifting up his eyes for a second, Josh wonders why Lorne doesn't use the word "shooting".

"Can I see the list of the candidates?" Taking his own key, Lorne opens the filing cabinet, takes their files and places them in front of him. Opening them impatiently, Josh considers the pictures one after the other and still looking down, asks his colleague: "Where is Shadow? Isn't she part of the group?"

"I've never heard of her. Who is she?" Taylor inquires but Josh, who is visibly angry, wants an answer from Lorne.

"I asked you months ago to get in touch with a girl named Shadow working over at the Ladder's refuge. Didn't you get her?"

"No, I did not." Simply replies the partner. Josh raises his head and keeps an unfathomable silence which only means one thing. "Oh Josh c'mon, don't be mad. I'm sorry, so many things happened!"

"What's going on? Who's that girl?" Taylor reproaches intrigued, turning his head at each of them in turn like a tennis game.

Forcefully tightening his jaw, Josh takes all the files and puts them back in the filing cabinet before locking it. "Hey! I said I'm sorry." Implores Lorne.

Josh starts walking toward the door but Taylor steps swiftly in front of him.

"Let me out!"

"Not before you tell me what this is all about."

"Josh Listen . . ." Begins Lorne.

"No you listen! I asked you one small favour months ago and *monsieur* says that he has a lot on his mind! Well let me tell you something, I had a lot on my mind including a tumor and two holes in my body. So don't give me any excuses for not contacting her."

"Why is she so important to you?" Taylor inquires turning his head again to him.

"Because I believe she's got aptitudes."

"She also works in a place where dope is as trivial as ordering a lagger!" Lorne shouts insistingly staring back at his partner.

"So you did go and see her."

"I did, I even brought Wilfrid with me." He finally reveals.

"And, what happened?"

"We had a chat." He claims sitting down. Josh turns to face him while Taylor approaches and stands right by Josh's side.

"She told me that I was the second policeman to approach her with the same request so naturally I asked her to describe who the other one was and she showed me your card. I didn't tell her that you had been shot but she saw it on the news and recognized you. When you went into a coma, I went to see her again and explained that we badly needed people with abilities but nothing seemed to move her. Was I supposed to argue with her all night?"

"You're damn right!"

That same evening, Wilfrid's car stops close to Ladder's refuge. Lorne is accompanying them and holds the door to let Josh walk out with his cane.

"I'll go alone but if I'm not back in twenty minutes, come and get me."

"Are you sure?"

"Yes." Walking up the stairs of the bar in casual attire, the doorman maliciously obstructs the entrance. "The place is full." He protests crossing his monstruous arms. "Is Shadow in tonight?" Josh snaps taking out a twenty pound bill.

"I don't know." The beast replies but Josh knew the pattern and pulls out another bill.

"Go in, her section is way back against the wall." He advises opening the door.

When he enters, a few heads turn but rapidly, everybody goes back to their business. Sitting at a table far from the stage where a guitarist plays his latest rhapsody under the beam of a single light, he looks for the waitress with scrutiny. While the smell of canabis is still lingering in the air, some other lady approaches his table. "What will it be?"

"Mineral water please."

"I'll be right back."

"Sorry, isn't Shadow here tonight?" Josh solicits promptly.

"She's having her break right now."

"I haven't seen her up front."

"She never takes her breaks up front . . . unless somebody interests her."

"You think I could pay her a visit?"

"I doubt that she'd mind. She's in the back alley. Just follow me."

Near the bar, a back door opens to a long set of stairs interrupted in the middle by a platform. Shadow is there, legs curled up under her, smoking a fag. When she sees Josh coming down the stairs, she looks surprised.

"May I?" He throws sitting beside her.

She slowly moves to the side to leave him some room.

"I thought you were dead." She supposes still looking in front of her, puffing out a last dash of smoke before crashing the butt under her high heel.

"My partners tell me that you are not interested in our proposal. Are you so well off working in a place like this?" She scratches her head and starts rocking herself.

"Listen, you must think that this is all a joke but we really need you." She lights another cigarette and ironically says: "I can't leave this place. It pays well." Her tone is nowhere near convincing and when she turns her head, the trace of a black eye under a ton of make-up and bruises on her left arm are visible.

"Who did that to you, the owner?"

A bitter-sweet expression appears on the young woman's face. "Shadow, your break is over!" They hear from the top of the stairs. Slowly rising from the wet improvised seat, she's about to go back in when he pleads one last time for her to accept his professional engagement.

"I've got two agents waiting in the alley for you to come and join us."

"I can't, I'm sorry."

Deception is all over his face and there is only one last thing for him to say.

"You still have my card?" He cuts short clearly hoping she would change her mind.

"Somewhere I guess."

"You have a paper and a pen?" She brings out her order pad and a pencil.

"Hey! Are you coming? Clients are thirsty!" The owner shouts even louder.

"I heard you dammit!" She yells back at him.

"Here, he says scribbling down. That's my personal number. Call anytime, day or night, otherwise just come to the London Police Headquarters and ask for Wilfrid, Lorne or me."

A last nod from the head, Josh climbs back the stairs and heads right out to the door. In the dark alley, Lorne holds the car door for the colleague who prefers to sit in the back and stretch his leg. A minute later, they are on the main street but again, a fine rain is dropping down its sorrow. The wipers dance over the windshield at a dull and regular pace that would make you fall into sleep mode.

"Tell me the truth Josh. I don't believe that you only want her because she has aptitudes. It's got to be more than that." Lorne teases.

His head resting against the comfortable seat, Josh speaks almost whispering, barely heard by his colleagues sitting up front.

"She's lost, like some kind of ship drifting far from the shore, just like I used to be. Can't you see that she has a gift?"

"You forget that I don't see people's aura buddy."

"Well anyway . . . I feel she's got something."

"She's, she has the colour turquoise and white a around her head . . . it's it's the s same as yours." Wilfrid shyly stutters, keeping his eyes on the road.

For a week, Josh meets with the group and sees why a few cases never resolved proposing solutions without linking. When the time came to decide on proceding with an issue as is or finding alternate methods, everyone relied on Josh's judgement. Taylor knew his man to be back on track and his worries about his welfare would be gone if it was not for a small change, something only he could notice standing outside the room, looking through the surveillance window.

"It's nice to have him back isn't it?"

Taylor suddenly turns to Wilkinson approaching.

"Of course, life is back to normal with him around. Are you happy about the terrorist prevention group?"

"It's more than I hoped for. They are very accurate and so less demanding than I expected. I'm very glad you brought both your agents to London."

"I'm happy to hear it Donovan."

As Wilkinson steps away from the glass, Taylor turns his head toward his protégé again noticing that his features have changed. His eyes now paler than before, his beard displays traces of grey and his hair is baring a paler patch where the mass was removed. It wasn't those physical changes that bothered him but his glance, filled with mistrust and skepticism. Somehow, the young man wasn't twenty-seven anymore but much older in the way he stared back. For a moment, he lets Lorne take the stand and address the group while his head rises and turns to meet Taylor's. Before the two-way mirror, Josh couldn't see who was on the other side but somehow knew his boss was there, standing vigil like a warrior standing guard at the height of a tower. Taylor creases his eyebrows wondering what is on the lad's mind suspecting he is hiding a dark secret.

Late at night, a few hours after dinner, alone in his office with only the desk lamp on and a simmering coffee in front of him, Josh is writing down comments about today's session when suddenly he feels the presence of someone near. He turns around and sees in the doorway, the man that started the shooting at the restaurant. Josh notices a dragon tattoo on the inside of the intruder's right wrist.

"Are you surprised to see me so close to you?"

Josh swallows heavily, thinking about how to protect himself since he doesn't have a gun. How the hell did this guy transgress all the security devices of the edifice? His metallic cane is close to the chair and briefly, he looks at it.

"Didn't you have enough of crippling me? What do you want now?"

"Nothing much, simply for you to stop searching for kids. There are far greater things to dig for." The intruder answers closing the door and locking it.

"Is that why you had someone shoot me?"

The red-haired man smiles, walks a few steps further inside the office.

"Everybody thinks that you saved Wilkinson but the truth is that *he* never was the target."

"What about the two bodyguards? One of them died!"

"Mere pawns on a checkerboard . . ."

"You could have hurt innocent people."

"No . . . I never miss and neither does my accomplice . . ."

"So why didn't he just kill me?"

"That was not his intention. You are a better asset alive than a crumbling pile of bone ashes. You . . . have something we both wish we had."

"And what's that?"

"You have the faculty to remember who you were in a past life but we won't rest or leave you alone until we have the jewels from the casket in our own hands." The stranger with red hair speaks with anger and violently charges toward him.

Josh wakes in a flash. Like thunder, he raises his head from the desk, his heart pounding so hard. Shaking, his hand lets go of the pen which drops to the floor. His coffee cup is now half empty and cold and the door of his office is wide open. Wilfrid appears and faintly knocks. Josh's head turns to him surprised as if he had seen a ghost.

"Agent Forge, I I hope I'm n not disturbing you but you had your ph phone on do not distrurb and the receptionist told me that some someone is here to see you."

"Who is it?" He warns afraid it would be the shooter from his dream.

"The receptionnist wouldn't gi give her name. She's downstairs in the lobby."

His eyebrow rises with surprise and he gets up, puts his papers away and turns off the light before taking his coat and cane. Locking the door behind him, he gets into the elevator with his co-worker.

"What time is it?"

"Al almost nine."

"What are you doing here so late Wilfrid?"

"I have no family to to get back to so I I may as well have some work done. B but I'll g go home now."

Josh smiles knowing that for some people, being a workaholic was the best way to survive. When the doors open to the ground floor, he sees a slim lady waiting. Surprisingly, he recognizes Shadow without her raven wig. She traded her plunging cleavage to a simple long cotton dress covered with a grey knitted vest.

"Hi! "He exclaims.

"Hi."

"Wilfrid, you remember Shadow?"

"Of of course, how how do do you do?"

"I'm fine thank you."

"You wanted to see me?" Josh demands the lady.

"Yes but not here, could we go for a coffee?"

"Sure."

"I'll I'll see you tomorrow." Affirms the colleague to Josh obviously intimitaded by the newcomer.

"Certainly, have a good evening."

"G g good night."

He brings his security card to the receptionist, pushing it slowly and he turns his head toward her. "Did you have problem finding the place?"

"Are you kidding me? You would have to be an outsider not to know this place." Astounded by the turn of events, he opens the door to the frail lady. She immediately lights up a cigarette. When she raises her hand, he sees that she has been battered again leaving a new blue trace on her wrist.

"What made you change your mind?" He begins looking at her sandy blond hair.

"I want a future; settle down with a husband and kids. The bar is no longer an option for me."

He doesn't smile, but a cheering sound of victory bursts inside of him. As if her chain were broken, she starts to reveal her life story, bit by bit, sparing him no details. When they arrive at the coffee shop, he chooses to sit far away from the door and the other patrons in a cozy corner allowing for deeper and more private revelations.

"Will I work with you?"

"It depends on your aptitudes Shadow; an evaluation will take place before they even decide upon hiring you. You are aware that there will be an investigation on your past?"

"I thought so."

"And do you have anything you'd like to share now?"

"Whatever happened with my father is a thing of the past. I did sell drugs but I never did drugs. I'm no angel, I know that but I was never arrested. Maybe I was just plain lucky after all. Are you single?"

It takes him a second to wonder if this was a flirting question.

"I'm not legally married but I'm not single either." He precises flatly but as she makes a chagrined mimic, he chuckles. And then, a serious conversation starts. Her life has been a mishap since her childhood but she was a fighter and found her strength in adversity. She probably was the best person to understand what teenagers on the run could go for. She sold drugs instead of her body afraid of getting AIDS and Josh just knew that her story was similar to the hundreds of others he had to face each week. After an hour of chatting, he brings her back home and reaches his own apartment.

Lorne is in the bathroom brushing his teeth and Josh stands without speaking, which obviously means he wants to catch his partner's attention. Lorne stops brushing, turning his head, his mouth filled with toothpaste.

"Shadow came to the office to see me. She wants to work with us."

Lorne spits out the foam and wipes his mouth dry before stowing his brush away. Immediately, Josh knows he's going to get a lecture.

"You have any idea what you're getting into?"

"I do."

"She's a drug dealer."

"She is also someone who tried to survive. Last time she saw her mother she was twelve and her father abused her until she left her place at fifteen. You really want me to put her back on the streets?"

"Why do you have to be so stubborn about her? What is it? You are not interested in Charlene anymore?"

"That couldn't be further from the truth. Give her a chance to prove you wrong . . . won't you?" Josh insists.

"Fine, but just remember that I'm not the only one she has to be approved by and if she messes up, it's your ass that will be on the line." Lorne answers after a long pause.

"Isn't it always . . ."

Climbing up the stairs to his room, Josh rubs the back of his neck feeling the pain of a sore body, even worse than when he came back from a karate fight.

During the following week, Lorne and Josh take care of introducing Shadow to the rest of the group and showing her the ropes after she signed a contract of confidentiality. No lies about her past, she figured. She told everything to Taylor and Hockart while Josh was sitting far away in the back of the room, contemplating the strong aura around the lady's blond hair. At the end of the encounter, she was dismissed and had to wait two days before knowing their decision. When Hockart finally shared his impressions with Josh, no convincing had to be imposed. The young lady was definitively a good asset to the child abduction prevention squad due to her sensitivity. Also, she had been living in the clandestine world of the drug dealing business, which would give her an edge. As days passed, the more she got involved with the group, the cheerier she became. Wilfrid turned out to be her best associate and after two weeks, he finally had the courage to ask her out to see a movie. She gladly accepted and they became unseparable. Awkwardly, he started to speak normally as if she had triggered some kind of self-confidence.

By that time, there was enough progress in Josh's health that his frequent check-ups at the hospital were getting sparse. He felt confident enough to venture out on new activities although he knew he was physically slower than before the accident. Accompanied by Taylor, they drive to Waterloo train station to get to another precinct where they will educate their counterparts on their working methods of child finding. In the station, a cacophony of boisterous noises is ubiquitous and is only punctuated by public address announcements. At his time of day, the place is bustling with people. Taylor is at the booth getting their tickets while Josh walks a few steps on the platform, trying to relieve the constant compression of the brace over his leg. Like a calling, his head pivots to a teenager, all crouched up behind a pillar while a guard is ordering him to leave. Hiding under a dirty hooded coat and wearing army boots, the kid stands up unhurriedly. Intrigued, Josh gets a few steps closer.

"Tommy?" He asks the young one. The teenager continues walking away from the agent. "Thomas Sacks, please wait!"

The teen under the black hood turns around while Taylor witnesses the scene from afar, wondering who his employee is talking to.

"Thomas, please. I just want a few words with you. Take some money and call your parents. They're worried sick. Your picture has been in our file for a year now."

"Who are you?"

"It doesn't matter. Here, take this, eat something and call them." He pleads handing the teen a few pounds.

"You're from the squad aren't you? Go fuck yourself!"

"I'm sorry but that's physically impossible." Josh comically replies.

The insulted teenager looks away, mad as hell but the agent still insists, getting one step closer.

"Your mother is really sad and worried. She's forgiven you . . ."

The runaway turns around once more. Josh limps a few more steps toward him.

"It wasn't your fault that your sister got hit by that car. She's fine now and both your parents only wish for you to come back . . . to be a family once more."

"Maybe 'Ma asked for me but certainly not the jackass that's supposed to be my father. He hates me, always has and always will."

Josh tilts his head a little on the side, rather disappointed by his statement.

"Please, take the money and call them or better yet, take the train and head back home."

The kid's look was nothing like the picture posted on the search data base, first of class, school uniform and crew cut.

"You're from the police?" The teen asks inquires.

"I am but I'm also someone who's been there, someone who thought that running away would solve my problems." Josh answers handing out the pounds again while his other hand is heavily leaning on his cane. Taylor is still standing, discretely watching how his agent is handling the intervention. Quiet as always, he is peeking from a distance. Without any thanks, the teen changes his mind and reaches for the money. As their hands close in, Josh covers the teen's wrist with his hand. Feeling uncommon warmth, Thomas raises his eyes to meet those of his benefactor.

"Pride is something we all have to swallow, once in a while." Josh adds on a peaceful tone, as Thomas gradually backs away, still facing him. There is no smile on the fugitive's face but something lit up before he swivels a hundred and eighty degrees and starts to walk in the other direction. The echo of the heavy boots resounding on the floor, the jingle of the chains at his waist, which match his ear pins, and the silhouette of the youngster whose green hair is sticking out from the hood, all prepped out like a Roman warrior's helmet, slowly fade away in the depths of the tunnel.

"Who was that?" Requests Taylor now coming near.

"Thomas Sacks disappeared last april from this city. His younger sister was hit by a car while he was babysitting her. She was brought in for care and his father put the blame on him. You can just imagine the rest. He didn't look anything like the picture we scanned from the private school."

Perplexed, Taylor hands him his train ticket. "So how did you recognize him?"

"No bright light was surrounding him anymore."

Taylor frowns. "You could not see that before, could you?"

Josh raises his lip to fake a smile. "Guess I'm getting closer to perfection . . ."

Because of his implication with the paranormal, the Lieutenant had to study the not-so-common courses related with criminality and psychology. With that last sentence, he realizes that the one he trained is getting nearer to the apogee of his existence, as per God's will, but he was eager to start a new meeting. "C'mon, we have other agents to meet."

"Gladly." Shouts the young lad, before the train flies on the tracks of the English panorama waking to dawn.

At the end of the long day, both get out of the train at Waterloo Station and Taylor drives Josh back to the office so he can drop off the day's report.

"Shall I wait for you or will Lorne take you back home with him?" The Lieutenant cuts short.

"I don't know yet but don't wait for me. Good night. See you tomorrow." He replies.

Josh barely has time to enter his office that Lorne bombards him with a thousand questions about his day.

"So, how was it? How many people were there? Were they receptive? Was anybody able to link?"

Tormented by other issues, Josh answers evasively and cuts things short.

"It was a good day but I'm really tired and I want to go home." He replies as he secures the files in his cabinet.

"OK, fine, I understand. I was just about to go home myself."

"No, you don't get it. I want to walk home."

"Oh, o.k. So, I guess I'll see you at the apartment. That's too bad! You're going to miss Robert and his brother. They're both coming over here to fetch me and we're going to have a guys' night out. Sure you don't want to change your mind?"

Indifferent, he walks away from the office without answering or looking back. Stepping out of the elevator, he continues right passed the receptionist, who bids him farewell as she always does, but he does not respond.

Needing some air after an eight-hour meeting, so many things rise in his mind.

As he strolls back to his apartment, he think about how easy it is for him to know who at the office was against the project just by staring above their heads. How easy it was for him to find the truth. Maybe walking home wasn't such a good idea after all with the excruciating pain he feels. When he reaches the corner of Broadway and Caxton Streets, he thinks of Lorne having fun with Robert, but as soon as his name pops in his head, a stupid sentence from Sylvia immerses: "The sense of smell is the one that is most strongly impregnated into our memory". His eyes widen as it all becomes clear: they could not find the assailants because they indisputably changed their appearances but the distinctive mixture of the two perfumes that Robert wore was unmistakably the same as he smelled during the attack. He dashes toward the grey building as fast as his legs allow. There, among the employees exiting the edifice, Josh recognizes Wilfrid walking beside Lorne exchanging what seems to be a pleasant conversation when a car parks near the sidewalk and two men step out. It's Robert and his brother whom he recognizes from the shooting.

"Lorne, Beware!" He shouts scrambling through the passing cars. Fire shots overpower all the other noises and taken by surprise, pedestrians are trapped within the deadly trajectory when the guard at the entrance of the edifice is shot dead. Robert and his brother turn toward Josh and aim but suddenly, Josh is pushed to the ground and other shots are heard, these ones so much closer. Looking up, he sees the siblings falling on the sidewalk surrounded by half a dozen policemen. Mouth open, he realizes that whoever pushed him to the ground just saved his life "Are you alright?" Barely recollecting what just happened, he turns to the voice of Taylor and doesn't answer. He begins limping to the other side street to see how Lorne and Wilfrid are doing while Taylor gets up still holding his weapon tight. Arkin steps out of an unidentified police car and other policemen secure the zone of the shooting. With the help of an officer, Wilfrid's back is leaned against the station's wall while Lorne is still lying flat on the cement sidewalk with a gunshot wound in his stomach. Flashing lights from police cars disturb the peaceful agglomeration and while some citizens are fleeing the scene, others are simply drawn in by curiosity. "Are you o.k.?" Josh asks his longtime partner. Through a grimace, Lorne answers that he's fine. Arkin steps in close and waits for Josh to turn around. "Agent Forge, whenever you're ready, I would like to have a conversation with you." From far, emergency vehicles can be heard and Josh decides to join Inspector Arkin only when both his buddies are on their way to the hospital.

Down at the station, Josh is sitting in Arkin's office beside Taylor. A coffee is placed in front of both while he waits for the conclusion of a long search for traitors within the prestigious organization. Ten pictures of people he met or worked with are laid in front of him, including one of his shooter and lastly one of Charlene. Frowning, Josh's eyes water wondering of her involvement in this affair. His body leans backwards and, struggling to compose his feelings, he lets Inspector Arkin explain the puzzle in which he was entangled, much to his astonishment. "A few years ago, a robbery took place in a jewellery store and three of London's agents were involved; Ralph Miller who still works in London, your colleague Wilfrid Armstrong and finally Colin Fraser. This last agent failed to conclude his mandate with the police force and resigned after the burglary in search for a job that was less hazardous to his health or so he said. Fraser was a perfect agent and received honouring distinctions but after being infiltrated as an undercover cop among the jewellers, an over-developed sense of greed controlled him. If you look closely at his prior education, you'll find that he was a student of Mrs Wilkinson in gems research. He was in the top five of his class and probably after one of their numerous receptions; she unfortunately and innocently spoke to him about the jewels covering the casket of the Book of Kells. We had a warrant to search his apartment today and it revealed that he concentrated all his time and efforts on this quest in the past years. When he realized he could not attain his goal alone, he sought the help of his brother Robert."

"Robert's family name is not Fraser." Interrupts Josh still in shock.

"He took his mother's maiden name when he entered the police force, probably an idea from his brother. When he was hired, all his papers were in order and his record was as pure as snow. Anyway, both of them started circling around the worst people including a network of child pornography prospectors evidently for lucrative reasons and their high living standards. Digging deeper into their possessions, we found out that they owned four cars estimated over 550,000 pounds. When they realized that common procedures could not reveal anything for the search of the gems, they both turned to historic facts and irregular practices such as transcendental imagery. They were looking for someone with an uncommon gift such as yours but they had to get close without being identified. That's where Charlene MacRae steps in. Colin Fraser had many identities and your lady knows him as Colin Blackburn from the Blackburn-Thornhill house of editing."

Josh's shoulders drop an inch. "Is she at all involved in this plot?"

"Of course not, she was only an innocent writer who was unfortunately approached by a wise and destabilized ex-agent. The main reason why we finally pinned them down was your Montreal colleague's drawing of Colin Fraser with a wig and brown contact lenses. We believe that she had no knowledge of the crimes of her brother-in-law, she probably never met him and Robert certainly hid the truth about his intentions. As we speak, she is being arrested for aiding and abetting a known felon even if we believe that he only used her to know more about you. At all times, we wanted to have a close watch on your activities just like today's earlier shooting where we stood right by about two hundred meters from your position. Lieutenant Taylor' implication was nothing but sheer luck."

Josh turns to Taylor and the shadow of something far greater obsesses his thoughts. "Didn't you say that it was Wilkinson who wanted me to work in London?"

Lips tightly sealed, the Lieutenant looks back and Josh immediately turns to Arkin. The young agent suddenly understands the proportion of the situation and remembers something odd Wilkinson said to him: "Some people would pay to possess half of your psychic faculties. Never thought about using them to the wrong essence?" The disturbing sentence just keeps hammering his brain incessantly. All the people he met or worked with in the past years had a connection, just like the intricate web trapping him in its midst. As if lightning struck, he now knew the reason for his attack. Arkin unvoluntarily raises his eyebrows in dismay. "While an investigation will take place, Mister Wilkinson will be relieved of his functions at midnight and an announcement will be broadcast over the nation. His own involvement in this case is obscure and as we speak, search warrants have been issued for both his office and residence. God only knows what we'll find because, according to his profile, I suspect him to be deliberately involved in his own son's abduction. He's a bright man and probably will deny any implication thus get rid of all incriminating evidence.

"That's insane! Is he guilty or not?"

"No one is above the law, not even him but let's just say that as police officers, we finally intercepted a network of child pornography and condemned a large amount of people including the person who wanted to attempt to your life. Despite the fact that honest citizens may lose confidence in our justice system, Wilkinson will be fairly tried and we will appoint a figure of authority worthy of such a prestigious and meaningful position. Corruption will always be part of a society that claims to be civilized and as long as I'll be wearing my Inspector badge, I'll do everything in my power to close up any Pandora's Box that I will come across.

"How did you manage to know my every move?"

"Look closely at your cross. You will find a piece of metal incrusted in the back that works as a transmitter. We only had to make sure that it would not beep in any of our security devices. Taylor asked an ex-colleague to put it there when you had your medical at the Headquarters in London. That's the reason you had a buzzing sound in your ears now and then. As well, we planted one in Lorne's wallet, which we had to replace when it became dysfunctional. You probably remember the day the taxi driver handed Lorne's wallet back to him. He was one of us.

"Who discovered all of this?"

"The one you always thought was against you, Sergeant Hockart of course. He would have done anything to corner Wilkinson."

Taylor approaches and includes his own comment. "Almost everything happened the way we thought it would except when you were shot at the restaurant. That incident was clearly something we could not foresee and I'm deeply sorry for it."

"So what am I supposed to do now?" Josh throws stupefied.

"How about taking a few days off and letting the dust settle until someone else sits in Wilkinson's chair?" Concludes Arkin.

Discouraged and visibly questioning himself about his future, Josh rises with the help of his cane and approaches the window.

"Agent Forge?" Shouts the Inspector now sitting at his desk facing Taylor. Shattered, Josh turns to his voice, crestfallen.

"Someone is waiting for you at the end of the corridor, last door on your right."

As his steps bring him closer to the designated area, he turns the knob and sees Charlene. They fall into each other's arms to find comfort and satiate an irrefutable need. "My God, you're alive and well! I couldn't believe the Inspector when he told me so. I was on my way to the hospital when I got his call." By her side, the precious original volume and its translation are resting on a table. Josh looks at them and keen to relieve some tension asks: ". . . I see that you went to fetch the original manuscript. It seems that you've got your hands on something you can't understand. Would you like me to help?" He smurks reiterating his offer to provide her with his translation skills services, as he did the first time he met her. "I think the safest place for it to be would be in my house. I've been had in so many ways I would just like to set this story aside for the moment. I never imagined that such a small and trivial object could trigger calamities of this magnitude." Through tears of joy, both embrace the moment in which they can finally wish for happiness.

Like a blaze, it submerges us.
Like a torrent, it engulfs us.
Like a storm, it swirls around us.
I battled against all odds not to lose the fight,
My thoughts are drawn to you, my sole reason and desire to live.
Some call it love . . . I call it my reason for living.

There was something about the city that I wanted to evade from.
Knowing I was on my way back home, my heart started to race, my
blood heating . . .
KMK

With Taylor's permission, Josh is granted a few weeks vacation and decides to fly back to Scotland bringing all his belongings with him to settle in Irma's B & B while his own house will be built at the far end of her land.

At night fall, hidden by bushes, surrounded by aromatic herbs strands laid over the robust plaid, their love is again shared. It was grandiose to be together again, united, feeling the warmth of her body against his. After a while, he turns on his back and she rests her head on his stomach. He gently presses his fingers over her waist.

"You know what's odd?" He claims.

"Please tell me."

"All this time that I couldn't move, it was you that I kept thinking of. I probably shouldn't say that because Taylor helped me out, but everytime I tried to move a finger, speak a single word, you were my drive. If I hadn't met you before this incident, I don't think that I would have had the strength to fight back. You certainly have made me breathless a couple of times and I owe it to you."

She smiles listening, enjoying the revelation that no one else has ever told her before. Crickets are playing their harmonious song as an owl is ululating its own complaint near by. He places his lips near her forehead, smelling her hair, falling into a deep sleep in the arms of the love he has been craving for.

Fortress of my dream
How many times did you and I go on the highest floors to discuss our future, our fate as a couple.
Look out the horizon and see nothing but challenges as a pair, a duo of lovers whom nothing could separate but God Himself.
KMK

Underneath the lone tree standing on the western side of Eilean Donan Castle, they finally bind their union before friends and family, Charlene wearing an off-white dress embroided with flowers matching the mauve ribbon on her head, gently dancing in the brisk wind. As for Josh, wearing a waist cut black jacket and a kilt is a first for him. Since no tartan is proclaimed for his family name, he opts for the MacKenzie plaid in hues of dark blue, forest green and black. Young Marie proudly stands as the flower girl and Lorne, sitting in his wheelchair, hands out the rings. As the priest recites his prayer and blesses the union of the newlyweds, he ties a silver ribbon around their joined hands, to symbolise the sacred vows pronounced in front of God.

"You may now kiss the bride." Sweetly, he takes Charlene's face and kisses her sublime peach lips, letting the cane drop which makes people laugh and cheer as flower petals are showering above them. His head then turns to the fortress, the one he drew so many times since his younger days, understanding the meaning of its call.

Sois moi et je serai toi. Soyons deux pour ne faire qu'un.
(Be me and I'll be you, let's be two so we can be as one)
KMK

Chapter Eleventh

The Londonian police organization decides to nominate Taylor as the following Chief Superintendant in charge which he gladly accepts even if the cloud of conspiracy still lingers above the institution. In the first week of his incarceration, Wilkinson was found dead in his cell, most likely from commiting suicide. Lorne returns to the Montreal office to now stand as their Lieutenant and Wilfrid takes over the Londonian child find section with a group of ten colleagues including Shadow.

After trying to have a child the natural way for many months without success, Charlene and Josh decide to turn to artificial insemination, which proved fruitful after a few trials. Josh continues to be involved with the child find program, working both from home and his Londonian office. Awareness campaigns were developed and widely spread. They were successful enough for a significant decrease in crime to be recorded. Years passed and Amanda died of old age, with a photograph of her late husband in her shriveled hand. Josh's son named Gabriel inherited his father's ability to draw and his mother's curiosity for historical facts. French, English and sign language were used everyday in this stone cottage, in front of which stood a huge rock immortalizing the Rampant Lion, official sign of the Scottish pride. Still, the feeling of unfinished business regarding the quest for the recovery of the jewels adorning the Book of Kells casket obsessed him. He would stand vigil at the top of the castle and dwell on the details he might have overlooked. Charlene gave him all the documents, tossing away that project which only reminded her of her naivete. Then one evening, after tucking his son into bed and kissing him on the forehead, the man with the grey-haired goatee looks nonchalantly at his wife's notes scattered over the oak desk. Something catches his attention; she voluntarily circled the date of the bombardment of the castle, 10th of May 1719, 10051719, the exact same numbers he chose for his security code to enter the police headquarters. An idea pops in his head, precarious and probably one that didn't make any sense, but something inside told him to try the impossible. Quickly, he scribbles something on the back of his latest painting and hides it underneath a fresh coat of gesso.

"I'm just going for a little walk." He precises to Charlene closing the door of their son's room. He stops, looks intently at his wife's lips before kissing her. It wasn't unusual for him to go for strolls by himself and she knew he needed to fill his lungs with the crisp Highland air. Taking the MacKenzie plaid, he rushes out the door with the key to the castle and enters the Banqueting Hall. After he has pushed the oak table to the side of the wall and rolled away the carpet, Josh lies down on the floor and crosses himself on the three shakras. He asks the Superior deities to fortune him with his search, not concentrating on people but on a certain date back three hundred years ago. Both his hands become loose, one is placed over his stomach and the other on the side of his body. Soon, the swirl of a blank dimension takes over, making him feel out of breath, fragile as a newborn but with a will to find the truth, a demand more powerful than anything else. The wind tunnel makes his breathing difficult and he has to protect his face with his shaky hands. No one is to make him lose grip, nothing can make him change his mind about going forward with his quest. His neck rises upward and his mouth opens to scream out the pain in which this state plunges him. Again, he screams, this time louder and his guide appears. The wind dwindles, relief is felt and breathing becomes easier. Within his linking MacKenzie appears speaking to his guards in the courtyard, in the mist of that unfortunate morning. Gaël approaches the castle master and soon, the tone of voice changes. Blasphemous words evade the landlord of Mull's lips.

"There is a traitor among us and I believe it to be Fraser, the one MacRae cast out of this bastion. The cautionary advice over the oak door and the saying above the fireplace mantle won't be enough to warn others about his treachery. I reckon he is planning an attack soon with the Brits. Just tell me where they are and I'll bring them somewhere else."

"Ney! (No!)" MacKenzie shouts with conviction.

"You don't trust me do you?" Gaël yells furious.

"You shut! It is my fault for not bringing them to Éire before. I'm on my way there right this instant." As his last word slips from the tip of his tongue, the shivering sound of a cannonball strikes in the humid air. "Attack! Attack! The Brits are here!" They hear from the height of the tower. The forty-six Spanish soldiers knew the position they had to keep and the bell was tolled repeatedly to warn the entire bastion. The master of the castle asks two soldiers to escort women and children to a cache in the mountains while the other men stay and protect the cherished castle. Kreg heads back to his room to take his own fighting sword off the wall and gives his wife the cross he sherished. "Give this to our child to pass on through generations." Sarah screams out his name while the iron welder is pressing her through the courtyard to climb her husband's horse. The man asked to protect the lady is about to mount his own but there is another blast. All duck their heads. Part of the northwestern wall is now destroyed, despite its impressive fourteen-foot thickness. The MacRae brothers are up on the first pavillion; soldiers are running back into the castle taking position . . . the noise from the cannons is awful. Kreg is rushing down the stairs, assisting his companions in the imminent foot attack. A blast comes through the eastern wall of the main building, shaking the thickest portion of the fortification. The protectors load their weapons to reply but all they see coming from the fog are soldiers in red uniforms running out to them like wasps, charging with their guns, placing the fortress under siege. Their huge vessels are far enough from the shore to be hit by their own ammunitions. MacRae's sons strike back with other garrison's men, loading up two bigger cannons to sink the closest ship, the Flamborough. Shots are fired back but the residents are outnumbered by five times. Three hundred and forty-three barrels of gun powder were originally destined to be used against the enemy, but since the Scottish warriors decipher the indisputable defeat, they decide to use the powder to blow their own castle. They prefer to provoke their own death rather than surrender to the enemy. Weapon in hand, Kreg starts fighting against the red coats that just came in by the hole in the wall. The battle is unequal but the fierceness of the Spanish fighting by the side of the Scottish makes them proud. He runs back to the shore to rescue one of his men from being captured by the English only to find that his companion has been riddled by a cluster of bullets. Eyes wide open, furious and converting his fear into survival mode, he returns to the castle hurrying up to the second floor, heart racing, he takes his blade, wipes the blood shed on it and kisses it warmly before taking off his féileadh-mór and places the blade within, hides it deep inside the fireplace. He then bends on both knees and opens his arms in a prayer. A blue beam enlightens his entire body before a cannonball comes across the window of the Banqueting Hall and hits him full blast while his mind recalls the last words he wrote:

Sitting in this chair, the one that welcomed me after painful, hard, intensely challenging battles, I am writing my last thoughts before I hide my memoirs. Lochland was so mad at Mise for taking so many chances, ones that were probably going to cost me my life. I knew it was because of his profound friendship that he shut the door back to our conversation. Still, I realized I had to do what lingered into Mo mind for I believed that if I did not accomplish that last task, my life would have been nothing but senseless.

The twelve stones representing the apostles have been gathered. Forgive me for not bringing them back to Éire and not elucidating the mystery of the lost amethyst gem representing God, which I did not have time to acquire. My sword will rest where the motto of my family takes all its sense:
Luceo Non Uro, I shine thus not burn.
If we are going to be attacked, parts of the castle will not burn. Rain and wind will not destroy the stash in which Mo blade will wait.
I will then rest my body inside the walls that I protected and which in return protected me. My last thoughts will be for my wife crossing the

ocean with Doray and whatever happens to my child, will be in the hands of God.
Honour, Diligence, Integrity.
Three words that mean everything and every task to be accomplished by.
KMK

Within the swirl of the transcendental voyage, Josh sees MacKenzie's wife Sarah entering a ship with the Irish iron welder sailing to France, where they will board a larger vessel carrying other refugees and exiled offenders, and then journey across the ocean to reach and colonize the new world, their hearts filled with hope and the promise of a better life.

Kanada (Canada), November 16, 1719.
"What is the child's name?" Asks a British controller at the Ville Marie harbour (now named Montreal). Without looking at Sarah holding an infant wrapped with the MacKenzie plaid, the iron welder replies hastily.
"Doray. D-O-R-A-Y."
The French lady turns to him in a flash but the iron welder dares not look at her right now. Understanding that it was the only way her child could be saved by not revealing his real family name, she does not argue.
"It sounds too English; this is a French speaking land and your name will be changed. From now on you will write it D-O-R-A-I-S. What about the child's first name?"
"Gabriel, he . . . I always liked that name." She adds precautiously.
"Date of birth?"
"Ten and a half weeks ago."
"That brings us to . . . September 2nd. Please sign here."
The controller dips his quill in the ink container and hands it back to the iron welder. Sarah's eyes fill with water as the name of her child will never bare his real father's name.
"You own a land already?" The controller asks the man standing in front of him.
"No sir."

"You look like a strong man. There won't be any problem for you to find a job and own a piece of land. Just go down the road and turn left. There will be a white sign with a red rooster above the door. Go in, apply to whatever they will tell you. That will get you started."

"What about me?" Sarah exclaims.

"God lady, you can have babies. Isn't that enough? Next!"

The way she looks back at him says a lot. Back in Scotland, she and her husband shared everything, either on the front or inside, taking care of the cannons or the injured, working the land or the fortification.

"Allez, venez Dame Sarah . . . Hushes Doray before walking down the dirty mud road. She kisses the silver cross incrusted with marcasite stones and then hides it deep inside between her breasts.

In Josh's mind, it was clear that the gems were still here. Their mention was true, vivid like the strength of the walls holding the bastion. Only the cross had been transmitted through generations. He gets up, reeling from the intensity of the linking and follows his instinct right through the master's bedroom. By knocking on the wood panels, nothing is discovered so he pushes away all the pieces of furniture to finally unveil on the main wall behind the resting place of the master, a six-legged star that time almost erased. He pushes the furniture further and with all his might, compresses the tile which suddenly draws back in. Part of the wall immediately opens to a steep descending staircase within the heart of the castle. Taking an oil lamp and lightening it, he carefully takes each step that draws him further down, right to a cave where foundations reflect the humidity proliferating for centuries. In the center, a circular well stands containing the cold and dark waters of the loch. Recalling his painting in hues of blue, he places the oil lamp on one of the steps and takes most of his clothes off. Setting foot on the ledge of the well, unaware of the depth or the path the tunnel underneath might take; he shuts his eyelids and plunges in feet first.

In the middle of the night, Charlene wakes as their son walks in the bedroom. "Maman, I had a weird dream." Rubbing her eyes, she invites Gabriel over to comfort him. "What is it honey?"

"Daddy was saying goodbye and walking away."

"You know your father would never do that."

"So where is he?"

Suddenly realizing that her husband is not beside her, she springs out of bed in search of him, calling out his name. She gets out on the porch, looks out to the road in both directions; no trace of him. She calls her mother over to watch Gabriel and rushes out with boots and a warm coat on. Instinctively, she sprints out to the castle, reaches it, sees the open gate and follows the path to the front door which is unlocked. Yelling out his name, she soon finds him resting on the floor of the Banqueting Hall. He is almost naked, covered only with the blue and green plaid. She races to reach him and kneels by his side. His body is so cold, his face pale and livid. "What have you done?" She screams before attempting to breathe life into him but the puppet-like mass, heavy and amorphous, does not respond to the inconsolable lady. Josh can hear his heartbeat becoming stronger then spacing out to a distant memorandum. Then a last, prolonged one laments. He feels a sense of peace while he takes a last look at his mortal envelope. For a second, the spirit contemplates his wife, the love of his life and promises. "I'll wait for you." Just then, he feels a warm current that makes him turn around and he willingly enters the threshold of his new boundary. Further on the stretch of brightness, three large celestial bodies come closer, just like the archangels he painted so long ago. They take both his hands and very gently invite him through a tunnel filled with warmth, where he recognizes his parents. Behind them are all the deceased kids he helped find over the years. No more pain, no more pain . . .

With a decrete from the Edinburgh Council, Charlene is granted the privilege to bury Josh's remains on Iona, in the cemetery near the huge Celtic cross. "Agent Jocelyn Laurent Forge has always been the uncommon type, one of intregrity and devotion until the very last days of his life. He left us better human beings, closer. He . . . (Taylor stops for awhile, breathing in), he was one in a million."

The Londonian Chief Superintendant stands beside friends and family on the small island of Iona to pay their respect. Honouring his last wishes, no flowers had been cut for his last voyage. He liked them too much to serve only one person. A sole bagpiper is there to render Auld Lang Syne and turns it to a song from Josh's most praised rock band. Gabriel clings on to his mother's hand a little stronger, lifting up a smile of appreciation. Taylor recognizes his agent's way of turning the most serious matters into something special and unique. It simply had to be . . .

After her husband's death, Charlene inherits all of Jocelyn's demise, including a fairly respectable monetary amount so she decides to quit her job and concentrate her time on raising their son. She gives his two sisters some memorabilia but cannot give any of his art work. Entering his studio, she takes down her favorite painting and places it on the window ledge to be closer to her. There was almost no furniture in that room except for his oak desk and antique chair so she lies on the floor like she saw him do so many times, hoping to cling on to his presence. The next morning when the call of the capercaillies wakes her with dawn, she slowly opens her eyes and detects through the painting what seems to look like grafitti. At first she thinks a letter must have slipped to the back of it so she turns it around. Nothing is in the back of the canvas so she brings the painting to the light once more and discovers that a text is filling the entire surface underneath the painting. She then recalls a sentence her husband told her decades ago: "There is a story behind each painting." She runs downstairs with the art work calling her son repeatedly.

A few hours later, both are waiting in the Edinburg science wing in charge of the preservation of historical documents and passing each painting under a digital scanner to discover Jocelyn's evolutive state. *"I feel lonely, awkward with my surroundings. I see dead people and speak to them."* With the painting about the archangels she finds the words: *"They will protect me like they protected the Lord above."* And so on . . . She could even retrace the painting he did when he first met her: *"Today, I met the woman of my life, her name is Charlotte but she doesn't like it and prefers to be called Charlene."* Underneath the painting about an eagle flying above the mountains Five Sisters of Kintail, Gabriel finds a letter addressed to him personally: *"Be kind and faithful my son, faithful to your own ideas and values and never let anyone discourage you from your goals."* And when the time comes for Charlene to scan the last painting Josh did, she pauses, wondering what she will find.

"Dear wife of mine. I believe that I will not live long enough to be a grandfather. The hammering in my head started again and my vision is declining so fast that you will certainly notice that this painting will not be rendered like the ones before. I want to die where MacKenzie had his last breath and will try to retrieve his sword and the jewels that are hidden in the bowels of the castle. Follow the six-legged star and you will find them."

The colleague she used to work with in the science department to scan the vellum, looks at her while she frowns and stays immobile. "I guess that's the last one Charlene. Do you want me to print this one too?" It takes her a minute to answer back. "Yes please, I would like that."

Returning home with all the paintings in the back of the car, Gabriel attempts to converse with his mother, who seems to be miles away. "Why didn't he just write all his messages on paper mom?"

"Because your father was like that, he was very discrete about his feelings. Maybe he was afraid people would laugh at him."

The following day, employees from the local Trust Fund bring in material to thoroughly look for the star as well as other signs to enable them to find both treasures. A magnetized stick reaching far inside the fireplace elucidates one of the mysteries and the sword that belonged to Kreg MacKenzie is finally brought out with immense care. The tapered iron blade which could be used with either hand was incrusted with gems and the famous motto of the family was engraved near the hilt. Without a doubt, the artifact was three hundred years old and much too precious to be kept in the dampness of the castle, so it was sent to the Edinburg Conservatory Museum to be cleaned until the necessary measures are taken to ensure the proper conservation of this factural discovery. As for the gems, employees of the reputed association finally find the six-legged star on the wall of the master's bedroom after weeks of searching for it. Following the quirky path down to the circular well, two divers locate a rusted iron box dropped at the bottom of it. They bring it up, open it with a chisel and discover twelve roughly cut gems but with incomparable value, the ones that used to decorate the Book of Kells's casket. That was probably the reason why MacKenzie did not want to bring back the treasure to Éire; one of the gems was still missing.

Chapter Twelfth

Four years later.

"C'mon let's hurry!" A group of children starts running toward the stairs to the Edinburg Museum of Fine Arts. Charlene is there with Gabriel, Taylor, Lucy, Lorne, Sylvia, Josh's sisters and their all grown-up children. Televison stations are filming the event and agents from the forces are all dressed up. Cameras are turned on. Taylor presents to Charlene the scissors that will cut the purple ribbon to the entrance as a journalist comments the presentation.

"We are here today to inaugurate the latest section added to this museum. In this vast gallery, the memorablia of the MacKenzie Trust Fund will be presented to the people of the world. Agent Forge was at the service of the London Police Force, and prior to that, of a child find organization in Montreal, Canada. He and his co-workers, Mister Lorne Landers and their supervisor Mister John Jacob Taylor, found over three hundred and seventy children, most of them alive and well. The widow of Mr. Forge, Mrs Charlene MacRae-Forge, used the deceased's trust fund to erect this pavillion and continue his spirited and acclaimed foundation. All the proceeds from this gallery will go to the U.K. Child Find Services."

"It's certainly very sad that mister Forge is not here to share this moment with us." Affirms one of the visitors.

"Oh don't worry . . . he's here alright." Charlene comments.

The visitor stops talking for a second, overwhelmed by the unexpected reply.

Gabriel smiles at his mother, taking her arm while getting close to the huge painting of the three Archangels. Beside it stands the recently recovered sword behind a bullet-proof glass.

"You shoudn't have said that maman." The teen lets out with a French punctuated accent and she simply turns to him with a smile. The painting of the three archangels is suspended so that when people entered the wing, this would be the first creation they would see coming up the stairs. The frame had been changed to a splendid golden plated one, surrounding a Marie-Louise of light linen canvas. The painting itself had been refurbished so the colours could emanate with exactitude all the nuances and luminosity they were intended to. The faces of the glorious ones were glowing just like her son's. Agents from the London Headquarters are present as well as Scottish effectives in their dark blue suits and checkered hats. On either side of the frame are two pictures of Josh. One where he stood all wet holding in his arms a young four-year old rescued from a boat accident in Canada and the other, a more recent one sitting on his motorcycle where his dark curly hair had started to turn to grey. Wearing his old leather jacket with the two badges sewed over his heart, one from Canada and one from Scotland, the picture shows him catching the autumn sunrays near the arched bridge of the glorious castle. He looked serene, proud of his life's accomplishments and family. Happy to have gone that far and reached most of his dreams. In his will, he did not forget his sisters both present with their children, ensuring a long education for them.

"Smile!" The newspaper photograph lets out.

Dozens of shots are taken and after a minute or two, the place breathes again.

"Tell me son." Begins a bystander to Gabriel. "Do you want to follow in your father's footsteps?"

Charlene's ear catches the sentence and she turns to her son. Gabriel exchanges a stare with his mother while Taylor turns his head as well, waiting for his response. The young man takes his time to answer, glancing at him nonchalantly, the same way his father would have.

"I ain't ready." He speaks out with a low tone voice.

"You are not ready to come and work with them?"

"I ain't ready to find out if father passed his gift on to me."

"Oh" replies the opulent man. "Well . . . if ever you happen to have it, I bet you'll let them know."

"I will sir." Replies Gabriel placing his head sideways like Josh used to do whenever he would feel annoyed about the people prying into personal affairs but had the decency not to argue.

"Mrs MacRae, it's been a pleasure." He claims grabbing Charlene's hand.

"Thank you for coming sir." She replies before he heads out of the museum.

Gabriel and Taylor exchange glances and the young man can't avoid showing his naughty grin to the protective British who was now to ensure the path of his « new protégé ». Charlene takes her son's arm. At seventeen, he was already taller than she was.

"So . . . where are you off to now?" She inquires.

"Home, I've got a ton of work to do."

He says his goodbyes to his aunts, uncles and cousins, kisses his mother on the cheeks and bows at Taylor who gives him a pat on the shoulder.

"I'll write you tonight."

"No problem Sir." Gabriel replies.

The lad heads out for the exit but, just before passing the archway between two paintings of Celtic soldiers, turns around. His father was there, close to his wife, smelling her hair. She turns her head, feeling the touch of something undetectable to the human eye. There was nothing there but her son smiling back, waving out a silent goodbye, but she knew perfectly whose presence she was feeling. On his left was the huge painting in hues of blue representing the body of a man seen from the back, head tilted forward. Charlene waves back at her son and, so does Josh.

It is a gorgeous September afternoon, one that he wishes would never end. Nature begins to slow its course before going to sleep for the winter. The cold air restrains the scent of the mauve heather close to the ground. His build is close to his father's, both in height and size, but his mustache reveals a little more red. Wearing his father's leather coat with the two badges, anyone could have been fooled to think the well-known agent was still alive and well. Their resemblance was uncanny. From up above, one could have sworn that a passenger had joined in, holding himself on the back seat, breathing in the invigorating Highland wind, offering his invisible protection.

There will be no bells to be tolled, for no more violent deaths shall be.
No roads to be shoveled, because every single one would have been built.
No weeds to be cut, for only flowers would spread all around.
I will be above, raised by wings.
Watching over you, protecting you, being a part of you.
Life is a perpetuous circle and it's up to us to make it sweeter at each turn.
Confront, bend, rise, but never abandon.
KMK

Deireadh

(The End)

Note from the Author

The names that appear on my baptismal paper are Marie Anita Jocelyne Forget. It's no accident that a name similar to mine was utilized for the main character. My father praised for a son all his life and unfortunatelly, never got him. Wanting to please him was a strong burden on my frail shoulders and that is probably the reason why I started dreaming about Kreg MacKenzie. Every night, I would imagine his unselfish protection and, as I was growing up, so was he.

At ten, I could see the aura of people, in fact, I still do. At thirteen, I started to have visions of disappeared children. Three times, I saw the bodies of people who reached another dimension. Three times I called the police telling them what I saw. They didn't laugh or think they were victims to prank calls. They knew about gifted people who would shed a little light on violent mysteries. I stopped asking the above deities for their help into the search of lost souls, it hurt and was unmistakably the worst feeling ever. Josh, my alter-ego, embraced and pushed further his gift while I only dared to scratch the surface of mine.

When things started to go wrong in my teenage years, when I realized that I could never please my father with the body I was born in, I started to run away. He would drink and smoke more as hold-ups would happen at the rate of one every two years. In a thirthy-two year career for the bank he served, he had sixteen of them and two attempts. He died of cancer at fifty-seven. For years, I grieved his loss, thinking that I didn't do enough to make him happy, that I was part of his miseries.

So, is there something to learn from all this? I believe so. Everyone is confronted by oppositions and it's our right to sink in or elevate ourselves. I don't let people into my life so easily, always defensive, always ready to counter-attack. But, I do let some people have their chance, make a connection, interchange or teach me values. When they do have my confidence, there is then no way back. This outside help I called Kreg would guide me through life.

Starting to write his story at ten, it first began by something very awkward but always, was there a blond-reddish-haired lady by his side and also, a faithful companion with dark raven hair. The story evolved to be worthy of the best Greek plays and took its toll when I learned after many years, that I really do have MacKenzies as ancestors. On my first visit to Scotland back in 1993, something lit up, opened inside of me, a confirmation of me having been there before. On my return visit with my fiancé and daughter of four in 1999, they too found why there is so much to like about this country. A glorious and animated past would always be rubbing shoulders with common daily life. Monuments about warriors who let their beliefs show what path they should take, surrounds you everywhere. And those mountains, clothed with mauve heather, embraced by low cumulus and caressed with the Scottish mist are something everyone should see at least once in their lifetime. There is nothing more breathtaking than this scenery. To have been blessed with looking at the sun go down on Eilean Donan, and posed my right hand, the one that has the six-legged star, on its western wall is one of the best moments of my life, this life. On this island, François my fiancé (with dark raven hair) and I exchanged fidelity vows under the sole tree on the western side of the castle.

Acknowledgements

I would like to thank Mrs Ellen O'Flaherty, Assistant Librarian (College Archives) at the Trinity College Library in Dublin, Ireland for giving me the authorization to use "The Book of Kells" within my own story. To Mr. David Win, Castle Keeper, to whom I want to give my best regards for letting me use the name of the famed Eilean Donan. Without their permissions, none of this work would have made any sense. I really need to thank my neighbours Nicole and Roger St-Louis who were patient enough to take pictures and scan the drawing of my hero. To my art teacher Mrs Sheila Cavanagh for her amazing talent for teaching the arts and bringing the knowledge of expressing myself through painting. To my dearest English literature teacher back in Western Laval High Scool, Mrs Nancy Vineberg who aroused the need to write. To Céline Béchamp, the person who corrected and made indispensable suggestions for this book, a true ally in this incredible adventure. To Doune Lyon-Weaver and her family, my Scottish friend who keeps telling me that *I'm* the one with the accent. To Shane John-Jacob Kelly, the one who inspired me for the character of Taylor, I would like to thank you for being there when I needed it the most. To my fiancé François Gladu who spiced up my life in so many ways. To my daughter Eve Laurence, who is the reason why I keep saying to never abandon any project. To my immediate family members who gave me permission to use their names, to my mother Thérèse and my father Lorenzo who taught me so much, to both my sisters Carole and Francine for their encouragements. To my grandfather Adrien Dorais, who is responsible for my link to the Celtic nation.

This story is my gift to the Scottish people, those who believe in the values of friendship, fidelity and integrity and to the English police force constantly repressing mischievous plots. This is my legacy to all the peace agents over the world who devote their energies to the recovery of lost children.

About the Author

Born and raised in the quiet suburb of Ste-Thérèse about 20 kilometers from Montréal, Jocelyne is a fervent amateur of martial arts, drawing, painting and of course, writing. Practising all these facets since her youth, and adding a few more like speaking the sign language because of an earring accident fearing she would become deaf, she also became a strong defender of youth protection and through her painting site: http://pages.videotron.com/forgeart/she collects funds for different organizations.

The author with her daughter Eve Laurence